PRAISE FOR MAR

~ The Hudson Sisters Series ~

THE LAST CHANCE MATINEE

"Prepare to fall in love with this amazing, endearing family of women."
—Robyn Carr, *New York Times* bestselling author

"The combination of a quirky small-town setting, a family mystery, a gentle romance, and three estranged sisters is catnip for women's fiction fans."

—*Booklist*

"If you like the Lucky Harbor series by Jill Shalvis, you will enjoy this one. Stewart's writing reminds me of Susan Wiggs, Luanne Rice, Susan Mallery, and Robyn Carr."

—*My Novelesque Life*

THE SUGARHOUSE BLUES

"A solid writer with so much talent, Mariah Stewart crafts wonderful stories that take us away to small-town America and build strong families we wish we were a part of."

—*A Midlife Wife*

"A heartwarming read full of surprising secrets, humor, and lessons about what it means to be a family."

—*That Book Lady Blog*

THE GOODBYE CAFÉ

"Stewart makes a charming return to tiny Hidden Falls, Pennsylvania, in this breezy contemporary, which is loaded with appealing down-home characters and tantalizing hints of mystery that will hook readers immediately. Stewart expertly combines the inevitable angst of a trio of sisters, a family secret, and a search for an heirloom necklace; it's an irresistible mix that will delight readers. Masterful characterizations and well-timed plot are sure to pull in fans of romantic small-town stories."

—*Publishers Weekly*

"Stewart [has] the amazing ability to weave a women's fiction story loaded with heart, grit, and enough secrets [that] you highly anticipate the next book coming up. I have read several books from her different series, and every one of them has been a delightful, satisfying read. Beautiful and heartwarming."

—*A Midlife Wife*

"Highly recommend this series for WF fans and even romance fans. There's plenty of that sweet small-town romance to make you swoon a little."

—*Novelgossip*

"These characters will charm your socks off! Thematic and highly entertaining."

—*Booktalk with Eileen*

~ The Chesapeake Diaries Series ~

COMING HOME

"One of the best women's contemporary authors of our time, Mariah Stewart serves the reader a beautiful romance with a delicious side dish of the suspense that has made her so deservingly popular. *Coming Home* is beautifully crafted with interesting, intelligent characters and pitch-perfect pacing. Ms. Stewart is, as always, at the top of her game with this sensuous, exhilarating, page-turning tale."

—Betty Cox, *Reader to Reader Reviews*

HOME AGAIN

"The town and the townspeople of St. Dennis, Maryland, come vividly to life under Stewart's skillful hands. The pace is gentle but the emotions are complex."

—RT Book Reviews

ALMOST HOME

"The characters seem like they could be a neighbor or friend . . . and it is because of that and Mariah Stewart's writing that I keep returning again and again to this series."

—*Heroes and Heartbreakers*

HOME FOR THE SUMMER

"If a book is by Mariah Stewart, it has a subliminal message of 'wonderful' stamped on every page."

—*Reader to Reader Reviews*

AT THE RIVER'S EDGE

"If you love romance stories set in a small seaside village, much like Debbie Macomber's Cedar Cove series, you will definitely want to grab [*At the River's Edge*]. I easily give this one a five out of five stars."

—*Reviews from the Heart*

ON SUNSET BEACH

"Mariah Stewart's rich characterization, charming setting, and a romance you'll never forget will have you packing your bags for St. Dennis."

—Robyn Carr, *New York Times* bestselling author

THAT CHESAPEAKE SUMMER

"Deftly uses the tools of the genre to explore issues of identity, truth, and small-town kinship. Stewart offers a strong statement on the power of love and trust, a fitting theme for this bighearted small-town romance."

—*Publishers Weekly*

DUNE DRIVE

"Rich with local history, familiar characters (practical, fierce, and often clairvoyant centenarian Ruby is a standout), and the slow-paced, down-home flavor of the bay, Stewart's latest is certain to please fans and add new ones."

—*Library Journal*

~ The Enright Series ~

DEVLIN'S LIGHT

"With her special brand of rich emotional content and compelling drama . . . Stewart is certain to delight readers everywhere."
—RT Book Reviews

An
Invincible
Summer

The Mercy Street Series (Suspense)

Mercy Street

Cry Mercy

Acts of Mercy

The FBI Series (Romantic Suspense)

Brown-Eyed Girl

Voices Carry

Until Dark

Dead Wrong

Dead Certain

Dead Even

Dead End

Cold Truth

Hard Truth

Dark Truth

Final Truth

Last Look

Last Words

Last Breath

Forgotten

The Enright Series (Contemporary Romance)

Devlin's Light

Wonderful You

Moon Dance

Stand-Alone Titles (Women's Fiction / Contemporary Romance)

Moments in Time

A Different Light

Carolina Mist

Priceless

The President's Daughter (Romantic Suspense)

Novellas

"Finn's Legacy" (in *Brandywine Brides*)

"If Only in My Dreams" (in *Upon a Midnight Clear*)

"Swept Away" (in *Under the Boardwalk*)

"'Til Death Do Us Part" (in *Wait Until Dark*)

Short Stories

"Justice Served" (in *Thriller 2: Stories You Just Can't Put Down*)

"Without Mercy" (in *Thriller 3: Love Is Murder*)

Stewart, Mariah,author.
Invincible summer

2021
33305252471119
ca   04/01/22

An
Invincible
Summer

MARIAH
STEWART

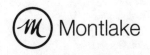 Montlake

This is a work of fiction. Names, characters, organizations, places, events, and incidents are either products of the author's imagination or are used fictitiously.

Text copyright © 2021 by Marti Robb
All rights reserved.

No part of this book may be reproduced, or stored in a retrieval system, or transmitted in any form or by any means, electronic, mechanical, photocopying, recording, or otherwise, without express written permission of the publisher.

Published by Montlake, Seattle

www.apub.com

Amazon, the Amazon logo, and Montlake are trademarks of Amazon.com, Inc., or its affiliates.

ISBN-13: 9781542025362
ISBN-10: 1542025362

Cover design by Caroline Teagle Johnson

Printed in the United States of America

For Charlotte Campbell Jones—welcome to the family!

In the midst of hate, I found there was, within me, an
invincible love.
In the midst of tears, I found there was, within me, an
invincible smile.
In the midst of chaos, I found there was, within me, an
invincible calm.
I realized, through it all, that . . .
In the midst of winter, I found there was, within me,
an invincible summer.

—Albert Camus

Prologue

Hi, all!

Hope this finds you all well (fat and happy for some of us!). Can you believe our FORTIETH HIGH SCHOOL REUNION is only ONE WEEK away? This is the last call! If you haven't already sent in your reservation, do it NOW. Dear friends, how could so many years have passed since we left the halls of Mid-Coast Regional High? I don't know about you, but I don't feel a day over eighteen! Okay, maybe a day or two, but I know I'm still a kid at heart. I'm betting you are, too.

Your reunion committee has been working hard to make this the absolute best weekend EVER. Rooms have been set aside at several local B&Bs (see attached list) but they're going quickly, so unless you're local or have family still in the area, I urge you to pick one and call as soon as possible to make your reservation.

Of course we've planned a full slate of activities, from the reception on Friday night to the homecoming football game at our alma mater on Saturday. If football's not your thing, there's a golf outing (email me if you're planning on golfing—we need to let the country club know how many to expect), a tour of the new(ish) art center, and a luncheon at Wyndham Beach's newest (and some say best!) eatery (I need to make reservations, so let me know if you want to attend). And of course there's the dinner on Saturday night. We've hired a DJ and given him the appropriate playlist. Long live the seventies!

Hope to see you all next week! It won't be the same without you.

Lydia Hess Bryant, Reunion Chair

Mid-Coast Regional Class of 1980

PS: I've attached a class list noting the friends we've lost over the years, may they rest in peace.

Chapter One

MAGGIE

From her window seat, Maggie Flynn watched the T. F. Green Airport in Warwick, Rhode Island, come into view through the parted clouds. She'd been looking forward to this weekend since she received the invitation to her high school class reunion. She'd immediately called her two oldest friends to make plans. Best friends since childhood, Liddy Bryant and Emma Dean had returned to their hometown, Wyndham Beach, after college, married local men, and stayed to raise their families while Maggie had moved on. But forty years! Maggie couldn't wrap her head around the fact so much time had passed since they'd graduated.

She slipped off her headphones, through which the soundtrack from her favorite movie, *Saturday Night Fever*, had been playing for the entire flight. Maggie firmly believed a trip back to the seventies had to begin and end with the Bee Gees. She placed the headphones in her bag, fastened her safety belt, and watched the runway come into view.

After the plane landed, she grabbed her luggage, picked up her rental car, and soon was behind the wheel of a midsize sedan, eagerly heading toward Providence, where she'd pick up Route 6 before swinging into Massachusetts. Happily singing along at the top of her voice—"Stayin'

Alive"—she drove the once-familiar highway that would take her past places that had been part of her life decades ago. Fall River, home of some of the best seafood on the planet and the flavors of Portugal, Cape Verde, and the Azores. Kayaking and hiking through Slocum's River Reserve in Dartmouth with Brett, breathing in the salt air, watching for fledgling ospreys, back in the day when they were young and in love and so sure about their future together—before things became so complicated. New Bedford, once the world's greatest whaling port and a major station on the Underground Railroad. Buying freshly caught lobster right off the boat in Fairhaven, her mother waiting at home to toss them into a steaming pot of water. Mattapoisett with its beautiful sandy beaches and Neds Point Lighthouse. The boat ramp from which her grandfather, Harvey Wakefield, used to launch his boat, *In My Wake*, and Shining Tides Beach, where many a summer day he'd taken Maggie and her sister, Sarah, crabbing and digging for quahogs. It all seemed so long ago—*Well, it was,* she reminded herself—yet the memories were as clear as yesterday. Funny how sometimes time and memory fed off each other, how some years flashed by in a hazy fast-forward blur, while others passed with such clarity, in slow motion and excruciatingly detailed.

For Maggie, the past two years had been painful and difficult and had left her feeling and looking wan and tired. She'd admittedly looked so bad that it had been months before she could recognize herself in the mirror. Being the primary caretaker for a terminally ill loved one would do that to a person.

Not that Maggie had complained. She'd devoted every waking hour to her late husband's care, and it had broken her heart to watch Art deteriorate so rapidly. He'd gone from a vibrant, active, intellectually sharp man of barely sixty to little more than a shell in a short time. When Art first shared the terrible, totally unexpected diagnosis, Maggie had vowed to be there for him every step of the way, through every day of the treatment they all hoped would defy the odds. She'd been true to her word, not leaving the house except to take him to his doctors' appointments and to drive him into Philadelphia for treatment. Despite offers from their daughters to stay with him while Maggie went . . . well, anywhere, to lunch with a friend or to the hairdresser, Maggie'd refused. Throughout thirty-two years of marriage, Art had taken care of his wife and daughters. Now it was Maggie's turn to take care of him. And she did, around the clock.

Her only focus had been Art and his care. She'd been too tired to realize the toll his illness had taken on her.

The day she'd really seen herself for the first time since the cursed day they'd gotten the bad news—five to seven months, the doctors had told them, and they'd been sadly and accurately prophetic—Maggie'd stared at her reflection, barely recognizing the woman who stared back. She'd been walking to the bakery to pick up a birthday cake for her granddaughter—the first real family celebration since Art's passing— when she'd paused to look at the window display. She'd been so shocked at her appearance she was embarrassed to go inside and identify herself as Maggie Flynn.

"Why didn't you say something?" she demanded of her daughters that night. "Why didn't you tell me?"

"Mom, we tried," Natalie, twenty-nine, the younger of Maggie's two daughters and mother of three-year-old Daisy, pointed out. "You didn't want to hear it. Remember when Grace and I offered to take you for a spa day?"

"Vaguely," Maggie admitted.

"We'd thought about tying you up and forcing you into the car, but we didn't want to alarm the neighbors," her thirty-two-year-old daughter Grace said. "You know how Mrs. Crenshaw next door is always looking out the window."

Natalie turned to her sister. "Maybe next time we should do that."

"I like it." Grace nodded solemnly.

"There isn't going to be a next time." Maggie's jaw set as she reached for her phone and scrolled through the preset numbers until she found the one she was looking for.

"Who are you calling?" asked Grace.

"My hairdresser," Maggie told them. "And tomorrow I'm going back to yoga and I'm renewing my membership at the gym." She paused, waiting for the call to be answered, inspecting her chewed and ragged nails. "Yes, hello. It's Maggie Flynn. When's the earliest I can see Kim? And can I get an appointment for my nails on the same day?"

It took more than an appointment with her hairdresser before Maggie felt like herself again, but even the smallest steps brought her back to the woman she used to be. Maggie harbored no illusions she'd look eighteen again—not that she'd want to, eighteen had been the worst year of her life—but she knew she could look good.

Good was an achievable goal.

~

Forty-five minutes after leaving the airport, the sign for the first of two turns into Wyndham Beach loomed straight ahead on the right. The first led directly to Liddy's, where she'd been invited to spend the long weekend. The second turn would take her past the harbor and eventually to her childhood home. She hesitated as she approached the first road before opting for the second.

She opened all the car windows and took deep breaths of sea air as she crept along Front Street, noting changes that had taken place since her last visit shortly before Art became ill. Since then, she'd hardly felt like going anywhere, but her fortieth reunion was too important to miss. Off to her left, the exclusive two-hundred-year-old all-boys private school, with its three-story, unexplainably Tudor-style buildings in this town where almost everything was built of clapboard or weathered cedar shakes, wrapped around the harbor like a tight hug. Through a break between buildings, she could see the *Jasper V*, the school-owned schooner, its sails folded at rest, moored at the same slip the *Jasper*s *I* through *IV* had called home. The boat rose and fell as the wake of a passing boat rolled toward the shore.

In the center of town, the Wyndham Beach General Store stood on the corner of Front and Church, and Maggie knew once inside everything would be just as she remembered. The bakery with its long glass shelves lined the right side of the building, the butcher shop ran straight across the back. The left side held refrigerated cases of dairy and frozen foods, and all other grocery items would be found on the aisles in between. The gift shops, the boutiques, the candy shop, the bookstore, all looked the same. There was one new restaurant—Mimi's—three blocks from Harbor House, which had been in business forever. Around the corner from the general store was a new coffee shop, Ground Me, which Liddy said had fabulous coffee and pastries. The pizzeria was still in the same place it had occupied when she was in high school, between the liquor store and a Realtor's office. The sign on the lawn of the tall-spired, white nondenominational church still read **ALL WELCOME**. A new sign hung over the door of Dusty's Pub, the only true watering hole in town. Otherwise, Wyndham Beach looked pretty much the same.

She slowed as she approached the point where Front Street veered off to the left and eased into Cottage, trying to remember who'd lived in which house when she was a girl, wondering who lived in them now. She pulled to the side of the road to let a panel truck pass, then crept along the curb a few more feet until she was almost directly in front of the gray-shingled house in which she'd grown up. A new sign out front proclaimed it to be **THE ISAIAH WAKEFIELD HOUSE, CIRCA 1796**—a sign obviously added by the new owners. The Blanchards? Something like that. Maggie's mother, Ellen Wakefield Lloyd, wouldn't have seen the need to advertise the provenance of her family's home. Just about everyone in town knew who'd built the house and when.

Maggie took it all in: not just the house but every tree and shrub. She'd hoped to get a peek of the backyard, since Liddy had told her the new people had built an addition, but a row of arborvitaes acted as a barrier between the front and back. They'd had to go to the historical society with their construction plans, Liddy'd said, and since she was on the architectural review board, she knew exactly what had been done (master bedroom, bath, closet, and sitting room on the second floor, and a family room, powder room, and expanded kitchen on the first) and how much they'd had to pay for all the work (close to $200,000— "But," Liddy'd confided, "you didn't hear that from me"). Maggie's curiosity got the best of her, and she got out of the car, feet crunching the dried fallen leaves on the sidewalk, and she tried unsuccessfully to peer around the green wall.

The front door opened and a child of eight or so came out, ran down the steps, and grabbed his bike from where it lay on the lawn before speeding off toward the center of town. Afraid she'd be caught craning her neck like a nosy neighbor, Maggie set off toward the end of the street.

When she was growing up, June and Jerry Gribbin had lived directly next door, a childless couple who decorated their home for every holiday. Mr. Gribbin had taught music at the academy, and Mrs. Gribbin had given piano lessons in their front parlor. While Maggie hadn't wanted to play the piano—Sarah had—she'd secretly loved hearing the music floating through the open parlor windows, and she'd fallen asleep many nights to the sound of "Für Elise" or songs her sister identified for her, Mozart's "Fantasia" in D minor and Beethoven's "Moonlight Sonata."

Maggie wondered who lived there now and if there was still a baby grand piano in the parlor.

Two houses past the Gribbins', Cottage Street came to an abrupt end and gave way to gravel that served as the parking lot for the beach. It had always been strictly "swim at your own risk"—which of course everyone did—but now Maggie noticed there was a lifeguard stand at the exact midpoint of the beach. She slipped off her shoes and walked through the coarse, pebbly sand for a closer look. She dropped her shoes and bag near the base, then climbed up to the lifeguard's seat. She sat leaning forward, resting her arms on her thighs, gusts of sea air blowing her hair across her face. At low tide, the harbor was calm, the whitecaps that flowed onto the shore languid, almost timid, though she knew the right circumstances could bring waves that flung angrily onto the beach and withdrew in a huffy snit. But today it was lovely, the sky a perfect early-autumn blue, the view clear all the way to the peninsula across the water. Between the harbor and Buzzards Bay, Shelby Island rose up like Bali Ha'i on days when the mist was thick. Such was late September along the Massachusetts coast below the arm of the Cape.

Maggie hopped down from the stand and headed for the water's edge, walked past the wrack line, and stepped over fat clumps of seaweed, broken shells, pieces of driftwood, and part of a shoe that had washed ashore. She paused to pick up a smooth piece of sea glass and rubbed it between her thumb and index finger before slipping it into the pocket of her denim skirt. Testing the water with her right foot and finding it chilly, she withdrew to a point the waves couldn't reach. At the end of the beach was the jetty, a random pile of rocks. She made her way carefully to the end and sat on the largest boulder, which marked the end of the jetty where once upon a time, she and Liddy and Emma had met to exchange gossip and discuss their social lives. She lost track of time in the flood of memories of the girl she had been and the faces of the people she'd loved. Liddy with her long skirts and long braid, a hippie before they'd ever heard the word. Emma, the minister's daughter, the peacemaker, who never rolled her skirts up above her knees and who always did the right thing. And of course there'd been the countless hours she'd sat there with Brett, the golden boy who could have had any girl in school but who'd only ever had eyes for Maggie. Beautiful Brett, the absolute love of Maggie's life, who'd shared her dreams and later a secret she'd never gotten over, one she'd never shared with even her closest friends. The secret that had driven them apart.

She wasn't going to think about that now—didn't want to think about *him* at all. She wanted to have a fun weekend and enjoy her time with her oldest and dearest friends. The last thing she wanted was to dwell on something that had, in the end, brought her nothing but pain and regret.

She picked her way back along the rocks to the sand and the lifeguard stand, where she retrieved her shoes and her bag. However mixed her feelings might be, she was still glad to be back in this town, on this street where she'd grown up, this beach she knew so well, immersed in the life she'd once lived here. She was grateful for the opportunity to come home, and she was going to enjoy every minute of her stay. Starting now.

Determined to make it so, she turned her back on the water, brushed the sand from her feet before sliding them into her shoes, and retraced the steps to her car, whistling "You Should Be Dancing."

Time to get the party started.

~

Liddy's deck overlooked the magnificent gardens she'd spent the past thirty years perfecting with perennial beds that swirled around rose bushes and set the stage for the tall backdrop of the last of the summer's delphiniums, monkshood, cannas, lilies, and hollyhocks. A riot of colorful annuals spilled from pretty pots on the deck and on the railings. A round table surrounded by four very comfy chairs was placed on the right side of the deck, and three lounges occupied almost all the left. Liddy had prepared a tableful of goodies—a baked brie, an artfully designed platter of crudités with a spicy dip, and a plate upon which a hefty slab of smoked bluefish rested on a bed of kale. For Maggie, it was sheer heaven to be sitting there on a beautiful late-September evening, inhaling the scent of the sweet autumn clematis that wound its way around the rails, and enjoying the company of her two oldest and dearest friends and the warmth of Liddy's hospitality, which was nothing short of fabulous.

"Refill, Mags?" Liddy held up the pitcher of margaritas.

"Oh, no. No. I shouldn't. I couldn't. Really," Maggie deadpanned and held up her glass. "Duh."

Liddy laughed and poured.

"Emma?"

"Oh, please. Yes." Emma turned, her glass in hand. "No one makes a better margarita."

"Thank you. Feel free to ring my doorbell anytime, day or night, and I'll be happy to whip up a batch." Liddy emptied the pitcher's remaining contents into her own glass, then set the pitcher on the table. The fingers of her left hand shuffled through her long, thick, salt-and-pepper hair, which flowed halfway down her back in one glorious wave. On some women, the color—or lack thereof—might have been aging, but Maggie thought on Liddy it was just right. Liddy'd always been all about honesty in everything, and that extended to how she presented herself to the world. On her last visit, Maggie had asked her when she was going to break down and color her hair, and Liddy had laughed. "Never. What you see is what you get. Besides, I don't have time for the upkeep. How often do you have your roots touched up?" she'd asked Maggie, who'd had to admit she had a standing appointment every six weeks.

"No time for that," Liddy'd declared. "Besides, I'm like Popeye in that old cartoon. 'I yam what I yam.'"

Maggie'd rolled her eyes and laughed, but she never brought it up again. She had to concede the look suited Liddy, who was taller than Maggie but who outweighed her by a good twenty-five pounds. Hers was a natural, comfortable look that sometimes still bordered on aging hippie, depending on what she was wearing, all of which went hand in glove with her mellow but tell-it-like-it-is personality. Tonight it was a long knit dress with three-quarter-length sleeves and knee-high slits. And it was orange belted with a wide swath of navy blue. Secretly, Maggie felt just a teensy bit frumpy, having chosen to wear conservative black pants, a teal tunic, and a plaid scarf around her neck. The closest she came to cool at that moment might have been the gold fringe earrings that dangled almost to her shoulders. Natalie had bought them for her birthday at the newest, hippest boutique on the Main Line. Liddy definitely took the prize for most colorful character, and always had.

Liddy regarded the empty pitcher. "I should go in and make more."

"In a few. Sit back and enjoy the night. You've been fussing since I got here. Your guest room looks like it belongs in a five-star hotel. It's absolutely luxurious." Maggie had arrived around four in the afternoon and had been led to Liddy's new guest suite. As promised, there was a new bed, new linens, totally new decor, and a newly redesigned bath. Flowers on the bedside table and fluffy white towels in a tall stack on the vanity. Maggie had rarely been treated so royally, and she'd said so.

"I do have a reputation to maintain. Besides, I couldn't have you wishing you'd booked a room at the inn CeCe Engle opened." Liddy's nose wrinkled. "I'd be plenty pissed off, I assure you."

"CeCe opened an inn?" Maggie hadn't heard this tidbit before. "Are we talking about the same CeCe Engle, the world's most unpleasant, unfriendly, nastiest gossip?"

"Not to mention the most slovenly and lazy person in Wyndham Beach. Well, from our class, anyway," Emma tossed in her two cents. Emma, who was the antithesis of slovenly, smoothed out the skirt of her denim shirtwaist dress. Always the lady, Emma *dressed* for every occasion—clothing, jewelry, nails, hair, all perfect before she ventured out of her house. *She's always been that way,* Maggie recalled. Emma had been the girl who showed up for the third-grade end-of-school picnic in neatly pressed white linen shorts and a tailored blouse—tucked in, of course—when everyone else was in cutoff jeans and T-shirts. Petite and pretty with a turned-up nose, wide blue eyes, and dark hair cut short in the same pixie style she'd sported all her life, Emma was always perfectly turned out.

"CeCe bought the old Ives place and has been working like a madwoman for the past year to pretty it up so it would be ready for reunion weekend," Liddy explained. "I understand only two couples have booked a room with her."

"I never thought I'd see the day when CeCe would consciously choose to do something that would require real exertion on her part. Does she know how hard innkeeping is?" Maggie took a sip of her drink before placing it on the table in front of her.

"If she doesn't, she soon will. I think this weekend is her virgin run," Emma said. "I ran into her at the post office a few days ago, and all she could talk about was getting the place perfect and who was staying with her."

"I wonder why she decided to open an inn," Maggie said. "She was never very industrious, and I never thought she liked people all that much. Maybe she's changed."

"Not that I can see." Liddy turned to Emma. "You?"

Emma shook her head. "Same old CeCe."

"I don't wish her ill, certainly, but I don't see that venture being very successful. The woman hardly has the temperament to deal with the public." Liddy paused before changing the subject. "Emma, should we share the latest about our police chief with Maggie?"

Maggie shot straight up in her chair in protest. "No, you should not. I don't want to know what he's doing, where he's living, who he's sleeping with, or who he's married to. Period."

"Oh, but Mags . . . ," Emma protested.

"No, I'm serious. I'm not interested. I don't want to know." Maggie clapped her hands over her ears. "All that with Brett happened a long time ago. I've moved way past it, and so has he. So should you. Can we please put it to rest?"

"Consider it done." Liddy exchanged a sly look with Emma. "But speaking of things being put to rest, did you see the list of deceased classmates I sent out?"

Maggie nodded. "I had no idea we'd lost so many over the past few years."

"Well, 'tis the season, I suppose." Emma swirled the remains of her margarita around in the bottom of her glass. "We're not getting any younger."

"Still, it seemed like a lot," Maggie said thoughtfully. "I had no idea Colleen Thompson had been sick. If I had, I'd have called her or at the very least sent a note."

"She hadn't been sick for long," Liddy told her. "It seemed like one day she had some testing done and the next week she was gone."

Maggie smiled sadly, remembering the girl they'd christened Tree, short for Treetop, because by sixth grade she'd towered over everyone, including most of the teachers. "Remember how the gym teachers and coaches all tried to get her to play basketball but she hated it? She wanted to play field hockey."

"At which she sucked." Emma added a second helping of brie to her plate. "God rest her soul. They had a lovely service for her at my father's church. He gave a stirring sermon."

"Your father always delivers the best sermons, Em. He was wonderful at my mother's memorial. So comforting," Maggie said, and Liddy nodded in agreement. "But I thought he stepped down as pastor."

"He did," Emma told her, "but her parents wanted him to do the service for Colleen, since the family had been members of the church for so long. You know my brother, Dan, is the pastor now, right? He took over when Dad retired."

Maggie nodded. "I do."

They fell silent, Maggie not only thinking of her mother but remembering other class members they'd lost over the years before

Emma said, "I think we're at the age where we can expect to hear about more friends passing on."

"You make us sound ancient. I'm not ready to think of myself as old. We're *not* old." Maggie frowned as she slid some fish onto a cracker. "Lid, what's in the sauce for the fish?"

"Sour cream, a little mayo, some lemon juice. Chopped fresh dill. I think that's it."

"It's delicious."

"Thanks. It's my mom's recipe."

Emma crunched a slice of red pepper. "Dying is a fact of life. We're all aware of that. I didn't expect to be a widow by my fiftieth birthday, and Maggie, I'll bet you thought you and Art had all the time in the world." She spoke softly, as always. The times when Maggie'd heard her raise her voice or lose her temper had been rare.

Before Maggie could respond, Liddy said pointedly, "And I never expected to bury a child."

Maggie reached over and squeezed Liddy's hands, which were folded together on the tabletop. Liddy's daughter Jessica's suicide three years ago had shocked everyone who had known her.

"I think a change of subject is in order right about now," Emma said, but Liddy shook her head.

"Not talking about it doesn't make it go away. For reasons I still don't understand, the fact remains that Jessie chose to end her life, and not a day passes when I wonder what I'd missed. There must have been signs I overlooked, things she'd said that should have tipped me off that she was in pain. How could I have not known?" Tears formed in the corners of Liddy's eyes. "What kind of a mother doesn't know her child is hurting so badly she'd rather die than continue to live?"

"Honey, you can only see what people choose to show you. For whatever reason, Jessie chose not to share." Maggie continued to hold on to Liddy's hands. "We'll probably never know what was going on, what she was thinking. Why she didn't confide in anyone. But we do know that you were a great mom to her. She adored you. You know that."

"She never acted depressed or troubled," Liddy continued on as if she hadn't heard Maggie's remarks. "She had days when she was down, like everyone does. I never thought there was something deeper going on. I've gone over and over every day I can remember for the weeks leading up to it, and I still don't see anything that should have set off an alarm that something was seriously wrong. She did seem to be a bit melancholy that last week, but not to the point where I was concerned. I knew she'd stopped dating Rob, and I thought maybe she was sad because he'd broken up with her. But afterward, he told me she'd broken up with him without any clear explanation." Her glass protested with a ping when she set it on the glass-topped table with a little too much force, and her voice cracked. *What did I miss?*

"Our kids don't share everything with us. Very often, they tell us what they think we want to hear." Maggie released her friend's hands. "There are things neither of my girls told me when they were growing up, things that made my hair stand on end when I heard about them later, which I did mostly by accident. Even now, I only know what they want me to know. I had no idea Gracie and Zach were having problems until she told me he'd moved out, and that was weeks after he'd gone. Frankly, I still don't understand why they divorced. And Natalie." Maggie rolled her eyes. "She didn't tell us she was pregnant until she was almost four months, and Jon had already walked out on her."

"Has she been able to locate him?" Liddy asked, as if grateful to change the subject.

"She isn't trying to. She says he'd gotten heavily involved with drugs, had no interest in stopping, and had no desire to go to rehab. She says she doesn't need his child support and doesn't want him in Daisy's life. Doesn't even want his family to know he has a daughter."

"Was he abusive to her?" Emma asked tentatively, as if she might be almost afraid of the answer.

"Not as far as I know. He was always sort of quiet, but amiable. He and Art got along well, and Art was always good at seeing things in people the rest of us missed. No." Maggie shook her head again, this time more emphatically. "Grace even asked her if Jon had ever 'gotten mean' with her, and Nat laughed in her face."

"Did you like him?" Emma asked.

Maggie blew out a long breath and thought before she answered. "He could be charming, and affectionate to Natalie, and he was always polite and well mannered. Art always said I'd never be satisfied with anyone either of the girls chose, but that's not true. I liked Zach. Loved him." She laughed ruefully. "And we know how that turned out."

"It sounds as if Natalie has good reasons for not wanting Jon to be in Daisy's life," Emma said.

"And I imagine she's still angry about the way he reacted when she told him she was pregnant." Liddy tossed a few grape tomatoes onto her plate.

"'Never wanted a kid, not about to have one now. You want it, you're on your own.' Can you imagine a man saying something like that to a woman he supposedly had been in love with for three years?"

"No. And you don't know what else went on that she hasn't told you about," Liddy pointed out. "And I'm sure you wouldn't want him around Natalie or Daisy if he's using drugs."

"Of course I don't. I still think he has the right to know he has a daughter, but that's not my call."

"Which reinforces what we've been trying to tell you about Jess, Liddy," Emma pointed out. Liddy acknowledged the remark with a slight nod but didn't comment. "You just don't always know what your kids are thinking or what's going on in their lives."

"I just hope Nat isn't going to regret her decision someday. Daisy is going to have questions about her father at some point."

"Those are her decisions to make. Natalie's an adult and she's going to do what she wants. I'd be happy if I could talk my son into coming home more than two or three times a year and staying for more than a long weekend." Emma drained her glass, then twirled the stem between her fingers.

"Well, when one is an international rock star, one has certain obligations," Liddy said, the hint of a tease in her voice.

"Yes, to everyone except one's mother." Emma made an exaggerated pouty face.

"You know, the whole rock star thing still tickles me." Maggie grinned. "Little Christopher Dean, who used to take music lessons at the house next door, has his name on a band and his face on album covers all over the world."

"It's crazy, right?" Emma laughed. "My sweet little boy now stands on stage and sings while girls throw their panties at him."

"Girls still do that?" Liddy asked. "I thought that went out with Tom Jones."

"Tom Jones is still around, and I'll bet women still toss their underwear at him," Maggie pointed out.

"Chris flew me to Los Angeles last year when the band kicked off their tour, and he plunked me right in the front row," Emma told them. "You wouldn't believe the things that went whizzing past my head. Everything from lacy bras to paper airplanes with phone numbers written on the wings to condoms. Also bearing phone numbers." She paused. "Not sure if the bras had writing on them."

"How'd you know their phone numbers were on the condoms?" Liddy asked.

"Someone swept them all up and piled them in a big bowl in the dressing room afterward, where I saw them. Oh, and hot tip: You're thinking about writing your number on a condom wrapper? Use a pen. Sharpies smear."

Liddy nodded. "Good to know."

"Well, I can't say I blame the girls for being excited. Chris was an adorable little boy, and he's handsome as sin now. Okay, maybe underwear and condoms are a bit much." Maggie recalled the sweet little towhead who used to pull her girls around the block in his red Radio Flyer wagon when they visited in the summers. "Of course, Natalie has all the band's CDs. She'll tell anyone who'll listen that she and Chris Dean, the lead singer of DEAN, were childhood friends, and that she used to call him Chrissy."

"Oh God, till my dying day, I will still see the look on Harry's face when Chris told him the name of the band was DEAN in capital letters." Emma's face reflected mock horror. "He was mortified. Told Chris the use of the Dean name, in any form, was absolutely forbidden."

"Unseemly for the son of the bank president to be the lead singer in a rock band," Maggie noted, "and so much more so for that band to carry the family name."

"Exactly. Oh, the arguments that ensued. Neither of them would budge an inch. You both know Harry wanted Chris to follow in his footsteps. He wanted him to go to Harvard, like he had, and his father and grandfather had, but Chris was having none of it. That boy knew what he wanted to do from the time he was eight years old, and it had nothing to do with banking." She grinned and added, "Except maybe banking his royalty checks once the band caught on and he actually started getting paid."

"I remember you telling me how the two of them would argue," Maggie said. "But with all due respect to Harry's memory, Chris seems to have done quite well for himself."

"Maybe too well. He makes an indecent amount of money, and I'm not sure what he does with it all. Not that he has to report his financial dealings to his mother, of course." Emma leaned close to one of the platters and cut a slim wedge of brie, which she topped on a cracker. "I just hope he's investing well. He can't play rock star forever."

"Are you kidding?" Liddy laughed. "Have you heard of the Rolling Stones? The Who? Rod Stewart? Eric Clapton?"

"Of course. But I didn't give birth to any of them, so I don't care what they do with their money or their lives. But my point was, I hope he's planning well for his future."

"I'm sure he has excellent financial advisers," Liddy pointed out.

"He mentioned he had someone who'd come highly recommended."

"Nothing to worry about then," Maggie assured her.

"You know what? We should go to one of his concerts sometime. The three of us together. Want to?" Emma looked from Maggie to Liddy.

"Of course," Liddy replied without hesitation.

"I'm in." Maggie toasted the idea with the last of her drink.

"Great. I'll call Chris and check the tour schedule. We'll see what date is best for each of us, and he can arrange it. Now, there's something fun to look forward to." She paused. "But you have to give me your solemn word: you will not remove articles of clothing to toss onto the stage."

"You have my word," Maggie promised. "No clothing, no condoms. Maybe a box of Junior Mints, though. I remember he loved those."

Emma smiled. "Still his favorite. I put a box in his Christmas stocking every year."

Liddy's face lit up. "It'll be such fun. Imagine the three of us rocking away in the front row, singing along with the band."

"I'll have to download some of his songs so I can sing, too." Maggie hadn't kept up with Chris's band over the past several years. All she knew was what she'd heard from Emma and from her daughter. "Natalie will be so jealous."

"She can go sometime on her own. I'm sure Chris would love to see her again. But this trip will be for us." Liddy picked up the pitcher and stood. "This calls for another round of margaritas. I'll be right back."

Maggie mused over what Chris might think, gazing down from the stage into a sea of adoring young female faces and finding not only his mother front and center, but her two oldest friends as well. "You think he'll be embarrassed?"

Emma waved a hand dismissively. "He'll love it. Trust me, nothing could be more embarrassing for him than the shenanigans that went on during the four days I spent at his house in LA last year. Even with his security, there were groupies climbing over the back fence day and night, sneaking into the house, hiding in his bedroom. One day, in broad daylight, a girl followed us home from the market, stripped naked right in front of me, then dove into the pool. And that's not the worst of it."

"Just what you want to see." Maggie grinned at the mental image that popped up in her head.

"I asked Chris what he'd have done if I hadn't been there, and he just laughed. I imagine he's leading quite the life." Emma shook her head almost imperceptibly. "Actually, I don't want to imagine it. If he's skinny-dipping with strangers or . . . whatever else . . . I don't want to know. It's his life, and I guess that all comes with the territory. Still, you know, you'd hope your son would be big enough to rise above it."

Maggie got up and opened the door for Liddy, who appeared to be struggling with another tray of snacks in one hand and a full pitcher in the other.

"Thanks, Mags." Liddy set the tray and the pitcher on the table. "We have some spicy Asian chicken thing I admit I bought frozen, and sweet-and-sour meatballs. Eat up, girls. This is what's passing for dinner tonight."

"Yum. This is perfect. Thank you." Maggie reached for a pick and speared a meatball.

Emma did the same as she continued on her rant. "Chris just turned thirty-three. Time to grow up. Meet a nice girl. Be responsible."

Maggie and Liddy looked at each other, then laughed.

"Em, my sweet, Chris is living his best life right now. A life any man under the age of, oh, maybe *eighty* would envy," Liddy said as she replenished the cracker tray from a box she'd brought out.

"I want him to settle down. Have children. I want to be a grand-mother," Emma grumbled. "I want him to come home."

"Ahhh, there's the heart of it." Maggie nodded knowingly. "You want him to come home."

"I can't help it. I'm a widow and he's my only child. Can you imag-ine how it feels to have one child that you almost never see?"

"Yes." Liddy refilled everyone's glass, including her own. "I had one child, and I will never see her again."

"Oh God, I'm sorry. I wasn't thinking." Emma's hand flew to her mouth.

"It's okay, Em."

"I swear, I just wasn't thinking. I wasn't comparing Chris touring with his band to Jessie." Emma appeared close to tears.

"Sweetie, I know," Liddy assured her. "Whatever the reason, we're both missing our kids, and living alone. Though the living alone part isn't so bad most of the time."

Emma nodded her agreement. "To be honest, I have to admit I don't miss Harry so much anymore. I mean, it has been eight years since he died. You adjust after a while."

"I'm still adjusting," Maggie admitted as she placed some brie on a cracker.

"Art's only been gone for two years. Of course you still miss him. But for me? No adjustment needed. I'm still angry. For all I know, Jim might have wanted a divorce for years, but his timing was just plain shitty." Liddy stabbed a celery stick into the dip with the vengeance of one spearing an elusive fish. One year and one day after their daughter had taken her life, Liddy's husband had walked out and wasted no time filing for divorce. "Jerk. And that's the nicest thing I can think to call him."

"That was a low blow," Maggie said softly.

"Insult to injury," Emma agreed.

"Kicked me while I was down." Liddy forced a half smile. "I can't think of any more clichés, but we all obviously agree it was a crappy thing for him to do."

"Have you heard from him at all?" Maggie asked.

"He sent me a card on my birthday. If I hadn't ripped it up and set fire to it, I'd share it with you." She took a vengeful bite from the celery stick and chewed. "It was totally generic. Like a card you'd send to your insurance agent. He signed his name, and that was it. After all the years we were married—all we'd gone through—and I get a *Hope you have a sunny day!* card with a picture of a sunflower on the front."

"That is cold," Maggie agreed, grateful that Art's image had suffered no such tarnishing since his passing. She still honored the man he'd been, and their daughters still believed he'd walked on water.

Liddy continued to bat Jim around for a while longer before talk turned to who all had declined to come to the reunion and who all they'd see over the weekend. They shared gossip—LeeAnn divorced her third husband and is looking for number four; Caroline had a mastectomy, but she's in remission and is doing really well; Kelly Sanger's daughter ran off with Kelly's pool boy and left Kelly to care for her two grandbabies. And there'd been much laughter and remembrances— *Remember the time Polly Landers brought her cat to school in her book bag because her brother threatened to take it to the beach? Remember the Memorial Day parade when Sue Merritt flipped her baton into the air, and it came down on Amy Thomas's head and knocked her out cold and they had to stop the parade?*

When at last the snacks had been consumed and the pitcher had been emptied for the last time, the leftovers had been packed away, and the dishwasher had been filled, Emma headed off to her own home and Maggie and Liddy retired to their respective rooms. Tired from her travels, once she'd tucked herself under the quilt Liddy'd left at the foot of the bed, Maggie closed her eyes. Her face still hurt from laughing, and for a while sleep seemed out of the question. So many images—faces and places and events—had been conjured up over the past hours. Voices and snippets of songs played inside her head, memories resurfaced, old feelings she'd thought long dead stirred. She pushed aside what she could and told herself she'd deal with the rest of it tomorrow. She drifted off to sleep still enveloped in the warmth and comfort of the love of her friends, effectively ignoring the certainty that before she left Wyndham Beach to return home on Monday, other emotions would be stirred up, other old feelings would surface—and those she would have to face alone.

Chapter Two

"I'd forgotten how nice it could be to have a day to just do whatever I feel like doing." Maggie finished strapping herself into the passenger seat of Liddy's car.

"You're still volunteering at fifty different places and substitute teaching?"

Maggie nodded. "It feels like fifty sometimes. I know I should cut back, but it's so difficult once you get entrenched and people start depending on you."

She'd quit teaching following Art's diagnosis, but after his death, she'd needed something to dig into, something to focus on other than herself and her lonely house, her empty bed. Someplace to go where she could meet people who'd never known Art, people who could talk about something besides her loss. Who could see her as someone other than half a broken circle.

"Well, you might think about what you'd miss the least, then slowly reduce your hours until you feel comfortable backing out gracefully."

"That's good advice. Maybe I'll cut back at . . . oh, hell. I don't know which one I like the least. I like all of the agencies and places and the people I've met."

"You'll figure it out. You can always use the excuse that you want to spend more time substitute teaching."

"Well, that is true. There have been times when I've had to turn down teaching opportunities because I've committed to one thing or another."

"Are you still the CEO of Art's law firm?"

"I am, though I don't know why. I mean, I know he wanted to keep the business in the family, but still. I don't do anything except pop in once a month, water the snake plant in Art's old office, and take his old assistant out to lunch."

"I'd have thought he'd have left the firm to Grace."

"Eventually, he would have. But at the time decisions had to be made, Art didn't feel comfortable putting Grace in such a position of power when her husband was working there, too." Maggie grimaced. "Of course, in retrospect, it was the right thing to do. Imagine if Gracie had the controlling interest in the firm, given the situation with Zach. If they'd stayed married even for a time, would he be entitled to half of the firm when they divorced? I don't know. I'm just glad that was one conversation we didn't have to have."

"And you're not tempted to exercise a little control yourself where Zach is concerned?"

"Of course I am. Zach was a huge part of our lives from the time he and Grace were in law school. He said he'd waited until after Art died to tell her he wanted a divorce because he didn't want to add to everyone's distress, but frankly, I think he waited because he couldn't look Art in the eye." Maggie shook her head, remembering how happy Art had been with his daughter's choice of husband, how he and Zach had gone to baseball and football games together. Just weeks before Art got sick, he and his son-in-law had gone deep-sea fishing, a first time for both of them, and they'd made plans to go again at the end of the summer. "He wasn't man enough to face Art with the truth. I also think he was hoping that, on his deathbed, Art would give him half the firm. Thank God he didn't."

"He isn't worthy of Grace," Liddy pronounced as if closing the door on that topic, then backed out of the driveway carefully, pausing at the curb to make sure nothing was coming either way. "So where to first? The beach? The harbor? Or we could check out a few of the new shops in town."

"I'm up for a little shopping. I stopped at the beach yesterday when I first arrived. I was surprised to see a lifeguard station there."

"Yes, there's a lifeguard from Memorial Day straight through till Labor Day, seven days a week, from nine in the morning till six at night. A dumb waste of taxpayers' money if you ask me. That beach has the worst sand. No one wants to sit on it. Everyone goes to the Island Road beach," Liddy all but harrumphed. "The Cottage Street beach has always been set aside for fishing and digging quahogs, and underage drinking. Everyone knows that."

"Then why . . . ?"

"Because three years ago, the stepnephew of our beloved mayor almost drowned when he stupidly jumped off the jetty into the water. Broke both legs when he hit the rocks. So now we have to pay to have someone sit up on that stand yelling 'Get off the rocks!' and watching the geezers fly-fish from the shore. The underage drinking doesn't usually start until closer to midnight, so the police get to deal with them."

Liddy made a turn into the municipal parking lot behind the Wyndham Beach General Store and cut the engine, and that quickly Maggie was out of the car, her head back and her eyes closed.

"I love how you can smell the water from anyplace in town," she said, relishing the moment. "The harbor here and the cove up by my family's old home, the bay from Island Road. It always smells like sunshine and the sea and salt to me. I've never stopped missing it."

"Then you should move back. There's lots more salt air where that came from. And great houses come up for sale all the time." Before Maggie could respond, Liddy took her arm and steered her in the direction of a brick path that ran behind several shops. "This is all new since the last time you were here. We call it 'the Stroll.' This little meandering path leads from one shop to another. Wait till you step inside Glinda's Corner. Cutest kids' clothes ever. You're going to want to buy everything for that sweet little Daisy."

As Liddy'd predicted, Maggie found several items for Daisy that would be tucked away until December. At Nibbles 'n' Such, she purchased some baked-that-morning cheese straws, a jar of locally sourced honey, and a fat round jar of fig jam made by the sister of the shop owner, all to share with Maggie's hostess. At Dazzle Me, Maggie bought a pair of malachite earrings for Natalie—green, to match her eyes—and huge gold citrine studs for Grace, with the hope that perhaps some sunshine in her ears might add a little sunshine to her life. At the Potter's Wheel, she found gorgeous vases for her daughters and a lovely bowl for Art's assistant, Lois, whom Maggie continued to remember on birthdays and holidays because of her devotion to Art and her kindness through the dark days of his illness.

"Did I lie?" Liddy demanded as they walked back to the car, laden with their purchases.

"You totally nailed it. I'm delighted with everything I picked up. You know, my mom always started her Christmas shopping immediately after Labor Day."

Liddy opened the back of her SUV and Maggie loaded her packages inside.

"Where to now?" Maggie asked as she got into the passenger seat.

"I thought maybe we'd visit Emma at the art center."

"I'd like that. I know Emma's been working her butt off to get it off the ground."

"She's done an incredible job. Wait till you see. You'll be so impressed." Liddy turned the key in the ignition, backed out onto High Street, and stopped at the intersection with Front just as a police cruiser rolled up to the opposing stop sign. The driver's window was down as the occupant exchanged words with a pedestrian who'd just come out of the post office. The brief conversation appeared to have been cordial, and a moment later the cruiser drove off in the direction of the harbor.

"He's coming to the reception tonight but not to the luncheon tomorrow, if you're wondering." Liddy followed Maggie's gaze toward the street, then proceeded through the intersection.

"Oh, I wasn't—" Maggie began to protest, but Liddy cut her off.

"Of course you were. But that wasn't . . . the chief." She smiled as she caught herself almost speaking the verboten name.

Maggie's cheeks reddened as she tried to deny she'd been staring at the police car. As much as she hated to admit it even to herself, *of course* she was curious about Brett, and of course she'd known for years he was the Wyndham Beach police chief. On the one hand, she'd hoped to avoid him all weekend. On the other, thinking about seeing him—or not seeing him, she couldn't decide which would be worse—caused a dull ache to settle in her chest.

God, I sound like a fifteen-year-old, she chastised herself even as she realized that was how old she'd been when she and Brett first met. It wasn't easy, but she managed to turn off the memory button in her head when Liddy entered the parking lot at the art center.

Emma's touch was everywhere in the art center, which was housed in a renovated white clapboard building sitting by itself on a spit of land overlooking Buzzards Bay. Exhibition space shared the first floor with two offices, and there were classrooms for painting, photography, sculpture, and children's art housed on the second. A small outbuilding was devoted to pottery and metalcraft.

"I can't believe you raised all the funds for the building's renovation by yourself, Emma," Maggie exclaimed. "You're amazing."

"The community has been very supportive, but most of the funding comes from Chris, to tell the truth. He paid for all the work in here and makes a monthly donation to keep the place heated in slow months,"

Emma confided. "I think *he* thinks it excuses him from not coming home more often."

"Or maybe it's just his way of showing support for his mama," Maggie said.

"Maybe," Emma replied. "We have the makings of a nice little artists' colony here. We're starting slow, only taking a few members this summer because we don't have living quarters to offer. There are no places in town for rent, so unless the applicants know someone who'll put them up, they're on their own until we can figure out something we can offer. I'd love to somehow get the Harrison family to open up that mansion of theirs. It's sitting there, no one's living in it, you know, and it would be perfect." Emma's eyes took on a dreamy glow.

"None of them have moved back to Wyndham Beach?" Maggie asked.

Emma shook her head. "Someone comes back to bring out the carousel every five years, plunks it out there in the park, lets all the local kiddies have a ride."

"That was in someone's will, right?" Maggie tried to remember the story. "They have to share the carousel with the town every fifth summer or the estate will be broken up and sold. Something like that?"

"Exactly. Harry's father was executor of the last Jasper Harrison's will. He was the one who bought the carousel back in the 1940s. After his father died, Harry cleaned out his desk and found a copy of the old man's will, which he showed me. The wording was 'no less than every fifth summer, preferably on the Fourth of July.' But it's never been brought out more than every five years."

"So I take it you haven't been able to track down the heirs yet?" Liddy turned her attention from a painting she'd been studying that hung in the foyer.

"Still trying. I have learned Owen Harrison inherited everything, but so far he hasn't returned my calls." She smiled slyly. "He can run but he can't hide. I will find him."

Maggie laughed. "My money's definitely on you, Em. Track him down and drag him back by the scruff of the neck if necessary."

"That's the plan." Emma took Maggie by the elbow and led her into the exhibition area. "Now, these are all works by local artists. Take your time looking around. I think you'll agree we have some true talent in our little town."

Maggie and Liddy spent almost an hour viewing and discussing the exhibited pieces, from the enormous freestanding hands sculpted from clay to the watercolor landscapes to the pottery that reflected all the colors of the bay beyond the art center. Liddy paused in front of a very large contemporary painting of muted grays and taupes, with sharp lightning bolts of red and gold slashed across the canvas.

"Wow, there's so much energy there," Maggie remarked. The swirls of color were almost electric. "The swashes of red and gold make such a bold statement against that subdued background."

Liddy pointed to the name of the artist: Jessica Christy Bryant.

"Oh. It's Jess . . ." Maggie's voice faded away momentarily. Of course, she'd known Jessie had been an artist. She'd started designing greeting cards when she was in middle school. Never sold commercially, the cards had been sent to relatives and friends. Following her mother's death, Maggie had cleaned out a desk drawer in the house on Cottage Street and found dozens of cards her mother had received from Jess over the years for various occasions. She'd taken them back to Bryn Mawr, and when Grace saw them, she mentioned she, too, had been the recipient of the wonderfully imaginative and colorful birthday and holiday cards. The Christmas card she'd received three years ago had been the last she'd gotten.

"This painting's the last thing she did before," Liddy was saying.

Maggie didn't need to ask *Before what?* "It's a remarkable piece," she said simply.

"Emma asked if I had any of her work I'd be willing to have on display. Ironically, this last piece of hers is my favorite. You'd think I'd hate it, but . . ." Liddy shrugged. "I think it reflects her state of mind better than anything she may have said at the time." She pointed to the name of the painting. *Last Stand.* "That's what I think this was. I think it's very emotional, don't you? I sense an overwhelming frustration when I look at it."

To Maggie, the painting seemed to scream, to rage against something nameless. But to Liddy, she said, "It's very moving. Eloquent. Jess was very talented."

"She was that." The sadness emanating from Liddy was palpable.

"She absolutely was." Emma had come up behind them quietly. "I've had several inquiries from interested buyers."

"It's not for sale," Liddy snapped. "I haven't decided if any of her work will ever be for sale."

"I cautioned the prospective buyers that it might not be." In contrast to Liddy's harsh response, Emma's voice was soothing. "I would never sell anything without your express permission, Lid."

"I do know that. Sorry for . . ."

"It's already forgotten," Emma assured her friend. "But if you agree, I'd like to showcase Jessie's work in a special exhibit over the winter. Perhaps January or February."

"That would be lovely, Em. I appreciate it."

"I'd like to include those white-on-white works in the December exhibit. They're so quiet and contemplative."

Liddy nodded. "Just let me know when you want them."

Emma patted Liddy on the shoulder before retreating to her office to take a phone call. Maggie took her friend's hand and together they finished their tour of the exhibit. Before leaving, they poked their heads into Emma's office to let her know they were going.

"I love this place," Maggie told her truthfully. "I want to come back before I leave."

"Come back anytime." Emma beamed. "Now, are you planning on going early to tonight's reception, or can we expect you to be fashionably late?"

"If I can get dinner on the table by six, we should be able to be on time. You're welcome to join us for dinner, Em," Liddy offered.

"Thanks, Lid, but I'll be here until six and will barely have time to get home and change."

"We'll look for you there." Liddy and Maggie made their way to the exit, then walked to the end of the boardwalk that led toward the bay.

"One of the best views ever, right here." Maggie paused at the head of the dune, where beach grass bent in the face of a breeze blowing in from the water. Rugosa roses, a few still stubbornly blooming, and beach plums, still bearing pink fruit, grew among the grasses.

Liddy checked the time on her phone. "Come on. We need to keep moving if we're going to get to that reception on time." She put an arm over Maggie's shoulder as they walked to the car. "Never know who we might run into."

"Oh?" Maggie raised an eyebrow. It wasn't like Liddy to be coy.

"Some of those yes responses were interesting." Liddy dropped her arm at the passenger's side and continued around the front of the car.

"Do tell," Maggie said as she opened the door and got in.

"Mark Renfield is coming. As is Rick Gallup." Liddy slid behind the wheel. "Both divorced. Rick's the head surgeon at a hospital in Chicago now, by the way."

"So . . . what are you saying?"

"I'm saying I've been sleeping alone since Jim left and the last time I saw Rick, he looked pretty damned good. One might even say hot." She put the car in drive. "And if I don't put a move on him, LeeAnn will."

"Are you sure you want a houseguest for the whole weekend? I wouldn't want to cramp your style," Maggie said. "Maybe I should consider a room at CeCe's inn after all."

"Don't be silly. For all I know, Rick's already on to wife number two. I'm just keeping my options open." She glanced across the console at Maggie. "You should, too."

Maggie waved a dismissive hand. "Not interested in putting the moves on anyone, thank you."

"Oh, come on. With all due respect to Art, he's been gone for two years. Are you telling me that you haven't thought about hooking up with someone tall, dark, and handsome since then?"

"'Hooking up'?" Maggie laughed out loud. "What are we, sixteen?"

"Call it whatever you want. You're widowed, I'm divorced, and neither of us are even close to being old or dried up. You want to spend the rest of your life sleeping alone?" Not waiting for an answer, Liddy added, "I for one do not."

Maggie looked out the window. She'd been so numb since Art's death she'd barely thought about what, if anything, came next as far as her love life was concerned. To do so felt disrespectful of her late husband. If she turned to someone else for whatever reason—friendship, companionship, sex—would he somehow know and think she'd forgotten him? Several times before he passed away, he'd made her promise to live a full life after he was gone, but still . . .

Liddy pulled all the way to the garage at the very end of her driveway and parked, then cut the ignition.

"Well, if you're thinking about getting lucky tonight, I suggest we get on with it. We have some work to do." Maggie opened the car door and got out. In Liddy's heart and in her wardrobe, the seventies were alive and well. It was part of her charm, but at the same time, it was a little predictable. The woman had so much going for her: smart, witty, so much fun. But her look—which might have been considered a little edgy in her teens—today looked tired, matronly. Her colorful clothes couldn't hide the sallowness of her skin or her crow's feet. Maggie knew it was a long shot, trying to talk Liddy into changing things up even a little.

As she slammed the car door closed, Liddy asked, "What do you mean, some work? What kind of work?" and followed her into the house.

~

"Seriously, Maggie? I haven't worn that stuff in a million years." Liddy staunchly declined Maggie's offer to share her makeup. "I'm not going to start now."

"What do you think will happen if you swiped on a little mascara?"

"I won't look like myself. I'll feel like I'm pretending to be someone I'm not."

"A little makeup isn't going to make you look like someone else. It just enhances what you already have. Who you already are."

"Not going to happen." Liddy was unmovable.

"Okay." Maggie ceremoniously dropped the eye shadow stick, mascara wand, and blush into her makeup bag and zipped it closed.

She could have reminded Liddy of all the nights the three of them—she, Liddy, and Emma—had crowded into the bathroom Maggie shared with her sister and passed around the latest cosmetic purchase one of them had made. Back in high school, they'd shared it all, experimented with it all, worn it all, especially for special events. Like when Liddy had wanted to attract the attention of a certain junior, or when Maggie wanted to catch the attention of . . . okay, she let herself mentally say his name. Brett. Brett Kyle Crawford. Even his name had sounded golden to her. She'd wanted to attract his attention the first time she'd laid eyes on him, wanted him to notice her before one of the other girls got her hooks into him. She'd known he was meant to be hers the minute he walked into homeroom on the first day of school sophomore year.

Hers to win, hers to lose.

Maggie brushed the memories aside and slid the dress she'd picked up at Nordstrom over her head. She'd decided to go low key tonight. Black sheath with elbow-length sleeves, a camel leather belt double-looped around her waist, and leopard print heels. A choker of oversize cat's-eye beads fit just inside the scooped neckline of the dress, and she chose large round gold discs for her ears.

"Wow. Sexy." Liddy wiggled her eyebrows when Maggie joined her in the kitchen.

Maggie made a face. "Hardly. There's no flesh showing above my knees or my elbows."

"Maybe so, but the overall impression is a wow." Liddy had donned a calf-length purple cotton skirt, which she'd paired with a plain white long-sleeve jersey knit top. Around her neck she'd wrapped several bead necklaces of various shapes, colors, and sizes. Long silver earrings dangled almost to her shoulders. She'd unbraided her hair and brushed it into a long ponytail that lay low on the back of her neck. Maggie bit her tongue. If Liddy was looking for action, the odds weren't in her favor tonight, but Liddy was . . . Liddy.

"Thank you. Natalie helped pick it out."

"The girl has good taste." Liddy opened the back door and stepped outside.

"She always has." Maggie followed Liddy out the door, down the back steps and to the car.

Maggie barely spoke on the drive to the Beach Club, built in 1860 as the home of the Wyndham Beach Ladies League of the Anti-Slavery Society. Her three-times-great-grandmother, Polly Wakefield, had been a charter member, her husband Henry having fought for the preservation of the Union. Maggie thought about Polly and Henry as she climbed the steps and approached the front door, wondering how they'd feel about the fact that none of their descendants now lived in Wyndham Beach. She suspected if they felt anything at all—and she wasn't sure they did—they'd not be very happy.

Thoughts of the distant past vanished when Liddy grabbed Maggie's elbow and steered her off to the right into the room known as the Fireside Room, which was set up with several round tables, a scattering of chairs, two long tables upon which an array of desserts had been displayed, and an open bar. The lights had been lowered to that precise point of bright enough to see but not harsh enough to make everyone look, well, harsh. The room was crowded, and the noise level ranged from happy chatter to boisterous laughter.

"Maggie. Three o'clock," Liddy whispered. "Blue blazer. White turtleneck. Yellow sweater."

Maggie looked off to her right, where a small group of men were animatedly chatting next to the bar.

"Who am I looking at?" Maggie kept her voice low as well.

"That's Rick. Don't you recognize him?"

"Ah, no." Maggie tried not to stare while at the same time trying to see something familiar about him.

Liddy took a hurried step in his direction, forcing Maggie to grab her by the arm to stop her forward motion.

"Uh-uh. Too soon," Maggie cautioned.

"Don't be silly. If I don't, someone else will. Come on." And with that Liddy took off like a shot in the direction of the bar, leaving a startled Maggie in her wake.

She watched Liddy approach the group of men without hesitation, a smile on her face and a spring in her step. She took a few steps in Liddy's direction but was waylaid by classmates who wanted to catch up. Distracted, Maggie tried to maintain attention to dual situations. She was happy to see old friends and wanted to talk, but at the same time, she had a sinking feeling in the pit of her stomach that things weren't going to end well for Liddy, especially after she saw a woman in a short tight blue dress cut down to *there* scoping out the same group Liddy had joined.

Tapping her target on the shoulder, Liddy stepped back as Rick turned and greeted her warmly with a hug, as did the others in the group. After a few moments of what appeared to be lively conversation, the woman in the blue dress who'd caught Maggie's eye drifted over and joined them, and one by one the attention of all five men began to swivel from Liddy to the newcomer.

LeeAnn . . . Maggie didn't know what the woman's last name was after three marriages . . . but it was pretty clear that LeeAnn was dressed for success, her impressive cleavage having led the way to the circle. The guys looked fascinated and hung on every word, and they slowly closed ranks, with LeeAnn in and Liddy gradually being eased out.

Maggie grabbed the hand of Caroline McNally, the latest friend to approach her, and said, "I told Liddy I'd meet her at the bar, and I see she's waiting. Let's join her for a drink."

Maggie made a beeline toward the bar, dragging Caroline with her.

"Time for a drink," Maggie said as she physically turned Liddy toward the bar.

"Did you see . . . ?" Liddy was understandably embarrassed.

"I did, but I don't think anyone else did," Maggie said under her breath. Aloud, she told Liddy, "Caroline was telling me how well she's doing now that she's in remission. Caroline, I think you're remarkably strong. And you look wonderful." Maggie signaled the bartender. "Wine, ladies? Or something else . . . ?"

When the bartender made his way to their end of the bar, Maggie ordered two glasses of pinot grigio and a sparkling water for Caroline. In the meantime, several others had gathered around them. Maggie fixed a smile on her face and let Caroline take center stage.

"Thank you. That was a really nice save," Liddy whispered when their drinks arrived. With a glance at the corner of the bar where the men still stood talking, laughing, and flirting with LeeAnn, she added, "You'd think none of them ever saw boobs before."

"None of them were worthy of you back then, and they're not worthy of you now."

"LeeAnn deliberately broke in on my conversation and she . . . she . . . oh, I'm so pissed." Liddy tossed back her wine as if it were water. "You know, she always was *obvious*. Remember the class trip junior year to New York City and the way she was making out with Tony Faselli in the back of the bus?"

"We can talk when we get back to your house and you can bitch and moan as much as you want, but right now, you need to act like you didn't even notice her."

"Right. You're right." Liddy took a sip of wine.

Emma made her way over, dressed as usual in a pretty but modest dress of navy knit with a white Peter Pan collar and plain navy leather heels.

"How does she do that?" Liddy wondered. "If I wore a dress like that, I'd look like a nun. She never does."

"That's just Emma. She always looks just right."

"Well, so do you. You couldn't have been blind to the fact that just about every head in this room turned when you came in," Liddy told her.

"You came in at the same time," Maggie reminded her. "Don't assume everyone was looking at me."

"Everyone's used to seeing me around. You haven't been to a reunion in years. Which makes you somewhat exotic."

Maggie laughed. "Believe me, there's nothing exotic about me or my life. But you're right. It's been too long. Let's mingle. Let's get a refill for our drinks—then we'll go and have a good time."

"Maybe I should have let you paint my face after all," Liddy said with apparent reluctance as she glanced over her shoulder to the corner of the bar where LeeAnn was now holding court.

"Don't be silly." Maggie leaned closer to Liddy's ear. "If you think you have to wear makeup to attract someone's attention, you're wearing it for the wrong reason, and you're trying to attract the wrong person."

"You were the one standing at the ready with the tools at hand," Liddy reminded her.

"I was doing it for you, not Rick or anyone else." Maggie slipped an arm through Liddy's. "I just remembered how much we loved doing our makeup when we were younger."

"You were trying to spruce me up and make me look more attractive, and I bitched at you." Liddy sighed. "I'm sorry for that. Looking around here at everyone else, I guess I look a little old and tired. I don't blame Rick for being lured away by LeeAnn's cleavage."

"I thought we were talking about makeup."

"That too." Liddy gestured toward the center of the room. "There's Kay Doran. Did you know she's working for the *Boston Globe* now? She covers the features desk. Let's go catch up . . ."

The room was crowded, but in the end Maggie made it a point to seek out everyone in it and chat, if only for a moment. Besides renewing old friendships that had sadly been allowed to fade away over the years, she was amused to see how some people had changed, while others had not. The mousy girl from AP English no one seemed to notice back then had turned into a beauty, stylish and confident in ways no one could have predicted. Conversely, the class beauty queen had really let herself go. The once exuberant, happy, beautiful girl now looked emaciated and sad. Alas, however, the class geek had avoided becoming a cliché by not growing up to be a handsome, rich lady-killer. He was still geeky, but he looked comfortable in his skin and seemed to be having a good time.

"He isn't coming." Liddy came up behind Maggie, startling her.

"Who isn't coming?"

Liddy rolled her eyes. "I've lost count of the number of times I caught you looking at the door."

"I wasn't aware I'd been looking. And if I was, I wasn't looking for anyone in particular."

"I just heard there was an accident out on Six. He's working."

Maggie cut her off, protesting she hadn't been looking for anyone in particular, but they both knew she'd been watching for Brett, dreading the moment he'd come through the door at the same time she was anxiously awaiting his arrival. Anybody'd be curious about an old boyfriend. It was nothing more than that, she'd told herself when they'd rehashed the evening later at Liddy's—who'd changed for the better, who the years had not been kind to. Who was unrecognizable, who hadn't changed a damn bit. Her protests aside, in her heart, Maggie knew the one face she'd most wanted to see was the one that hadn't shown.

Chapter Three

For Maggie, deciding in which of the Saturday events to take part had been a no-brainer. She hated golf—she'd learned to play because Art wanted her to, but she'd never taken to it. There was no way she was going to sit in the stands and watch a football game—too many memories there. So while Liddy played golf and Emma tended to the art center, Maggie joined some old friends for lunch at Mimi's. New since Maggie's last visit to Wyndham Beach, the restaurant was bright and pretty, with lots of glass overlooking the water and lush green plants in every window.

There were eighteen women in the group, divided between three tables positioned closely enough to each other that the diners could take part in nearby conversations. As Liddy promised, the food was delicious, and the company engaging and downright fun. Maggie found herself seated next to Dee Olson, who, after having raised five children, trained to run marathons.

"You run *marathons?*" Maggie had a vague recollection of Dee having been somewhat athletic back in the day, but marathons were a far cry from the track events they'd all been forced to participate in.

Dee nodded, a smile on her face. "At least two a year. Sometimes three."

"When I was younger, I used to run every morning for about forty minutes," Maggie confessed to Dee, "but I was never good enough to run a marathon. It's been on my bucket list for a couple of years, though."

"I'm not sure what you mean by 'good enough,'" Dee replied. "Marathon running is really more a discipline. Taking your training seriously enough to make a schedule and stick to it." She smiled wryly. "Which is why I didn't run my first until I was in my forties. I just couldn't stick to a schedule while my kids were still in school. At least, that was the excuse I gave myself. After the last kid left for college, I had no excuses left. I realized if I really wanted to do this, I had to stop talking about it and start taking the steps I needed to make it happen."

"I'm sure it was really hard," Maggie said.

"It got easier." That wry smile again. "Here's the thing. The more you run, the more you can run."

"Well, I admire the fact that you have the willpower to do something so demanding. I'm really impressed."

"If you ever get serious about it, let me know, and I'll give you some pointers." Dee wrote her number down on a piece of paper and handed it to Maggie. "You might like it."

Maggie looked at the number before slipping it into the pocket of the navy cable cardigan she'd worn over a white shirt and pants with a subtle navy-and-gray plaid. "Thanks. I just might do that." She thought she really might. Probably would. Maybe.

On the drive back to Liddy's, Maggie thought more about running marathons and decided if she lived closer, she definitely would take up Dee on her offer. Before Art had fallen ill, they'd talked about joining a local running club. Now would be a good time to explore distance running. Maybe she could make it a goal to run a 5K in the spring. Several nearby towns sponsored such runs—she'd seen the advertising. She wouldn't be up to the speed of the other runners, to be sure, but would it matter if she came in last, other than possibly a minor blow to her pride?

Intrigued by the possibility, she made a mental note to check after she arrived home on Monday. She was also going to dig out that bucket list she'd made when she'd turned forty.

~

"You made a bucket list? What else was on it?" Liddy asked when they'd reconvened in her kitchen before heading out to the dinner dance at the Harbor Inn.

Maggie reached for one of the cheese straws she'd purchased the day before at Nibbles 'n' Such. "Oh, buying a vacation house somewhere near the water. Writing a novel. Taking a photography class. Brushing up on my sailing skills. Traveling. Spain. Egypt. Spending a summer in Tuscany." She shrugged. "Stuff you think about when you turn forty. How 'bout you? You have a list of things you want to do before you die?"

"Not really. I've done pretty much everything I've ever wanted to do." Liddy looked away, then smiled. "I guess the only thing I really want to do before I die is have sex again."

Maggie rolled her eyes. "It's supposed to be something you've always wanted, Lids. Not something you've wanted since last week."

"There are no rules when it comes to the bucket list. You put on it what you want. That's what I want. I want to have sex again. Preferably soon."

"Let me know if you think you're going to get lucky later. I can probably bunk in with Emma for the night."

Liddy laughed. "Not to worry. I'm not going to bring anyone home tonight."

"Good to know. We should leave if we're going to pick up Emma."

"Good point. Wrap up those cheese sticks, would you?" Liddy grabbed their wineglasses and rinsed them out before putting them into the dishwasher. "And once again, you're going to turn heads. That dress is gorgeous on you."

"This old thing?" Maggie quipped, then laughed. "Found it on sale in Neiman Marcus three weeks ago. I've had to practically starve myself since to make sure it would fit, but I love it."

"Blue is definitely your color."

"Thank you. And that black sheath you're wearing is perfect, if I may say so. I can't remember the last time you wore a fitted dress. You look wonderful. Ten years younger." Maggie grabbed her bag off the table as Liddy turned off all the lights except the one over the stove. "And I love your hair like that. You definitely rock the bun, Lids."

"Thank you for the kind words and thank you for pinning my hair up for me. It's a bit more than I can handle on my own. I should probably get it trimmed sometime soon." She gestured to the door, and Maggie opened it. "I bought this dress for Jessie's funeral and never thought I'd wear it again. Then I saw all those girls decked out in black last night, and I decided my daughter would be pissed if she knew I'd only worn this dress that one time."

"I don't know if she'd be pissed, but I do know she'd agree that you look really lovely." Maggie peered closer. "Are you wearing . . . did you . . . ?"

"Yes. Mascara. I've decided to walk on the wild side." Liddy laughed. "I found an old tube in the bathroom and figured what the heck. And before you ask, no, I didn't do it to attract Rick. Though I wouldn't mind if he . . . never mind." She brushed past Maggie and went down the back steps. "Close the door behind you, please."

"How old is the tube?" Maggie asked.

"A couple of years."

"At the risk of sounding critical, old cosmetics can carry bacteria. You could get an infection in your eye from using old makeup."

"You're the one who told me I should use it. So I use it, and you tell me I'm probably going to go blind?" Liddy opened the driver's-side door and slid behind the wheel. When Maggie got into the passenger seat, Liddy said, "Make up your mind."

Liddy started the car and had her hand on the shift. They sat in silence, then they both began to laugh.

"Sorry. For a minute there, it was almost like having Ruthie back. Even after all these years, I miss my sister. I miss arguing with her. Damn, but that girl could argue about anything, anytime. Sometimes I still miss that, you know?"

"I do know. I miss Sarah a lot, especially when I'm in Wyndham Beach. We didn't fight much, though." Maggie bit the inside of her lip. *Except for the day she died.*

"It wasn't your fault."

"If she hadn't been so mad at me, she wouldn't have left the house in a snit. She would have been more cautious."

"Come on, Maggie. You were twelve. Sisters argue all the time." Liddy raised her hand to stop whatever it was Maggie was about to say. "Okay, so you borrowed something of hers without asking, and it pissed her off."

"Something she'd told me not to touch. Ever."

In her mind's eye, Maggie could still see the pretty blue sweater their grandmother had sent Sarah for her birthday. Maggie'd been so jealous. What had her grandmother sent her? A doll. Granted, it was a Madame Alexander doll, but it was a doll all the same. As if Maggie were still a child and played with dolls. Then five weeks later, Sarah's birthday gift had arrived: a cashmere sweater in the most glorious shade of pale blue. Sarah was only three years older than Maggie. It wasn't fair that she got something so grown-up and Maggie got a little girl's toy.

Maggie had wanted only to try on the sweater, but Sarah had come home early from the library. She'd thrown an absolute fit when she walked into her room and found her little sister with the beautiful sweater pulled over her head. She'd screamed at Maggie, wrenched the sweater away, and bodily thrown Maggie out of her room. She'd landed in the hallway, her pride and her feelings more injured than her butt. Sarah had returned the sweater to the box, put the box on the top shelf of her closet, slammed her bedroom door, and stomped down the stairs, yelling, "Stay out of my room! Don't you ever touch any of my things again!" She'd run out the front door, jumped on her bike, and taken off, pedaling furiously.

Maggie never saw her alive again. Sarah, highly allergic to insect stings, had taken a shortcut through a field on her way to her best friend's house, no doubt to complain about what a pain in the ass her little sister was. She'd ridden her bike directly over a yellow jackets' nest, sending several of the small wasps after her. When their father found her lying in the field after she'd failed to come home that night, Sarah had eleven stings on the backs of her legs. Any one of the stings could have killed her.

Maggie had never gotten over the guilt for the part she'd played in her sister's death.

"Drive." Maggie pointed to the shift.

Liddy put the car into reverse but didn't drop the subject. "You were a kid, acting like a kid. It wasn't your fault."

Turning her face to the window, Maggie said, "It doesn't matter now. Just drive. We're going to be late. Emma's going to be pacing the front porch."

They drove without speaking until Liddy made the turn onto Emma's street.

Liddy pulled into Emma's driveway. "And there she is, as predicted. Waiting on the porch."

A moment later, Emma opened the rear passenger door and got in. "You're late. Were you having a cocktail party without me?"

"We had one little glass of wine and a couple of cheese straws. Hardly a party." Liddy backed out of the driveway.

"Candy Shultz has called twice wondering where we were and what we were doing. She said she was saving us seats at her table for dinner,"

Emma told them, eliciting groans from both Liddy and Maggie. "That was pretty much my reaction as well, and I figured you two wouldn't want to sit with her, either, but how do you tell someone you don't like their company?"

"We can live with it for one dinner," Liddy said. "Then we hit the bar."

"Sounds like a plan." Maggie turned in her seat to face Emma, who, as always, was meticulously outfitted. Tonight she wore a navy-blue dress with a wide skirt and a pretty belt, and black kitten heels. Pearl studs in her ears, opera-length pearls around her neck, and a wide gold band circling her wrist. Understated makeup and hair. Perfectly Emma, and Maggie said so. "You're always so put together."

"And you always look so cool, so beautiful," Emma countered. "And Liddy, you always look so . . . wait, are you wearing a black dress? Black, Liddy?" They'd driven into the parking lot at the Harbor Inn, and Liddy was preparing to turn over her car to the valet. Emma released her seat belt and leaned over the front-seat console and stared. "Liddy, you're wearing a black dress. No purple. No red. No miles of colorful beads. Where's the rainbow?"

The three women got out of the car and convened behind it before heading toward the entrance of the restaurant.

"And your hair. It's so . . . neat." Emma hadn't quite finished her commentary.

"It's our forty-year reunion. I was thinking tonight was a good time to put the tie-dyes and the gypsy skirts and the love beads away. I wanted to look like an adult tonight, to show a new side of me. So tonight I'm Lydia. We're leaving Liddy home with her mom's old Bob Dylan and Joan Baez albums." Liddy stopped and turned to Emma. "Tell me what you really think. About the way I look."

Emma took in the sight of Liddy standing with her hands on her hips, wearing a dress that was just tight enough to show off her voluptuous curves.

46

"I think you look fabulous."

"Thank you. Maggie agrees. And so do I." Liddy linked arms with Maggie and Emma, and together the three old friends joined the reunion.

"But I hope Liddy hasn't been put on the shelf permanently." Maggie paused in the doorway. "She's so much fun."

"Of course she is." Liddy grinned. "You know you can't keep a good woman down."

~

The room was festooned with balloons and flowers and reminded Maggie way too much of their senior prom.

"Gah." She tapped Liddy on the arm. "This looks like prom night."

"It's supposed to. Shelly Jaffe's idea, and since she was in charge of decorating, it was her call." Liddy looked around. "You have to admit, she's got a good memory."

"Almost too good," Emma agreed. "Lest we forget our glory days, I suppose."

As if Maggie could forget. She and Brett had been crowned king and queen. She'd worn a gorgeous pale-blue strapless gown she'd begged her mother to buy when they'd gone into Boston to shop for something special. The look on Brett's face when he'd seen her coming down the stairway in her family home had been pure lust tempered by the freshness of first love. The entire evening had been enchanted.

And oh, yes—that was the night she'd lost her virginity. Just what she wanted to be reminded of right at that moment, when she could run into him at any second.

She successfully blocked out the memory through the salad and main courses, but just as dessert was being served, she heard a familiar voice behind her, and the chocolate mousse she'd just oohed and aahed over suddenly lost its appeal.

Maggie held her breath, her heart in her throat, steeling herself against the sound of hearing her name fall from his lips, but the flutter she felt a moment later was that of—dare she admit it, even to herself?—disappointment when he'd walked right past her to lean over the shoulder of Lisa Merritt, who sat at the opposite side of the table. She pretended not to notice his presence, turning to Liddy and asking her to pass the cream for her coffee. Liddy rolled her eyes and Maggie kicked her under the table. Despite her resolve to ignore his presence, she couldn't help her gaze from wandering across the table, where Brett was still chatting amicably with a couple of classmates. The third or fourth time she glanced in that direction, she noticed a woman standing slightly behind Brett. She was a good twenty years younger than most of the other women in the room, and prettier. Her long blonde hair curved over one shoulder even as her left arm curved over Brett's.

Maggie put her head down and lifted her coffee cup. Out of the corner of her mouth, she whispered, "Is that . . . ?"

"Um-hmm. Wife number three. Kayla," Liddy whispered back.

"She looks sort of familiar." Maggie narrowed her eyes. "But I don't know where I'd have met her." She paused, trying to recall who'd been seated next to Brett at her mother's funeral, but in that moment she'd turned around, as if sensing him there, she'd seen only him.

Liddy snorted. Another eye roll, causing Maggie to frown and ask, "What?"

"Seriously? You don't see it?" Liddy made a face and leaned behind Maggie. Tugging on Emma's sleeve to get her attention, she said, "Em, Maggie's trying to figure out why Kayla Crawford looks familiar."

Emma smiled and said softly, "Maggie, she looks like you."

"Oh, for crying out loud, she most certainly does not." Maggie protested a little too loudly. The woman on the other side of Emma turned at the sharp outburst. Maggie smiled at her, and the woman—the sister of someone at the table but right then Maggie couldn't remember who—smiled back and returned to her conversation.

Maggie lowered her voice. "Okay, she's blonde. I'll give you that. But Brett always liked blondes."

"The last two wives were blonde, too," Emma told her.

"That has nothing to do with me." Maggie attacked her coffee cup, stirring in more cream in a vicious swirl.

"Maggie"—Liddy touched her arm—"we've been friends our entire lives. I don't make up this shit. All you have to do is look at that woman and you can see the resemblance."

"I am looking at her. I still don't see it. For one thing, she's gotta be twenty years younger," Maggie pointed out.

"There are none so blind as those who would not see." Liddy sat up in her seat and proceeded to drink her coffee. She made a face. "It's cold. I need to find a waiter." She looked around the room. "Ah. I see one with a coffeepot in hand. I'll be right back. Maggie, Emma? Coffee?"

"I'm switching to wine, thanks," Maggie said.

"Me too." Emma reached for the bottle on the table and poured into first Maggie's glass, then her own.

The DJ, who'd played soft music during dinner, now started to play livelier songs. Maggie watched Liddy disappear into the crowd and turned to Emma, who was now chatting with the woman on her right. She reached for her phone to see if either of her daughters had sent her a text—unlikely but it beat sitting there pointedly not looking at the other side of the table—when she had the sense she was being watched. She turned on her phone and made a pretense of scrolling through emails while trying not to look, but her curiosity got the best of her. Glancing up, she caught the blatant stare of Kayla Crawford. Maggie looked away and continued scrolling. *I'm sure she's heard my name over the years,* Maggie told herself, *and I suppose it's natural to want to know what your husband's high school sweetheart looks like.*

She had to sneak another peek. Kayla was chatting amicably with Lisa, her attention diverted, which gave Maggie a few seconds to get a better look even while ignoring her own internal question of why she

49

felt the need to. *Well, she's certainly younger, and maybe a little taller . . . and hmm, maybe she does look just a teensy bit like me. Or like the me I was years ago. Not that that means anything . . .*

Maggie couldn't help wondering just how young Kayla was.

"Don't think I didn't catch you in the act," Liddy said as she took her seat, a pot of coffee in her hand. "Coffee, anyone?"

Three people at the table raised their hands, and after pouring into her own cup, Liddy passed the pot to her left.

"What are you talking about? What act?"

"Checking out Kayla Crawford." Liddy smiled. "I knew you wouldn't be able to resist."

"Liddy, I was not . . . ," Maggie protested.

"Please. Remember who you're talking to. Besides, I saw you. But what's the big deal? If you weren't the least bit curious, I'd think there was something wrong with you."

"But I—" Maggie was interrupted by an announcement from the DJ.

"I'm happy to see all you folks having such a good time. Nothing like reliving your high school years, am I right?" He paused for a spattering of applause and a cheer from the other side of the room. "And how 'bout that seventies music, eh? What's better than listening to those songs that you listened to as you drove along in your car with the windows down, singing along at the top of your lungs? Or dancing till you dropped? Or snuggled up with the one you loved? Ah, yeah, those high school days were special, weren't they? Makes me nostalgic for you. And to bring back all those special moments, here's your class president, Francie Peterson."

From the podium, Francie motioned with both hands for the applause to die down. She looked very authoritative in a high-necked, sparkly green dress that fit just a little snugly around the hips and black-rimmed glasses, her frosted brown hair tucked behind her ears. In her hand she held a sheaf of papers.

"Thanks, everyone. What DJ Steve was saying about the music of our times is so, so true," Francie continued. "Seventies music was magical, am I right? So let's relive a little of that high school magic, shall we?" As the crowd cheered, Francie nodded to someone near the doorway, and the lights dimmed. "Your attention, please, to the screen being lowered at the front of the room."

Maggie flinched. The first slide was . . .

"First, we have to pay homage to our state champion football team, right? Three years in a row!" A picture of the entire team flashed onto the screen. Maggie closed her eyes. "Were they awesome or what?" Francie led the crowd in enthusiastic applause. On cue, the DJ began to play Queen's "We Will Rock You / We Are the Champions."

Wild hoots rang out from every corner, and someone on the opposite side of the room yelled, "Yeah! Three-peat!" Lest she appear to lack that old high school spirit, Maggie smiled and applauded along with the others at her table while avoiding looking at the picture on the screen. She knew exactly where Brett stood: back row, in the center, as if anchoring the team's defense. Which, inarguably, he'd done. She of all people did not need Francie's reminder of his accomplishments. All-state three years. Second team all-American his junior and senior years. A full ride to Ohio State. Drafted by the Seattle Seahawks in the second round. Eight years playing pro.

"I understand many members of that team are here tonight. Stand up, please, so we can show our appreciation," Francie urged as the DJ played Springsteen's "Glory Days."

The appreciation was loud and long. Maggie averted her eyes even as she half-heartedly cheered.

The cheers finally faded, the football team sat, and the screen changed to display other teams. Maggie was recognized as the captain of the field hockey and lacrosse teams, and when her name was called—"I know Maggie Lloyd—Maggie Flynn—is here because I saw her. Maggie, stand up so . . . oh, there she is"—Maggie stood with her heart in her mouth. Never one to be comfortable in the spotlight, tonight she felt she was carrying her teenage self on her back. She gave a half-hearted wave, then sat before the applause died out as Francie moved on to after-school activities. The chess, journalism, art, photography, and pep clubs. Theater. Chorus. By the time she got to the school orchestra, the applause was beginning to sound tired and forced after twenty solid minutes.

It was all in fun, celebrating good times, until the DJ started to play the Trammps's "Disco Inferno"—the theme of their senior prom—and Maggie's stomach went into a knot. The first few photos on screen were group shots not focused on any one particular person. And then suddenly there it was: the crowning of the prom king and queen. Maggie in her blue gown, her hair piled atop her head, loose tendrils drifting down almost to her shoulders, Brett in his rented white tux, the two of them standing like royalty, holding hands, and beaming at each other. The next picture—and Maggie prayed the last—was the couple leading off the dancing, lost in their own beautiful world of love and glory. Maggie held her breath and waited for the buzzing in her head to stop. All she needed now was for the DJ to start playing their song.

And then Francie was saying, "For the first time in forty years, if you can believe that, we have *both* our king and our queen back with us. So Brett—Maggie—start off the dancing for us."

Oh . . . no. Just . . . no.

But there was no easy way to decline in front of the entire group, all of whom seemed to be applauding as Brett, still golden, still the best-looking guy in the class, walked across the room in her direction— *Damn him, why hasn't he aged a little more?*—his smile only slightly less forced than hers. One hand held out to her, he asked, "May I have this dance?"

"Of course." She smiled for the benefit of the crowd even as she tried unsuccessfully to avoid making eye contact. They walked to the middle of the floor, her heart beating rapidly. His hand was a light presence on the small of her back when the music began to swell around them, and Maggie had to force herself to remember to breathe. She hadn't been this close to him since she'd walked out on him thirty-four years ago.

Annoyingly, his arms around her felt the same.

His right arm wrapped around her, and his left hand held hers, as Ambrosia began to sing "Biggest Part of Me." The song they'd danced to at the prom, and later that night, on the beach at the end of Cottage Street. Their song.

God, how she hated that song.

"Did you know Francie was going to . . . ?" she asked between clenched teeth even as she tried to ignore that it all felt so familiar. Hauntingly so.

And she wished that at some point in his life he'd changed his damned aftershave.

"No," he replied. "But thanks for being such a good sport. For a moment, when I first looked at your face, I thought you were going to bolt for the door."

"If I'd had time, I just might have."

"Sorry."

"Not your fault, Brett. Just dance. The song's not all that long."

"You can count the minutes if it makes it more bearable," he said softly.

"I didn't mean it that way." *Okay, yes, I did.*

"Sure you did." There was a touch of humor in his voice. "But it's okay. Only one more verse, I think."

A moment later, he said, "I was sorry to hear about your husband."

"Thank you."

"How've you been?" he asked.

"Good. Thanks."

"How are your kids? Two daughters, right?"

"Yes. They're fine. Thanks for asking." And then, because she knew it was expected of her, she asked, "How about you?"

"Three daughters." He smiled wryly. "One from each wife."

Maggie froze in his embrace, her feet suddenly unable to move. If they'd been alone, she'd have slapped him.

She pushed his arms away and turned her back on him.

"Maggie, wait," he said as she walked toward the table where Liddy and Emma watched. "There's something I need to tell you." He tried to take her arm, but she shook him off as if she hadn't heard. "Maggie, there's something you need to know. It's important."

She ignored him and lifted the glass of wine Emma wisely had waiting for her. She took a long drink, waited to make sure he'd given up and walked away, then turned to Liddy and said, "I'm going to walk home."

"You'll do nothing of the sort. Sit down for a few minutes. If you leave now, it'll look like . . ."

"I couldn't care less what it will look like. I'm done." She needed to move, needed air, needed to put space between herself and this room and the music and her memories. The feel of his arms around her, the feel of his body. The prickle of his five-o'clock shadow against her skin. The sorrow that came with remembering.

"Come on, Maggie." Emma stood. "Bring your glass and we'll go for a walk."

Maggie nodded, kissed Liddy on the top of her head, and said, "I'll see you back at the house."

"The doors are locked." Liddy sighed. "I'll come with you."

"No need. I know you've been looking forward to this for months, and I know how hard you've worked. You and your committee have done a great job. Stay and enjoy the compliments. I'll wait on the back porch." Knowing there were eyes on her, she forced the biggest smile she could muster and patted her friend on the shoulder.

"Maggie, I swear to God I had no idea Francie was going to do that." Liddy gestured toward the dance floor, which was now filling up with couples. "I'd have shot that idea right down if she'd told me."

"I know you would have. It's okay. It was awkward, but it's okay. No one died. I just need some air. And I don't want to be here right now."

Maggie grabbed her bag and her wineglass from the table and glanced at Emma to let her know she was ready to go.

"Ladies' room," Emma said in response to someone asking her where they were going. "Just like old times. A pack of two."

When they reached the hall, Emma told Maggie, "I wasn't kidding. I really would like to hit the ladies' room before we go outside."

"Go ahead. I'll wait in the lobby."

The inn's lobby was small and dark, with wood paneling that was original to the building, as was the large fireplace that covered most of the inner wall. Maggie drifted toward the large picture window overlooking the harbor and peered into the night. Lights from a boat moored at the dock cast a yellow glow upon the water. Her gaze followed a large schooner that eased past on its way to Buzzards Bay.

"Tom Harrison." The voice behind her startled her.

"What?" She didn't have to turn to know it was Brett. Had he followed her?

"Tom Harrison's boat. You know, the Harrisons that own—"

"The house no one lives in and the carousel that they drag out every five years or so and set up in the park so all the little local kids could have a ride." She still didn't bother to turn around. "I know the story."

"Listen, Maggie. I'm really sorry. About everything. Mostly, I'm sorry that . . ."

She could feel him behind her, close enough to touch if she leaned back just a little. Which she'd die before she'd do.

"Please don't. Just . . . *don't*. We're a lifetime away from apologies, Brett." She still faced the window.

"I was hoping that . . ."

"There were things I'd hoped for, too," she snapped, "so I guess we'll both have to live with our disappointment."

"Look," he said, lowering his voice. "Something's happened. Something you need to know about."

She glanced over her shoulder, and they came face-to-face. In the low light, his expression was solemn, his blue eyes dark and haunted. He looked shaken. Which was ridiculous. She'd only seen him look shaken once, and that was over something a whole lot more serious than whatever was on his mind now.

"Ready, Mags?" Emma came out of the bathroom, the door closing softly behind her.

"I am." Maggie looked up at Brett and dismissed him with a blithe, "Nice seeing you again, Brett."

She had to step around him to join up with Emma, who was already near the front door, but as she did so, from the corner of her eye, she saw a shadow in the doorway that opened onto the hall. Kayla Crawford stood still as a stone, her eyes flitting from her husband to Maggie and back again. Brett hadn't noticed. He was watching Maggie walk away.

That doesn't look good. Maggie wondered just how much Kayla had heard.

"Nice night for a walk along the harbor," Emma was saying as they walked toward the water. "They put in a walkway—cement—a few years back because so many people liked to walk along here at night."

"Um-hmm," Maggie replied.

"And a lot of people like to take their boats out at night," Emma continued.

Maggie nodded absently.

"At least, they used to. Not so much these days, since we lost so many to the sea monsters out in Buzzards Bay. Used to think they were just fairy tales, but nope. They're real. Huge, ugly, mean suckers. My dad has video he took from the bow of his boat a few weeks ago. Just barely made it back to the dock."

Another silent nod.

"And they're getting so bold, you know." Emma took Maggie's arm as they strolled along. "Snatched a couple of kids right off Emerson's dock on Wednesday. Sad, you know?"

"Sure."

"Maggie." Emma laughed. "Where are you?"

"What?"

"You're off somewhere. Your mind definitely isn't here. What's up? You need to talk about something?"

"Oh, no. I think I'm just a little tired." Maggie averted her eyes.

"You're the worst liar on two feet. So he rattled you. It's okay. You don't have to pretend with me."

"Maybe a little," Maggie admitted. "I guess it's been so long since I've been that close to him—well, it was odd, that's all." She paused, then added, "It was that damned dance thing. Who thought that would be a good idea? And Brett's wife . . ." She rolled her eyes. "God only knows what she's heard about me. What she thought watching us dancing. Grrrr."

"Down, girl." Emma laughed and squeezed Maggie's arm before dropping her hand. "I'm sure Kayla knows all about you. She's living in Brett's hometown with people who knew you both back then and who witnessed everything but the breakup, which around here accounted for high drama." Emma lowered her voice. "The golden couple who were destined for one another, and then tragically, they weren't. Who—or what—came between them?"

"Stop." Maggie laughed in spite of herself.

"Please. You have no idea how many times Liddy and I have been asked about what caused the breakup. No one believes us when we say we don't know." Emma sounded wistful, as if wishing she had been taken into Maggie's confidence.

"Well, at least you're not lying."

"I can't say I haven't wondered, all these years. What could have been so big you couldn't have confided in either of us?" There it was. Clearly, Emma had been hurt by Maggie's refusal to discuss her breakup and sudden move to Philadelphia without so much as an "Oh, by the way . . ."

"I'm sorry, Em. I really am. It was something I just couldn't bring myself to talk about." She tried to smile, but her mouth wouldn't cooperate. "Besides, it doesn't matter now. We're worlds apart, he and I, and we always will be." Maggie's throat tightened even as she protested.

"You sure about that?"

"Positive." Maggie drained her glass of wine and held it up to the light at the end of the dock. "Let's go in and have one more drink. I think I've had a long enough walk down memory lane."

That walk had been painful, full of emotions that had been tucked away in the dark corners of her mind and her heart for a lifetime, and Maggie'd had enough. She felt an overwhelming desire to shake off the past, to run home and bury herself in the present, her daughters and her granddaughter, her volunteer work and her teaching. Tomorrow was Sunday, and she and Liddy would have brunch with Emma, then hang out together for the rest of the day. Maybe drive to the Cape for dinner. By Monday afternoon she'd be home, and the weekend, along with its ghosts, would be behind her. It would take her a while, but she would shake Brett out of her head and get on with her life, just as she'd done thirty-four years ago.

Chapter Four

GRACE

The sound of her ex-husband's laughter through her half-open door made Grace want to scream. Or cry. Crying might be better, since if he happened to push open her door and see her weeping softly at her desk, the full weight of what he'd done to her might finally shame him into forgetting about that little slut paralegal and remembering why he'd fallen in love with Grace in the first place.

Right. Fat chance.

Grace coughed, then rustled papers, hoping he'd hear, but he and his girlfriend just kept on walking. She wished she'd gotten her father to fire that girl before he died. She sighed. That wouldn't have happened. Two years ago, Zach was still the faithful husband, still the doting son-in-law. Still hoping, no doubt, that Art was going to leave the firm to Grace, and therefore, by marriage, to Zach. But no one knew that shortly before he'd died, her father had changed his will, leaving the firm to her mother, of all people. Grace had been shocked and hurt, but in retrospect, she supposed it had worked out okay. Grace was still on the fast track to own the firm, and Zach . . . was not. She knew her dad had been about to elevate her husband's position before he fell ill, but the exhausting treatments had pushed aside all thoughts of everything but survival.

She hadn't known then about Zach's betrayal with Amber, a paralegal she herself had hired.

Why the two of them stubbornly stayed at Flynn Law was anyone's guess. Rumor had it that now that her father was gone, Zach and Amber were counting on Grace's humiliation at the situation to drive her out, which only proved to her that neither of them was half as smart as they thought they were. Art Flynn had built this firm from the ground up into a highly regarded legal team. He had the goodwill and respect of the legal community in Philadelphia. Why would his daughter leave the firm she was sure her mother would eventually hand over to her? She'd already been humiliated beyond anything she could have possibly imagined. Everyone in the office had known about his infidelity before she had, had witnessed all the many ways she'd tried to win him back. Her face burned with shame every time she thought about the lengths she'd gone to, how she'd embarrassed herself.

When her father had been offered an experimental treatment for his cancer, he'd said, "Well, when you've got nothing to lose—you've got nothing to lose." That was sort of the way Grace felt. She'd already lost her father, her husband, and probably the respect of many if not most of her colleagues for the way she'd tried to hang on to Zach. The firm was meant to be hers. She was now the face of Flynn Law, and dammit, she intended to keep it that way.

She'd thought about asking her mother to fire them both, but she knew that without cause they could sue her and the firm. They were both outstanding at their jobs. In Grace's mind, it was a matter of who was going to blink first. It wasn't going to be her.

The fact that she was sick to her stomach every morning when she stepped off the elevator wasn't as important to her as being the last one standing.

She'd tried everything she could think of to win him back, but nothing had worked. He had made it very clear they were over by filing for divorce two months after Art died.

"I'm sorry to have to deliver the second blow, Gracie, but I held off while your dad was sick." Zach had looked up from packing a suitcase when she'd walked into the bedroom one evening to let him know dinner was ready, but it hadn't taken her long to realize she'd be eating alone. There had been several bags sitting by the door already packed and ready to go. "I didn't want to upset anyone any more than they were. But I don't love you, and I haven't for a long time."

She'd been stunned. Had he really just said he didn't love her? That couldn't be right. When had that happened? Why?

She'd broken down and begged him to try to work things out. They could go to counseling, she'd said through her tears, but then he'd hit her with, "Stop demeaning yourself. I'm in love with someone else. I've moved on, and I suggest you do, too."

He'd picked up his bags and walked down the stairs and out the front door without saying goodbye. Or maybe he had. All she'd been able to hear inside her head was, *I don't love you . . . I'm in love with someone else.*

They'd been together since law school, married for almost ten years. *This isn't real,* she'd told herself. *He'll be back.*

At first, after he'd moved out, she'd tried to pretend that everything was normal, not mentioning their impending divorce to anyone. She'd waited weeks to tell her mother and sister that she and Zach had separated, but added they were trying to work things out, which was true only in her own mind. Still, at work she'd directed cases to Zach that she believed would require her input, but he'd declined her offers to assist. Then one morning, weeks after he'd left, Grace had been in the break room, where someone had left a box of doughnuts on the table. She'd peered into the box, then picked up a chocolate frosted and said to no one in particular, "I think I'll take this in to Zach. Chocolate frosted are his favorites."

An awkward silence had fallen over the room. Then Amber had smirked, taken the doughnut from Grace's hand, and walked out, still smirking. One by one, wordlessly, the others had left the room, leaving Grace with chocolate on her thumb and the feeling she'd missed something important.

About a half hour later, her assistant, Terri, had come into Grace's office, closed the door behind her, taken a deep breath, and said, "Grace, there's something you need to know. It's about Zach." Another deep breath. "And Amber."

"What about Zach?" she'd asked. "And Amber?"

Terri had stood at the front of Grace's desk with a pleading look. "Grace. It's not Zach. And Amber. It's *Zach and Amber*. They're together. Like, living together."

The punch to Grace's gut had been so fierce and so sudden she couldn't speak. Finally, "Zach and Amber? They're together? Like, *together* together? Are you sure?"

"Do you really think I'd come in here with idle gossip?"

"How do you know . . . ?"

"Grace, everyone in the office knows. They've made no effort to hide it. Haven't you noticed she's always in his office?"

"She works on some of his cases . . . ," Grace had replied weakly.

"She's working on his case, all right."

Grace had looked down at the report she'd been reading. All she'd seen was a black blur.

"Thanks. I appreciate the heads-up." Grace had tilted her head in the direction of the door.

Terri had gotten the hint, but before she'd opened the door, she'd added, "I'm sorry to be the one to tell you, but someone had to. I can't stand watching you humiliate yourself every day."

Grace had nodded slowly, her eyes downcast. She'd wanted to thank Terri for clueing her in, but her voice had seemed to have gone AWOL. The door had closed softly, but Grace hadn't been able to move. She'd thought back on moments over the past few months when she should have picked up on what everyone else apparently knew. Motionless at her desk until shadows began to ease across the room hours later, finally she'd stood. Outside her office, she'd been able to hear the sounds of the workday shutting down: the ping of the elevator, the *good nights* and the *see you tomorrows* of her coworkers. When the voices had gone silent, she'd gathered her briefcase, stuffing in work she'd wanted to take home even as she knew she wouldn't look at it, grabbed her purse, and slung it over her shoulder. Turned off the lights, closed up her office. Passed Zach's half-open door, through which a giggle escaped. Grace had paused in the hall, listened for a moment, then gone back to her office, into her private bathroom, and thrown up.

By the time she'd pulled herself together, most of the office suites were dark. She'd gotten into the elevator and punched the button for the lobby with more force than was necessary. Once home, she'd allowed herself to cry until she was hoarse. After she'd dried her face, she'd poured a glass of wine and considered her options.

Her first thought had been to fire them both. But she had no grounds to take to HR, and she'd known that to fire two extremely competent employees without cause was tantamount to putting out the welcome mat for a lawsuit she couldn't defend.

"Ms. Flynn." The judge would look her straight in the eye—and with her luck, the judge would be Judge Borden, the only judge in the Philadelphia Court of Common Pleas who hadn't liked her father. "Can you tell this court why you fired Amber Costanza?"

"Yes, Your Honor. She stole my husband."

"And why you fired your ex-husband?"

"He allowed himself to be stolen."

The judge would have stared her down. "Your paralegal boinking your husband is not legal grounds for termination of the employment of either party. I find for the plaintiffs in the amount of eight trillion dollars." At which time he'd bang his gavel and uniformed officers of the court would drag her away in chains. She'd be dressed in orange—so not her color—and her hair would be a mess. Her picture would be on the front page of the *Philadelphia Inquirer* and the *Main Line Times* and all over the internet the following morning and would be front and center in every Wawa from Center City to the Jersey Shore and the Delaware beaches.

She was pretty sure firing their asses was probably not a defensible option.

She'd looked for subtle ways to make Amber's job unbearable and thought she'd found the solution by reassigning Amber to work for Paul Groh, the oldest, grumpiest attorney in the firm, but somehow she'd charmed him right out of his get-off-my-lawn sign, for which everyone in the office blessed Amber.

Since Grace wasn't about to leave the firm her father had founded, and Zach had laughed at her suggestion that he quit and take Amber with him, she had to find another means of venting her anger, frustration, and humiliation.

Hence the birth of her blog, *TheLast2No*.

It had started as something she'd done only for herself. She'd found it cathartic to write out her feelings and say the things she really wanted to say when her desire to save face demanded civility. Then one day it had occurred to her that there had to be dozens—hundreds—probably thousands of other women who'd been dumped by their significant others in favor of another woman who'd like a safe place to vent their anger, a place where they could just let it rip where no one would tell them to calm down or get over it. So, Grace had set up a blog under the name of Annie Boleyn (no way was Grace Flynn going public with her humiliation!) and invited others to share their tales of betrayal at the hands of their ex.

The blog had just about blown up the first week.

She'd grossly underestimated how many men had stepped out on their wives/fiancées/girlfriends, and every one of them seemed to want to tell their story on her blog. She tried to make it a place where women could complain anonymously, could vent without being told to grow up or move on. A place to express their rage and humiliation and frustration and know they weren't alone, that it had happened just as unfairly to other women, and that some of those women were there for them, to commiserate and remind them it wasn't their fault, that their life didn't have to end with a breakup.

From merely commiserating and offering a virtual hug and an uplifting word, the blog had expanded after several women mentioned how they missed going out with their friends on the weekend, but it seemed that once their divorces were final, the invitations eventually stopped coming. So every Friday night Grace hosted a virtual happy hour, and she'd select one of that week's commenters as her Woman of the Week. Everyone at happy hour would toast this one woman and wish her the fulfillment of her every desire after cursing out her rotten ex (and his little honey, too). It cost Grace nothing but seemed to make a lot of women happy. There were days when she had trouble getting her real work done.

It was all very harmless and gave Grace something to focus on other than the great love story that was playing out under her nose and the pain it caused her every single day.

Next, she'd invited her followers to Saturday night at the movies. Every Monday, she'd suggest three movies to be voted on during the week, then on Friday, she'd announce the movie that had garnered the most votes. On Saturday night, they'd all watch the selected movie and share their thoughts on her blog. It was a way for them to cope, to get their feet back on the ground. Even Grace felt a lot better after a few months of getting *TheLast2No* up and running.

It seemed harmless enough. Okay, so a few of her followers maybe got a little carried away now and then when describing what they'd like to do to their ex or to the woman who broke up their happy life, but of course no one would ever follow through. And Grace tried to defuse any violent sentiments as best she could, either by talking the person down, if possible, and if not, by blocking them from commenting.

There had been a few who protested being blocked by rejoining under another name, and once or twice had threatened Grace personally, but she figured that came with the territory. Anytime you tried to shut down someone who wanted to have their say on a topic they felt particularly passionate about, there could be protests, emotions could run understandably high, but she never took them seriously and never felt she was in danger.

The only thing she was afraid of was being found out.

~

She'd have been hard pressed to admit it, but Grace actually enjoyed her Friday and Saturday nights with her virtual friends more than she enjoyed being with people face-to-face over the weekend. The followers of her blog deferred to her in ways no one in her real life ever did, and her blog gave her total control over that one small corner of her life. She wasn't interested in meeting anyone, had no desire for romance—she thought of her heart as having shrunk to the size of a walnut—and the friends she'd had hadn't proved themselves to be as understanding as she expected good friends to be.

"Gracie, he doesn't love you. You can't spend your life pining for someone who doesn't love you," her supposed best friend Michelle had told her every time Grace had confided a possible new how-to-win-Zach-back scheme. "Why would you even *want* to be with someone who doesn't want you?"

After showing her childhood friend Rosemary the sexy card she'd bought for Zach's birthday, she'd invited Grace to lunch, during which time she'd leaned across the table, taken Grace's hand, and said, "Grace, you're better than this."

Even her own sister had tried—in typical blunt Natalie fashion—to get Grace to give up her dream of getting Zach back. "Girl, you're making a fool out of yourself. Let him go. You deserve so much more than a guy who would walk out on you two months after you buried your father."

"Oh, this from my sister whose baby daddy walked out on her the minute he found out she was pregnant?" Grace had snapped.

Nat's eyes had flashed with indignation, and she'd snapped back, "Oh, yes, I most certainly deserve more than a drug-addicted man who would make me choose between him and my child. I will never regret choosing Daisy. I was happy about the baby, so I expected Jonathan to be as well. But I'd never for a second even think about crawling back to him. He's not worth it. Neither is Zach. Stop crawling."

Grace had walked out of Natalie's apartment, and it had been weeks before she'd spoken to her again.

She sighed. She knew her sister loved her, knew she meant well. Grace loved Natalie, too, and she adored her niece. She missed her friends, but she couldn't be in their company. No one understood how she felt. She'd been in love with Zach since she'd walked into her first-year law school class and he'd turned and smiled at her. With her whole heart and soul she believed that he was her one true love, her meant-to-be, her happy-ever-after. Her parents had had that sort of love, so for Grace nothing else would be acceptable. And once you found that person, you were supposed to stay together, till death do you part. That was what soul mates did: they stayed together forever. That was what she'd expected from her marriage.

What she hadn't expected was that things between her and Zach would end the way they had. It was inconceivable that he'd go behind her back and have an affair right under her nose and show absolutely no remorse. She'd waited for him to come to his senses and come back home to the house they shared in Haverford, but with every passing week, it became more obvious that *that* was not going to happen.

Grace hadn't tossed in the towel until she realized he hadn't cared who knew—and apparently everyone at Flynn Law had, except her. He hadn't tried to hide his new relationship, hadn't cared how humiliating it was for her. Grace had accepted the end of her marriage—the end of her happy-ever-after—with a sense of overwhelming sadness and bitter disappointment, because she had no choice. *TheLast2No* gave her a sense of control she had nowhere else in her life, and for now that was going to have to be enough.

Chapter Five

NATALIE

Natalie thought of Friday nights as a portal that opened onto two days she could make into whatever she wanted. Tonight she'd shared dinner with Daisy at six thirty and by eight had smoothly nailed playtime, bath time, and bedtime—including the reading of one of their favorite books, *On the Night You Were Born*, which was so wonderful she silently thanked the author, Nancy Tillman, every time she read it. After closing the bedroom door on the sleeping three-year-old, Natalie poured herself a glass of wine and decided she'd like company. Specifically, she'd like the company of her sister. She picked up her phone and sent Grace a text.

Wanna come over and hang out?

Five minutes later, Grace replied, Sorry. Plans for tonight.

Whatcha doing?

Drinks with friends.

Anyone I know?

Nope.

Dinner on Sunday at Mom's?

See you there.

While Natalie would have enjoyed Grace's company, she was happy to hear her sister was beginning to socialize again. While Grace appeared to have accepted the fact that Zach would not be coming back, she'd kept to herself so much that their mother confessed to Nat she'd discussed Grace's situation with Isabelle Finley, a friend from college who was a psychologist. Isabelle had offered to refer Grace to a therapist who specialized in dealing with the aftermath of failed marriages, but Grace had declined. So Natalie was gratified to see her sister making new friends and getting out of the house she and Zach had shared (which both Maggie and Nat agreed Grace should sell and find a new place, one with no ties to the life she'd been forced to leave behind). The hope was that Grace soon would move on and make a new life for herself.

Natalie turned on the TV as she scrolled through her emails and half watched the last half hour of a crime show. She responded to emails from several students. As a teacher of freshman English at a community college, she tried to be accessible. Having gone through those in a timely manner, she exited her email and opened the genealogy website where, several months ago, she'd submitted her saliva for a DNA test. She hadn't had high expectations from the results, though she did discover several second cousins she hadn't known about, one who lived near State College, a Nittany Lion like Natalie, whose enrollment at Penn State had overlapped Nat's for two years. They'd spoken on the phone several times and were making plans to get together sometime later in the fall at a Penn State football game. Nat's main genealogical goal was to find her father's maternal great-grandparents, whose names and places of birth had somehow been lost over the years.

Her bare feet crossed at the ankles and rested on the edge of the coffee table, she scanned the DNA matches, searching for names that might have been added since her last visit to her page, but there was nothing new. She opened the family tree she'd started for Daisy, thinking the day might come when she might want to know about both sides of her family. Jonathan had made it clear he wanted nothing to do with their daughter, which was fine with Natalie. The last year they'd been together he'd grown increasingly distant. Nothing had changed in their lives that she could see, though in retrospect she'd realized there'd been much he'd taken pains to hide from her. She'd discovered he'd been using and selling drugs the day she found out she was pregnant, and she had delivered her ultimatum: stop using, stop selling if he wanted to stay with her. But as soon as he'd heard the word *baby*, he was packing. After he left, she had no regrets. From that moment on, she'd known she'd be raising her baby alone. It had never occurred to her to beg Jon to be part of Daisy's life. She didn't need the child support—she could support herself and Daisy with no help from him, thank you very much—and her father had left her and Grace each a generous inheritance, so financially she was fine.

Until Natalie had finally broken down and told her mother about Jon's drug problems, Maggie'd insisted that she locate Jon and let him know he had a daughter. The last thing she wanted was to have that negative, criminal influence in her daughter's life. It well may have been that Daisy would have questions later and she'd do her best to answer them as honestly as she could. If Daisy chose to seek out her father and/or his family when she became an adult, Natalie wouldn't stand in her way.

Once she'd realized what he was using and how often, his strange disappearances had begun to make more sense. But since Daisy's birth, she'd had recurring nightmares about Jon taking her daughter with him when he drove to Kensington, that section of Philadelphia where heavy drug use was most rampant and lethal, and losing the baby somewhere in the maze of abandoned houses that made up the warren of shooting galleries. Of him putting Daisy down in the midst of a trash-strewn room and forgetting about her. Of someone stealing her and taking her God knew where.

Natalie had definitely inherited a wild imagination from someone.

She skimmed the list of mostly third, fourth, and fifth cousins, and finding nothing new returned to her research to locate James Flynn, her fraternal great-great-grandfather. Two hours had passed, and while she'd identified four possibilities, she couldn't differentiate between them, James Flynn apparently being a relatively common name in Ireland in the eighteen hundreds. Tired of staring at her computer screen, she decided to give up the search for the night and pick it up again at some point over the weekend. Maybe if Daisy napped on Saturday.

Natalie's phone buzzed, alerting her to an incoming call. She glanced at the screen, then smiled.

"Hello, Mom," she said.

"Hey, pet. How're my girls tonight?"

"Your one and only granddarling is sleeping like the angel she sometimes is. She had a full day at nursery school, so she's beat. She was out like a light by eight."

"She's a growing girl. How 'bout you? How was your week?"

"Busy. We have midterms in two weeks, and I have a stack of papers to read. But I didn't make any big plans for the weekend. I just want to take it easy and hang out with my baby girl tomorrow."

"But you'll be here on Sunday for dinner, right?"

"Of course. Dinner at Mom's on Sunday is a great American tradition. We'll be over around three, if that's okay."

"Sure. Whatever time works." Maggie paused. "Have you spoken with Grace recently?"

"Not spoken, but we did text a little tonight. She said she was going out for drinks with some friends, but she'd see us at your house on Sunday."

"Oh, good. I tried calling her, but she didn't pick up. I wonder who she went out with."

"I had the feeling it might have been some new friends, but as long as she's out of that house and socializing and hopefully having a good time, I don't care who she's with." Natalie sighed. "I almost wish she'd go get another job. I mean, I realize why she doesn't—the firm was Dad's baby. But for her to have to face that shithead Zach every day—well, it has to be killing her. You know how much she loved him. I think she still does."

"I can't help but wonder if he'd have left her if your father had left the firm to her outright instead of to me. Someday she'll be the senior and managing partner, but I understand why your dad didn't hand it over to her now. He felt she needed more experience, needed to make her own name, not just get by on his." She fell silent before adding, "Now I can't help but wonder if he'd had some sense of things not being right between Grace and Zach. He thought Zach was a brilliant lawyer. Why wouldn't he have made some provision for his brilliant son-in-law to have a larger profile within the firm? Art made that new will a week before he died. I'd have expected him to have provided for Zach, but there was no mention of him."

"You think he left the firm in your hands to see how things played out between Grace and Zach."

"I have my suspicions. I'll be going into the office soon for my monthly walk-around, when I smile at everyone as if I had a true purpose there. Mostly I meet new employees. Water the plants in your father's office, dust his bookshelves. Then I close it up again, take Lois to lunch, then try to catch a train by two thirty or so."

"What exactly does Lois do there these days?"

"Anything she wants," Maggie quipped. "She was your father's first hire when he started the firm. She was his right hand for thirty-two years."

"Yeah, I know all that, but what does she actually *do*?"

"Mostly, she keeps his spirit alive. She's there to reassure the old clients that even though Art's gone, the firm still is behind them one hundred percent and the clients are comfortable with that." Maggie laughed softly. "And yeah, whatever all that means. The bottom line is that I promised your father that I'd keep her on until she decided to retire, and that's what I'll do. Now and then, I ask her to look up something inane for me. Most recently I've asked her to go through your dad's files and make a list of the firm's oldest clients so I could be sure they're on the Christmas card list. What can I say, Nat? She was faithful to him, so we're faithful to her."

Nat was still thinking about her father while she checked for any new DNA matches and pondered how randomly certain traits were passed through DNA. Nat looked like her mother, her hair the same honey-blonde, her eyes the same green, but her build—tall and lanky—was her father's. Her no-nonsense approach to life was Art's as well. Grace, on the other hand, who was a traditionist down to her toes, was a dead ringer for a younger version of their father's mother—dark hair and blue eyes, like Art—but she had the soul of a romantic, like their mother. And like Maggie, Grace was long waisted and petite. From their father, Grace had inherited a love of the law, Italian food, and Paris, while Natalie shared his love of crime shows on TV, hiking, and an appreciation for sixties rock bands. Reading the names of past generations on her computer screen, Nat wondered which of her ancestors had passed on her free spirit, and who, like Grace, never colored outside the lines.

She had only one really cool find through her research, but it was a beauty. Lily Mullin, their father's Irish immigrant maternal great-grandmother, had been a cook at the home of one of Philadelphia's most prominent families. She'd disappeared from the household at the next census, but Natalie later discovered her in the home of her great-great-grandfather, John McKeller—as his wife. How, Natalie mused, did one rise from a young cook's apprentice—sixteen years old!—to become the wife of a man who was heir to a fortune and years older? Whatever the story, she was certain it was a romantic one: Lily and John had gone on to have nine children, all of whom were alive to celebrate their parents' fiftieth wedding anniversary. Natalie pondered the list of her DNA matches, wondering if the story was known to any of her second, third, and fourth cousins. It wouldn't be difficult to figure out which of the names were connected to her father's side of the family—just a little checking to see who had a McKeller in their family tree.

"A task for another day," she muttered as she exited the site and did a quick check of her email before turning off her computer. She'd promised Daisy a visit to the Please Touch Museum on Saturday, and she hoped to get an early start.

But first—baking for the weekend.

Scones for the morning, cupcakes for dessert after dinner tomorrow night, and some to take to Maggie's on Sunday. Daisy loved cupcakes, any flavor, any color frosting—fancy or otherwise—with or without sprinkles, gummy bears, or chocolate shavings (Natalie's favorite). This weekend they'd celebrate autumn: the scones would be pumpkin spice, and the cupcakes would be chocolate with cream cheese frosting and orange, yellow, and brown sprinkles. Natalie would bake the cupcakes tonight, and Daisy would help frost and decorate tomorrow after they returned from their outing.

Four years ago Natalie would have laughed if anyone'd predicted she'd be spending her Friday nights baking and her Saturday nights home tucked under a cozy throw sharing popcorn with a three-year-old. But then came Daisy, and Natalie's life did a complete one-eighty. Even when she was with Jon, Friday nights were usually girls' nights for her and her besties. And before Jon, her dance card was always filled. These days, if she occasionally missed male companionship, well, there were any number of men who'd be happy to date her and who weren't put off by the fact that she had a three-year-old. Unfortunately, she hadn't met anyone who appealed to her on every level that mattered to her.

Natalie's father was the standard by which all men were measured. Art Flynn had been handsome, intelligent, warm, kind, thoughtful—and had a playful humor that she'd adored. For a while, she'd thought Jon had measured up, but once the facade had begun to crumble, he'd been left with nothing but his handsome face, and even that had begun to show the wear and tear of an addict's life. While she wished she'd recognized the signs sooner, Natalie refused to beat herself up over it. Jon's sins were not hers, nor would she take any responsibility for them. Her father had been one hundred percent in her corner when she'd opted to have her baby and to raise Daisy on her own, whereas Maggie had wanted her to pursue Jonathan for support. Art had disagreed, and his last gift to Natalie had made Jon's help unnecessary. She didn't live extravagantly, but she and Daisy were comfortable, and there'd be money for her daughter's education.

"Jonathan Banks is out of our life now and forever," Natalie declared when she turned on the kitchen light and picked up Boo Boo Kitty, the stuffed cat Daisy had dropped. "Case closed."

She pulled the spiral-bound notebook containing her grandmother Lloyd's recipes from the shelf and slapped it onto the counter and repeated, "Case closed." She located the recipe for the scones and began to gather the ingredients and line them up next to the notebook. She'd been happy to hear her mother sound so upbeat on the phone, because in Natalie's opinion, Maggie hadn't been herself since she returned from her high school reunion over a month ago. There'd been nothing Nat could put her finger on, but it seemed a sadness had followed her home from Wyndham Beach. When asked, Maggie said she'd had a great time in Wyndham Beach, had spent several delightful days with her two oldest and dearest friends, and had renewed friendships with people she hadn't seen or heard from in years.

"It was a wonderful weekend," Maggie had told her. "I should go back more often. No one knows you like the people you grew up with, and no friends ever love you more."

Liddy and Emma were fine, she'd told Natalie, and everything in her hometown was just swell. So why did Natalie have the feeling that something happened that had dimmed her mother's usual sparkle just a touch? Maybe she could get her mother to talk about the reunion a little more on Sunday, see if she could intuit some slight or incident that had been unsettling. Maybe it had saddened her to visit her hometown without her husband—Nat knew it was the first time her mother had returned since her father had passed away. Or maybe she'd visited the cemetery where her mother and sister were buried.

Natalie had no way of knowing what Maggie may have found in Wyndham Beach. But just in case, she doubled the scone recipe so she'd have extras to take with her on Sunday. She'd drive to Bryn Mawr early and hopefully arrive before her sister, so she and her mom could sit in the sunroom, drink coffee, nibble on scones, and chat. Maybe without Grace's ever-present drama, Maggie might be more inclined to talk about herself for a change. At the very least, Natalie could look forward to a pleasant hour spent with her mother and her daughter over good coffee and homemade scones, all of which added up to win-win in her book.

Chapter Six

MAGGIE

Sitting in her pretty sunroom, surrounded by her jungle of plants, with her granddaughter curled up next to her with a book and Grace and Natalie chatting amiably was Maggie's idea of the perfect evening. There were few things that made her happier than having her girls home. Dinner had been drama-free, and her daughters had gone an entire afternoon without arguing about something inane.

"Mom, are you ready for a little more?" Grace stood, the bottle of pinot grigio poised over her own glass.

"Oh, just a splash. Thanks, Gracie." Maggie held out her glass as Daisy slid to the floor, speaking softly to the illustrations in her board book, an owl and squirrel, both of whom wore dark glasses and berets.

"That's about all that's left." Grace emptied the bottle and set it on the table.

"Wait just a moment while I get a pen and paper." Maggie got up and went into the kitchen.

"Let me guess." Natalie pulled a few yellowed leaves off a trailing pothos on the table next to her. "Time to make the list for Thanksgiving dinner."

"Why do we have to make a list?" Grace frowned. "We have the exact same meal every year."

"It's more for me to remember what to put on my shopping list." Maggie returned with a notepad and a pen. "Unless you'd rather go out this year for Thanksgiving dinner?"

"No," both daughters replied at the same time.

"But we know what's on the list, Mom. Turkey. Some of that packaged stuffing," Natalie began.

"The cornbread kind," Grace interjected.

"And dried cranberries and sage sausage." Maggie began to write.

"Mashed potatoes. Roasted sweet potatoes. Green beans." Grace ticked off on her fingers.

"And cawotts?" Daisy piped up.

"Yes. You like carrots with orange juice, so we'll have those." Maggie continued making notes. "And homemade cranberry sauce." She looked up from her list. "You guys can toss a coin to see who gets to bring the appetizers and who brings dessert."

Natalie looked at Grace. "Why don't we both make one of each?"

"Why don't we just plan on eating from the second we get up until we have to head for the nearest vomitorium?" Grace rolled her eyes. "There are three adults and one child here. How much food do we need?"

"Actually, I invited Liddy and Emma to join us this year." Maggie glanced from one daughter to the other. "We're saving Liddy from potluck Thanksgiving with a group of friends, and Emma's going to be alone because Chris is touring with his band. Actually, on Friday, the three of us are going to—"

"Oh, cool. I haven't seen Liddy or Emma since Gram died," Natalie interrupted. "That was the last time I was in Wyndham Beach. So we'll be five ladies and one girl."

"Oh, we could get tickets for the special holiday display at Longwood Gardens. I'll go online right now and reserve tickets for Friday for the five of us and Daisy." Grace dug in her bag for her phone.

"No, that's not going to work. Emma and Liddy and I are leaving on Friday afternoon for Charlotte." Maggie looked up from her note-pad. "I started to tell you."

Natalie and Grace exchanged blank looks. "What's in Charlotte?"

"Chris invited the three of us to his concert on Friday night, and we're staying for the weekend. He's arranged everything, right down to having a car pick us up here on Friday morning and drive us to the air-port, where we'll take a private jet to North Carolina. Accommodations at the number one inn in the city. Oh, and did I mention front-row seats at his show?"

"Mom!" Grace exclaimed. "What? When—how did this all come about?"

"We've been talking about doing it someday since the reunion. Emma called yesterday to tell me Chris had it all arranged if I was available."

"If she's available." Natalie rolled her eyes. "Duh."

"Duh," Daisy repeated, nodding for emphasis.

"And we're just hearing about this now because . . . ?" Grace was wide eyed.

"I'm so jealous I could weep." Natalie looked as if she was in fact about to cry. "Little Chrissy Dean, rock star and international man of mystery."

Grace scoffed. "No mystery. I read he nails everything that comes within ten feet of him."

"One wonders. Emma visited him in California, and she said there were women following him home and climbing over his back fence and sneaking into his house, all manner of goings-on that Emma . . . well, let's just say she wasn't happy to see the kind of girls who were stalking her son."

"What does she expect? He's gorgeous, rich, the lead singer in an enormously popular band, and oh, yeah, he really can sing." Grace ticked off his attributes on the fingers of her right hand. "Emma should know better than to expect him to be different from any other guy who's gorgeous, rich, yada yada yada."

"He's her baby. Her only child," Maggie reminded her, then changed the subject. "Anyway, we're looking forward to having a grand time that weekend."

"I'm really jealous, Mom. I wasn't kidding," Natalie said again.

"I'll bring you a T-shirt."

"Me too." Grace raised her hand.

"Me too," Daisy chimed in.

"I'll see if I can find one small enough for you, pet," Maggie said. "Oh, Grace, could you pick up the wine for Thanksgiving?"

"Sure. I'll plan on extra since Liddy and Emma will be here."

"Well, it sounds as if we have our holiday weekend pretty much planned. Good for us." Maggie rose and collected the empty glasses and headed for the kitchen, which had been renovated the year before Art died. A gourmet cook, he'd picked out everything himself, from the tall white cabinets to the granite countertops, the tiles for the backsplash, the appliances, and the flooring. The new kitchen had pleased him every time he came into the room, and he would run his hand over the smooth counters or stop to wipe away a smear from the front of the stainless steel refrigerator every time he passed by.

"I wonder what Chris is like now," Natalie mused as they all followed Maggie.

"He was such a pain in the butt when we were little," Grace said.

"Who was a pain in the butt?" Maggie rinsed out the wineglasses.

"Chris." Grace leaned on the counter.

"Why would you say that? He was always nice to you. And he was only a year older than you, Grace. Don't you remember, he used to take you both for rides in his wagon?" Maggie began to stack the dinner dishes in the dishwasher. "Nat? Do you remember?"

Natalie frowned as if searching her memory. "Not really."

"I remember." Grace pulled a chair out from the kitchen table, sat, and pulled her niece onto her lap. "Sort of."

"We have pictures somewhere. You were all so cute when you were little."

"Too bad we grew up to be such beasts, right, Nat? Except for Chris, who grew up to be the golden boy."

Natalie nodded. "Chris was always the golden boy. There always was something special about him. Like you knew he was going to be someone when he grew up."

"He worked pretty hard to get where he is, remember. Emma says they played a lot of tiny clubs for years before they could even get a record deal. It didn't all fall into his lap, you know," Maggie reminded them.

"Unlike the redheaded starlet I saw on his arm at the Billboard Music Awards a few months back. I bet she fell into his lap easily enough." Grace reached across the table for the book Daisy was straining to grab.

"Just cut all that talk when Emma's here, okay?"

"Sure, Mom. I wouldn't do anything to upset her," Grace said. "On the other hand, I'd have loved if we could have been included in that round trip to Charlotte."

"Maybe next time," Maggie told her. "This time is for the moms."

Natalie turned to her mother. "When was the last time you were at a rock concert?"

Maggie turned and leaned back against the counter, thinking. "It was at the old Spectrum in Philadelphia, but I don't remember what year. Your father and I and the Larsons went to see Steve Winwood. Warren Zevon was the opening act."

"I saw my first concert there. Britney Spears. I loved that place," Natalie said. "What a shame they knocked it down."

"Progress, sister," Grace told her. She turned to her mother and asked, "And what does the well-dressed fiftysomething woman wear to a rock concert?"

"That's a good question. I'll ask Emma what she thinks."

"Oh gosh, look at the time," Grace said suddenly. She lifted Daisy from her lap and stood her on the floor next to the table. "I need to go."

"Where do you need to be at seven on a Sunday night?" Natalie asked.

"I need to check in on a couple of friends." Grace walked into the hall and grabbed her coat from the closet. "Mom, thanks for dinner. It was delish, as always."

"We should probably go, too." Natalie guided Daisy in the direction of the hall.

"Come here, my Daisy girl. Give me a big kiss." Grace scooped up the little girl and planted kisses all over her face, then handed her over to her mother. "Do you believe our mom scored front-row tickets to a major rock concert while we languish at home?"

"Yeah, what's wrong with this picture?" Natalie struck an indignant pose.

Grace sighed. "Maybe if we're lucky, she'll remember to bring us those T-shirts."

"Maybe." Maggie slung an arm over Grace's shoulder and walked her to the door. "If you're really lucky, maybe Chris will autograph them for you."

Natalie faked a squeal. "Oh, Gracie, did you hear that? Maybe we'll get *autographed T-shirts* from our childhood friend."

"Yeah, our childhood friend who grew up to be one of the hottest guys on the planet." Grace opened the closet and took out her coat, which she slid over her arms. She reached back for Natalie's and Daisy's jackets, then tossed them to Natalie.

"You didn't think he was hot back then. You just said you thought he was a PITA." Natalie knelt to help Daisy into her jacket.

"You sure didn't." Grace smirked.

"I don't remember either of you being particularly enamored of Chris when you were younger." Maggie opened the front door and stood off to one side.

"Nat was." Grace stood on the front step and grinned at her sister. "Deny it now, but there was a time . . ."

Natalie laughed. "We were friends. We were always just friends."

"If you say so," Grace whispered.

"Mom, is everything all right? Are you all right?" Natalie asked softly as she buttoned her jacket.

"Why, do I look ill? Am I pale?" She stepped in front of the hall mirror and examined her reflection. "Everything's fine. Why would you ask me that?"

"You look great. You just seem . . . I don't know, maybe just a bit distracted?" Natalie appeared to struggle to put her finger on what seemed off about her mother. "And you've been neglecting your plants."

Maggie frowned, her hands now on her hips. "What are you talking about? I certainly have not been neglecting anything."

"Mom, I pulled dead leaves off several plants in the sunroom. I don't remember ever in my entire life seeing a dead leaf on anything green in this house."

"I haven't noticed any dead leaves," Maggie protested.

"That's my point. You've always been so meticulous about your plants. It just made me wonder if there was something on your mind, that's all." Chastised, Natalie softened. "It wasn't an accusation. I asked because it isn't like you not to notice. You haven't been the same since you came back from Wyndham Beach."

Maggie waved a hand as if to dismiss the conversation. She was pretty sure she knew why she hadn't been the same since the reunion, but she wasn't about to get into that with her kids. It was something she'd have to work her way through, something that had nothing to do with her daughters. Something she'd been avoiding thinking about. "I guess maybe I'm just distracted by the holidays being so close and your father not being with us."

"Oh. Well, that makes sense." Natalie glanced at Grace, who'd watched the exchange but hadn't commented. "We'll all be missing Daddy even more at Thanksgiving. Remember how he loved to put the turkey on that big white platter—"

"The one with the big turkey on it." Grace nodded.

"—and bring it into the dining room and make this big show of carving it." Natalie smiled at the memory.

"Dad really went all out for every holiday," Grace reminisced. "He loved seeing the dining room all dressed up for Thanksgiving. That plum tablecloth and the dark gold napkins and the dishes with the cornucopia in the middle. The table was always so gorgeous."

"Mom always made these fabulous centerpieces," Natalie added.

"And she always got those little pumpkins and stood up little candles in them and put them at every place," Grace said.

"Mom is right here, and she can hear you," Maggie said lightly, hoping to lift the nostalgic mood that was threatening to turn somber. "And yes, your dad loved to go all out for the holidays, and yes, before you ask, I still have the plum-colored tablecloth, and I can buy little pumpkins at the farmers' market."

"Excellent." Grace made a thumbs-up.

"I can't wait. Thanks again for dinner."

Natalie turned to Daisy. "Dais, what do you say to Nana?"

"Thank you for my book." Daisy reached up for a hug and planted a big kiss on Maggie's cheek.

Maggie's heart melted. "You're most welcome. Come back and see me again."

Daisy looked up at her, nodded, and said, "I will."

Natalie kissed her mom and followed her sister outside.

Maggie stood on the front step and watched her girls walk down the path to the driveway while she deadheaded the colorful mums she'd bought at a local farm to bring some autumnal touches to her porch, observing that the mums, too, appeared sadly neglected. The jack-o'-lanterns she'd carved for Halloween had collapsed upon themselves and should have been put into the trash days ago. Maggie made a mental note to bag them up and take them to the curb before the next trash day.

She folded her arms across her chest and watched Grace lean on the side of Natalie's car while Daisy was strapped into her car seat. Her daughters spoke for another minute before hugging, Natalie getting into her car and Grace walking to the end of the driveway to hers. One last wave and Maggie stepped back inside the house and proceeded to straighten the kitchen, returning Daisy's discarded toys to the basket she kept in the family room and setting the gas fireplace to a low flame as she finished picking up the last pieces of their visit. A photo out of place here, a magazine tossed carelessly onto the coffee table there. She settled into a chair near the fireplace, where she'd left the book she was supposed to read for her book club, and turned on a nearby lamp. She read almost a dozen pages before admitting neither the story nor the characters were appealing to her. She closed the book and stared into the fire, then grabbed her phone and tapped Emma's number.

"What are we supposed to wear to Chris's show?" she asked when Emma picked up. "My girls were here for dinner tonight, and I think they're concerned that I'm going to dress like a nineteen-year-old. Or worse, a fifty-eight-year-old. What are three women who are closing in on sixty supposed to wear to a rock concert?"

"We wear T-shirts with my son's picture on them, which Chris already sent, and your favorite jeans," Emma told her.

They discussed the travel arrangements Chris had made for them, and then, travel and wardrobe issues settled, they said good night. Maggie closed up the house, turning on the security system before turning off the downstairs lights, then slowly climbed the steps to the second floor, her heart heavy. All night she'd tried to forget that tomorrow would be the anniversary of the worst day of her life. In its honor, she'd allow herself a good cry in the shower, which was a habit she'd developed while Art was alive. She'd turn the water on high to muffle her sobs, and if Art noticed the red blotches on her cheeks, she'd pass it off as the water having gotten too hot. Over the years, she'd become so accustomed to crying on her own that she'd long since stopped wishing for someone to hold her and to comfort her, someone who would understand. But that someone was the only other living soul who knew of her heartache, and when it had mattered, even he hadn't understood. So she'd learned to weep alone and mourn in silence and tried not to wish that the day would ever be marked by anyone except herself.

∼

The Flynns' normally sedate Thanksgiving dinner turned out to be anything but. While Maggie had to accept the fact that her turkey would never be as golden brown and juicy as Art's, her sweet potato casserole never quite as delicious as his, her cranberry sauce somehow not quite as sweet even though she followed his recipe to a T, the day had been a success. Grace drove to the airport to pick up Liddy and Emma, and they'd arrived at the house just as the florist delivered a gorgeous centerpiece in autumnal shades. When Maggie had read aloud the card—*Wish I was there with you. See you soon. Love to all, Chris*—Emma had sighed and said, "Ah, my boy."

"Just imagine how much that card would be worth if Chris had signed it himself," Grace noted. "You could auction it off."

"And if you'd had the presence of mind to save all his dirty socks over the years instead of laundering them," Maggie said, "you'd make a fortune."

"Yes, well, if only I'd known." Emma laughed. "I should have learned to read tea leaves like my mother."

"I say we toast Chris for sending those flowers." Not bothering to wait for a response, Grace opened a kitchen drawer and brought out the corkscrew. "Nat, grab some glasses."

Nat passed around the glasses, and Grace filled them.

"To Chris," Grace said. "With thanks for his thoughtfulness."

"And may he be with us next year," his mother added as she lifted her glass.

"Thank you, Chris. You're a good boy," Liddy said, at which everyone laughed and patted Emma on the back. "We know it's because you raised him right, Em."

"Thank you." Emma took a sip of wine.

"Credit where it's due," Maggie added.

"So what shall we do between now and dinner?" Grace asked.

"Cards?" Natalie offered. "Or Monopoly?"

"Monopoly!"

Everyone agreed.

Maggie found the game box and brought it into the kitchen, setting it up on the table overlooking the yard. As the Monopoly money was distributed, they finished the bottle of wine they'd opened to toast Chris and opened a second between trips to the oven to check the turkey's progress, then a third. They paused the game long enough to eat dinner on the beautifully appointed table, the traditional china and silver, the golden turkey on the white platter. After they'd tasted each of the pies—a pumpkin and a pecan—they cleared the table and loaded the dishwasher before playing three games of Candyland so Daisy could take part in the festivities. But once Daisy had been tucked into bed, the unfinished game of cutthroat Monopoly was resumed.

Shortly before eleven, after having cornered the market on the three orange properties and all four railroads, Grace was declared winner and real estate mogul.

"Wow. That was an impressive win," Natalie conceded. "Congratulations, but I don't remember you being so serious about Monopoly."

"You played that game like your life depended on it," Maggie said as she watched Grace count her winnings.

"Zach and I used to play a lot," Grace told them as she held up her play money gleefully. "He was really into it in a big way. There are sites online where you can go to learn strategy and how to maximize your winnings."

"Oh, really?" Natalie sat back against the cushioned banquette. "Do tell."

"Yeah, they're really informative. I had to make him stop looking stuff up because then he'd use that information to cheat when we played."

"Did you just use what he learned to cheat just now?" Natalie narrowed her eyes.

"Maybe." Grace grinned.

Natalie tossed her game piece—the Scottie dog—onto the board. "Cheater."

"You're just pissed because you don't know the inside dirt," Grace told her.

"The least you can do is share what you know, now that the game is over," Emma said.

Grace began sorting the money in piles to return to the box. "Statistically, the most frequently landed-on spot is Illinois Avenue. So if you can put a house or two there—or better still, a hotel—you'll be collecting a lot of rent. Also, orange is good. Always buy the orange places—Tennessee and New York Avenues and St. James Place."

"Someone actually sat down and figured out the probability of landing on which spaces?" Emma asked.

Grace nodded. "And as we've just seen, the odds were in my favor."

"Okay, that's it for me tonight." Liddy stood and stretched. "Early morning tomorrow. Fun game, ladies—cheating aside. And Maggie, thanks so much for making such a delicious dinner."

"Not quite up to Art's standards, but we all survived another of my attempts to re-create the perfection of my late husband's turkey." Maggie had risen when Liddy had.

"Mom, stop. It was fine," Natalie told her.

"Sweetheart, Thanksgiving dinner is supposed to be more than just 'fine.' But it's okay. I'm a work in progress where holiday meals are concerned."

"Dad set impossibly high standards," Grace reminded her. "That said, don't put yourself down. You did a great job."

"Thanks, Gracie."

"Listen to your daughters." Emma kissed first Maggie, then each of the girls good night. "This was the best Thanksgiving I've had in . . . oh, years. Chris usually is somewhere else, so I'm at the mercy of any kindhearted soul who'll have me."

"And for the last few years, I've done potluck with my book club," Liddy said.

"You both have a standing invitation at my house," Maggie assured them. It hadn't been the kind of holiday the Flynns used to have, but it had been fun. More fun than the last two had been. *Change is good,* she reminded herself. Maybe her life could use a little more of it.

"Excellent. I was hoping you'd say that." Liddy gave Maggie a hug before she headed for the stairs. "I'm over that whole potluck thing. Maureen Harper's green bean casserole and Deb Burke's runny pumpkin pie." She turned to Emma. "I'm ready to turn in. How 'bout you?"

Emma nodded. "The car is supposed to pick us up early tomorrow."

"You two go on up. I'm just going to close up down here, and then I'll be going to bed, too."

"Mom, we'll finish cleaning up in the kitchen and straightening the dining room," Natalie said as Liddy and Emma went upstairs. "You have a big day tomorrow."

"Yes, go. Shoo." Grace motioned with both hands toward the stairs. "It's not every day you get picked up by a private car and flown in a private jet to see a concert. Go get rested. We've got this."

"Thank you both. It's been a long day, and I am tired. I'll see you in the morning, assuming you're up before we leave." Maggie kissed Grace, then Natalie, on their cheeks and headed for her room on the second floor.

~

Early Friday morning, a long black car pulled up in front of the house, and the stout driver got out. Maggie opened the front door before he reached the porch. He tipped his hat, then pointed to the women's bags piled in the foyer. "This all the stuff that's going?" he asked, pointing to the luggage.

Maggie nodded. "That's it."

Without another word, he gathered it up and headed for the car.

"We'll be out in a minute," Maggie called after him.

Emma came out of the kitchen carrying a travel mug of coffee in one hand and a danish in the other. Liddy, late as always, flew down the steps, retreated to the kitchen for the coffee Maggie had waiting for her, then followed her friends out the door, pausing while Maggie locked up behind them. Within five minutes of his arrival, the driver was on his way to the airport, three excited, giddy, middle-aged women in the back seat, singing songs from the seventies and laughing like kindergartners.

Maggie had never flown in a private jet before, and she entered the plane with her curiosity on alert.

"This is going to ruin me for anything less," she said when the flight attendant, who introduced herself as Ginger, handed her a glass of champagne. "Even first class is going to seem like a downgrade after this."

Emma swiveled her chair around to face her friends and raised her glass. "To us. To road trips. To friendship."

"To us." Liddy nodded.

"To friendship. And to sons who send private planes to bring his mama and her buds to see him play with his band." Maggie touched the rim of her glass to the others, then took a sip.

Emma took out her phone and held it up. "I have all the songs from Chris's playlist right here. I'm going to play them until we know them at least well enough to sing the chorus."

"You have to be kidding." Liddy glared over the top of her glass. "Em, the only person I know whose singing is worse than mine is you. Do you really want to inflict that on the people around us tonight?"

"They won't be able to hear anything over the band, believe me. So okay. The first one is called 'If You See Me.'" Emma increased the volume and repeated the line from the chorus, "If you see me, keep on walkin', don't come knockin' on my door."

"See how easy? We don't have to know the whole song, just enough so that if Chris looks down and sees us, he'll think we know his songs, and it'll make him happy," Emma explained.

"Em, honey, Chris is going to have about eighteen thousand screaming girls in various stages of undress in the audience," Liddy said. "I don't think he really gives a crap about whether or not his mother and her friends know his lyrics."

"You just wait. He'll be glad." Emma turned her attention back to her phone. "Okay, so we're good on that one, right? Now here's the next one. It's called 'Living My Best Life . . .'"

Ginger served Cobb salads followed by individual pumpkin soufflés, and for a few minutes the singing stopped. But once their plates had been cleared away, Emma insisted on resuming the crash course in DEAN's greatest hits.

Two hours later, the plane landed, and they were escorted off, their bags in their hands.

"Who's picking us up?" Maggie followed Ginger across the tarmac.

Emma shrugged. "Chris said he'd send someone."

"You don't know who?" Liddy asked.

"No." Emma kept walking.

"How will we find our ride?" Liddy caught up to her.

"I think she's found us." Maggie grabbed Emma's arm and pointed off to the left, where a young woman held up a sign that said, **WELCOME MAMA DEAN & FRIENDS**.

"Yup. That's us." Emma made a beeline for the woman with the sign, and Liddy and Maggie trailed behind. "We're here." She waved.

The smiling driver—who introduced herself as Penelope—led them to the car, and it was off to their lodgings. Chris had found a special place, he'd told his mother, close to the concert venue but small and luxurious. When they arrived at the small boutique hotel, they discovered he'd bought out all the rooms on the top floor so they wouldn't be disturbed.

"Oh, now he's just showing off," Maggie teased Emma when they were led to their suite. There was a large vase of dahlias along with a tray of fruit and cheese and a bottle of wine on the round table that sat by the windows in the common sitting room. "This is amazing. Remind me to thank your son for being so good to Mama Dean and her friends."

"You can thank him yourself later. He'd wanted to make it over here to have dinner with us, but he has some TV interviews to do. But we'll definitely see him after the show." Emma settled into one of the overstuffed chairs near a gas fireplace. "I can't wait. I haven't seen him since my birthday."

"That was two months ago." Liddy held up the unopened bottle of wine. "Anyone?"

"None for me, but feel free." Emma added wistfully, "Two months is a long time."

"I'll pass for now, too." Maggie cozied up on the sofa, her legs tucked under her. "I'd hate to go even two weeks without seeing my girls."

"I think daughters are different. You guys go shopping together, you meet for dinner." Emma toed off her shoes. "Sometimes you even have breakfast together just because. The last time I had breakfast with Chris, he was just getting in from the night before."

"Different lifestyles, Em." Maggie held up the brochure she'd picked up in the hotel lobby. "I looked up things to do in Charlotte. There's a self-guided walking tour called the Liberty Tour. Nineteen historic sites from the American Revolution. There are carriage tours, too. Oh, and the NASCAR Hall of Fame is in Charlotte."

"*Ruvvvv, ruvvvv.*" Liddy mimicked what she apparently thought was the sound of a roaring engine. "I'd go for the walking tour. The liberty thing."

"Yeah, me too." Maggie set down the brochure.

"Okay, me three." Emma appeared deep in thought. A few moments later she said, "But I think we should do something special to commemorate our trip. Something different. Something . . . memorable."

"Like what?" Liddy joined Maggie on the sofa and sat facing Emma. "We can ask someone to take pictures with our phones at every stop of that walking tour."

"We can. But I'm thinking something more permanent." Emma's eyes began to twinkle.

Maggie laughed. "What exactly do you have in mind? And will it involve calling your son to bail us out?"

"I don't think you can get arrested for getting a tattoo." Emma looked first to Maggie, then to Liddy.

"You want to get a tattoo?" Maggie's eyebrows raised in exaggerated shock. "Em, that's so unlike you."

"I was thinking all three of us should get tattoos. The same tattoo."

"Matching tattoos," Liddy said flatly.

"Yeah. Why not?"

"Because we're . . . ," Liddy began, then stopped. "I don't know why not. Maggie?"

Maggie shrugged. "I never thought about getting one, but I could be persuaded. Depending, of course, on what you have in mind."

"I was thinking something small and tasteful that would be meaningful to the three of us. Something that represents our years of friendship," Emma said softly.

"Like what?" Liddy asked.

Emma shrugged. "I don't know. I was hoping one of you would have an idea."

They sat in a prolonged silence, each apparently contemplating the possibilities. Finally, Maggie said, "Well, maybe it should have three parts. Like a shamrock. Or a triangle. Or a Celtic knot."

"Or three stars. Three hearts. Three tiny kayaks," Liddy said.

"Lid, we haven't kayaked together in years," Emma reminded her.

"Yes, but we used to. And we could again." Liddy seemed to think twice about that. "Okay, scratch the kayaks."

"Or it could be something that we share, like, we could get the same rose. Or the same butterfly." Emma was still pondering the choices. "A single feather. A sandpiper. A dragonfly."

"Sun, moon, and stars." Liddy tossed out another. "The sun with three tiny planets, for the three of us."

"This is more difficult than you'd think. Maybe we should find a tattoo artist and see what he or she has. You know, like a design book," Emma suggested.

"You really think we'd be able to agree on a choice while we're standing there?" Maggie looked up from her phone. "There are several artists in Charlotte. I'm reading the review comments right now." She read silently for a moment, then aloud. "'Botched a simple design. Avoid at all costs.'

Okay, nix Main Street Anthony. Here's another. 'Spent a month on anti-biotics after S. did my tats.' Ah, thank you, but no, Mr. S. We'll pass." Maggie scanned a few more. "Oh, here we go. Nicole's Tattoos. Mostly four- and five-star reviews. One negative because the customer thought Nicole was expensive, though he admitted the work was perfect." She looked up from her phone. "Nicole gets my vote."

Liddy and Emma both nodded their agreement.

"I'm going to call and get some information. Like, do we need an appointment?" Maggie tapped in the number, then waited while the call went through. When Nicole herself answered, Maggie went through her list of want-to-knows. When she hung up, she didn't look happy.

"What?" Liddy asked.

"Nicole can't take three of us tomorrow at the same time. And unless we have something drawn out, we would have to select one of her designs."

"If we can't go together, it sort of takes the fun out of it," Emma said as her phone played the ringtone signaling a call was coming in from her son. "Oh, there's Chris." She grinned broadly. "Hello, yes, we're here and we can't wait to see you."

While Emma spoke with her son, Maggie picked at the fruit in the basket, snagging a few grapes. She poured herself a glass of wine and returned to the seating area in time to hear Emma say, "Oh, that would be great. Call me right back. And thanks, son."

Emma turned an excited face to the others. "Chris thinks the tattoo idea is very cool. He's going to call Nicole and see if he can bribe her with concert tickets or something if she'll fit us in together tomorrow."

"Great idea. I bet that works." Maggie returned to the sofa.

"He isn't going to be able to get here in time to eat and get back to the arena, but he's going to send a car for us. Also gave me instructions on where to go once we get there." Emma laughed. "And he also sent someone out to find earplugs for us. I assured him we wouldn't need them—it's not like none of us has been to a concert before—but the thought was really sweet."

Maggie nodded. "It's the thought that counts."

"Really sweet of him," Liddy agreed. "But yeah. I've been to dozens of concerts in my time. I saw the Who a few years ago, and they were *loud*."

Emma's phone rang and she glanced at the screen. "It's Chris . . . hi. Okay. Oh, terrific. Thank you!" She gave Liddy and Maggie a thumbs-up. "That's so nice of you. I will. Thanks. See you soon."

She held up the phone in a triumphant gesture. "We're good to go for noon tomorrow."

"Did he have to promise Nicole his firstborn?" Maggie asked.

"She extorted four tickets and backstage passes for tomorrow night, but he said no big deal. And he's looking forward to seeing all three of us tonight." Emma got up and went to the table and picked up the menus. "So how 'bout we look into a quick dinner. Something light, maybe. We're getting picked up in about ninety minutes, and I'm going to need some of that time to get into my 'rock star mom' look."

"What's a rock star mom look like?" Liddy asked.

"We wear makeup and good jewelry."

Liddy looked at Maggie and deadpanned, "She's going to do it. She's going to wear pearls with her concert tee."

They pored over the menu before Emma called in their order. When she finished, she turned back to Liddy and Maggie and said, "So we need to decide where we want to have it."

Maggie glanced at the table, then back to Emma. "I guess the dining table."

Emma laughed. "Not dinner. I meant the tattoo. We should all have the same thing in the same place. Preferably someplace where it won't sag."

"Honey, sooner or later, everything's going to sag," Liddy pointed out.

"So we find some discreet place for this little tattoo where the sagging won't be noticeable to anyone except ourselves," Maggie said.

"What's the point in having a tattoo if no one sees it?" Liddy asked.

"We're not getting it for anyone else," Emma said. "We're getting it for ourselves."

"Good point." Maggie thought for a moment. "How 'bout between our shoulder blades? We'll always know it's there—whatever *it* turns out to be."

Emma rose to answer the door. "I'd like to be able to see it. If it's in the middle of my back, I'll only be able to see it in a mirror, and what's the fun of that?"

Room service wheeled in a cart laden with dishes hidden beneath shiny covers as the three women gathered at the table. In no time, the women had devoured their omelets and fruit salad, and after they'd finished, Emma passed out the T-shirts her son had sent for them.

The short-sleeve black cotton shirts bore Chris's face front and center, with the members of his band behind him. DEAN was written in pale-blue cursive under the image. Maggie and Liddy both made a fuss over them before heading off to their rooms to change for the main event.

"I love that Chris had this shirt designed and made special for you, Em." Maggie stood in front of a mirror and fluffed her hair after they'd regrouped in the sitting room. "Makes me feel like I'm twenty-one again and on my way to a Bruce Springsteen concert with a sorority sister from Hartford. Her aunt worked for the promoter and got us great seats."

A bittersweet memory struck Maggie without warning, and she almost doubled up from the pain of it. She walked to the window and craned her neck, pretending to look for the limo while she tamped it back down. Brett had left for football camp in Ohio the week before, and she'd been crying on and off every day, even as she packed for her return to Pittsburgh for her senior year. He'd gone back early to get in some extra training, because word was there'd be several pro scouts at camp, and he'd wanted to make sure he was ready.

"This is for us," he'd told her before getting into his car and driving off. "For our future. If I sign with a pro team, we'll have it made." He'd kissed her long and hard, then set off on the drive to Columbus, the car radio blasting, his fingers tapping out the beat on the steering wheel. She'd stood at the end of their driveway until the car disappeared down the road at the point where Cottage merged with Front Street.

"Where was that?" Emma asked.

Maggie snapped back to the present. "Sorry. Where was what?"

"The concert."

"East Rutherford, New Jersey. The Brendan Byrne Arena. It was August and hot as blazes. Like, ninety-five degrees. We were on our way back to school and the air-conditioning in my old car died. The concert was amazing, though. One of the best ever. After it was over, we went out for burgers. Then, since I drove us to New Jersey, she drove the rest of the way to Pittsburgh that night. Made it to school in time for breakfast."

The knock at the door saved her from sharing other memories.

"That must be our driver." Emma's eyes shone with excitement as she picked up her bag and slung it over her shoulder. "Ready, girls?"

"Let's do it." Maggie went to the door and opened it. The same young woman who'd driven them from the airport stood in the hall.

"Lead on, Penelope." Emma paused to lock the door behind them. "I'm so excited I can't stand it."

"You've seen Chris in concert before," Liddy reminded her.

"Yes, but not with my two best friends." Emma clutched their hands as they got into the elevator. "And I can't wait to see my boy."

"Her boy." Liddy elbowed Maggie. "Her boy who will have thousands of women screaming his name in about ninety minutes. Tossing him condoms with their names on the wrappers."

Penelope grinned without commenting and hit the button to send the elevator to the lobby.

~

Charlotte's Spectrum Center arena was mobbed from the parking lot to the brightly lit concourse. Maggie, Liddy, and Emma were whisked away to a guarded back entrance to the building and ushered inside and down a hall.

"There are guards everywhere," Liddy whispered.

"So no one can sneak in and harass the performers. Chris told me we'd need to show our passes about four times before we got to him." Emma held up her pass to the tall, beefy, bearded guard at the dressing room door.

He reached behind him and opened the door, and Emma disappeared into the arms of her grinning son. Chris held her for a moment, then turned the grin to Maggie and Liddy, gesturing for them to follow him. The door closed behind them as Chris lifted his mother off her feet and swung her around.

"Put me down," Emma protested, though not, Maggie thought, very convincingly.

"You look great, Mom." He planted a loud kiss on her cheek, then turned to his visitors. "Mrs. Flynn! I'm so happy to see you." He kissed Maggie, then leaned over to kiss Liddy as well. "Looking good, Mrs. Bryant."

Chris looked to Maggie like the kid who'd gotten an air rifle for Christmas. He was beaming, one arm around his mother. With his other arm, he reached out and hugged Maggie.

"Mrs. Flynn, I was so sorry to hear about your husband. I wanted to come to the service, but—"

Maggie cut him off. "Your mom told me you were out of the country, Chris. We didn't expect you. But the flowers were gorgeous. Just perfect. Dahlias were Art's favorites. And thank you for the centerpiece yesterday. It was lovely."

"You're welcome. But I still would have liked to have been there." Before Maggie could again reassure him, he added, "How's Natalie? I haven't seen her in . . . damn, years."

"Nat's fine. Teaching remedial English and creative writing at a community college. She hasn't changed much," Maggie said. "Same old Nat."

"And Grace? How's Grace?"

Maggie paused, wondering if she should tell the truth, then reminded herself that most of the time when people asked how you were, they were being polite and not really expecting much of anything beyond "okay."

Maggie opted for simplicity. "Gracie's well, thanks. I'll let her know you were asking about her."

"Mom said she has a daughter. Natalie, that is."

"She does. Daisy is three, and the smartest, most beautiful child on the planet," Maggie told him.

"I bet you've got pictures," he said.

"Of course I have pictures." Maggie laughed. "What kind of a grandmother would I be if I didn't have pictures?"

He held out a hand, wiggled his fingers. "Hand 'em over."

"You don't need to . . . ," Maggie began to protest, thinking how nice it was for him to ask, but asking was sufficient.

"Yeah, I do. I want to see what Nat's kid looks like." That grin again. Maggie remembered that grin getting him out of all sorts of scrapes when he was younger. She took her phone from her bag, scrolled till she found her photos of Daisy, then handed it over to Chris. "If you insist . . ."

He swiped the screen several times, his smile spreading with each swipe. "She looks like Nat."

"She does. Hey, you don't have to look at them all," Maggie told him.

He looked at a few more, paused at one or two, then handed the phone back to Maggie.

"Nat looks good. Please tell her I said hi." He gave Maggie a quick hug. "And give her that from me. Maybe we'll all be in Wyndham Beach one of these days and we can get together."

"She'd love that. Both the girls would." Then remembering that this wasn't just their childhood friend Chris but Chris Dean, lead singer of DEAN, she added, "They're hoping to catch one of your shows, one of these days." She picked at the front of her shirt. "And they were plotting behind my back, trying to figure out how to get this away from me. Thank you for the shirts, by the way."

"You're welcome, but tell Nat I'd love to see her anytime. She's still in Philly?"

"Outside of the city, but yes, they both are."

"I think we're playing there in the spring. I'll get in touch. And those shirts were designed and made just for you and Mom and Mrs. Bryant, but I'll have a few more made up."

"That would be such a fun surprise for them."

"Mrs. Bryant, I was hoping to get a moment to talk to you . . ." He skillfully led her a few steps away, his arm around her as if to shelter her.

Maggie couldn't hear what he was saying, but she knew instinctively he would be speaking to her about Jessie, offering words of comfort even though Maggie knew he'd canceled a show to come home for her funeral.

"You've raised a remarkable boy, Em," Maggie said quietly.

"He is that," Emma whispered.

A moment later, someone shouted, "Chris! It's time, man."

Chris raised a hand behind Liddy's back to acknowledge he'd heard but finished whatever it was he was saying before giving her one more hug. When Liddy turned back to Maggie and Emma, her eyes were brimming, but she was smiling.

"Some kid," she said simply.

"And now that kid's going to work." Chris touched Emma on the shoulder. "Mom, I got you all earplugs."

"Earplugs? Pshaw," Emma said dismissively. "I was going to concerts long before you were born."

"Maybe, but that was back in the day, before speakers and electric guitars, right?" he teased, nodding at someone behind Maggie.

She turned to find two large, burly men, tattooed sleeves from their wrists to their shoulders, wearing black T-shirts with DEAN SECURITY in big white letters on front and back.

"Ladies," Chris was saying, "this is Turk, and this is Brando. They're your guides for tonight." He looked over Maggie's head and said, "This is my mom and her two friends. Guard them with your lives, guys."

He turned back to Emma. "Have fun. See you after the show."

Liddy looked from one of the guards to the other, then back again. "Brando, huh?" she asked.

"Yes, ma'am." He nodded solemnly.

"Well, I do see a slight resemblance." Liddy rubbed her hands in anticipation. "Okay, let's go, fellas. We've got a show to watch."

Chris had offered them special box seats from which to watch the show, but they'd declined because they wanted "the whole concert experience." So instead of comfy box seats, Maggie, Liddy, and Emma found themselves dead center in the first row on the floor, "spitting distance," as Liddy had said, from the stage. When the band appeared to take their places, the entire arena erupted in screams and shouts, and Maggie began to second-guess Emma's blithe dismissal of earplugs. The level of noise was unlike anything she'd ever heard. When she slapped her hands over her ears, Turk—or Brando, she wasn't sure who was who—offered her a small box.

"Plugs," he said, pointing to his ears. "Won't block out everything, but they will make it tolerable."

"What?" She'd leaned forward to ask, then said, "Never mind." She took the box and popped it open to reveal two small tan-color knobs, which she proceeded to slide into her ears. The effect was immediate. The noise level dropped dramatically, but she could still hear. She tapped her friends on the arm and pointed to her ears, then to the guard who'd offered the earplugs to her. Emma and Liddy nodded, Turk (or Brando) handed over the tiny boxes, and everyone was smiling just as the band began to play.

As promised, Chris followed the set list he'd sent Emma. If members of the audience sitting around them were amused by the fact that the three older ladies in the front row knew the chorus of every song DEAN played, they gave no sign, even when the arm waving began and the ladies began to get into the spirit of the music, dancing and singing along. When the lights in the arena went low and the audience held up their lit phones, Maggie looked at Liddy and Emma, shrugged, and pulled out her phone as well. Laughing, Liddy and Emma followed suit. When objects began to fly past them to land on the stage, Maggie pulled a small box of Junior Mints from her bag and tossed them directly at Chris, who caught the box on his chest with one hand, then doubled over with laughter before tucking it into the pocket of his jeans.

At the midway point of the show, he gestured for the crowd to settle down. When he began to speak, the arena went as close to silent as it ever would.

"If you've been to our shows before, you know I like to take a little breather and share a little personal story with you all. Tonight, I have my most special girl with me. The woman who stood behind me—always—who took my part when I know how hard it was sometimes for her to do that."

Boy, was it ever, Maggie thought, recalling how Emma and her husband had fought over Chris's rejection of a career at the bank, how

Harry'd dismissed Chris's love of music and his instinctive ability to play any instrument he picked up. The arguments had left Emma raw and gutted.

Chris stepped to the edge of the stage, microphone in hand, looking down to the first row with much love in his eyes. "Guys, say hello to my mom, the ageless, beautiful Emma Dean."

Applause was swiftly followed by chants of *Em-ma, Em-ma*, which made Emma cover her face as she burst into tears. Chris nimbly jumped down from the stage and put his arms around his mother. After a few words meant only for her, he rubbed her back for a second before he hoisted himself back to the stage, signaled the band, and launched into the second half of the set list.

After the show ended, Maggie, Emma, and Liddy were ushered back to the crowded dressing room, where bandmates, roadies, several important-looking men in suits, and various women congregated.

One of Chris's bandmates, Todd, told them Chris had jumped in the shower to clean up and had appointed him to keep the dressing room decent—"no bad cursing, no nudity"—till he was dressed.

"Good of him to appoint a chaperone," Liddy muttered. "Like we don't curse like sailors when it's called for, and we've seen plenty of naked people in our time. Including Chris. Not since he was a baby, but still."

"Trust me, ma'am," Todd told her, "you don't want to be here during an all-out free-for-all. Bottom line, the boss said no one misbehaves while his mom is here."

And for the most part, no one did. Someone did bring in several large paper bags and dumped the contents on the floor. Maggie watched with some amusement as all manner of items fell out, everything from lacy bras to, yes, condom wrappers with writing on them. She was just about to comment when Chris emerged from the actual dressing area, grabbed a beer from a cooler as he passed, and made a beeline for his mother.

"So whatcha think?" he asked as he approached.

"It was great, sweetie. It really was." Emma would have loved it even if Chris had sounded like a cat whose tail was caught in a closed door.

He grinned and pulled the box of Junior Mints from his pocket. "Only you, Mrs. Flynn." He kissed Maggie on the side of her forehead. "I can't believe you remembered."

"Are you kidding? You used to live on those things. You and Ted . . . I can't think of his last name, but his father used to be the barber down on Front Street."

"Ted Affonseca." Chris opened the box of candy and shook a few pieces into his hand, then promptly popped them into his mouth. "These are still my favorite. And Ted's dad is still the barber. I need to get back there soon and see him." He ran a hand through his blond hair, which reached the top of his collar. Someone tapped him on the shoulder and leaned in to whisper something. Chris nodded and said, "Tell him I'll be with him in one minute."

He turned back to Emma. "I forgot I agreed to do an interview after the show. I don't mean to kick you out. You're welcome to hang around, but I don't know how long I'll be."

"Don't be silly. We'll be on our way," Emma said. "I know you have other obligations."

"None more important than you, but yeah, I'd like to get this over with, and then I want to get something to eat. And hey, it's already after midnight." He elbowed his mother lightly. "Past your bedtime, Mom."

"It is, but it was worth it." Emma hugged her son. "So will we see you before we leave on Sunday morning? No pressure."

"I have to check with my manager to see what else is on the schedule, but if I can hook up with you guys before you leave, I will." He walked them toward the door. "Tomorrow's a big milestone for you guys, right? First tats?" He walked them to the door.

"It is. For each of us." Emma tucked a hand through his arm, and he squeezed it.

"Pick something awesome," he said as the guard opened the door and stood aside for them. "Pick something that shows who you guys are to each other."

And that, Maggie thought as they walked through the crowded corridor to their ride, *is the whole point of the tattoo.* She still wasn't sure what it would be, but it would, in fact, be awesome.

Chapter Seven

GRACE

The Christmas lights adorning the well-kept houses on Linden Circle cast a cheery glow over every porch and driveway, from the corner all the way to the end of the block where Grace's pretty Cape Cod sat in bleak and total darkness. There'd been a time not so long ago when the sight of the neighborhood all sparkly with holiday joy had lifted her spirits, but this year every beautifully lit house seemed to mock her. She stopped at the mailbox to gather the few catalogs of last-minute gift ideas tucked among the bills and a few Christmas cards before heading to the end of the driveway, where a motion-sensor light came on to illuminate the area between the garage and the back deck. With her house keys and the mail in one hand and her handbag and her briefcase in the other, she slammed the car door with her shoulder. Up the four steps to the deck, her heels tapping across the boards, and then she unlocked the back door and went inside the silent house.

Grace had not entered the house she'd shared with Zach without feeling like a failure since the night he had packed his belongings. She'd married him believing in their happy-ever-after and had bought this house with an unquestioned assurance of undying domestic bliss. After closing that first day, he'd carried her over the front door threshold, and they'd begun their life together under this roof. Grace had never—not even for an instant—suspected there'd ever be an end to the fairy tale of their marriage. She still didn't understand what had happened, what had caused Zach to fall out of love with her and into love with someone else. She must have done something to make him not love her anymore. Not that it mattered now, but still, she'd like to know what it was that had made her suddenly so unlovable.

She flicked on the light, dumped her bag and the mail on the kitchen counter, set her briefcase on the floor next to the table, and draped her coat over a nearby chair. The thought of the impending holiday exhausted her. She went into the living room and plugged in the Christmas tree, pausing to watch the blinking lights. She hadn't planned on having a tree this year—really, she hadn't wanted one—but her mother and sister had insisted it would cheer her up. She hadn't been able to explain how the tree had the opposite effect on her. Every time she looked at it, with its graceful arms laden with cheery ornaments and the beautiful angel that sat on the uppermost branch, she wanted to cry because of all the memories the tree evoked. Their first Christmas, she and Zach had walked on the frozen ground of the tree farm as snow had fallen lightly. They'd examined every tree of a certain height until they'd found the perfect one. They'd fought to get the tree into the stand, laughing as the trunk wobbled and crashed not once but twice before they'd managed to secure it. Zach had carefully draped the lights while Grace sorted through the boxes of ornaments, some bought new together, some gifted by her mother or his. There'd been angels she'd made in kindergarten from pipe cleaners and crepe paper, and a print of his small hand impressed inside a plaster heart he'd made in nursery school and hung by a red satin ribbon. Even last year—well after he'd left her—she'd hung that heart on the tree, still hoping against hope that he'd get over whatever it was that had made him leave her and he'd come home. Having spent the last twelve months watching Amber lead him around by his nose—if not by another portion of his anatomy—Grace'd given up any notion of a reconciliation.

A week ago, Zach had had the nerve to ask her if she'd give him that little plaster heart for the tree he and Amber were going to put up that weekend in her apartment. Grace had promised to look for it when she got home, which she'd done. When she'd found it, she'd smashed it into dust with a meat tenderizer.

"Sorry," she'd told him on Monday when he'd again asked about his treasured ornament. "I guess it got lost or something." It gave her perverse pleasure to know that he knew she was lying, but he couldn't do a damned thing about it.

She sat on the sofa and pulled her legs up under her. She couldn't help how sad she felt at how disappointing her life had turned out to be. Even sitting in this room she loved in the house she loved made her sad. She'd lost her heart to the house from the moment she first saw it, and she prized every piece of furniture and every work of art. Now all those lovely things she and Zach had picked out together had been left behind, just as she had been. He'd taken nothing but his clothes and a few personal items, discarding every trace of their marriage as if wanting to erase it all from his life. And yet every day he reported to work at the law firm that carried her father's name.

She thought about how her father would have handled a cheating son-in-law who worked for him. Then again, there'd been no cheating while Art was alive. At least, she was pretty sure there hadn't been. Zach had been perfectly happy to be married to the boss's daughter—until the boss died. She'd been easy enough to love when Zach thought she—and therefore, he—would be inheriting the firm. Her father's death had changed everything.

Her stomach rumbled, a reminder she'd skipped lunch to work on a brief, and it was now almost seven. She went into the kitchen in search of last night's leftovers, still lamenting the turn her life had taken. She just didn't understand why she and Zach couldn't have had the same kind of marriage her parents had. They'd been soul mates. Perfect together. Meant to be. They were each other's one and only. She wondered if her mother ever felt this deep bitterness when she thought about losing her husband. If she ever wondered why he'd been taken from her. Why they couldn't have grown old together.

There were times when Grace was angry with her father for dying, not just for the upheaval in her mother's life, but for what it had done to hers. Had his death been the catalyst for the breakup of her marriage, or had he been the only thing keeping it together? She wasn't sure. He'd been so proud to walk her down the aisle on her wedding day as she floated in a Vera Wang ocean of tulle. He'd been so pleased with her choice of husband. And then poof! Her father was gone, and Zach was gone, and she had nothing except this house and her job. She went into the office every day, closed her door, did her work, kept her head down, and then came home. It was killing her.

The only thing that was keeping her sane was *TheLast2No*.

She ate Thai takeout from two nights ago straight out of the container, standing at the kitchen counter while she turned on her laptop and went directly to her blog. Scanning the comment section, she found a discussion had been ongoing, apparently for the last hour.

> JK-Taurus: I've always been a good person. I've never hurt a soul in my life. But all I can think about lately is—well, doing something bad.

> BlackWido55: Like what kind of bad?

> JK-Taurus: Like, hurting him.

> JanieJoPa: You mean, like, physically?

> JK-Taurus: Yeah. In a really big way.

LizzieCake_25: I can so relate. I think about smashing my ex's knees with a big hammer.

Grace had to jump in and remind them that any talk of violent behavior was a no-no.

Annie Boleyn: Yow, LizzieCake_25! Remember the blog rules! No violence!

LizzieCake_25: I didn't say I'd do it. I just said I think about it. And I do. I thought the purpose of this blog was to be a place where we could vent and not be judged.

Annie Boleyn: No one's judging you, LizzieCake_25.

LizzieCake_25: Sure sounds as if you are.

Annie Boleyn: Just reminding you.

BlackWido55: So JK-Taurus, what's stopping you from putting a big hurt on the bastard?

JK-Taurus: The thought of spending the rest of my life behind bars? Never seeing my kids again? Their jerk father gaining sole custody so he and his new wife can raise my children?

BlackWido55: Only if you get caught, girl.

JK-Taurus: My luck, I'd be caught. I've never gotten away with a damned thing in my life.

> BlackWido55: There are ways if you're smart. DM me if you want to know.

> OurMissArden: Guys! I can't believe you're having this conversation! I hope you're not serious.

> BlackWido55: He ruined her life and he's getting away with it. That POS gave her three kids and then walked off into the sunset with another woman. Why shouldn't he be punished?

Grace stared at the screen. Was BlackWido55 actually encouraging JK-Taurus to physically harm her ex-husband? Time to jump in again. She donned her Annie persona and began to type.

> Annie Boleyn: Guys, I started this blog as a place where we could offer support to each other. Trust me, no one was dumped more painfully than I was. But I'm going to have to shut you down if you keep talking about hurting someone.

Grace watched as first BlackWido55 then JK-Taurus left the conversation.

> OurMissArden: Am I the only one who got a little worried there for a minute?

> LizzieCake_25: You know how BlackWido55 likes to talk tough. She always has an edge.

Grace monitored the conversation a little longer, adding one last reminder that talks of actual violence were verboten before closing the laptop. The blog had been her saving grace—no pun—but lately a few of her followers had developed a sharper tone, suggesting if not outright advocating some sort of retaliation against their or someone's ex that crossed the line from unpleasant to possibly criminal. She'd have to keep a closer eye on BlackWido55. If she kept it up, Grace would have to block her completely.

She poured herself a glass of wine and tried to decide how to spend the rest of the night. She could watch a movie on TV. Wrap Christmas presents and put them under the tree. Write out those few Christmas cards she sent every year. She recalled there'd been a few cards in the stack of mail she'd brought in earlier, so she culled them from the pile and opened them to see if she needed to add anyone else to her list. Christmas was still a few weeks away, so she could still mail a few cards. There was one from a friend from college, another from a lawyer who'd left the firm and moved to Memphis right after her father had died and didn't know that she and Zach were no longer together ("Wishing you both the merriest of holidays! Love, June"), and one from Emma Dean, the envelope of which was marked PHOTOS. DO NOT BEND. She opened the card and let the photos fall onto the counter.

The photos were all from her mother's Thanksgiving road trip with her friends to Charlotte. There were photos of the three women standing in the front row of the audience as other concert-goers filed in around them. A photo of Chris on stage—she paused over this one and smiled because he was so damned cute and looked *so* like a rock star. Next, the three women in a horse-drawn carriage. Another at the NASCAR museum. A picture in the tattoo shop—what had ever possessed her mother to go along with that? At least the tattoo was cute and was in a discreet place. Grace would have bet that had been Liddy's idea, but her mother had said Emma had suggested it. The last one was of her mother and Chris. He had his arm around her, his hand holding a box of Junior Mints. She looked through the pictures a second time before leaving them on the counter with the realization that her mother was having more fun and a way better life than she was. Which she acknowledged was a good thing for her mother. She knew Maggie'd had a hard time since Art died.

It occurred to Grace, not for the first time, that the Flynn women had really, *really* bad luck with men. Maggie's husband had died a week before he'd have turned sixty. Grace's own husband had left her for the office floozy. Natalie . . . well, Nat never had a husband, but her baby daddy—a term Grace would never use in the presence of her mother— had walked out on her, and whether it had bothered Nat or not, the fact remained that if her luck had been better, she'd have gotten involved with the kind of man who would have stayed, who would have wanted the child he'd made with the woman he supposedly loved. One who hadn't turned out to be a drug addict.

Yeah. Bad luck all around.

She rinsed out her glass, turned off the kitchen light, and settled herself back in the living room. She wanted to take one more look at *TheLast2No* before she headed upstairs to get ready for bed. She clicked on her blog, scanned today's entries, and was dismayed to find that not only had BlackWid055 reappeared, but others had joined the conversation after she'd signed off, and it was taking an ugly turn.

LilacLadyNJ: I don't know . . . I . . .

BlackWido55: Girl, you need to take matters into your own hands and teach that bitch a lesson she won't forget.

Annie Boleyn: I think that's enough for tonight, ladies. I'm shutting this down for a while.

LilacLadyNJ: Oh, but Annie, this is my only place where I feel like I can say what I think and what I feel about what happened to me.

Annie Boleyn: I understand that, I really do. But there's a tone here tonight that is setting off all kinds of alarms, and I need to clear the air.

BlackWido55: She's talking about me. And by clear the air, she means she wants to shut me up.

Annie Boleyn: Not shut you up as much as tone you down. We're supposed to be supportive here, help each other vent so we can move on eventually.

BlackWido55: Oh, really? How close are you to moving on, Annie? I bet if you had the chance, you'd deepsix that little hottie that stole your man.

Annie Boleyn: I'd like her out of my life, yes. Or more accurately, out of his life, but not literally. I mean, I don't want anything bad to happen to her. I wouldn't do anything to hurt her.

BlackWido55: Sure you would. If you could get away with it, there's any number of things you'd do to her. And to him. Want to know what I'm going to do to my ex?

Annie Boleyn: No. And that's it for tonight, ladies. I'll be here by 8 on Friday for happy hour if you're free and want some company.

With shaking hands, Grace closed and locked the blog's comments for the night, effectively shutting everyone out, and signed off. BlackWido55 always seemed to take things right to the edge. Her story was a familiar one: she was happily married to the love of her life until her ex fell in love with her yoga instructor and left her. She'd quipped that she'd lost not only her man but the best yoga teacher she'd ever had. She'd vented hard, but all Grace's followers did that, especially in the beginning. It was why they came to *TheLast2No*, to bitch and whine and put curses on their exes—hence the relatively new feature on the blog, the Ex Hex, where those curses could be spelled out. Once in a while someone got a little carried away with their revenge fantasies, but that was all they were. Fantasies. God knew Grace had had plenty of those herself, none of which she'd shared, but she wasn't going to judge someone else for having them. And for most of her followers, just putting those fantasies out there had been enough to banish them from subsequent conversations. But BlackWido55 seemed unable to drop the baggage, and her aggressive rhetoric seemed to increase as time went on.

One way or another, Grace was going to have to rein her in. The last thing she wanted was for someone in her space encouraging others to acts of violence. Maybe something had set her off earlier in the day, and maybe by Friday she'd be over it. If not, Grace was going to have to block BlackWido55 from the site. Grace was a lawyer, for God's sake. She couldn't have anyone on her blog openly encouraging others to commit criminal acts.

Someone could get hurt. It wasn't a stretch to imagine the blog being discovered in an investigation. And if the blog was traced back to her, no one had more to lose than Grace.

Chapter Eight

NATALIE

"Hey, Natalie. Wait up."

Natalie glanced over her shoulder at the sound of her name. She'd been about to open the door to the room into which her freshman remedial English students would soon be filing. Glenn Patton, the second-year creative writing professor at the community college where Natalie taught, closed the gap between them in four quick strides of his long legs.

"Just wanted to give you an update on Ava Beech." He was a little out of breath. It made her wonder how long he'd been trying to catch up with her.

"Is there a problem?" Natalie opened the door and leaned in to turn on the overhead lights. "Last I heard, she was doing really well in your class. In all her classes, actually."

"She's doing fine. More than fine. Her classwork isn't the problem." He ran a hand through hair the color of very dark tea. "I asked her if she was going to be taking my class next semester, because I didn't see her name on the roster that came out yesterday. She said she wasn't able to come back. Out of funds. Already has two jobs." He followed Natalie into the room. "I hate to see her quit school. She's a gem of a student, and she has tremendous talent. She—"

Natalie held up a hand to halt his concerned rush. "You don't have to sell me on Ava's ability. She is exactly the type of student my program hopes to help. She had all the talent in the world, but she just needed a little boost to get her where she should be. I love the kid and I totally agree. She shouldn't even be thinking of quitting school. A girl like her . . ." Natalie shook her head.

"I thought maybe since you worked closely with the first-year kids, you might know of a scholarship or work-study program or something we could recommend her for."

"Not off the top of my head, but let me give it some thought."

Several students made their way into the room, chatting and swinging their backpacks onto the floor in front of their chosen seats with little more than a glance at their instructor. It was the last day of the semester, and they were all antsy to leave for the holiday break.

"By the way, there's a jazz group playing at the Hungry Bee tomorrow night. I was wondering if you'd like to go." He paused, somewhat awkwardly, which Natalie thought was adorable. "With me. After Yvonne's Christmas party."

"I'd like that. If I can find someone to watch Daisy." She flashed him her best smile. Their colleague from the history department, Yvonne Connor, had a holiday party every year for the faculty. Natalie had gone in years past but hadn't decided on whether to go this year. "Can I get back to you? Let me see if I can arrange something?"

"Sure. Just text me. Or call. Whichever." More students were walking past, so he backed out of the room. "I should let you go . . ."

She smiled again, then set her bag on her desk. Glenn was the nicest guy, hands down the most eligible bachelor on the faculty. He was tall and good looking and personable and smart and cared about his students—everything she'd be looking for in a man, if she were looking—and she knew he'd been wanting to ask her out since last year. She liked his easygoing personality and the fact that he didn't seem to think his good looks entitled him to be a jackass. He always treated the women on the faculty with respect, even that odious Belinda West, who hadn't said a pleasant word to anyone for as long as Natalie had known her. Still, while Glenn was interesting and nice, there was no spark there as far as she was concerned, and she hated to agree to go out with him and have him think there might be. She'd dated only two men since Jonathan had split, and while they were both nice enough, she hadn't wanted a third date with either of them. Actually, she hadn't wanted to date anyone but resisted becoming a once-bitten, twice-shy cliché, so she dated just enough to prove to herself that she could. She understood there were good—great—men in the world. She simply wasn't looking for one just yet.

At the close of her last class, she checked her mail in the main building before walking to the parking lot, hunching against the fierce wind that had blown in while she'd been inside. There was a chance of snow, which Daisy was very much looking forward to. Natalie, not so much.

She got into her car and turned the ignition before calling up the heat along with the heated seat and steering wheel. She remembered learning to drive in an old Jeep that her father had, which suffered from a faulty heating system. As one who hated being cold, the advances in seat and steering wheel winter comfort were greatly appreciated. While she waited for the heater to do its job, she thought about Ava. The young woman would be anyone's prize student. Natalie hated the thought that she'd have to suspend her education, but a third job wouldn't give her any time to study. The steering wheel was slowly beginning to warm as she tapped her fingers on it. There'd been a thought nagging at the back of her mind since Glenn had given her the news that morning. She reached for her phone and speed-dialed her mother's number.

Maggie answered the phone with a cheerful, "Hi, Nat. I was just thinking about you."

"And here I am. What's up?"

"No, you called me. You first." In the background, classical music was playing. Natalie pictured her mother in the sunroom, a cup of coffee in one hand, the book she'd been reading facedown on her lap.

"Do you remember Dad talking about setting aside some money to establish a few scholarships at local colleges?"

"Of course. You were in on those discussions. You know he very much believed in paying it forward. He'd gotten his entire education through scholarships." Maggie paused. "What's the real question?"

"Did he ever actually do it? Set money aside for needy students?" Natalie stared out the windshield as light flakes began to sail by on the wind that continued to pick up.

Her mother was slow to answer. Finally, she said, "I'm not sure."

Natalie laughed out loud. "Mom, how can you not be sure? You know where every penny of Dad's estate went."

"I know what your father's intent was. I just don't know . . . Let me talk to Alvin and get back to you." Alvin had handled the firm's finances for the past twenty-five years. "Or did you need an answer right now?"

"Tomorrow's soon enough."

Maggie sighed. "So are you going to tell me what's going on? Why the sudden interest?"

"There's a student here—a terrific student, a great girl with tons of potential. One of those kids who had a rough start in life but is working her ass off to make it. I just heard she's dropping out of school because she's out of money. Mom, she already has two jobs. I thought if Dad had followed through . . ." It was Natalie's turn to sigh. "I know we'd talked about it several times, but I couldn't remember if he'd actually done it."

"So we're talking about one student? For the rest of the year?" Natalie could almost hear the wheels turning in her mother's head. "But then what happens after next year? Won't she be transferring to a four-year college once she graduates from community?"

"That would be the hope."

"Let me look into a few things. I'll talk to you tomorrow."

"Okay, thanks, Mom. And . . . well, *thanks*."

"You're most welcome. This is exactly the sort of thing your father wanted to do—the sort of kid he'd wanted to help." Maggie hung up, and Natalie was certain she'd heard a tear in her mother's voice.

It wasn't until she'd picked up Daisy from day care that she realized she'd forgotten to ask her mother if she'd be available tomorrow night to babysit. She still hadn't decided if she'd wanted to go on that date, though she did need to make a decision.

The storm that kicked up later that evening made Natalie's decision for her. By morning, there was over a foot of snow outside the first-floor window of her apartment, and according to the forecast, more snow was on the way. She sent Glenn a text declining his invitation—Roads impassable here. Thank you—maybe another time—and settled in for the first snow day of the winter. With Daisy happily playing day care with her stuffed animals, Natalie snuggled into a deep armchair, her laptop in hand. With a click of the remote, the gas fireplace came to life. Whoever had invented such a thing—fire at the touch of a button!—should be in the inventors' Hall of Fame, if there was such a thing. Warm and comfortable, her daughter chatting merrily with her friends, Natalie turned on the laptop. After reading and responding to several emails related to work, she switched to the genealogy site where she'd sent her DNA several months earlier.

The stories her father had told about his great-aunt Lola Barnes had run the gamut. After she'd run away from home at fifteen—this much they knew to be true—the stories became muddled. Depending on who in Art's family was telling the story, Lola'd gone to Chicago and become a stage actress. She'd moved out west and run a brothel. She'd been one of the first women to play professional baseball. Maybe all of the above. Maybe none of the above. Natalie was no closer now to finding the truth than she'd been when she'd first started, but she was finding the search to be fascinating.

The first thing Natalie noticed when she signed on was that a message had been left on her account page. She clicked on the mail symbol, hoping for news about one of the relatives she was researching. She skimmed the text once before reading it through from the start, then twice more. Someone had obviously gotten a bogus DNA result. That, she thought, or someone was trying to run some sort of scam. She read the message once more before deleting it.

Hi—

I've been trying for weeks now to find a clever way to write this—but it seems I'm just not as clever as I thought, so I'll just put it out there. My name is Joe Miller and I think I'm your half brother. Actually, according to the DNA results, I'm pretty positive I am. Unless someone has told you more than anyone's ever told me—except that I'm adopted, which I always knew—this could be a shock to you, and while I'm sorry to be the bearer, as the only child of parents who are now deceased, finding someone who shares my history in any form would be amazing. Hearing from you would mean the world to me. I always wanted a sister.

It has to be a hoax, Natalie told herself. *Most definitely. Like I'd write back to some random person pretending to be related to me? A half brother, no less? Like I'd fall for that long-lost relative thing?*

She snorted. "Yes, because I was born yesterday."

Daisy looked up from the book she was reading to her favorite stuffie, Elle E. Fant. "Mommy, you were born in the summer. Nana said so."

"So I was. Thank you for reminding me." Natalie went back to scrolling the list of DNA matches, identifying her cousins Lainey and Alex, several second cousins, and a bunch of third, fourth, and fifth cousins. Dismissing the message from her "half brother Joe Miller," she resumed her search into the family trees of the more distant matches, hoping for clues to her search for the elusive Lola Barnes.

The snow stopped for a brief time, during which Natalie bundled up herself and Daisy and went outside to build a snowman. They'd managed to get all three round sections rolled and stacked before the storm resumed with a vengeance.

"He has no face, Mama," Daisy protested when Natalie said they'd have to go back inside for a while. "And he needs buttons. See?" She'd pointed to the middle snowball that made up the snowman's abdomen.

"We'll give him a face later when the snow stops falling for good and the wind has died down." Natalie ushered her daughter to the door and, once inside, stripped them both of wet boots, mittens, hats, and hooded winter jackets. She made hot chocolate, and they drank it in front of the fireplace, where the heat chased the cold and damp from their feet and faces. Lulled by the warmth, Natalie snuggled Daisy's small body next to her own and watched her daughter unsuccessfully fight sleep. Almost against her will, the note from the man calling himself Joe Miller popped back into her head. She'd been quick to assume the message a hoax, but it occurred to her that he'd have had to be on the website legitimately to even have access to her. But a half brother? Nah. Whoever read the test results hadn't done a very good job. He might be a second cousin, but not a brother, half or otherwise.

Still, she couldn't help but wonder. The possibilities were, well, not possible in her world. She wondered how old Joe Miller was. Was he older, maybe the result of a relationship her father had had before he'd met her mother? But no, there was no way in hell Art Flynn would have not been in the life of any child he'd fathered, which meant he wouldn't have known about his son.

The thought that either of her parents could have had an affair while they were married to each other simply wasn't an option. Could

Joe Miller be the child of a long-ago liaison between her father and his mother?

She soon dismissed even that possibility as not plausible. Later she'd try to recover the message she'd deleted, and she'd respond to Mr. Miller and suggest he contact the research site to report they'd made a mistake. She wasn't his half sister, but she'd wish him luck in his search.

Chapter Nine

MAGGIE

On the first Monday in January, Maggie dressed appropriately for a Center City Philadelphia law office—a well-tailored suit, heels, and a silk blouse—and headed for the train at the Bryn Mawr station for her monthly visit to Flynn Law. She boarded, then took her seat and opened the newspaper she'd grabbed on the way out her front door, crossed her legs, and settled in behind the arts section. A moment later she lowered the paper, pushed back her left sleeve, and turned her forearm to admire the tattoo she, Liddy, and Emma had agreed on after much discussion.

That Saturday in Charlotte, they'd filed into the small but neat shop promptly at noon. The artist had been waiting for them, though it appeared to Maggie she was still somewhat skeptical that one of the well-dressed middle-aged ladies standing before her could possibly be the woman who'd given birth to the infinitely cool Chris Dean and therefore given the world DEAN.

"Which one of you is Emma?" The tattooist sat in a small leather chair at a desk that was way too large for her tiny frame.

She was a walking advertisement for her art. Vines entwined her thin arms all the way to her neck, which they wrapped around. Roses bloomed on her arms alongside angel wings. A larger pair of wings embracing a flowery heart covered what they could see of her chest.

Emma, whose stare was fixed on the vines, raised her hand. "Emma here."

"I'm Nicole. Your son called and said he's running late. I hope you guys aren't playing me, because I'm going to be pissed if someone walks in here and says he's a roadie for DEAN and Chris got tied up and he's not coming, and I've closed my shop and canceled my other appointments. I hate to be scammed."

"If Chris said he'll be here, he'll be here." Emma leveled the not-so-young woman with her laser gaze.

"You ladies know what you want?"

"Not really." Maggie looked from Emma to Liddy and back again. "We thought you might have some ideas we could look at."

"Fortunately for you, I do." Nicole opened a drawer and took out several catalogs, which she tossed on the desktop. "No ideas? Theme? Anything you like, don't like. Help me out here."

"Something with a three theme," Liddy said as she reached for one of the catalogs.

"You mean, three of something?" Without waiting for a response, Nicole flipped one of the catalogs open, thumbed through for a second, and turned the book around to show her customers. "Three hearts. A shamrock. Three stars." She turned the page before any of the three women could get a close look. "Three monkeys—you know, see no evil, hear no evil, speak no evil."

"I'm not sure that applies," Emma murmured just as Liddy said, "A distinct possibility."

"Then you have your Celtic cross. Celtic knot. A Celtic spiral." She glanced up at them. "Represents the three stages of a woman's life. Maid, mother, crone."

"You lost me at crone." Maggie frowned and gestured for her to go on to something else.

"So call her the matriarch. It's a beautiful tattoo, very popular. It's a symbol of female power." Nicole straightened up as the shop door opened. Seconds later her eyes widened.

"You probably should have led with matriarch." Emma leaned over the desk for a better look.

"Tell me you're still deciding," Chris said as he walked toward the desk, an envelope in his hand.

"Oh. Hi." Emma barely looked up from the catalog. "No, we haven't decided yet. Nicole—this is Nicole. Chris, she's going to do our tattoos."

He reached beyond his mother to shake Nicole's hand.

"Oh my God, you really are Chris Dean." Nicole sounded as if she was going to need oxygen sometime soon.

He nodded. "And this really is my mom and her friends. I'm hoping you can help them out a little here."

"I'm trying." Nicole was clearly starstruck.

"Herding cats?" He raised an eyebrow and smiled.

"Not yet, but close." Nicole smiled back and seemed to relax.

"So let's see what we've got here." Chris looked over his mother's shoulder, then flipped a few pages. "Mrs. Flynn, anything jump out at you?"

"You mean, have I found something I want on my body from this day until the day I die?" Maggie shook her head. "Not yet."

"Mrs. Bryant?" He turned to Liddy.

"I liked the 'see no evil, hear no evil' monkey thing, but your mother nixed it," Liddy told him.

She pointed to the tattoo of the three monkeys, and he laughed. "You would each get one, though, right? You wouldn't have all three monkeys on your . . . where are you getting this tattoo, anyway?"

"Inside left ankle," Emma spoke up. "How about a feather? As in birds of a feather." She held up the catalog.

"It looks more like a phallic symbol," Maggie noted.

Emma held the book out at arm's length. "Maybe. It's been a while, though, so I'm not sure how accurate my memory is."

Chris coughed. "Mom. Move on."

They pored over several more pages before Maggie said, "Wait. Go back to the last page. I saw something . . ."

Emma flipped the page, turned it around. They all leaned closer.

Chris tapped on one image. "This one."

"That's the one I wanted to look at." Maggie studied the image. There were three curlicues, their curves representing ocean waves. "I like it. Three waves, sailing on the sea of life together. The sea is eternal—there's some quote about that, but I don't remember what it is."

"Good call, Mrs. Flynn. You grew up in a bay town together, and you've weathered life's storms together." Chris looked from his mother to each of her friends.

"I like it. It's small enough to be discreet, and it's pretty, and it has significance. But not on my ankle." Maggie pointed to her inner left wrist. "Here. I want to see it whenever I want without pulling up my pant leg, rolling down my sock, or taking off my boot every time. Easier to pull up a sleeve."

Liddy nodded. "I agree." She held up the catalog. "This is what we're celebrating with our tattoos, right? The fact that all our lives we've gone through all manner of shit together and yet we're still rolling on together?"

"Mrs. Bryant," Chris said, obviously amused, "one thing I always liked about you, you always put it right out there."

"I like it. Waves on the same sea," Emma agreed. "Good job, Maggie. You saved poor Nicole here an afternoon of the three of us going round and round and . . ."

Chris laughed and held up a hand as if to stop her flow of words. "Please. I've been there. This young woman has a business to run. So you're set? This is it?"

Emma, Liddy, and Maggie nodded.

"Great. Glad that's settled." He handed Nicole the envelope. "As promised. Four front-row seats and backstage passes. I can't thank you enough for accommodating my mom and her friends. I'll give you a shout-out at the show tonight, in case anyone's looking for a tattoo."

"You might want to wait to see if I do a good job." Nicole took the envelope with shaking hands. "You wouldn't want to be remembered in Charlotte as the guy who gave everyone a bum rec on a tat."

"I think you'll do fine." He turned and kissed first his mother—"Love you, Mom"—then Liddy and Maggie in turn. "Guys, it's been great to see you. I'm glad you made it to the show. I've gotta go—I have an appointment in fifteen minutes, and I can't be late. Nicole, thanks again. I'll see you tonight." He was almost to the door when he paused and turned back. "Hey, Mrs. Flynn, don't forget to tell Nat I said any show, anytime. I'd love to see her again."

"She'll take you up on that, I'm sure," Maggie said. He nodded and left, the bell over the door ringing softly.

"Phew." Nicole slid back into her chair, fanning herself with the envelope.

"Take a drink of water and calm yourself," Emma told her. "You're not going to be sticking a needle in my skin with those shaky hands."

"Sorry. I'm fine. He's just . . . so . . ." Nicole was still a little wide eyed.

"I know." Emma patted her on the arm. "He's a good boy."

It was such a mom thing to say, Maggie'd laughed at the time, and she laughed at the memory as she got off the train at her Center City stop and walked the three blocks to Flynn Law.

Once at the office, she greeted the receptionist and several staff members who passed in the hall. She chatted with Lois as she unlocked the door Art's assistant had guarded like a pit bull since the day Art went out sick. Maggie sat at her late husband's desk in the office she'd taken over as her own those times when she'd ventured into Flynn Law to take care of the responsibilities Art had unexpectedly left to her. When he was dying, he'd told her he'd changed the structure of the firm so that while Alvin Cummins was in charge of the finances, and George Young was effectively the senior partner and managing attorney, she, Maggie, would be the final word on any matter of substance.

"Trust them to do their jobs," Art had told her. "You won't need to get involved in most issues. The accountants will give you a year-end report, and if you have any questions, they or Alvin can answer them. George will oversee the work product, hiring and firing, but I'm leaving the firm in your hands. If you ever decide to sell it, get an appraisal of what it's worth, then give George first right of refusal and give him a ten percent discount off the appraised price. You could also decide to simply dissolve it—though that might not be as easy as it sounds. There are steps that would have to be taken. I'm hoping you keep it going as it is, but as we've learned over the past few months, you never know what's around the next corner. Eventually, I'd like to see Gracie become the face of Flynn Law, but she's not ready to take over. And if you ever, for any reason, feel the need to pull the plug, do it and don't worry that somehow you've let me down. You're the one who has to live with this from now on. Don't be afraid to move on, Maggie. You'll know when— and if—something needs to be done, and you'll do the right thing."

She'd done the right thing by effectively doing very little. She looked over the reports Alvin and George sent her quarterly, asked the occasional question, and went into the office on the first Monday of every month mostly to remind the firm's employees that there was still a Flynn at the helm.

It drove her crazy that Zach was still there after he'd left her daughter so suddenly. He always managed to be out of the office on the days Maggie would be in, or he'd make himself very scarce so at least she didn't have to look at him. She still had no clue as to why he'd dumped Grace the way he had, how he could have fallen out of love with her, as he claimed, so soon after Art's death. Had he been banking on Art leaving the firm outright to Grace—and therefore through marriage to him? Had he been so disappointed in Art's decision to leave the firm to Maggie that he'd taken it out on Grace? She might not ever know.

Maggie accomplished what she'd set out to do that morning, meeting with Alvin and George to arrange for the firm to underwrite several scholarships for students who excelled in their work at the local community college.

"I'd like the money from the stipend the firm pays me as CEO to be used for tuition and books for the two-year college, and if the recipients maintained an A average, tuition, books, and room and board for the final two years at a four-year college," she told them.

"That's very generous of you," Alvin said. "I know Art mentioned several times he wanted to do something along these lines, but are you sure . . . ?"

"Positive. Art left me more than enough to live comfortably," she told them. "I believe he would have wanted me to do this."

The two men looked at each other and nodded.

"Consider it done," George said.

Pleased, Maggie returned to Art's old office, where she watered the large snake plant in the corner and the fern on the table next to the sofa. She'd stopped in to see Grace but found she was in court, so with one last glance around the office, Maggie gathered her coat and her bag and locked the door behind her. After she and Lois shared their customary lunch at one of Art's favorite restaurants, Maggie headed for the afternoon train.

The minute she situated herself in her seat, she called Natalie.

"Mission accomplished," Maggie said after Natalie answered the phone.

"Mom, that's incredibly generous. I can't even begin to tell you what this will mean for Ava." Natalie had all but wept when Maggie told her what had been agreed to.

"Well, keep in mind we're awarding two scholarships each year, so if you don't have another worthy student in mind, you might want to confer with your colleagues."

"Oh, no, I could recommend any one of a dozen students," Natalie had said, "but I do have another kid in mind. Thanks a million, Mom."

"You think on that second recipient, and I'll contact the college. We should go through them to set this up, though I'm sure there won't be a problem. A prestigious law firm wants to reward your students with some healthy financial aid, you don't turn it down. I'll make the calls in the morning."

"Dad would have been really happy."

"Somehow, I think he knows, and he *is* happy. And he'd have been proud that you made sure this happened. Thanks so much for the reminder, Nat. A scholarship in his name was a dream of his. It's exactly the sort of thing that became more important to him toward the end of his life." Maggie cleared her throat, which had tightened at the thought that her late husband might still be taking a peek at the goings-on he'd left behind.

She didn't know what happened once you left this plane—this *dimension*, as a self-proclaimed psychic had once referred to life on earth as we knew it—but she hoped wherever Art was, he knew she was doing the best she could, and that he approved. "Now, you remember I'm driving up to Wyndham Beach on Tuesday for the opening of the showing of Jessie Bryant's paintings at Emma's art center?"

"And that you asked me to water the plants in the sunroom on Friday? Yes, of course I remembered. Daisy is ready with that little watering can you gave her for Christmas."

"Bless her little heart," Maggie murmured.

"So you're just going to spend like, what, a week up there with Liddy and Emma?"

"More or less a week. I haven't decided how long yet. I want to see how Liddy feels after the exhibit." Maggie fell silent. "She'll need someone to be there for her emotionally. It still eats at her that Jessie died the way she did. Not that I blame her. I can't even imagine the pain." Maggie shivered. Knowing your child chose to leave this life must certainly add a whole different level of suffering. Not knowing why had to add even more.

Maggie opted to drive to Wyndham Beach this time around, the weather maps showing mostly clear though cold weather for the next week, with only an occasional rainy day in the forecast. It would take a good seven to eight hours, depending on traffic, but she needed the time to de-stress from the holidays, which had held moments of sadness as well as moments of joy.

She missed Art the most during the Christmas season. He'd loved everything about the month between Thanksgiving—when he pulled out all his favorite Christmas CDs—and the new year. He took great pains to decorate the house inside and out, loved the cooking and baking for their family meals as much as he loved preparing for their annual parties—one for friends and neighbors, one for business associates. When the girls were little, he'd hired a Santa to come to the house on Christmas Eve and give them each a special present, and he'd wondered every time that they never realized it had been their friend from the office, Alvin, behind the beard. Art had made special dishes for Christmas Eve and had insisted Maggie and the girls bake cookies with him to distribute to the neighbors. The holidays since his death had seemed flat and colorless, and the need to keep up the traditions he'd established for their family exhausted Maggie. She baked and cooked and decorated the house to honor his memory, but once the holidays were over and everything was packed away, she wanted to collapse.

Art's death had left her untethered, and at first, she didn't know what to do with the rest of her life. She had periods when she did nothing, when she'd stay in her house for days, only to emerge and dive into something headfirst. She would cut back on her volunteering and her substitute teaching for a while, then sign up for several of the charity benefits she'd once chaired. She'd wear herself out, then step back again for a few months. She'd putter around the house, then jump back into the thick of it all over again. There was a randomness to her days, and while she knew her life had become unbalanced, it had taken her months to find her footing. But even after settling into a workable schedule of volunteer activities, she'd lately been having more and more-frequent *Is that all there is?* moments.

She'd been Art's wife for more than thirty years, and now that she wasn't, she wasn't sure what to do with herself. The trip to Wyndham Beach had come at a good time. Worn out from the holiday and all the emotions it had dredged up, a week away was exactly what she needed.

She drove along the New Jersey Turnpike and followed her old route to Wyndham Beach, through New York State and Connecticut, Rhode Island into Massachusetts. She'd hoped the drive would be long enough to think through her situation, but she was starting to realize the length of the ride wasn't the issue. *A week home* was how she'd secretly thought of it. Somewhere, in the back of her mind, she still thought of Wyndham Beach as home. In her heart, she knew she needed the cold salty air like she needed sleep and food. The fact that she was coming home because Liddy needed her made the trip even more meaningful. It had been a while since she felt truly needed by someone she loved.

And then there was the elephant in the room: Brett. Seeing him had had a powerful effect on her. Denial would be a big fat lie, and she knew it. It seemed after all this time, all those things she'd forced herself to forget really hadn't been forgotten. All it had taken to remind her had been the feel of his arms around her, his voice soft in her ear.

The truth was that he'd been in her head since the reunion, and nothing she'd told herself about their past—not even the memory of the worst day of her life—had pushed him out. She wasn't sure which man was more to blame for the funk she was in: Art for dying or Brett for reminding her of the life she might have had—and that she still had a life to live.

~

"Lid, you sure you're up to this?" Maggie had insisted on driving her car to the art center in case Liddy became too emotional, but she should have known better. Liddy was facing the display of her daughter's art with more pride than pain.

"Are you kidding? My girl would have loved this. She's not here, so I'll stand for her. You and Emma will stand for her." Liddy's eyes were wet, but no tears fell. "She was a hell of an artist, and I'm proud that her work will finally get some recognition." She smiled wryly. "Even if it's only from locals."

"Emma seems to think the opening will attract interest from more than just the home front. She said she'd had inquiries from several dealers, so we'll see. It would be nice for Jess, though, if she had a showing at a big Boston gallery."

"I'd be happy with even a small Boston gallery," Liddy said. "Something Jess hadn't been able to arrange while she was still alive. Though I suppose Chris's letters to the gallery owners touting the talent of his childhood friend and personally asking for their support could have had something to do with their interest in this showing."

"That was a nice touch on his part," Maggie agreed.

"He's a good boy," Liddy said solemnly. She and Maggie looked at each other and broke into laughter. "Would he die if he heard me say that?"

"Nah. He'd roll his eyes and chalk it up to the mom in you. He knows Emma says it all the time." Maggie turned onto the sand-and-shell road that led up to the art center. "Oh. The parking lot is full. I don't see an empty spot. Looks like half the town is here already." She turned to Liddy, who'd rolled down the window for a better look. "How 'bout I let you out here, and I'll park on Bay Street and walk up?"

"Are you sure? I can walk with you from the street." Liddy's neck was craned to see who was getting out of the black BMW sedan that had taken the last spot.

"Go on in," Maggie commanded good-naturedly, knowing how excited Liddy was about the showing. "I'll only be a minute."

"Okay. If you're sure." Liddy already had the door open and was on her way.

Maggie was glad she'd talked Liddy out of the severe black sheath she'd worn to the reunion and into the midcalf purple skirt that, over the years, had become almost her signature. Despite her efforts to push aside the hippie and dress—her words—"more like someone her age," Liddy never quite looked herself without the ropes of beads around her neck and her hair flowing behind her or in a braid draped over one shoulder. At her core, Liddy was still a would-be flower child, albeit an aging one, and she was beginning to not only acknowledge but embrace her inner goddess.

"You've always had your own style," Maggie had told her that morning. "I think you need to be true to it. Not that it isn't a good thing sometimes to dress up. You did look smashing at the reunion dinner in that black dress, but this is an art event, and let's face it, no one rocks that artsy look better than you."

"True." Liddy'd tossed the black dress aside without even watching to see where it landed. "So you think the purple skirt?"

The purple skirt combined with an ivory cashmere sweater, topped with acres of colored beads, paired with knee-high brown leather boots, was quintessential Liddy. Maggie sat and watched her friend hustle through the cold wind that blew in off the bay, her skirt billowing in the breeze, her brown puffy jacket clutched tightly around her as she made her way to the squat white building.

"You go, Lids," Maggie murmured as she turned around in the parking lot and headed for the street. She found a spot not too far from the center, then walked back up the drive, crushed clamshells crunching beneath her feet.

Once inside the center, she found Emma in the midst of discussing a painting with a tall man with a receding hairline and what looked like a recent tan. He wore wire-rimmed glasses and a navy sport jacket with khaki pants, and he appeared to be totally engrossed in the conversation, or in Emma—Maggie wasn't sure which. Either way, it had to be good, she told herself as she glanced around the room for Liddy. She found her standing next to a short balding man in a black turtleneck sweater and dark jeans, deep in conversation in front of one of Jessie's largest canvases, the one Liddy had named *Snowfall.*

"The use of whites is remarkable," the man was saying, the index finger of his right hand held as if instructing her. "The spatter of the lighter white upon the darker gives the illusion of a blizzard. I can see the flakes falling, falling, swirling around in the wind. Yes, I see them." He was nodding. "Just so. Brilliant."

Liddy turned when Maggie touched her on the back, and crossed her eyes before turning back to her companion.

"Go on, Darren," Liddy told him with a straight face. "This is fascinating."

"Yes, of course." He nodded as if acknowledging his own importance and expertise. "Now, in this corner of the canvas, she's added a remarkable touch . . ."

Maggie stifled a giggle. *Remarkable* must be the man's word of the day. She wandered around the exhibit, pausing to listen to conversations here and there. Jessie's paintings were well received, judging from the comments Maggie overheard.

Good, she thought. *Good for Jessie, great for Liddy.* Maggie knew how badly her friend needed to hear the accolades for her daughter's work.

She wandered till she found herself standing in front of another all-white canvas, thinking while she didn't completely get the whole white-on-white thing the way the art people seemed to be doing, she did find them soothing, when she felt a tap on her shoulder.

"Maggie? You are Maggie, aren't you?"

Maggie turned to the voice and found herself face-to-face with Brett Crawford's wife.

"Maggie, I'm Kayla. Kayla Crawford. We haven't been introduced, but I know who you are."

"Oh, well. How are you?" Maggie faked her most pleasant smile. "Enjoying the exhibit? Jessie did some remarkable"—*heh*—"work, don't you think?"

"Brett and I are separated. We're getting a divorce. I just thought you should know." Kayla Crawford's expression was unreadable.

"Why are you telling me this, Kayla?" Maggie lowered her voice and tried to move back, away from the displayed paintings, while trying not to appear stunned.

"Because you should know. You're both free now." There were tears in her eyes, and Maggie couldn't help but feel sorry for her.

"Kayla, I don't know what you've heard, or what you believe, or what you think you know . . . ," Maggie began.

"I know he's never loved anyone but you." She spoke the words flatly, as if stating an accepted fact, no accusation intended.

"Why would you think that? He married you."

"Only because he couldn't have you. It's always been you, Maggie. He told me. I heard your husband died. Now you can have mine back. He always belonged to you anyway."

Before Maggie could respond, Kayla turned her back and left the building.

Puffing her cheeks as if trying to expel a deep breath and compose herself after the unexpected confrontation, Maggie stepped around the crowd to find her way to Emma's office, in search of a few minutes of solitude to process what had just happened. She opened the door and stepped inside to find Emma seated at her desk and engrossed in a conversation with the man in the navy jacket.

"Oh, Em. Sorry. I didn't know . . ."

"Maggie, come in. Meet Owen Harrison." Emma smiled. "Owen, this is my very dear friend, Maggie Flynn. Maggie grew up here in Wyndham Beach, but she's been living in Pennsylvania for years. Maggie, Owen is . . ."

Before Maggie could ask, he said, "Yes, that Harrison."

Owen extended a hand in Maggie's direction. "And yes, you needn't ask—thanks to Emma, the carousel will be brought out and assembled for the Fourth of July. Tell you the truth, I'd forgotten about it, but she's been reminding me relentlessly in her yearly calls."

Maggie nodded. "Emma can be quite persuasive when she wants something."

"Apparently so." He turned to look out into the gallery area. "She's certainly managed to get the word out on this obscure artist, didn't she? I see people here from several very influential galleries in the city. How on earth did you get them to leave Boston and drive all the way out here to look at the work of an unknown?"

"I prefer to think of Jessie as undiscovered." Emma smiled graciously. "And we'll leave the story of how I got their attention till summer, when you come back to bring out the carousel." She opened a desk drawer and took out a card, which she handed to him. "My address is here, and my cell number. So you can let us know when to expect you. I'd hate to publicize something I have to apologize for later when it doesn't happen."

"Oh, trust me. I'll be back. I appreciate your tenacity—and your concern for the community." He slipped a hand into his back pocket and removed his wallet, opened it, stuck in the card, and returned the wallet to its place. "You have my word."

He turned to Maggie and, with a somewhat formal nod, said, "A pleasure, Maggie Flynn." And to Emma, "You'll be hearing from me."

One last smile meant to be shared by both women, and he was out the door.

"Well, well." Maggie sat on the edge of Emma's desk. "That was interesting. Did you really contact him every year reminding him about the carousel?"

Emma nodded. "I sure did. I just wanted to make sure someone whose last name is Harrison remembered and was planning on making it happen."

"Sounds more like harassment to me," Maggie teased.

"Worked, didn't it?" Emma grinned.

"Apparently. And I'm betting Owen will make sure he's back from wherever it is he goes to make sure it happens." Maggie grinned. "I saw the way he looked at you."

"Really? I hadn't noticed." The color of Emma's cheeks rose just a little.

Maggie laughed out loud. "Bull."

"I wouldn't mind. He's nice. Much nicer than I expected. And I had no idea how old or young the current Harrison heir was," Emma told her. "But we'll see come summer whether he's all talk or not. Now, was there something you wanted to tell me, or were you seeking refuge from the crowd?"

"Yes. And yes."

"I don't blame you. Some of those artsy folks can get a bit tedious. I don't mind if it helps get the word out on Jessie's work." Emma went to the door and looked out onto the room. "It would mean so much to Liddy."

"I guess you won't know for a while if anyone's interested in her paintings?"

"Oh, no. Several people already have expressed an interest in moving the exhibition to their gallery, doing a showing in the city. I'm taking their information, and I'll go over everything with Liddy after I know who's offering to do what."

"So the show's successful."

"More than I could have hoped for," Emma said softly.

"You're a good friend to do this for her, Em."

"You're a good friend to be here for her, Mags."

"Friends to the very end, the three of us."

"And we have the tattoos to prove it." Emma stretched out her forearm and turned it to show off the three crested waves that rose alongside each other. "Waves of the same sea, rising and falling together." Emma admired the ink for another second or two. "So what was the other 'yes'?"

"The other . . . oh." Maggie nodded, remembering why she'd come into Emma's office in the first place. "Did you know Brett and Kayla Crawford are separated? Getting divorced?"

"What? No!" Emma's eyes widened at the news. "Who told you that?"

"She did. Kayla. Just a few minutes ago."

"Did she say why? And why she told you?" Emma frowned. "Wait, why *would* she tell you?"

Maggie hadn't wanted to say it out loud. If she said it out loud, it would be real.

"Maggie? What did she say?"

"She said"—Maggie sighed deeply—"that it was because of me. That he only ever loved me."

Emma stared at her for a moment. "That's not news. Everyone's always known that." She made a face. "But why is it a problem now?"

~

Emma's words rang in Maggie's ears for the rest of the week. While the news of Brett Crawford's latest—third!—divorce spread like wildfire, the real talk of the town was the successful showing of Jessica Bryant's paintings at the art center, the number of bigwigs from the art world who'd attended, how many important galleries in Boston were vying to exhibit the collection, and how much Liddy had been offered for this painting or that. Winter White, as Emma had decided to call the collection of all-white canvases, had become a sensation, and Liddy was still reeling from the news. Maggie was grateful for just about anything that diverted attention from the fact that the gossips were looking to make something out of the fact that Brett and Kayla's announcement had come while Maggie just happened to be in Wyndham Beach.

Emma popped into Liddy's for coffee the morning Maggie was set to leave for home. She'd stopped at the bakery and picked up a selection of gorgeous pastries, which she'd plated almost the minute she'd walked into Liddy's kitchen.

"They're almost too pretty to eat," Maggie declared as she looked over the offerings.

"Almost, but not quite." Liddy poured a cup of coffee for Emma and passed it to her. "Thanks for those. They all look luscious."

"Madeline is back from vacation," Emma said as she sat. Addressing Maggie, she added, "Madeline Affonseca is the best baker ever. She left for a well-deserved vacation right after New Year's, and she just got back."

"I know that name, Affonseca." Maggie tried to place it.

"She's married to Lou Affonseca, the barber." Emma took a bite of lemony danish and rolled her eyes. "Perfection. Their son Teddy is a good friend of Chris's. They get together every time Chris gets home."

Maggie picked up an almond pastry and sniffed. "It even smells delectable."

"Oh! I almost forgot!" Emma smacked herself in the forehead with an open hand. "I drove up Cottage to drop off the key with my assistant, Marian, so she can open the center this morning. She lives at the other end of Cottage, and she's only part-time, so she doesn't have a key, and I knew I'd be late getting there, because I wanted to see you before you left. Anyway—guess what I saw!"

"I give up. What?" Maggie licked sugary white frosting from her fingertips.

"A sale sign on your old house," Emma announced, then sat back in her chair. "The house you grew up in is for sale."

"Wait! What?" Liddy took her seat. "When did that happen?"

"Apparently very recently." Emma took another bite of her danish. "The sign wasn't there yesterday morning when I picked up Marian."

"Didn't they just dump a ton of money into it? Renovated from stem to stern?" Maggie nudged Liddy. "Didn't you say . . . ?"

Liddy nodded. "Yeah. They redid everything. Even put on a gorgeous addition in the back."

"Why would they be selling so soon after putting so much money into it?" Maggie wondered.

"Maybe the Wakefield ghosts were more than they could handle." Liddy wagged her eyebrows.

"The Wakefield ghosts are harmless." Maggie waved a dismissive hand. "Except for Great-Aunt Ida. I understand she was a beast."

"Define *beast*." Liddy added a little more sugar to her coffee.

"She was a 'vengeful serpent of a woman.'" Maggie eyed a second danish. It *was* a long drive back to Pennsylvania. "That was a quote from my great-grandmother. Mom said my great-grandmother didn't care for Ida, so I have no idea what it really means."

"Maybe Ida got after the Blanchards' kids," Emma suggested. "Maybe that's why they're leaving."

"More likely Peter—that's the husband—got transferred somewhere," Liddy said. "You don't just pack up and leave a house you've spent lots of money to renovate unless you have a damned good reason."

"Ida sounded like a good enough reason to me." Emma wiped the corners of her mouth with her napkin, then stood. "I hate to leave before you, but I promised Marian I wouldn't be long. Since the showing, we've had endless calls from people wanting to know how much longer the collection would be available for viewing and when we're open." She patted Liddy on the shoulder. "If you decide to sell any of Jess's paintings, you're going to clean up. I've had offers for every single canvas. The numbers are eye-popping."

"I'm still thinking about it. But thanks, Em."

"You take your time. There's no hurry. We can keep them here as long as you like." Emma leaned over to kiss Maggie on the cheek. "Safe trip, Mags. Keep in touch."

"Will do." Maggie stood to hug her friend. "I'll be back sometime in the spring."

"Glad we're seeing more of you. We miss you when you're not around." To Liddy, Emma said, "I'll let myself out." She was halfway to the front door when she called back to the kitchen. "Maggie, you ought to think about buying your mom's house."

Maggie rolled her eyes. As much as she loved Wyndham Beach, her life was in Bryn Mawr, wasn't it? Her kids were there, the home she'd shared with Art was there.

"Emma's right, you know," Liddy said after they heard the front door open, then close.

"You're glad to see more of me, too?"

"Smart-ass. No. Well, yes, I am, but you should at least look at your mom's house."

"Why would I do that?"

"Idle curiosity if nothing else. Don't you want to see the renovations?"

"I kind of liked the house the way it was. Besides, even if I was interested—which I'm not—I'm leaving as soon as I finish this danish." Maggie held up the last bite. "So there's really no time."

"You could make time."

"Liddy."

"Okay." Liddy held up both hands in surrender. "I won't bring it up again."

And Liddy hadn't. Still, Maggie found herself turning onto Cottage Street on her way out of town, though technically it was out of her way. She just wanted to see the house one more time before she went home. She parked across the street and took it in, its innate hominess, its weathered cedar siding, long since grayed by the salt air. Even in the chill of a late January morning, the shrubs and trees deep in hibernation, it was still beautiful, and deep in her heart of hearts, it was still home.

She wondered who would end up buying it and living in the rooms where she'd grown up.

On a whim, she wrote down the name and number of the Realtor, then sat for a few more minutes, thinking about the years she'd spent under that roof, the happy years when her sister was still alive, and before her parents' divorce. She glanced at the clock on the dashboard. She'd already decided she was going to stop at the pastry shop to pick up some goodies to take home to share with Natalie and Daisy, who'd spent the weekend at her house to enjoy her wide-screen TV and the story hour at the Bryn Mawr Library.

She'd not been completely honest with Liddy or Emma. The truth was Maggie was dying to see inside the house. She'd wondered about the renovations and couldn't deny her curiosity. This could be her one and only chance to check it out. She took her phone from her bag and dialed the number, which went to voice mail.

"Hello, Ms. Brock, my name is Maggie Flynn. I'm in Wyndham Beach for a very limited time this morning, but if at all possible, I'd love to view your listing on Cottage Street. You can call me back at this number if you're available to show the property. Otherwise, perhaps it will still be on the market the next time I'm in town." Maggie ended the call and tucked the phone into her coat pocket.

There. If it's meant to be, I'll hear from her before I leave. Otherwise—not meant to be.

She turned the car around in the parking lot next to the beach and headed toward town and the bakery. She was almost to Front Street when her phone rang.

She pulled it out of her pocket. "This is Maggie."

"Ms. Flynn, this is Barbara Brock, Brock Realtors, returning your call about the house on Cottage in Wyndham Beach."

"Oh, yes. Thank you for returning my call."

"I'd love to show you the property. It's one of a kind, really. One of the oldest homes in town, built by one of the town's oldest families. Continuously family owned, by the way, until eight years ago." The Realtor paused. "Are you familiar with the town?"

"Yes. I was born here," Maggie told her.

"Well, if you're still interested in a quick walk-through, I'm on my way to the house now."

"I can be there in three minutes."

Maggie pulled into the driveway of the old Wakefield house, got out of the car, and walked along the once-familiar brick walk to the front porch. Up the well-worn steps to the refinished door. She was about to knock when a pleasant-looking woman around her age opened the door.

"Ms. Flynn? You're right on time. I'm Barb Brock. Please come in." She stepped aside for Maggie to enter.

"Thanks so much for fitting me in." Maggie smiled and tried to look over the Realtor's shoulder to the space beyond the entryway. She could only see what appeared to be a blinding sea of white.

"I'm happy to do it. I had an early morning showing and I have another at noon, so this worked out well for me." She smiled brightly. "There's been a ton of interest, as I'm sure you can imagine." She gestured toward the living room and dining room area. "A house with so much charm and history and yet one that is totally renovated and fully functional for the modern family . . . well, such a buy doesn't come along very often." Barbara's phone buzzed in her hand. She glanced at the incoming call and said to Maggie, "Why don't you wander around down here while I take this?" At that, she stepped out onto the porch, leaving Maggie alone in a house full of memories.

Maggie stood at the entrance to the living room for a long moment. The room was, like the entry, white. White walls, white furniture, white throw rugs and white throw pillows. She felt momentarily disoriented as her eyes scanned the room for something familiar. Her searching eyes located the fireplace, but it, too, had been painted . . . white. The only touch of color in the room came from two tall green leafy plants that flanked the entry to the dining room, itself adrift in an all-white sea.

She was riveted to the spot—the same spot where she'd stood when her father, seated in the long-gone leather wing chair, had announced that he and her mother were divorcing, and he was moving to Michigan. Forty years ago almost to the day. She'd been so stunned by the news she'd been unable to breathe for a very long moment. Her mother had sat stoically on the middle cushion of the sofa and stared into space, not a muscle moving, not even blinking. Maggie'd never been able to get a true read on what her mother had been feeling at that moment. But for Maggie, the walls of her life, her security, had quietly tumbled down, piece by piece. She had still been emerging from her own private hell and was about to begin her first year of college a semester late when her father had decided he'd had enough of Massachusetts coastal living and was going back home to the Upper Peninsula, where he'd been born, and where he'd apparently reconnected with a former neighbor when he'd returned for a family reunion—without her mother—the previous summer. Maggie had turned heel and run up the steps and locked herself in Sarah's old bedroom. By that time, Sarah had been gone for six years, but Maggie had never missed her—needed her—as much as she had on that day. She'd lain on Sarah's bed, holding her sister's pillow to her face. Her father had left the following morning and hadn't bothered to return, not even for Maggie's mother's funeral, for which Maggie would never forgive him. They hadn't spoken in years. It was as if he'd forgotten he'd once had a life—a family—in Massachusetts. She and her mother had been erased as neatly and as quickly as a fourth grader would erase the wrong answer on a homework assignment.

"Ready to see the kitchen?" Barbara touched Maggie on the shoulder.

"What?" Maggie blinked and the tableau faded into the all-white room. "Oh, yes."

She followed the Realtor past the staircase that still retained its original oak glory. It and the floor were the only touches of natural wood left that Maggie could see.

"Now, are you ready for this?" Barbara stood in the kitchen doorway, one arm extended like a TV shopping host displaying her next item. "This is all new. The addition is only four years old, all the latest technology, top-of-the-line appliances. What do you think?"

"I think it's . . . white." Maggie felt like she'd stumbled into a snow globe. Everything in the room was blindingly white.

"Absolutely on trend, every inch of it." Barbara was positively glowing. "A true gourmet chef's dream. I'd kill for a kitchen like this in my house. The owners sank a fortune into it." She ran a possessive hand along the counter covering the island.

"Granite?" Maggie asked to have something to say.

Barbara shook her head. "So last year. This is quartz. Much trendier. Easier to care for with the look of marble." She lowered her voice. "Those beams overhead? Planed from a tree in the backyard that came down in a storm a few years back."

Maggie went to the french doors that opened to the yard and peered out. Gone were her mother's flower beds and the vegetable garden she'd planted every summer, and there was no trace of the ageless peonies she'd prized. Maggie fought a wave of nausea. This might not have been as good an idea as she'd first thought.

"Wait till you see the master bedroom."

Maggie started to follow Barbara from the room when the Realtor stopped and said, "Oh, the dining room. It's this way."

The door to the dining room had been moved when the addition was built. Maggie felt even more disoriented approaching the room from a different direction. It pained her to see that her mother's beautiful wallpaper had been stripped off, and the gorgeous crystal chandelier that had hung over the dining room table for three generations was gone, replaced by a chrome-and-glass fixture that took Maggie's breath away with its starkness.

"I know, right?" Barbara apparently noticed Maggie's reaction and had mistaken shock for awe. "That fixture is to die for."

Maggie bit her bottom lip. "I'd have expected a house of this age and style to have a more classic fixture."

"They said there had been an old chandelier there but, of course, during the remodeling, it had to go. It was so yesterday."

"Any idea what they did with it?" Maggie asked.

Barbara shook her head. "My guess would be that they sold it to a dealer, but I don't really know."

Maggie left the room and headed for the staircase, her head pounding.

"Now get ready for the most amazing master suite. Honestly, it has everything." Barbara went up the steps ahead of Maggie and proceeded to the end of the hall when she reached the second floor. "This is truly to die for. If you're looking for luxury, look no further." She opened the bedroom door with a grand sweeping motion and stepped in.

For a moment, Maggie felt lost as she tried to remember the exact layout of the second floor.

"This is of course all new," Barbara was saying. "The original bedrooms are across the hall and next door to this one."

Maggie wandered from the bedroom with its contemporary furnishings—all white to match the walls—into the bath with its overload of chrome. But the layout was actually functional, with the soaking tub and the large glass shower. The double vanity held a surprise: the bowls of the twin sinks were embellished with flowers that seemed almost incongruous with the starkness of the rest of the house, but they were lovely. Along one wall was a gas fireplace, which Maggie had to admit made the room pretty much perfect. Painting the walls a pretty color—palest blue or sea glass green, maybe—would elevate the room to perfection.

"Aren't you blown away?" Barbara asked anxiously, as if just realizing her would-be buyer had been mostly silent.

"That would be one way to describe it." Maggie paused at the wall of windows that looked out on the bay. At least they'd kept the view.

"It's beautiful, right? Like a painting."

Maggie nodded and left the master suite and stepped into the hall. She opened the door to what had been her parents' room and what was now apparently home to two boys. The bunk beds in the corner were built to look like a pirate ship, and the interior wall had been painted—hallelujah!—navy blue. She took a few steps across the hall to her old room, which was now an office with a chrome-and-glass desk and a white fuzzy rug on the refinished heart pine floor. She paused at Sarah's old room before stepping inside to find a nicely appointed guest room with a colorful quilt on the bed.

"Seen enough?" Barbara poked her head into the room.

"I think so." Maggie left the room without a backward glance and went directly downstairs.

"I'm sure you're overwhelmed," Barbara was saying as she followed in Maggie's wake. "There's so much to see here. If you'd like to take a minute to . . ." Her phone rang. "Oh, let me take this. I'll just be a moment."

Maggie went into the kitchen and tried to conjure up a memory that would reassure her that this was in fact the house in which she'd grown up. Closing her eyes, she breathed in, her senses searching for a familiar scent. Vanilla and cinnamon, the staples of her mother's basic cookie recipe. Her mother's stuffing for the turkey on Thanksgiving morning, sage and onion and celery. She wanted to be able to see herself and Sarah, their elbows leaning on the kitchen table, watching their mother roll out cookie dough until she had it exactly the way she wanted it. The memories remained even if the room had been transformed.

And everywhere she felt the ghosts of everyone who'd lived in this house watching anxiously from the shadows. For the first time in her life, she understood the meaning of something her grandmother Lloyd used to say: *Sad ties you to a place as sure as happy.*

⁓

Maggie turned the car around at the end of the street and headed for the center of town, her head still reeling from the house tour. It was strange that while everything had changed, the feelings that had been conjured up had been the same. Somehow the innate warmth that had defined her home still lived below the stark white surface. It had tugged at her with every step she'd taken inside those walls. It had been a somewhat surreal experience. On the one hand, she'd been saddened to see how the owners had tried to transform the house, but on the other, it retained its warmth and welcome.

She slowed as she approached Front Street and found a spot in the public lot across the street from the bakery. When she pushed open the pastry shop door, her senses were overcome by so many delectable aromas that she couldn't decide which of the glass display cases to look into first.

"Oh my God," she muttered as she wandered from one case to the next, four in all. Cakes, pies, and cupcakes, of course, but fancy fruit tarts, napoleons, colorful macarons, and some of the most intricately decorated cookies and sugary small bites she'd ever seen. It took her a while, but she finally made a selection. While she waited for her order, she helped herself to a cup of complimentary coffee, then went to the counter to pay for her goodies.

"Guess you still have that sweet tooth."

The voice went through her like the sharp jab of a knife.

Without turning around, she merely nodded and replied, "Guess so."

"How was your weekend at Liddy's? I heard you were back for a few days."

Maggie turned and faced Brett. "Oh, I guess you heard that from your wife. I ran into her at the art center on Sunday."

"Yeah, she told me." Brett took her by the arm and tried to lead her a few steps away from the counter, but she didn't budge. "You look great, Maggie."

"Thanks. Now if you'll excuse me, I have to . . ." She started to turn back to the counter to pick up her package, but he took her arm a second time. His touch was light, and no pressure was exerted, but his hand on her arm felt like a vise. "Let go, Brett."

He dropped his hand.

"Maggie, I need to talk to you." He lowered his voice. "It's important."

"I doubt it." She didn't want to hear his declaration of love, didn't want to hear from his lips that he'd always loved her, only her. It had been hard enough hearing it from Kayla.

"You don't understand," he insisted quietly.

"I understand plenty, thank you. I need to go." The last thing she needed was to deal with Brett, coming on the heels of witnessing what she considered a desecration of her family's ancestral home and the emotions that had been stirred up—her sister's death, her parents' divorce, her father's abandonment of her and her mother. Brett was part of everything that had been churned up in her life that morning. She already knew what he was going to say—*Thanks, Kayla*—and she couldn't bear it. Her heart couldn't take one more look back right at that moment.

"There's something you need to know, Mags."

"I'm going to say this one more time." She looked into his eyes and ignored that she saw anything that would make the past disappear. "I don't have anything to say to you, and I don't want to hear anything you have to say. Now—"

"Maggie, please."

She grabbed her box of pastries off the counter and headed for the door as an elderly gentleman was preparing to open it to come in. He held the door for her, and she smiled a thank-you.

Maggie checked traffic both ways, then crossed to the parking lot, refusing to look back at the shop. She could feel Brett's eyes on her as she walked to her car on shaking legs. She'd been thrown off-kilter by what she was certain would have been Brett's declaration of undying love. She'd wanted to cover her ears rather than hear that from him now, after they'd been apart for so long and she'd taught herself to live with the aftermath of their relationship. She'd had more than she could handle already that morning, and she couldn't get out of town fast enough.

She sighed with relief when she reached Route 6, determined to put as many miles behind her as quickly as she could. But the farther she drove, the closer she felt the ghosts that had watched her from the shadows in the house on Cottage Street. She had the feeling they'd followed her and were crowded shoulder to shoulder in the back seat. The more she glanced into the rearview mirror, the larger the past loomed, the good and the bad.

Kayla's words were in her head. Seeing Brett, walking the floors of her childhood home, had taken her back to the time when she'd believed she knew where her life was headed. College in September. After graduation, she'd marry Brett and they'd live together in whichever city's football team drafted him—there was never a doubt in anyone's mind, least of all hers, that he'd play professionally. She'd teach for two years—three at the most—and then they'd start their family. After football, they'd move back to Wyndham Beach, and they would assuredly live happily ever after.

It had never occurred to her that anything could happen that would change what she'd been so sure of, that there could be forces in the universe that could misdirect everything in the blink of an eye.

She'd moved to Seattle with Brett after college graduation, but she'd been unable to shake off the pain of a life-changing decision she'd been forced to make, the stress of keeping a secret that was eating her alive. She was unable to forgive him for not understanding her grief, unable to go through with a wedding to a man who'd seemed to close his eyes to her devastation. In the end, the only thing she could do was leave Brett and the dreams they'd shared to find her own way.

Her solitary journey had taken her to Philadelphia and a man who'd loved her and who'd offered her a life, a family, a home. She'd loved Art in her own way, maybe not with the passion she'd felt for Brett but with a steadiness and a resolve to never let him know he'd been second in her heart. She'd taken one last look over her shoulder at the life she could have had before she moved on and said *I do*.

Sad ties you to a place as sure as happy.

"Amen, Nana," she said aloud. "Amen."

As sure as happy. She had to admit there'd been equal measures of both, and it was the happy that sat on the shoulders of the ghosts in the back seat, begging her to take a good long look—and she'd do that. But not today. Today had been about nostalgia and feeling the losses that had marked her life. There would be other days to remember the joy and the laughter that house—that family—had once known. There was much to remember. But not today.

Chapter Ten

GRACE

Grace read the online news article for the third time before getting up from her desk to close her office door.

This had to be a mistake. *Please* let this be a mistake.

Someone had left a column printed out from Philly News and Views Online and left it smack in the middle of her desk. The gossip site item was dated yesterday, and the section circled in red made her blood run cold.

> Rumor has it that the online blog known as *TheLast2No*—a private members-only spot where women go to bitch about their lyin', cheatin' ex-partners—was set up by a well-known Center City attorney who was dumped by her husband who'd been having an affair with one of their paralegals. The attorney, who identifies herself on the site as Annie Boleyn (cute, no?), was reportedly devastated to have been—yes, I'll say it—the last to know, and obviously had not taken the news of the affair well. It's been said that the spurned attorney had continued to pretend all was fine with her marriage for several months after

the husband left seeking greener—read **younger**—
pastures, but everyone in the firm knew otherwise.
Talk about a fall from grace! It's only a matter of time
before Annie Boleyn is unmasked and the entire legal
community will know what a desperate woman looks
like. Next time—and there probably will be a next
time—skip the humiliation and #justletgo.

Grace felt sick, a wave of nausea overtaking her. She closed her
eyes and tried to will it away. How, she wondered, had anyone found
out? She hadn't told anyone—not one person!—about *TheLast2No*.
Who could have figured it out? And who had given—she checked the
byline—Amy Spinelli the news?

She was sure by this time tomorrow her name would be out there
in connection with the blog. "Talk about a fall from grace!" Seriously?
Could it have been more obvious? Combined with the other information in the piece, it was clear as glass that she was Annie Boleyn, that
TheLast2No was her blog, and that she was the desperate woman who
hadn't seen what everyone else in her office had known. Amy Spinelli
might just as well have written "Grace Flynn" in parentheses after "a
well-known Center City attorney who was dumped by her husband
who'd been having an affair with one of their paralegals."

Grace held her head in her hands but wouldn't let the tears fall. She
couldn't take any more humiliation. She just didn't have the strength.

Closing her laptop and packing it with a few files in her tote bag,
she cleared her desk, turned out the light, and, closing the door behind
her, walked to the elevator with her head high. In the parking garage,
she loaded her bag into the back seat, started the car, and drove off as
if nothing were wrong. She made it all the way to Spruce Street before
she let the tears fall.

She'd thought her humiliation had been complete before, thought
she'd managed to salvage a certain amount of dignity by ignoring the

happy couple in the office and going about her business. Apparently, someone was determined to ensure that she wasn't going to be able to maintain whatever pride she still had.

Without thinking about where she was headed, she found herself on the Schuylkill Expressway headed for Bryn Mawr.

Once in her mother's driveway, she broke down and sobbed for twenty minutes. Finally, hiccuping and blotchy faced, she got out of the car and started toward the front door.

"Gracie? That you?" her mother called from the top of the driveway. Maggie wore old jeans with dirty knees, one of Art's old Penn State sweatshirts, and sunglasses. "I was just trying to take advantage of this beautiful weather to get a jump on my garden. Whoever heard of sixty-five sunny degrees in February?"

Grace walked up the drive slowly. Now that she was here, what could she possibly say to her mother to prepare her for the embarrassment headed their way?

"I thought I'd . . ." Maggie paused. "Grace? Are you all right?"

Grace shook her head. "No, Mom. I'm not all right . . ."

Forty minutes later, the dam having burst, Grace had told her mother everything, from Zach admitting he was in love with someone else to the humiliation she'd suffered at Zach's and Amber's hands to setting up the blog and letting her feelings rip.

"It felt like such a safe place to unload it all. It made me feel like I had some control over one small part of my life when everything else was out of control." Grace sat at the kitchen table, the picture of total dejection. "I could talk about how devastated I'd been when Zach left me and how horrified I was when I found out he and Amber were a couple. I had no idea, Mom. But apparently everyone else in the office knew. I made a total fool out of myself."

"Sweetheart, why didn't you tell me? Why did you hide all this . . . this pain? And for the love of all that's holy, why didn't you tell me about Zach and Amber?"

"I didn't want you to know what a failure I was at marriage. You and Dad had such a perfect life together, and that's what I wanted. It was just too hard to admit I'd failed."

"Grace, you didn't fail. Zach failed. Look, your dad and I had a great marriage, but it wasn't perfect. We had our challenges, just like everyone does." Maggie sighed. "I just wish you'd talked to me about it."

"I just couldn't face you. I was afraid you'd think I was flat-out stupid for the way I handled it. Mom, I pretended we were still together weeks after he moved out, but everyone knew we weren't—but I didn't know that—so I looked like a lying fool. And I did everything I could possibly think of to win him back. There was nothing I wouldn't have done, like, I had no pride left whatsoever. When I found out everyone had known not only about him leaving, but about his relationship with Amber, I just wanted to die." Grace grabbed a tissue from the box her mother offered her. "I was so hurt. I had to go in there every day and face him, with her. Everyone knew he'd dumped me for her."

"I wish you'd talked to me." Maggie rubbed Grace's back to comfort her the way she had when Grace was a child.

"I don't know what you could have done. And besides, running to my mom to fix it somehow would only have made things worse."

"Well, he's got to go, Gracie. He and his girlfriend. Both of them. Outta there." Maggie's temper was starting to build, but her voice remained calm. Grace knew that the angrier Maggie was, the lower her voice. "Believe me, if I'd known, she'd have been gone long before now."

"We can't out and out fire them. They haven't done anything that fits the definition of the firm's grounds for termination. Believe me, I've been waiting for them to screw up."

"It's inhuman to ask you to continue to work under those conditions. God, I had no idea he was such a bastard. And I am so, so very sorry that you didn't feel you could talk to me."

"I was too humiliated." Grace started to cry again. "I'm still humiliated, just talking about it. But that's why I started this blog. It was my safe place. The one place I didn't have to pretend I wasn't angry. It was a place where other women could unload their anger and their humiliation, too. Where we could encourage each other to move on and remind each other that our lives didn't need to be defined by our divorce. Mom, some of these women were even more depressed and lonely than I was. We started doing movie nights and happy hours—all online—and after a while, it became more than just a place to bitch. Now . . ."

"Now you're shutting it down. Get rid of it, preferably some way that no one can dig it up again."

"I can delete it, Mom, but I think it can still appear on other people's computers."

"Talk to the IT guy at the office. Timothy? Maybe he knows some way to just make it disappear."

"I'll call him in the morning. I can't talk to anyone right now. By tomorrow, this story will be everywhere. I don't think I can take any more embarrassment. When it gets around that I was so pathetic I started a blog under an assumed name to rail about Zach . . ." Grace shook her head. "I don't think I can face anyone ever again."

"Grace, how could anyone have known it was you?" Maggie got up and went to the coffee machine. She dropped in a pod and hit the button after putting a mug in place.

"I have no idea. I swear I never told anyone—not even Natalie— that I'd set up that site. I didn't even tell Nat about Zach's affair with Amber."

Maggie paced while the coffee dripped. "And you did all this on your laptop?"

"Mostly. I used my old desktop in the office a time or two."

"Who would know that? That you used it?" She set a pitcher of cream and the sugar bowl on the table.

Grace shrugged. "I guess anyone who ever saw me working on it."

"Zach?"

"Sure. He used to tease me about . . ." Grace's eyes widened. "You don't think he would . . ."

"Why wouldn't he?" Maggie handed Grace the mug of coffee, then began to prepare one for herself.

Grace knew her mouth was hanging open, but it never had occurred to her that Zach would snoop on her computer.

"Maybe he thought he'd find something relative to the disposition of the firm," Maggie said. "Maybe he thought there were emails between you and your dad spelling out when you might be taking over."

"Maybe." It didn't feel right to Grace. "But he already knew where things stood. Dad's will had made it clear. Remember, we were still together when Dad died. I told him everything. He had no reason to snoop."

"How about Amber?"

"Do I think Amber would hack into my computer?" Grace laughed. "Duh."

"So how would we find out?" Grace watched her mother's wheels turning. Maggie took her phone from her pocket and speed-dialed a number.

To Grace, she said, "We're not waiting until tomorrow."

Then apparently the call had been connected. "Timothy? It's Maggie Flynn. Are you still at the office? Good. I wonder if I could ask you to do a favor for me . . ."

~

Grace had spent the night at Maggie's after an ill-advised check of the comments on Philly News and Views Online. She scanned the responses to the article, looking for her name. When she found it, she wanted to throw up.

Oh God.

—Is there anyone in Philadelphia who doesn't know this is about Grace Flynn?

—Everyone knows Grace Flynn's man left her for something better. But did she give up, bow out gracefully? Nope. I know someone who works at Flynn Law and she said it was painful to watch how she pretended they hadn't split up.

—She should have gotten an Oscar for the way she acted like she and her ex were still together.

—I checked out the blog. Be careful out there, guys. There are some really sad, desperate women.

—I'd kill myself before I humiliated myself the way this woman did. Shame on her. She should have just let him go and gotten on with her life.

—Would you want this lawyer handling your case? I wouldn't. She sounds unstable. No wonder her old man dumped her.

And on it went.

"Oh, sweetheart." Maggie had come up behind her and read over her shoulder.

"Well, I guess my humiliation is now complete. I give up. Zach and Amber have won. I am done, Mom." Grace's eyes filled with tears. "I can never show my face in Philadelphia again. There is not one courtroom I could walk into where everyone doesn't know how pathetic I am. My law career is over."

"Grace . . ."

"Mom, you know how small the legal community is in Philly. Who could continue to practice here after this? I can't. I've been dealing with this for months, and I just don't have it in me anymore." Grace got up from the table and went into the hall, up the steps, and crawled into the guest room bed. She pulled the covers up to her chin and spent the night staring at the ceiling.

She meant what she'd said. She was over the entire mess, done with pretending it didn't hurt and done with ignoring the whispers. She just didn't care anymore.

At some point in the morning, her mother came into the room, but Grace pretended to be sleeping. A few minutes later, she heard Maggie leave the house. Grace barely moved for the next couple of hours. It was unhealthy and stupid—she knew that, but she couldn't make herself get up, and she couldn't fall asleep.

She should get up and call George and let him know she wouldn't be in today—or any day. It was cowardly to resign over the phone, but she wasn't going anywhere near the office, not after this. From time to time during the night, she'd gotten up and checked the site where the offending article had been posted and found hundreds— hundreds!—of comments, almost all as nasty as the ones she'd read the night before. Shockingly, several were written by people she knew, some she'd thought were friends. She'd taken a peek at her email earlier and found Amy Spinelli, the author of the article, asking for an interview, or at the very least a comment. Grace deleted the email.

Downstairs, a door slammed, and Grace assumed her mother had returned from whatever errand she'd gone on. But the footsteps running up the stairs were too quick to be Maggie's, and before Grace could once again feign sleep, Natalie burst into the room.

"What the hell, Grace?"

Grace rolled over and put her pillow over her face. The last thing she needed was a lecture from her younger sister.

"Go away, Nat," she muttered.

"Like hell." Natalie grabbed the pillow and won the tug-of-war, forcibly removing it from Grace's grip.

Grace sat up and pushed her hair out of her face. "Mom called you, didn't she?"

"Actually, I heard it first from one of my colleagues. He sent me a text this morning." Natalie sat on the side of the bed.

"I can explain . . ." Grace sat up slowly and leaned back against the headboard.

"You don't have to explain anything to me. I get it. I did talk to Mom. Frankly, I think it was a stroke of genius on your part—the blog?—finding a way to cope with a horrible situation, dealing with that moron you used to be married to." Natalie paused. "You do realize how lucky you are to be rid of such a two-faced, cheating asshat, right? His little girlfriend deserves him. He does not deserve you."

The last thing Grace had expected was such a deeply felt show of love and loyalty from her sister. Fat tears rolled from her eyes and dripped onto the T-shirt she'd slept in.

"I thought you'd be appalled that I'd done this blog thing. I thought you'd be disgusted with me for being so weak. I thought you'd be embarrassed and . . ."

Natalie moved close quickly to grab Grace's face and make her look into her eyes. "I will never be embarrassed to be your sister. And I don't think you're weak at all. I think you've shown remarkable strength, and I'm proud of that. I don't know if I'd have been as strong. I hate that someone has found a way to turn that against you. Believe me, when we find out who sold you out to Philly News and Views Online, they will feel the full force of the Flynns."

"What did Mom say?" Grace wiped her face with the back of her hand, which she then wiped on the blue comforter. "Wait, where is Mom?"

"She said she had something she needed to do this morning and asked me to keep you company."

"Did she say what?"

"Nope. Just that she might be gone for a while." Natalie leaned over and grabbed the box of tissues from the bedside table and handed it to Grace.

"You don't think she left town in a cloud of humiliation, do you?" Grace was only half-kidding.

"Not a chance. But I'll tell you this: she sounded really pissed off."

"Oh God," Grace groaned. "She went into the office. She called Timothy yesterday . . ."

"The IT guy at the firm?"

Grace nodded. "We're pretty sure someone hacked into my office computer, and that's how they found out about the blog." When she saw Natalie's frown, Grace hastened to add, "I didn't really use that computer to post on the blog, but there were some references to it. Like I kept my passwords in a file." She sheepishly added, "And I did use it to work out the initial introduction to *TheLast2No*, so if someone had my password . . ."

". . . this someone would know that you set up the blog in the first place."

"Yup." She wiggled her fingers. "My prints are all over it."

"And do we have any thoughts on who this someone might be?"

"The obvious is Amber. She's the sneaky type."

"You don't suspect Zach?" Natalie asked.

"I thought about that, but the truth is he's too over me to do something like that. He's not interested in what I'm doing. Plus he wouldn't care. I'd be willing to bet big money that Amber's behind this, and when she told Zach, he laughed and said something like, 'Yeah, my ex-wife's a loser,' and promptly forgot about it." Grace shrugged. "He just doesn't care enough to get worked up over something like this."

"But you think she does?"

"No question about it. She can't dig her claws in deep enough or often enough. It's her, not him."

Natalie appeared skeptical. "You don't think he'd use something like this to urge you out of the firm?"

"Well, if he did, he'd have been right."

"What do you mean, he'd be right?" Skepticism turned into indignation. "That's your firm."

Grace shook her head. "Not anymore. I can't go back there. I just can't take any more, Nat. I've been dealing with this shit for months. Got myself to a place where I tried to let it all roll off my back, but that sanctuary is gone now. I just don't want to do it anymore. You can't imagine what it's been like."

"I get it. At least, I think I do. But still . . ." Natalie's voice softened.

"Put yourself in my place. Imagine being publicly betrayed by the man you loved. Your husband of ten years. Well, almost ten years. He's having an affair right under your nose, and you refuse to see it while everyone around you knows what's going on. Humiliating enough?" Grace's laugh was harsh and held no touch of humor. "No, of course not. You try to cope by looking for a safe place where you can howl and gnash your teeth, and when you don't find one, you make one and invite other women to join you and do their own howling. And it helped, that community, that sense of not being quite so alone. I had no idea there were so many people hurting." Grace stopped, remembering she had to shut down the blog, the sooner the better. "And then someone finds out that you're behind this and makes sure the entire world knows that you—who have spent your adult life building an admirable, I'm even gonna say respected, career in a professional field—you are a pathetic whiner who can't get over the fact that the man you love dumped you and turned you into someone who couldn't handle the rejection and you had to band together with a bunch of other losers."

"Stop saying 'loser.' You're not a loser."

"I am in the opinion of the Philadelphia legal community. Have you seen the comments on Philly News and Views Online? Everyone knows I've been hiding behind a fake name. Everyone knows I did not deal with the end of my marriage in a mature fashion. If you read some of the comments I made on my blog, you'll think I'm unstable. Last night I read some of the things I've written, and I cringed. I don't sound intelligent or rational. Anyone reading that shit will know I'd lost it for a while." Grace shook her head slowly. "I'm done in Philly, Nat. How can I look anyone in the eye after this? No one will ever take me seriously again. Not my clients, not the judges, not my fellow lawyers—a bunch of whom were among the commenters, by the way."

When Natalie opened her mouth to speak, Grace shut her down. "Don't bother. There's nothing you or anyone else can say that would change my mind. I'm moving on. I'm leaving Flynn Law."

"You're letting Zach win."

"Zach has already won." Grace grabbed a tissue and blew her nose. "I'm finished."

Chapter Eleven

NATALIE

By the time she'd picked up Daisy from day care on her way home from Maggie's, Natalie was exhausted. Her sister had gotten herself into deep waters—not for the first time in her life—and the bailout had apparently just begun. Their mother had returned home around four in the afternoon, and when Grace had asked Maggie where she'd been, she'd just said, "Not now," and gone upstairs. They'd heard the shower running in the master bathroom for what seemed like a long time, then . . . nothing. Before leaving to get Daisy, Natalie'd stood outside Maggie's door for a moment, then, hearing nothing from the other side, knocked softly. When there had been no response, she cracked the door just a bit and saw her mother sound asleep, lying crosswise on the bed, a pillow under her head, her favorite soft throw covering her to her shoulders. Natalie'd closed the door quietly and crept down the steps.

"She's dead to the world," Natalie told Grace. "Out cold."

"I doubt she slept last night. She was really agitated." Grace looked remorseful. "I really did it this time, didn't I." It wasn't a question. She started to say something else when her phone buzzed on the kitchen counter, and she sighed. "Someone else wanting to know if it's true: Am I really Annie Boleyn? And for all the years I've practiced in this city, not one person has called or emailed to offer support."

Natalie picked up the phone and turned it off. "If you want to speak to anyone, you can call them. In the meantime, it's just more aggravation. Leave it off."

Grace nodded as she walked Natalie to the door. "Thanks, Nat. I don't say it often enough, but I love you. I don't deserve a sister as good as you."

"Shut up." Natalie gave her a hug. "I love you, too, and neither of us say it enough."

"Give Daisy a big hug for me."

"Will do. Now get some sleep. We'll talk tomorrow about what comes next. For the rest of the day, and tonight, let's just take a very deep breath and let it all go for a while, okay?"

Grace nodded, standing in the doorway as Natalie made her way to her car. She stopped midway along the path and called back over her shoulder. "Yoga."

"You think it would help?" Grace called back.

"It couldn't hurt."

Natalie took her own advice and rolled out her mat on the family room floor after she got home and started dinner. Daisy had her own little mat from their mommy-and-me yoga classes last summer, and she rolled it out next to Natalie's and managed to keep up for all of ten minutes before her wandering eye settled on a stuffed llama she'd left on the sofa, and she decided he should be doing yoga instead of her. Natalie continued her own routine while Daisy chatted happily nearby with her silent friend.

Once they'd gotten through dinner, bath, and story time, Natalie tucked in her sleepy girl and tiptoed down the stairs. It had been an emotional day, and while thirty minutes of yoga had helped, she was still a little hyped from spending the day with Grace. She cleaned the kitchen before turning on her laptop and reading first her emails, then, belatedly, her horoscope for the day.

"The trials of the morning will extend through the next several days, all of which will have their own challenges."

"Swell," she muttered. "Like I couldn't have figured that out on my own."

"There will be a break in the clouds, but you might not like what you see at first. Trust the universe to bring you what you need and keep faith that decisions made by others will eventually lead you to your destiny."

She rolled her eyes and clicked on the link to her genealogy website. The first thing she noticed was the blinking icon that signaled a new message.

Hi, Natalie—

Joe Miller here again. Hope you're well. Not to belabor a point, but I did want you to know I had another DNA test run and I'm still getting the same feedback. So unless something is really screwy somewhere, I have to believe we are definitely half siblings. I'm hoping this doesn't upset you in any way, and I will certainly understand if you don't care to open what could be one enormous and potentially ugly can of worms on your end, but as I mentioned in my last email, I was adopted at birth, so it's been a long twisty road for me to find any birth relatives. I will respect whatever decision you make. But if you want to explore this further, you can reach me at this e-address or call me at the number below if you ever want to talk (I wish!), but I won't contact you again.

If I don't hear from you, I wish you a beautiful happy life.

Joe

Without understanding why, Natalie burst into tears. If she'd ever had a brother, Joe Miller sounded exactly like the sort of guy she'd have wanted. She still wasn't convinced, but she knew there was a conversation she was going to have to have with her mother. If her father had had an affair, or, more likely to Natalie's mind, a child born of a relationship before he'd married her mother, Maggie should probably know. Under other circumstances, she'd be on the phone with Grace to figure out what to do. Tell Maggie? Delete the email and pretend she'd never gotten it? How would Maggie react if she discovered her husband had had a son she hadn't known about? In light of Grace's current drama, there was no way Natalie could discuss Joe Miller's messages with her sister or her mother just yet. Their family had enough to deal with right now, but it was a conversation that would have to be had when Grace's dust settled.

She still hadn't decided whether to respond to the email, but as she locked the front door and made her way upstairs to bed, the thought that Joe Miller sounded like someone she'd like to know followed her every step of the way.

Chapter Twelve

MAGGIE

Maggie had flown into Flynn Law like an avenging angel, walking past the receptionist and going directly to George's door, which she entered without her customary courtesy knocking and which she slammed behind her. But once she saw George—kindly, good-natured, soft-spoken George, Art's best friend since law school—she lost a bit of her edge.

"George, we need to talk."

"Good morning, Maggie. Somehow I knew I'd be seeing you today." George greeted her with a warm hug and a resigned smile.

"So you know . . ." Maggie pulled a visitor's chair closer to his desk while he seated himself in the one next to her.

"I know what I've heard, and what I've read. Now you tell me what the truth is, and we'll discuss what we'll do about it," he said gently.

Over the next twenty minutes, Maggie shared everything Grace had told her.

George leaned his elbow on the desk and covered his face with his right hand. "I had no idea . . . oh, dear God, Maggie. I didn't know all this was going on." His face had drained of color. "I should have known. Should have been more diligent. I promised Art I'd watch out for her, and I failed him."

"It isn't your . . . wait, what do you mean, you promised Art . . . ?"

"Toward the end, Art confided he'd been picking up strange vibes from Zach. He asked me if I'd noticed anything different at the office, and I told him truthfully I had not. Though, in retrospect, I probably wasn't the one to ask. You know I've never been one to socialize in the office or pay attention to gossip. I'm always the last person to know what's going on in anyone's personal life." He added sadly, "Obviously."

"Still the first one in and the last one out?"

George nodded. "Pretty much. This craziness, this thing with the paralegal—I honestly didn't know." The poor man looked so distressed Maggie felt compelled to lean over and pat him on the arm to comfort him. "I just didn't notice, Maggie. I am so sorry. I let you all down."

"Don't be silly." She gave his arm one last pat, then stood. "It isn't your fault. The blame belongs on Zach and Amber. There are more issues at stake right now and steps to be taken to mitigate each one. First: this whole mess with Grace being revealed as the person behind this blog. I asked Timothy if he could determine who, if anyone, accessed Grace's computer files, and surprise, surprise, he did."

"Please tell me Zach did not hack into her computer."

"Amber did. She discovered Grace's hobby as a blogger and contacted the woman who reports for Philly News and Views Online."

"Confirmed?" If anything, George went another shade paler.

"Absolutely. Timothy found where she'd even sent some of Grace's emails and files to her own computer."

"Then she's gone. Not only is that unethical, it's a federal crime." He got up and reached for his phone.

"I agree. But if you wouldn't mind, I'd like to be the one to break the news."

"And that's your right. But I'm calling the local FBI office. I have a neighbor who works in cybercrimes. We can't give her a pass for breaking the law." He plopped down in the chair behind his desk, suddenly looking every one of his sixty-three years. Maggie sat by quietly while he made the call. When this latest scandal began to make the rounds, Flynn Law would take another hit. The thought was sobering.

"We can expect a visit from my neighbor soon. We're going to let law enforcement deal with this." He shook his head. "More bad news for the firm."

"I was just thinking that exact thing. But it can't be helped. And of course this news will only perpetuate the story about Grace and her blog and all the reasons why she set it up in the first place." Maggie rubbed her forehead, where a killer headache was taking over. "But of course there's no way in hell we're going to let that little snit get away with what she's done," Maggie said with more force than she'd intended. She continued, her voice softer. "Grace's name has already been dragged through the mud. It's Amber's turn. At least my daughter didn't break any laws."

"I'm so sorry, Maggie. How is Grace taking all this?"

"Not well. Actually, you'll be hearing from her soon, but I might as well tell you, she's going to be resigning. She feels her ability to practice law in Philly has been greatly compromised, and her professional reputation has been ruined."

"This is wrong, Maggie. So wrong. Art wanted . . ."

"Art isn't here anymore, and Grace isn't coming back. Which means there's no longer a Flynn at Flynn Law." Maggie took a deep breath. "Which brings me to the second issue we need to discuss." Deep breath number two followed. "I'm sorry, George, but I'm going to sell the firm. Not the name, but the clientele. I'm not certain how all that will work. The best thing for everyone would be if you bought the firm and simply changed the name."

He was silent for a very long moment. "Maggie, you have to know this firm is worth a fortune. And I don't know that Art would have wanted me to take over."

"Art did, in fact, want you to take care of his clients. You know he—and you—have represented some VIPs. They trusted him, and they trust you. One of the last long conversations Art and I had was about going forward with the firm. He said if for any reason I wanted to dissolve the business, I was to talk to you first and give you first right of refusal." George started to speak, but she held up a hand to stop him. "He told me to have the business appraised, then offer it to you at a discount."

"That's . . . very generous, Maggie. But—wow, this is the last thing I expected today. I don't know what to say."

"You can take some time to think it over. But I would like to resolve it. I will be calling Jacobs and Biddle to appraise the business. I'd like to hold on to the building, though."

George nodded. "Whatever you want, Maggie."

"I'm hoping you'll come around to the idea. There's no one I'd rather have take over for Art, and it was his wish."

"I need time to think about it. But are you sure . . . ?"

Maggie could see his wheels beginning to turn. "Oh, I'm very sure. Art told me I'd know when the right time is, and if this isn't it, I don't know when. He trusted me to use my best judgment, and I believe I am. In the meantime, until the appraisal comes back, we'll keep this between us, if you don't mind."

"Not at all. I think if word gets out the firm is for sale, it could be detrimental. If anyone thinks this thing with Grace has diminished the value . . ." He stopped in midsentence. "Oh, Maggie, I'm sorry. I didn't mean to imply . . ."

She waved a hand in his direction. "No need to apologize. I thought the same thing myself. I'd never want Grace to hear me say it, but it's true. The damage has been done. But when it becomes apparent that life is going on here, I think things will settle down."

"Why don't you suggest that Grace take a leave of absence instead of resigning? It doesn't feel right that she should be the one to leave."

"I agree it isn't right, but she's adamant that her career here is over." Maggie stood and picked up her bag from the corner of the desk.

"What will she do?"

"That remains to be seen. I have a few ideas, but I haven't discussed them with her just yet. One thing at a time." She walked to the door. "And right now, it's time for me to have a little chat with Amber and with Zach. I'll stop back to say goodbye on my way out, but don't be surprised if they come running to you after our little talk."

"Oh, I hope they do. I can find her for you if you give me a minute."

"I have a pretty good idea where to look, but thanks. See you in a while."

She walked out into the hall and took a right, which led her past the break room, where several of the younger women were busy with the doughnuts and danishes someone had brought in. Maggie thought she heard Grace's name followed by uneasy laughter, so she stuck her head through the doorway and said, "Morning, ladies."

"Ah, hi, Mrs. Flynn."

"Good morning, Mrs. Flynn."

Maggie forced a smile and continued on her way, trying to think calming thoughts and practice deep breathing. The last thing she wanted was to come off like a shrieking banshee. There were other ways to get the point across. She didn't want to add to the office gossip.

And then Mrs. Flynn came in and she was screaming and yelling and acting like a crazy woman. It was scary.

Nope. No scary crazy woman here. Only a woman who was in complete control of herself and her anger.

At Zach's door, she paused. Hearing voices, she knocked once quickly, then stepped inside, closing the door behind her. A giggling Amber sat on the edge of Zach's desk, his hand up her skirt.

"Well, good morning. Glad you're together so I can take care of all my business at one time."

Zach went white and removed his hand so quickly Maggie was amazed it didn't snap off at the wrist. Amber took her time turning to the voice but jumped off the desk the second she saw Maggie.

"Mrs. Flynn," Amber stammered.

Zach looked terrified, as if he knew the boom was about to be lowered. He wasn't wrong.

"You." Maggie pointed a finger at Amber and spoke slowly and calmly. "You are fired. Your last paycheck will be mailed to you. And if I were you, I wouldn't bother asking for a recommendation from anyone associated with this firm."

"What?" Amber narrowed her eyes as if about to take Maggie on. "You can't fire me."

"Ahhh, Amber . . ." Zach stood but looked as if he were about to pass out.

"She can't fire me. She doesn't even work here," Amber snapped.

"Maggie . . ." Zach took two steps in Maggie's direction, and she stopped him right there with a sharp, "It's Mrs. Flynn."

"Mrs. Flynn." Still the color of paste, Zach swallowed hard. "May I ask . . . ?"

Turning back to Amber, Maggie ignored him. "The FBI will be here to talk to you in . . ." Maggie glanced at her watch. "About another twenty minutes, which should give you enough time to clear out your desk and check in with HR."

"The FBI? What are you talking about?" Amber looked at Zach as if for support. He was strangely silent, so she turned back to Maggie. "I haven't done anything wrong. And I certainly haven't done anything that would require the freaking FBI."

"Au contraire." Maggie's smile was lethal. "You hacked into Grace's computer and stole some files."

"That's ridiculous." Amber smirked. "You have no proof."

"Actually, we do have proof. Dates, times, and files copied and sent to your laptop." Maggie folded her arms over her chest and tried to project a calm she did not feel. "You're welcome to ask the HR rep about that. She's already been given confirmation, which I'm sure she'll be more than happy to share with you."

"Amber . . . did you . . . ?" Zach came around the side of the desk slowly. "Tell me you didn't . . ."

"You used the information you stole to go to Amy Spinelli," Maggie continued, "and you ruined my daughter's career. You can bet your ass we called the FBI."

Amber's mouth dropped open.

"Amber." Zach grabbed her by the shoulders. "You're a paralegal. You know that shit's against the law. It's a federal crime, for God's sake. What the hell were you thinking?"

"I was thinking I wanted her out of our lives." She pushed him away. "I hate her being here every day, giving me dirty looks. Watching every move I make, hoping I'll screw up somehow."

"Well, you did," he said. "You screwed up big-time."

"You did indeed." Maggie nodded toward the door.

Amber wet her lips, apparently readying a plea. "Mrs. Flynn, if I could explain . . ."

"You may not. Out, now, or I will call building security to escort you down to HR. I would think you'd rather walk out of here and make your way to the office on your own, but it's your choice."

Her eyes flickered from Zach to Maggie and back to Zach. "I'll see you at home," she told him as she left.

"But maybe not for a while." Maggie walked behind her to close the door.

"Mag . . . Mrs. Flynn . . . ," Zach began.

"Please don't. Just listen." Maggie fought to keep her voice level, but it was a battle. "You're going to need to look for a job. You should probably start today."

"I can't be fired for falling in love with someone," he protested. "I didn't mean for it to happen. It just . . . happened."

"Right." She nodded slowly. "The heart wants what the heart wants, and all that."

He nodded, perhaps for a tiny moment thinking she understood.

"Well, Zach, I'll tell you what my heart wants." Maggie leaned a hip against his desk. "My heart wants my daughter to be happy. My heart wants *her* heart to have not been broken by you. My heart wants her life to be sane again."

"I never meant to hurt her. And you can't blame me for what Amber did. I swear I had nothing to do with that. I never would have let her hack into Grace's computer." He swallowed hard, his Adam's apple moving nervously above the knot of his tie. "Please, believe me. I'm not responsible for what Amber did."

"I don't hold you directly responsible for Amber ruining Grace's career. But I do blame you for ruining her life." Maggie was not going to give him the satisfaction of knowing all the ways his actions had affected Grace.

"I didn't think she'd take the divorce as hard as she did." He slumped in his chair, looking both confused and defeated.

Maggie laughed. "Really? Tell me how you thought she might take it." She slipped into her Mama Bear persona and pinned him to his chair with her gaze. "Come on, Zach, we both know you never thought about how she'd feel when her husband of ten years openly cheated on her in her own home. And make no mistake, Flynn Law *is* her home. But wait, make that *almost* ten years, and keep that thought in mind because it will be relevant in a minute. You didn't care how she felt, Zach." God, she even hated saying his name. "Once you realized this firm had not fallen into your lap—and thank God it hadn't—there was no longer any reason for you to pretend to be in love with her. No reason to hang around if there wasn't going to be a big payoff."

"I didn't think it would hit her so hard. And I didn't think she'd act like a lovestruck kid who couldn't let go, whiny and pathet—" The look on Maggie's face told him he'd gone too far.

"I'll tell you what I think. I think you had Amber in your sights for a while before my husband died. I think you stayed with Grace because you thought once he was gone, she would inherit the firm, and by 'she' you thought 'you.' That had been Art's plan all along, by the way, that the firm would someday be Grace's. That someday *she* would be the face of Flynn Law. But toward the end of his life, some little alarm began to ring. Something told him not to trust you. You, his brilliant protégé, the young man who showed so much potential. The man who wooed and married our daughter not for love, but for his own gain. You, who betrayed not only Grace, but the man who'd believed in you, who'd loved you like a son. Who welcomed you into his family and his business." She had to stop and cover her eyes. Zach's betrayal of her family—not only Grace, but Art as well—had been one of the most painful truths she'd had to face.

Maggie swallowed hard before continuing.

"So at the last minute, he left the firm in my hands to do whatever I thought best. And what I think is best is for you to be gone. You could wait until George calls you in, but I think you should be a man and leave on your own before Amber's shit hits the fan."

He flinched. Had she ever cursed in front of him before?

"Make some calls." She straightened up. "You should want to get out in front of this whole Amber-hacking-into-Grace's-computer story. Some people might suspect you put her up to it. A lot of them will believe that you did."

"That would be a lie. You're not going to tell people that . . ."

"Of course not. I won't have to. They'll come up with that on their own. There'll always be people who will want to believe the worst, whether it's true or not. It's a good lesson to learn, Zach. One worth remembering."

She started toward the door, then snapped her fingers. "Oh—and about that ten-year thing. You and Grace never made it to your tenth anniversary. Which would have been in seventeen days."

"So?"

"So while Art was beginning to get bad vibes about you, he still wasn't sure if he was really picking up on something, or if the meds he was on were messing with his head. So he had a clause added to his will to the effect that if you and Grace were still married on your tenth anniversary, the firm would belong to you both. Equally." She opened the door and, without turning around, whispered, "Looks like you blew it."

She closed the door behind her, proud of herself for not losing her temper or saying some of the really ugly things she'd wanted to say. It had taken every bit of her willpower not to. But the look on Zach's face just before she closed the door had been priceless. The satisfaction she felt would go a long way toward making up for all the things she'd wanted to throw at him but didn't. He was a lying, cheating snake, and he deserved to fall flat on his face.

Then again, Maggie wasn't above a little lie of her own now and then. Zach would never know she'd made up that part about Art changing his will and the ten-year thing. She didn't lie often, but sometimes you just had to make sure your opponent understood that you'd gotten in the last punch.

~

"I can't believe you left him standing," Natalie said when Maggie called her from the train. "Didn't you want to kill him?"

"I did, almost as much as I wanted to slap Amber's smirking face. But we both know that's not my style. I thought I'd get the point across better if I just laid it all out there calmly. Doesn't mean I liked doing it that way, but I felt the room needed an adult. Besides, I don't think I would have been able to rein myself back in once I'd lost it. And I must say, my instincts were right. I was very effective."

"Sort of like when Grace and I were little. When you stopped yelling and got really quiet, we knew we were in trouble."

"Something like that."

"Calling the FBI was brilliant. Bless George."

"Hacking into someone else's computer is a federal offense. I honestly don't know how it's going to play out. They may look at it and think it isn't worth prosecuting because there was no money involved."

"Of course there's money involved. Grace lost her standing in the community and doesn't feel she can be taken seriously ever again. She's leaving her job over this. That has to be worth something."

"I agree, but I don't know how such things work on that level. I've never dealt with the FBI before. But the look on her face when the two agents showed up to talk to her was . . ." Maggie paused, then smiled. "It was a thing of beauty."

Later, after Maggie awoke from her much-needed nap, she repeated the story for Grace.

"You think they'll put her in prison for such a small offense?" Grace asked.

Maggie shrugged. "I don't know. They could. I have no idea. I called Larry Gleason to act as your lawyer, by the way. There's no one else Dad would have wanted to represent the firm and you. Of course, if you'd rather have someone else, you're free to call him or her."

"No, that's fine. Larry would have been my first choice, so thank you for sparing me from making that call." Grace smiled for the first time since she'd arrived at Maggie's the day before. "I hope she goes to prison. I hope they put her away for a very long time. Him too." Her smile broadened. "I can't believe George actually called the FBI. He's the best. And you're my hero. On the one hand, I wish I'd been the one to confront her. But on the other . . . you know people would just see the wife who was dumped being a shrew. Like the blog wasn't enough. Dad would have hated this, but he'd really have hated it if we'd embarrassed the firm even more than it has been."

"That was one of the things that kept me from hurling heavy objects at the two of them. All we needed this week would have been for me to be arrested for assault. Not that it might not have been worth it, but I didn't think it would be a good look for the Flynns. Now get into the shower, clean up, and get dressed. I picked up takeout for dinner from your dad's favorite Italian place in town, and I'm starving."

Later, after dinner had been eaten and the dishes stacked in the dishwasher, Grace said, "Mom, what do you think Dad would have done?"

"I think Dad would have shot them both."

"No, seriously. What do you think he would have done?"

Maggie chose her words carefully. "I don't believe we'd be having this conversation if your father was still alive."

"Because Zach wouldn't have left me. We'd still be married."

"Possibly."

"But he still wouldn't have been in love with me." Grace looked overwhelmingly sad. "Our marriage still would have been a sham, and I'd still have been the last to know."

~

It took Maggie several days to work everything out in her head, but once she made up her mind, the path ahead seemed very clear. The decision hadn't been easy, but all things considered, it was the best option for everyone: she needed to sell the house in Bryn Mawr and move back to Wyndham Beach.

First consideration: it was crystal clear that Grace couldn't return to her job even if she wanted to. Her reputation had been shattered, and her self-image had been destroyed. She needed to make a new start somewhere else, but she could see no clear path ahead.

Second consideration: since Maggie had toured her old family home, she'd been haunted by memories—faces, voices—and couldn't stop thinking about how gratifying it would be to repaint every one of those white walls. She imagined where every piece of furniture she owned would go, where she'd hang every photo and every painting.

She'd been drawn more and more back to Wyndham Beach, to her beloved friends, and to the chance to move her life forward.

Third: something was missing in her life, even if she wasn't sure what, but she knew there was only one place to go if she wanted to find it.

Still—there were so many memories in the house she'd shared with Art and their children. There'd been great times, joyful times. Their first days, the rooms empty because they had so little to bring with them. The fun of finding just the right—everything. She remembered where they'd bought every piece of furniture, some banged-up rejects they'd taught themselves to refinish, some precious antiques they'd saved for. They'd brought their babies home from the hospital to that house (Art liked to tell the story of how Natalie'd been so eager to be born they'd barely made it to the hospital). There had been festivities of every kind under that roof: birthday, anniversary, Christmas, New Year's Eve, graduation, Grace's engagement party. They'd marked their girls' growth on the pantry wall—even when the kitchen was renovated, they'd instructed the painters to paint around the chart. Maggie had walked the floors here, holding a sick baby while she prayed for a fever to go down, and, years later, when one or both girls had missed their curfew. Their daughters' first dates had nervously rung their doorbell and stood in the foyer holding thin bouquets of limp flowers. They'd made their way down the wide staircase in prom gowns, and Grace had descended the wide staircase in a white wedding gown that had made her look like a princess.

And there'd been some not-so-joyful times as well. Maggie knew that, but Art's sickness and his passing here had blotted out everything else. She still found it painful to walk into the guest room, where his hospital bed had been set up, his choice because, he'd said, he'd wanted to look out into the trees and watch the birds. Maggie suspected the real reason was that he'd wanted her to be able to sleep without waking every time he coughed or moved. He'd said he wanted to pass quietly, watching the sun rise over the rose bower in the backyard, with Maggie holding his hand, and that was exactly what he'd done.

Maggie had walked through the house, room to room, remembering all those little moments that made up a life, savoring some more than others. When she was certain her decision was final and there'd be no change of heart, she called the Realtor in Wyndham Beach. Then she called Natalie and asked her to get a babysitter for Saturday afternoon and come to the house. Grace was still there, having gone home once over the past week and found notes from several reporters from local TV stations taped to her front door.

"Mom"—Grace had called from her house—"would it be okay if I stayed with you for a bit longer? Just until I decide on my next move."

"Of course. I love your company." Maggie had expected the call, had hoped Grace wouldn't go back to her house, where she'd probably lock herself in and try to disappear for a while. It wasn't healthy, and it wasn't necessary. Grace hadn't done anything to deserve the negative attention she'd been getting. At least at Maggie's there was someone to talk to and someone to make sure she ate something healthy at least once a day, because a mom never stopped being a mom.

Besides, Maggie had a few thoughts on what Grace's next move might be. She was hoping to be able to steer her in that direction.

~

"So what's going on, Mom?" Natalie had come into the kitchen around one on Saturday afternoon, an hour earlier than Maggie had expected her.

"Oh, you're early. That's fine. Grace is upstairs. Will you call her for me? I just have to put some coffee on." Maggie suspected before the day was over—and depending on how her plan was received—wine would be more appropriate, but for now, coffee would serve just fine.

"Where do you want us?" Grace came into the kitchen, followed by her sister.

"I think in here is fine." Maggie pointed to the alcove with the built-in banquette and the harvest table she and Art had found at a barn sale five years ago. It had languished in the basement until the kitchen renovation had been completed. With its plush bench cushions and view of the bird feeders hanging from shepherd's hooks on the deck, the cozy nook was one of Maggie's favorite places.

Maggie poured coffee, placed cream and sugar on the table along with a plate of brownies she'd made the night before.

"Must be serious." Natalie selected a brownie and placed it on a napkin she retrieved from its holder. "Mom's bringing out the chocolate."

"It is serious. But before I tell you why I wanted us to get together, I just want to say how much I love you both."

"We love you, too, Mom." Grace helped herself to a brownie, immediately biting into it. "Yum."

"Mom, you're not sick, are you?" Natalie gripped the edge of the table anxiously.

"No, no. I just want you to remember that and know that whatever decisions I've made over the past week, I've made with the best interests of this family in mind."

Grace and Natalie exchanged a questioning look.

"You already told us you're selling the firm to George," Natalie said. "And we're fine with that."

"What I didn't tell you is that I've decided to sell the house as well." There. She'd put it out there. Maggie studied the expressions on both daughters' faces.

Natalie frowned. "What house?"

Before Maggie could respond, Grace said, "Wait. This house?" A look of disbelief crossed Grace's face. "You want to sell *this* house? The house we grew up in?"

Maggie nodded. "Yes. This house."

"Why?" Natalie looked stunned. "Why would you do that?"

"It's because of me, isn't it? Because of the big scandal about me, you had to sell Dad's firm, and now you want to sell the house." Grace was on the verge of tears.

"No. It's not because of you. Well, only to the extent that I decided to sell the firm now, but it would have happened at some point. If you'd stayed there, eventually it would have gone to you. But you don't know what else might have happened between now and then. And if I've learned anything over the past two years, it's that nothing is forever. Sometimes change is good. Sometimes it's necessary." Maggie blew out a long breath. Her daughters were staring at her as if she had two heads. "For me, it's necessary. I've always loved this house, from the moment your father brought me here to 'just take a look.' I brought both of you home from the hospital to this house. We lived and loved each other and argued and made up in this house." Her voice dropped. "I said goodbye to your father in this house. This hasn't been an easy decision for me. But I need to make a life for myself now. I need to be somewhere that's mine. Somewhere I can start over and shake off everything that's happened since your dad got sick."

"I get that. Okay. So are you looking to downsize, Mom? I have to agree, it's a big house for one person. We can help you find a place," Grace offered. "There are a lot of great houses around."

"That's true. But I've already found my house, and it isn't around here."

"You already found a place? What do you mean, not around here?" Natalie appeared dismayed. "Aren't you going to show us before you make a final decision?"

"The final decision has been made. I have the house under contract. And it's a house you're well familiar with."

"I'm confused." Grace shook her head as if to clear it.

"So am I." Natalie grabbed on to her mug as if to anchor herself to the spot.

"When I visited Liddy in January, I saw that my mom's old house—the house I grew up in, the house my great-great-grandfather built—was for sale. Liddy'd told me the place had been totally renovated, all new everything, top of the line, yada yada yada. Before I left Wyndham Beach, I called the Realtor. I just wanted to see the place one more time before someone else bought it. The Realtor met me at the house and gave me a tour."

"Please tell me you are not moving to Massachusetts." Natalie's eyes were wide as saucers.

"Actually, I am moving to Massachusetts. I'm moving back to my hometown, my old home. That's where I belong. It's where I always belonged."

"But . . . Mom." Grace's voice held a plea. "Why now? Because of me?"

"Grace, everything isn't about you," Natalie snapped.

"I think the timing is a bit suspect, Natalie," Grace snapped back.

"Please. Girls." Maggie rubbed her temples. "Don't."

"What did you expect, Mom? You call us together and drop this bomb on us? You're selling the house we both love, where we grew up, so you can buy the house *you* grew up in? And you never said a word about this until today, and then you tell us you're moving eight hours away?" Grace's ire was beginning to show.

"Why would you do this without telling us, Mom?"

"Because I don't need your consent, nor do I need your approval." Maggie realized how harsh her words must have sounded. Both girls had sat back as if slapped. "But I do need your understanding. Your father is gone. My best friends are hours away. I need them. I need to go home."

"Don't you need us?" Natalie asked.

"Of course I do, sweetie." Maggie covered Natalie's hand with one of her own. "But you have your own life. A job you love. One of these days, you're going to meet someone, and your life will be taking off in another direction. Both of you will." She tried to force a smile. "And I'll be left in the dust."

"What about me?" Grace was on the verge of tears. "I had a home I used to love. A job I used to love. A husband I used to love."

"Gracie, I know you're sort of adrift right now. Actually, I thought I'd ask you to come with me and help me get the house straightened out. The seller painted everything white—stark raving white—which means I'll need to do over every room. I could use your decorating skills."

"Did you do this to give me busy work?"

"No, Grace. I did it because I haven't thought about anything else in weeks. When I went home in September for my reunion, I really did feel like I'd come home. That feeling was intensified when I went back in January." Maggie looked from one daughter to the other. "Please understand, this is what I need to do. Please respect that and wish me well. And know that the door is always open. You can spend your summers there. We can celebrate all our holidays together just as we always have." She turned to Grace. "This is the perfect time and place for you to make a new start. If you want, you can take the Massachusetts bar and practice law there if that appeals to you. Or you can stay here and practice. Or do something else entirely, leave the law behind. Your life is your own now, Gracie. You can choose what comes next. I'm asking that you extend the same courtesy to me. Recognize that my life is mine again. Let me choose what's next for me."

"Damn, you should have been a lawyer." Natalie wiped away tears.

"Yeah, that was as good a closing argument as I've ever made." Grace was weepy, too. "Maybe better."

"I'm hoping to put this house on the market in six weeks. I know I need to have some areas painted and the bathrooms refreshed, but I don't see any reason to drag this out. Can I count on you to help me get it ready?" Maggie directed her question to Grace.

Grace nodded. "Of course."

"Me too," Natalie said. "Winter break starts on Friday. I can come over and help over weekends and next week."

"That would be wonderful. Thank you both. Now, I'm sure there will be some things you will want to have. I'm going to tag everything I'm taking with me, but everything else is up for grabs. If there's something you want, put your name on it with a sticky note. I'll be having my stuff moved into storage in four weeks, then I'm having a house sale."

"Like a garage sale? It'll make you nuts, Mom, everyone running through the house, picking up your stuff." Natalie wrinkled her nose. "Sure you want to do that?"

"I've hired someone to run the sale. I won't be here because you're right. The process would make me insane. So we'll have the sale, and anything that doesn't sell gets donated. I suggest you start thinking about what you want from this place before then."

"Do you already know what you want to keep, Mom?" Natalie asked.

"Yes, for the most part. I've more or less inventoried in my head, so I'm clear on what I want to take."

"How 'bout we take a few hours now to tag whatever you're taking with you, so Grace and I know what's left for us to fight over?"

"No fighting. There's plenty for both of you. But yes, I should tag my things sooner rather than later. You can help with that. Thanks."

Well, that didn't go too badly, Maggie thought as she searched a desk drawer for a pad of sticky notes. Could have been worse. For a moment she did think it was going to spin out in a flood of tears, but it ended well.

She turned back to the table and realized Grace was crying.

"What, Gracie?" Maggie asked.

"I was just thinking how this has been my home my entire life." Grace reached for the box of tissues that sat on the wide window ledge. Maggie had left it there when she'd had a crying spell of her own in the wee hours of the morning. "Everything that ever happened to me started here."

Natalie sat next to Grace and nodded. "She's right, you know," she told Maggie. "Our whole lives have revolved around this house."

"I understand that, girls, I do. This house has been the hub of my life for thirty years. Some of the most important times of my life began—or ended—under this roof. But I'll never move forward with my life as long as I stay here." She watched her daughters' faces as she spoke. "And it's time for me to do that."

"Do you think Daddy would understand?" Grace blew her nose, then got up to toss the tissue in the trash.

Maggie nodded. "I do. He was the last person in the world who would have held any of us back from doing something we believed in."

"Yeah, he was great about things like that." Natalie wiped away a tear of her own. "Even when I told him I was pregnant and that I'd kicked Jonathan out, but I was keeping the baby, he never questioned me. Never asked if I knew what I was doing. He just told me to be true to myself and do what I felt was right and he'd be there for me one hundred percent. And he was."

"He always said that. And think before you act because you'll have to take responsibility for your actions." Grace winced. "No small bit of irony there."

"Well, I do believe if he were here now, he'd encourage us each to live our lives and be true to ourselves." Maggie leaned back against the counter. "Don't think I haven't been hearing his words in my head these past few days."

"Mom, if you're okay with selling the house and moving back to Wyndham Beach, I'm okay with it, too. I'll miss having dinner with you on Sundays, and Daisy will miss seeing you so often, but you're right. It's your life. Your choice." Natalie tapped her fingers on the tabletop. "I remember that house. I always loved visiting Gramma in the summer."

"Me too. It was always fun," Grace agreed.

"Well, don't expect it to look much like what you remember. The new owners changed it a lot. Thank God, we can paint over most of the whiteness, which made the house seem so cold. And of course there's the addition, which changed the second floor and the kitchen. But in retrospect I kind of like the new master bedroom and the bath, and the kitchen could be fun to cook in. Once we get rid of all the white, of course."

"Mom, no offense, but you're not much of a cook," Natalie pointed out. "Dad and takeout saved us when we were growing up."

"I can't argue that your father was the real cook in the family, but I don't remember any complaints the nights I put dinner on the table. Besides, I can learn. Yesterday I ordered all Ina Garten's cookbooks. I've been watching her shows on TV," Maggie replied. "She makes everything look easy, so I'm game."

"Well, as long as you're happy, I'm happy." Natalie raised her coffee mug in a toast. "Here's to your new life, Mom. May it shine."

"I'm with Nat." Grace joined the toast, then rinsed her empty mug out under the faucet and set it aside. "So let's put that pack of sticky notes to work. Can we start in the dining room? There are a few things I'd love to have if you're not taking them with you."

"Me too. I've had my eye on that soup tureen you and Dad bought in Italy that time." Natalie led the way.

"Wait, you mean the white one with the painted flowers?" Grace followed, her voice trailing behind. "I wanted that . . ."

Maggie smiled. She'd planned on taking the tureen with her. There would no doubt be negotiations ongoing all day—and hopefully no arguments—but in the end, it would all work out just fine.

Chapter Thirteen

GRACE

"Will you be living in Wyndham Beach?" the Realtor asked Grace after they'd completed the closing on the house on Cottage Street.

"I told my mother I'd stay and help her get settled, but I have a home in Pennsylvania," Grace replied. A home she'd put on the market and was hoping to sell sooner rather than later, but no need to get into all that. And there was still that question of a job. Thank God for the rainy-day fund her father had left her.

"Well, it was good of you to stand in for her today. How lucky is she to have an attorney in the family." Barbara closed her briefcase with a snap.

"I'm not here as her lawyer, just her proxy," Grace explained. "Mom's gotten several offers on her Bryn Mawr house, and she's trying to decide among them. As soon as that house is under contract, she'll be here. Most of her furniture will be arriving today, so I'll have my hands full." She glanced at her phone for the time. "Actually, I should be getting back to the house. The movers are due in about an hour, so I need to be there."

"I will let you go then. Here are the keys." Barbara handed Grace an envelope. "And a list of contractors who worked on the house, as your mother requested, so she'll know who to call if she has any questions about any of the systems or whatever."

Grace picked up the folder of documents that she'd signed in her mother's stead. Once the FOR SALE sign on the Bryn Mawr house had been placed on the lawn, the phone had begun to ring nonstop. With the closing of the Wyndham Beach house imminent, Maggie had signed a power of attorney in order that Grace might take her place at the closing table in Massachusetts. She'd also asked Grace to oversee the arrival of the moving van. There'd be furniture to place and a number of boxes to be emptied. Since leaving her law office behind, Grace hadn't had much to do other than help her mother pack up a lifetime of possessions. It had taken several weeks, but much had been donated, much had been sold, and much had found its way to the rented storage unit Grace and Natalie were sharing. Maggie's house in Bryn Mawr was now empty—even the stager's furniture had been removed. Maggie was staying with Natalie until the house was sold and she could leave Bryn Mawr behind.

Sometimes Grace secretly thought it was just a little strange that her mother could turn her back on thirty-some years of her life and move on—or move back, depending on how you looked at Maggie's return to Wyndham Beach. She'd admitted as much to Liddy, with whom she was staying until the house was ready for her mother's arrival.

"I can't help it. I just think it's out of character for Mom to just decide on the spur of the moment to leave Bryn Mawr behind and move here," Grace had said over breakfast at Beach Fries, the new beachside café Liddy had taken her to the morning after the settlement.

"Your mother's family has very deep roots here, as you know. She grew up in that house and has a strong connection to it," Liddy reminded her. "Just as you'll always feel a pull toward the house you grew up in. Who's to say that someday you might see that house for sale and want to buy it?"

"I get that part. It just seemed so sudden. I'm a little concerned that maybe she didn't think it through all the way. Like it was just something that occurred to her, and she thought it sounded like a good idea."

Liddy laughed. "You know your mother better than that. She doesn't act on a whim when something important is at stake. I think she's missed Wyndham Beach for a long time. I'm pretty sure she's wanted to come back more often than she had over the years."

"She could have. I don't know what stopped her."

"When you and your sister were still in school, and your grandmother was still alive, the trips back here made a lot of sense. You spent most of those summers here. Once you were in college and doing summers abroad, your parents were free to travel to other places. I don't think you or Natalie have been here since your grandmother passed."

Grace frowned, trying to remember. "We haven't. At least, I haven't. But you know, we always traveled as a family," Grace reminded her. "The four of us took lots of trips together when we were kids."

"Yes, but once you two were out of the house, your mom and dad no longer had to plan their trips around school vacations. They could go anywhere, anytime they wanted."

"And they sure did. They went everywhere." Grace smiled, remembering. She never knew when she'd get a call asking her to pop in at her parents' home once or twice to bring in mail and water plants.

"It's no secret your father preferred Europe to Wyndham Beach. Not that I blame him. We don't have any grand museums or historic places to visit. We're just a small beach town here on the Massachusetts coast."

"Well, it's a charming town. In that respect, I do understand why Mom wants to come back. The house itself has changed so much, though. I hardly recognized the place. The addition has seriously tripped up my memory. Nothing looks the same." Grace took a bite of the excellent french toast.

"At least the previous owners had great taste and enough money to do the job right," Liddy said. "I'd kill for a kitchen like the one they put in. Top-of-the-line everything. It would be an absolute joy to cook in that kitchen."

The door at the front of the café opened and a tall, well-built blond man wearing jeans and a black long-sleeve T-shirt came in. His glance went from table to table, as if taking inventory. It stopped at the table where Grace sat with Liddy. A moment later, he walked toward them.

"Morning, Lydia," he said.

Liddy turned and looked up at him. "Where's your uniform, Chief?"

"I took the morning off." He smiled at Liddy, then at Grace. "Hi."

"Oh, Grace, this is our chief of police, Brett Crawford." Liddy looked up at the chief, one eyebrow raised. "Grace is Maggie Flynn's daughter."

"I thought you looked familiar," he said to Grace. "I saw you and your sister at your grandmother's funeral."

"Chief Crawford went to school with your mom and me," Liddy told her.

"There's a rumor going around that your mother bought the old Wakefield place, your grandmother's house." He leaned on the back of an empty chair that sat tucked under their table for four.

"Not a rumor," Grace said. "She closed on the house yesterday. Well, I closed for her. She's tying up some loose ends on the house she's selling in Pennsylvania."

"So she'll be moving back, then."

Close up, Grace could see silver woven through his blond hair, but even so, he was exceptionally good looking. "I'd guess within the next month or so."

"I'll be sure to stop by and see her after she gets settled. In the meantime, if you need anything, help at the house, whatever, you can call me at the police station." He straightened up.

"I'm hoping I don't need to call the police while I'm here, but thanks."

"Don't hesitate if you need to. Liddy, I'll be seeing you."

"You betcha."

After he walked to the counter to put in a takeout order, Grace turned to Liddy. "He seems nice."

"Yeah, he's a nice guy. Good police chief. He cares a lot about the community." Liddy looked as if she wanted to say something else but thought better of it.

"Well, at least I know who'll show up if I ever have to call 911." Grace finished the last few bites of her french toast. "That was delicious, Liddy. Thank you so much for recommending this place. I'll definitely be back."

"There are several really good restaurants in town. Wyndham Beach has changed over the past few years. New businesses opening up. Young families moving in. The new art center that Emma opened last year is doing very well. Stop over and see the exhibition of Jessie's work before some of the paintings are moved to the gallery in Boston in a few weeks."

"My mom told me the show is stunning and that several galleries in Boston have been vying to show her paintings. We always knew Jess had a lot of talent. I'm so glad people in other places are going to get to see her work. I will definitely go while I'm here."

Thinking about Jessie's suicide made Grace sick to her stomach. The girls had been the same age, and Jess had been Grace's best summer friend for years until their lives took them in different directions. Once out of high school, Grace had studied abroad in the summers. She tried to recall the last time she and Jessie had spent time together and couldn't. She wished she'd kept in closer touch. The fact of her suicide had hit Grace like a runaway train. She'd never known Jessie to be depressed, but then they hadn't been close in years. She knew the loss of her daughter had broken Liddy's heart. Maggie hadn't shared the details, but Grace did know that Liddy's husband left her a year after Jessie's death.

Grace and Liddy parted in front of the café, Liddy to head home after promising to stop over later to help, Grace to make a quick stop at the general store to pick up a few things for the house—eggs, bread, peanut butter, ice tea mix, and pretzels. She had a list of things she wanted to accomplish and needed to get started.

The movers placed the furniture in the dining room and the living room after putting down the oriental rugs, though Grace knew eventually everything would be moved once painters were hired. She wasn't sure where Maggie would want the wingback chairs, so she set them to flank the fireplace. Maggie had told her to pick one of the bedrooms on the second floor for herself, and she'd chosen the one in the back. It had a perfect view of not only the backyard, but the bay as well. When she opened the window, the crisp, salty air drifted in on the spring breeze, and she closed her eyes and inhaled several times before she recalled having seen her mother do exactly the same thing. She found sheets for her bed in one of the boxes, then went across the hall and made up the bed in the master bedroom. She posed herself lounging on her mother's bed, took a picture with her phone, and sent it to Maggie in a text.

You told me I could have any bedroom I wanted. I picked this one. Love the glass shower in the bathroom, btw—and that walk-in closet is the size of my first apartment! Love it! Thanks, Mom!

Minutes later, Maggie texted back, Hahahaha. Get off my bed. Xoxo

After spending that first week in Wyndham Beach, Grace began to understand why her mother was so attached to the town. She'd gotten into the habit of walking to the beach after dinner with her mug of coffee and sitting on the rocks before the sun set. She'd closed her eyes and listened to the waves roll softly onto the sand. She'd watched the small birds chase the retreating water and poke at the sand and made a mental note to buy a bird guide so she knew what they were, and so she could tell one gull from another. She'd stayed as long as her coffee lasted before heading back to the house. For the first time she could remember, every day belonged only to her. There were no demands being made, and no one to answer to, and she was determined to make the most of it.

And she had time to breathe, time to reflect on the life she'd be leaving behind if she chose to stay once Maggie was settled. She'd thought she'd miss Zach, but she found that being away from him and the close quarters of the firm had put things in perspective in a way she doubted would have happened had she stayed in Pennsylvania. Amber had been arrested but made bail and was a long way from a trial—probably years away. She knew cases like this didn't hit the docket quickly—and Grace's lawyer had told her there was still a debate about whether or not Amber'd spend time in prison even if she were to be convicted. Grace had given her statement to the FBI, grateful for the small favor of the agent being a woman who appeared more sympathetic than appalled at the purpose of the blog. Art's former partner, George, had purchased the firm and had kept most of their clients. Zach had left Center City and was working with a firm in West Chester. Grace had no second thoughts about having resigned from Flynn Law or her decision to sell the house she and Zach had bought together. The only thing she wasn't sure about was her next move, but as her mother had pointed out, she could take time to figure out what she wanted to do and where she wanted to be. May was a beautiful month in Wyndham Beach, and for now, that was where Grace wanted to be.

It wasn't long before Grace remembered why she'd loved visiting her grandmother every summer—the smell of the sea and the way the sun shone on the water. How could she have forgotten how much she'd loved this place?

Once the stress from her departure from Flynn Law eased a bit, Grace wanted to revisit her blog to offer her apologies to her followers for having gone on hiatus so suddenly, but she found that after Timothy had shut it down, the FBI had frozen it as part of the evidence against Amber. She wished she'd had a chance to let her online friends know she wished them all well.

Maggie arrived on Memorial Day weekend, bringing with her a few things she hadn't wanted to trust to the movers—her grandmother's china and her jewelry, and a few pieces of art she especially prized. She approved of everything Grace had done to make the house livable and hadn't moved so much as a vase. Liddy and Emma had been waiting for Maggie at the house, and after a tour, the three of them made their way into the backyard to inspect the flower beds, discuss where Maggie would plant what, and whether or not her mother's once-beautiful perennial beds had survived the last owners.

Once the garden planning began, Grace took herself out to the front steps. She thought about the pretty pink polish she'd picked up at the drugstore the day before. Now would be a good time to tend to those fingernails that had barely survived all the work she'd done over the past few weeks. She went inside and grabbed the drugstore bag off the kitchen counter and went back out. She'd barely gotten three nails buffed and polished when she heard someone coming across the lawn.

She looked up to see a blond guy wearing cargo shorts, a Grateful Dead T-shirt, flip-flops, aviator glasses, and a goofy grin.

"Chris?" She narrowed her eyes, squinting into the afternoon sun. "Chris Dean?"

"Gracie Flynn!" He jogged the last fifty feet. "Honest to God, I thought I was hallucinating for a minute. You look just like your mom used to look, back in the day. Well, your mom with dark hair."

"Don't you know better than to tell a woman she looks just like her mother?" Grace screwed the cap back on the polish and put the bottle on the step. "I'd think a sophisticated world traveler such as yourself would know that."

"You have me confused with that guy who calls himself DEAN. Besides, your mom was always beautiful. Like mother, like daughter." He picked her up in a bear hug. "How are you, Gracie?"

"I'm good. You?" She leaned back to look at him, and he kissed her on the forehead, a loud smacking kiss, before setting her down.

"I'm okay. Hanging in there."

Grace laughed. "Please. Don't make me admit I know you're an international superstar."

"Not when I'm in Wyndham Beach." He sat on the top step and pulled her down to sit next to him. "Here, I'm Emma's kid who grew up two streets over and spent many summer hours pulling you and your sister around in an old red wagon." He paused. "Is she here? Nat?"

Grace shook her head.

"I was hoping she'd be around. It's been a long time since I've seen her. How's she doing? Your mom showed me pictures of her little girl. She's a cutie."

"Daisy's the world's most perfect three-year-old."

"And the guy she was living with split?"

"Yeah. Jerk took off as soon as she told him she was pregnant."

He was quiet for a moment, then said softly, "Bastard."

"You have no idea, Chris."

He blew out a long breath. "Natalie deserved better. And you?" He picked up her left hand. "I thought you were married."

"Was married." She made a face.

"Your choice or his?"

"Oh, his, definitely. As in his choosing to fall in love with someone else."

"That sucks, Gracie. I'm sorry. You deserved better, too. He's obviously a fool and an asshole."

"What can I say? The Flynn sisters have shit luck when it comes to picking men."

"I don't know what's wrong with those Pennsylvania guys." He put an arm over her shoulder. "What you need is some time out with some old friends. I'm on my way to Dusty's to meet Ted for a few beers. Come with me."

"Ted . . . Teddy Affonseca? He's around?"

"Just for a few days. We try to get back home for the same few days a couple of times a year. This is one of those weekends. Come on, Gracie. He'd love to see you, I know."

"Chris . . ." She paused. "I'm not the best company right now."

"What are you talking about? You're great company." He took her hand and squeezed it. "I'm really happy to see you." He glanced at the house. "My mom's still here, right?"

"Yes. She and Liddy are out back helping my mom move some plants around. She didn't tell me you were going to be home."

"She doesn't know. I thought I'd surprise her." He stood.

"They're out back planning Mom's garden."

"Coming with me?"

"I need to finish up something. You go on around. I'll meet you here in a few."

Chris trotted around the side of the house, and Grace finished giving her nails a quick polish, waved her hands to speed up the drying, then went inside, ran upstairs, and made a quick change into shorts that weren't sandy and a tank top that didn't have coffee stains dribbled down the front. She took a minute to brush her hair and pull it back into a ponytail. She made it to the porch with a minute to spare.

"You ready?" Chris came through the front door.

"I should run back and tell my mom I'm leaving."

"I already told her."

"Was Emma surprised to see you?" she asked as she stood.

Chris grinned. "You didn't hear the screaming?" He took her arm. "Come on. Let's head into town."

"Maybe just for one beer."

"Two beers. It's not worth walking all that way for one beer."

Grace couldn't resist. She'd be lying to herself if she said she wasn't flattered that Chris wanted to spend some time with her.

On their walk to the bar, she sneaked an occasional glance at him. He was taller than she remembered, and he'd filled out a lot since the last time she saw him. His hair had been longer, shaggier when they were in their teens, but now was well trimmed, a cut she knew cost a bundle. His five-o'clock shadow gave him a rugged look his younger self hadn't had. Walking leisurely along Cottage Street, his hands in the pockets of his shorts, his eyes hidden behind his dark glasses, he could be any thirtysomething-year-old resident of Wyndham Beach out to enjoy an afternoon stroll.

Teddy was waiting for them at the bar and was obviously happy to see Grace. They exchanged condensed versions of their lives since they'd last seen each other.

"Long story short, I'm an actuary with an insurance company in Boston, married to a pediatrician, and father to three-year-old twin girls. I consider it a vacation when I get to come back here to check on my parents and spend a few hours with an old friend or two," Ted told her.

"My sister, Natalie, has a three-year-old girl as well," Grace told him.

At the mention of her sister's name, Chris said, "Let's call her. What's her number?"

She seemed to remember there'd been something between Chris and her sister during their teen years—she was never really sure what that something was—but as far as she knew, nothing ever came of it. She'd secretly hoped that Chris wanted her to come along tonight because he wanted to reconnect with her. Had that been a ploy to get Natalie's number? Nah. If all he'd wanted was Nat's number, he could have gotten it through Emma.

Chris punched Natalie's number into his phone, and Grace noticed he'd entered her as a contact, saving the number. He hit "Call" and waited. The phone rang but went to voice mail.

"She doesn't recognize the number, so she's not going to pick up," Grace told him. "Let me call on my phone." She did, and Natalie picked up right away.

"What's going on?" Nat asked. "Did you just call me from a different phone? Is everything all right? Mom's okay?"

"Everything's fine, but I ran into an old friend who wanted to say hi. Hold on." Grace put the call on speaker, then passed the phone to Chris.

"Hey! Is this the Nat in the Hat?"

There was a pause followed by a giggle. "Oh my God! Is this Pissy Chrissy?"

Chris tossed his head back and laughed. "You do know that no one has ever been allowed to call me that but you."

"A right that was well earned, lo, those many years ago." Natalie laughed. "How are you, Chris?"

"I'm great. Sitting here in Dusty's having a beer with Gracie and Ted Affonseca. Remember him?"

"Of course I do. Hiya, Ted!"

"Hiya, Natalie. Don't you wish you were here?" Ted leaned over Grace's shoulder to make sure he was heard.

"I do. You guys sound like you're having a great time. But how did you get my sister to agree to a trip to the local tavern?"

Grace frowned and rolled her eyes.

"Must be the old Dean charm," Chris said.

"I've been reading a lot about that Dean charm lately. You really do get around, don't you?" Natalie teased.

"I don't know what you've been reading, so I'll just say a man's gotta do what a man's gotta do," Chris replied good-naturedly.

"Which in your case is apparently to retreat to the nearest cliché. Got it," Natalie continued to tease Chris. "Though one would think that someone who could write songs like 'Into the Summer' and 'I Will Remember' could come up with something better than 'a man's gotta do what a man's gotta do.'"

"Hey, you caught me off guard, what can I say?" He paused, then said, "So you liked those songs?"

"Two of my favorites. Not just favorites of my favorite DEAN songs, but of my all-time favorites by anyone, any group, anywhere."

"Tell you what. We're playing in Philly next month. We don't usually do those two anymore, but if you come to the concert, I promise they will be on the set list. What do you say? I'll make all the arrangements. Transportation, tickets, backstage passes." His eyes flickered to Grace, as if remembering she was there and he was on her phone. "You and Grace." He looked directly at Grace and raised an eyebrow. "You still live near Philly, right?"

Grace hesitated. Did she still live there? Rather than answer the question, she said, "I'm in. Nat?"

"How could I turn down an offer like that? Damn right, I'm in. Thanks, Chris. I'm already looking forward to it."

His voice softened just a little. "So am I. It'll be great to see you again, Natalie. And now, I'm giving your sister her phone and buying her another beer. See what you're missing?"

"Are you coming up this weekend?" Grace asked after taking the phone off speaker.

"I wish I could, but it's the end of the semester. Professor Flynn has papers to read and grades to send out. Can I call you tonight?"

"Sure. I'm not planning on staying out too late with these two."

"Oh, you should. How long's it been since you just went out for a good time?"

"It's been a while. But I think the guys are ready for some guy talk, so I'll be heading back to Mom's."

"How's she doing? Does she seem to be adjusting to the move?"

Grace laughed. "She's already lined up painters and planned new garden beds. She's fine. Better than fine. She seems happier than she's been since before Dad died."

"That's good. I was afraid maybe she'd get up there and realize the Bryn Mawr house really was gone for good and . . ."

"Yeah, I wondered, but she really seems at peace with the decision."

"Great. Look, I'll talk to you tonight. I have to run to pick up Daisy at day care."

Grace ended the call and put her phone on the bar.

"I meant to ask her if she was going to be coming up this weekend," Chris said. "Do you know if she has plans?"

She shook her head. "Yes. She plans on working because it's the end of the semester. Papers and tests to grade. You know that she teaches in a community college, right?"

"I do. Mom keeps me up to date. Sorry to miss her this trip. Guess I'll have to wait till we can hook up in Philly."

Grace studied Chris's expression. He really *did* look sorry to be missing Natalie. *Too bad for me,* she thought, *but lucky Nat.* The rock-god thing aside, he'd sure grown up nice, as her grandmother Lloyd would have said.

Chapter Fourteen

Natalie

"Done." Natalie posted the last of the grades and breathed a sigh of relief.

The semester was over, and almost all her students did well, or at least reasonably well. There were a few standouts and a few who never did catch on, but that was to be expected in any class. Before shutting down her laptop, she reread the emails from the two recipients of the Arthur J. Flynn Merit Scholarships and smiled. Her father would have been so proud to see his dream become a reality.

The house was quiet as she checked the doors and windows and turned off the downstairs lights. She'd opted not to teach over the summer as she had in the past because she wanted to spend some time with her mother and sister in Wyndham Beach. She was in constant contact with them, usually FaceTiming with Daisy before bath and book time. It sounded like such a lazy, peaceful life they had, and she wanted to join them. Grace would be back in two days for the concert Chris had promised them, and the Flynn sisters were excited by the prospect. Grace had seen Chris in person about a month ago, but Natalie had to be content with FaceTime, and when it was Chris Dean she'd been FaceTiming with, it was pretty damned cool.

She showered and got into bed, and stacked the pillows behind her before she pulled up the light spread. She gazed out the window at the night sky, dark and dotted with stars, easily visible in the country town she lived in where there was little ambient light. She picked one and made a wish, something she wasn't sure she'd admit to, but old habits were hard to break. Earlier she and Daisy had sat on their little patio, and Daisy had recited her version of "Star Light, Star Bright," ending with a wish she could find her glowworm, which she'd been looking for all afternoon. Natalie suspected Daisy had sneaked the toy into day care and left it there. Natalie would check in the morning when she dropped her daughter off.

Natalie hadn't seen Grace since she'd left for Wyndham Beach, but she sounded so much better than she had when she'd left. Natalie still couldn't believe the shitstorm that had hit out of the blue, forcing her sister from her job and her home. She hoped Amber faced a prison sentence for her part in ruining Grace's life. Still, things were looking better for Grace right then than they were for Amber, a fact that Natalie found gratifying.

She stretched out and closed her eyes, but all she could think about was the upcoming concert and seeing Chris Dean again. It had been about twelve years since she'd seen him, and that last night they had been together had left her confused and unsettled. She had been seventeen and about to go abroad for six weeks in Italy, touring art museums with a friend from school—a combined graduation gift and early eighteenth-birthday present from her parents—and Chris had been twenty-one and about to embark on his band's first legit tour. They'd sat side by side, elbows touching, on the big rock overlooking the harbor, watching the sun set. Darkness had slowly grown around them as the lights came on in the houses across the water.

"We're just the opening-opening-*opening* act," he'd told her, "but you walk before you run, right?"

"I'm not sure what that means, exactly, but nonetheless, I am impressed."

Chris had laughed. "It means there are two other opening acts after us and before the main event. They always put the least known act on first. That would be us. But that's one of the things I've always liked about you, Nat. Everyone else just said 'Cool' when I told them. You're the only one who was interested enough to ask."

"My dad always says, 'If you don't ask, you don't learn.'"

"So it's my turn to ask. What exactly will you be doing this summer, besides fighting off all those Italian guys who'll be following you around, begging for a date?" He'd slipped into an exaggerated accent. "Ciao, bella. You are beautiful. Will you marry me?"

Natalie had laughed. "Right. I'm sure I'll be pursued by scores of Italian lovers."

"Would-be lovers," he'd said. "You're too smart to fall for a line."

"Maybe I'll want to, before I come home. Why go to Italy if you're not going to sample the local talent?"

"Natalie Flynn. We both know that would never happen."

"We *don't* know. That's the fun of a summer abroad without my parents. Maybe I'll meet someone tall, dark, and handsome, and he'll sweep me off my feet."

"Don't," he'd said with less levity than she'd expected. "If that happened, you wouldn't come back."

"And?"

"And I'm going to be thinking about you being here, in Wyndham Beach."

"Why? You won't be here. You'll be flying all over the world, with groupies begging to sleep with you, selling out arenas. Becoming an international rock star. You won't have time to think about me here or anywhere else." She'd risked a quick peek at his face, to see if she could tell what he was thinking.

"I'm hoping you're right about the international thing. Our band is so good. We deserve to make it, Nat. But the rest of that . . . the groupie thing, I'm not so sure. And I don't think there's ever going to be a time when I don't think about you."

They'd spent so much time together that summer, even their mothers had commented on it. Natalie had heard them discussing the relationship between their offspring and wondering just what it meant.

"Chris goes out with several girls, and I know Natalie has been seeing Andy Simmons this summer, but Chris seems to be spending an awful lot of time with Natalie." Emma had been sitting on her front porch with Maggie. "Not that it wouldn't make me happy to see him with Natalie. She's perfect."

Maggie had laughed. "The girl is not perfect, but I'm pleased to see them together. I think they're just friends. They go to the beach together and that sort of thing. But I don't see them dating. Nat's only seventeen and Chris is four years older."

"A good age difference," Emma had said, "but I agree, they seem to be more interested in just being friends."

And for most of the summer, they had been. Natalie would never have admitted to Chris or to anyone else—not even her best friend—that he was the only guy who attracted her in *that* way, that the crush she had on him was killing her. She liked him so much, had so much fun in his company, was so happy in his company, that she wouldn't risk ruining it with a confession that would have been humiliating because he would inevitably have told her he thought of her only as a friend.

"What do you want to do someday, Nat?" he'd asked her that last night. "After college."

"I'm not sure, but I think I might like to teach. Maybe something that would help kids to learn something important."

"You mean like special ed? Something like that?"

"Maybe. How 'bout you? If you weren't going to be a rock star, what would you do?"

"Something to do with music. Teach, maybe." He'd smiled. "So when everything falls through and I come back to Wyndham Beach, dragging my guitar behind me in defeat, maybe we both can teach here."

"There's no way you are going to fail, Chris. You are going to soar like . . ." She'd looked up at the sky, where a star shot across the night in a flash of light. "Like that shooting star. Did you see it? Quick, make a wish, and I will, too."

He'd closed his eyes. When he'd opened them, he'd asked, "What did you wish for, Nat? A summer full of Italian lovers?"

"I wished that your dream would come true. That your band would be what you hoped for."

"Aw, Nat, that's sweet. But you shouldn't have wasted your wish on me," he'd teased. "Wish something for yourself."

"That is for me. I wish for you to be happy, and that will make me happy. Besides, if you wished that, too, that's a double wish. Double wishes always come true, so it wasn't a wasted wish."

He'd turned her face to his and stared into her eyes for a long time. Finally, he'd said, "I will never forget you, Nat. And I will always remember this . . ." And then he'd kissed her. One long, slow, perfect kiss, the very one she'd dreamed of all summer, one that had left her wanting more. "I'll remember, I swear it. No matter where I go, whenever I see a shooting star, I'll think of you."

From time to time over the years, whenever she saw a shooting star, she remembered that night, and she wondered if he remembered, too.

~

"Can you believe we're actually doing this?" Natalie opened her front door when she saw Grace's car pull up. They hugged quickly before Natalie closed the door behind them. "Going to a rock concert together. And not any concert."

"Honestly, I almost thought he wouldn't come through with all this, but he did." Grace went straight to the hall mirror and checked her makeup and her hair, which she wore in a very high ponytail, one that matched her sister's. "Oh God, do we look like the Flynn twins or what?"

Natalie laughed. They'd both worn jeans, ankle boots, and long silver earrings. They wore the matching T-shirts Chris had sent them, with his face in the center and the date and venue under his likeness.

"It's too late to change." Natalie pointed out the window to the street, where a long white car had stopped. "Let me run in the kitchen and kiss Daisy good night. I was lucky to get her favorite sitter for the night, so she doesn't care that I'm leaving."

"Tell Daisy I'll see her in the morning," Grace said as she dashed out the door.

Natalie hadn't been exaggerating. Daisy barely lifted her head for a goodbye kiss. The babysitter had brought a bag of finger puppets, and they were busy telling a story.

Natalie and Grace sat in the back seat of the limo, holding hands and giggling like schoolgirls.

"Do you have your backstage pass?" Grace asked.

"Are you kidding?" Natalie laughed. "I've been sleeping with it so I wouldn't lose it."

"Me too. I've never been backstage after a concert. I read it's wild."

"I don't know. It's hard for me to think of Chris as wild," Natalie said.

"I can. Remember, I saw him not too long ago. Went drinking with him. The guy's a stud, Nat. Why he'd be excited about having two of his childhood friends at his concert is beyond me."

"What makes you think he's excited?"

"I was there when you two were on the phone, talking about it. I saw the look on his face after he passed the phone back to me." Grace narrowed her eyes. "Are you sure there wasn't something going on between you and Chris back then?"

"Nothing really. I mean, we were friends. Close friends for a while." Natalie shrugged. "I don't think it would ever have been more than that. Oh, look." She changed the subject adroitly. "Is that a cooler of drinks for us?" She switched her seat and opened the cooler. "OMG. Champagne!"

She slid up to the panel separating the passengers from the driver and moved the glass to one side.

"Excuse me."

The driver's eyes reflected in the rearview mirror. "Miss?"

"There's a bottle of champagne back here, and we were wondering . . ."

"Oh, yes, miss. That's for you. There are glasses in there, too." He smiled. "Just please close the panel before you pop the cork."

"Will do." She turned to her sister. "It's for us. Let's open it."

Grace grabbed the bottle. "You don't have to tell me twice."

The bottle opened and the drinks poured, they toasted each other and their luck in sharing such a fun adventure.

"When was the last time we went out together to have a good time?" Natalie sank back into the seat and sipped her champagne.

"Before I was married. Back when we were in college. One of those weekends you were home from Penn State and came down to see me at Delaware." Grace appeared to be debating whether to pour another drink.

"Your sorority had some epic parties."

"We did."

The sound of a horn blowing got their attention. Their driver had cut off another car on Broad Street and was now apologizing for it.

"Oh, we're here." Natalie drained her glass and put it back into the cooler as the limo rounded a corner and crept slowly behind the Wells Fargo Center. "You don't happen to have a Taser, a torch, fireworks, or brass knuckles on you, do you?"

"What?" Grace stared at Natalie.

"How 'bout a box cutter? A drone? Skateboard?"

"Are you crazy? What are you talking about?"

Natalie laughed. "Chris sent me a list of all the things that are prohibited at the arena. Those were just a few items on the no-no list."

"Good to know. Nope. No contraband."

"Ladies, I'll be stopping by a door up here soon. You're going to wait until I open your door before you get out, okay?"

"Sure." Natalie nodded and grinned at her sister. They were here. After so many years, she'd see her old friend again. Her long-ago wish for him had come true, and she couldn't be happier.

They were escorted to their seats—front row center, same location their mother had occupied with her friends some months ago—and soaked up the excitement of the crowd.

"I love listening to music at home and in the car, but boy, nothing is like being on the floor during a live concert," Natalie said over the rumble of voices surrounding them.

There were two opening acts: the first, one Natalie had never heard of; the second, an up-and-coming singer she'd seen on one of the late-night shows. And then the lights went down, pyrotechnics went off on the stage, and Chris appeared, looking so much like the lead singer of a world-famous rock band that Natalie had tears in her eyes. The boy from the small town few people had heard of, who'd had such a huge dream, had made it come true. It really was a Cinderella story. He glanced down into the crowd and winked. She was hoping it was for her, but there were so many screaming women around her she couldn't be sure. Grace had told her he'd been dating a Brazilian model for months. Natalie looked around but didn't see anyone who looked like a Brazilian model, but you never knew.

Still, Natalie smiled when the band began to play all the songs she'd listened to and knew by heart. She sang along with the crowd as it sang along with the band and danced with Grace in the space between their seats and the stage.

After a long version of "If You See Me," Chris stood alone at the front of the stage, the microphone in his hand, and motioned for the crowd to quiet down. When finally the cheers and applause faded, he took a few steps closer to the audience.

"You all know I like to stop about halfway through the show for a little story time. So settle down, boys and girls. This is a story I've never told anyone before and may never tell again. But tonight is special, so here goes." He paused, the crowd in expectant silence. "A long time ago I had a friend. We only saw each other in the summers, but every summer, we'd spend time together. Mostly talking. I was a little older, and I never wanted to take advantage of that, because she was a very special friend. A very special girl." There were a few hoots from the crowd, and Chris stopped for a moment, smiled. "The last time I saw her, we were sitting on a big rock on the beach down the road from her house, and it was growing dark. The stars were coming out overhead, and it was a perfect night. She was leaving the next day, and we knew we wouldn't be together there again for a long, long time. But we're sitting there, and I'm teasing her about something, and we look up and there's a shooting star going right across the sky, and she said, 'Make a wish.' And we did. Turns out we both wished for the same thing, and that wish came true. But I remember, and I wrote this . . ."

He turned and gestured to the band, and the music began. "We've never done this song before in public. It's called 'Shooting Star.'"

"Natalie, he's talking about you." Grace elbowed her. "What the hell's he referring to?"

Natalie couldn't respond. She stood stock-still, staring up at the stage, seeing only Chris. He really had remembered. He'd promised he would, and he had. She barely heard the words of the song, but she knew it was about that night, about watching the sky together and sharing their dreams and that one perfect kiss. The rest of the concert went by in a blur, and before they knew it, they were ushered back to the band's dressing room, where Chris gathered her in a bear hug and kissed her face.

"You really did remember," she said when her feet finally touched the ground.

Chris nodded, but he didn't let go. "A double wish has to come true."

"Hello? Remember me? Grace? The big sister?" Grace waved to Natalie.

Chris laughed and hugged Grace. "How lucky am I to have both the Flynn girls here? You two are gorgeous. I think I'm in love with you both."

Chris introduced them to the other members of his band, several celebrities who'd flown to Philly for the show, and a number of local professional athletes, careful all the while to keep Natalie at his side and Grace in his sight. But before they knew it, Chris had a plane to catch, and the limo driver who'd brought Natalie and Grace arrived to take them home.

"This summer, right?" Chris had whispered to Natalie when he hugged her goodbye. "You'll be back this summer?"

"I'll be at my mom's for a while, yes." She'd leaned back to look into his eyes, and she was seventeen all over again.

"You let me know when, and I'll be there. I'll take time off." He smiled, and she could see the boy he'd been. The boy who'd grown into this man who still had the same effect on her as he'd had when she was a girl. "You should know, you've stayed in my head all these years. I think we need to figure out why."

Natalie had nodded, too overcome to tell him he was still in her head as well. But this time when she left, she knew she'd see him again. This time, she wasn't seventeen, and he was no longer too old for her.

The last thing he said to her was, "I'll be in touch."

~

Their driver had pressed an unopened bottle of champagne on them as they were getting out of the limo the night before ("From the boss"), so after Natalie took Daisy to day care in the morning, she and Grace had mimosas along with the omelets Grace made. They relived the night before and laughed at how little it had taken for them to act like teenagers again, singing and dancing in the area between their seats and the stage.

"It probably looked better on the teens and the girls who were in their early twenties than it did on my thirty-two years, but honestly, I can't remember the last time I had that much fun," Grace declared when she'd finished eating.

"Me either. And the concert was amazing. The band is everything Chris always wanted it to be."

"Oh, really? And how would we know that, missy?"

"You heard him last night. We were good friends that last summer. We talked a lot. Life. Our goals."

"Sounded to me like you guys were doing more than talking."

"He kissed me one time. That last night."

"Must have been a wowzer of a kiss for him to remember it for, what? Ten years?"

"Twelve, but who's counting?" Natalie got up and cleared the table. "But to set the record straight, it was a double-wowzer."

"Huh. You and Chris Dean." Grace grinned. "He'd not be a good bet these days, though."

"What do you mean?"

"He's a player, Nat. He dates A-list celebrities. I see his picture in *People* with someone different every other week."

Natalie shrugged. "It's not like there's anything but friendship between us."

"You can call it whatever you want, but he not only remembered kissing you, he wrote a freaking song about it."

"I think what he remembered was the fact I believed in him back then. And back then, it was probably only me and Emma who did. Remember how his father treated him so badly because Chris didn't want to go to Harvard and become a banker?"

"Not really. I wasn't around that summer at all. I interned at Dad's office and only came to Wyndham Beach for Memorial Day and Labor Day weekends."

"Mr. Dean was just awful. It was like he was embarrassed to have a son who believed he could make a living making music. A couple times that summer, I heard Mom and his mom talking about it, how she—Emma—was stuck between her husband and her son, and it was tearing her apart. I think that's why Chris decided to take his band on the road, to get out of the house. He was hoping his father would let up on his mother if he was gone, but I don't think he did." Natalie paused. "And then a few years later, Mr. Dean had a heart attack and died. Mom said Chris and Emma both blamed themselves, but Mom said he'd had a heart condition for years."

Natalie poured herself a second cup of coffee, scooted back to her place on the banquette, positioned a pillow behind her, and settled in.

"Have you made a decision yet about the house? Keeping it? Selling it?"

"I'm going to sell it. I don't want to live there again. It represents a time in my life when I was happy and settled and knew who I was and who Zach was. We were a team there."

"I don't think Zach was much of a team player, Gracie," Natalie said as tactfully as she could. "I think he played for himself."

"You're right. But back then, it didn't feel that way. Whatever he was scheming, I never saw it." She forced a smile. "Love really is blind, kiddo."

"If it were me, I could never be happy in that place again."

219

"I sure wasn't happy there after Zach left. Which is why I started that stupid blog to begin with."

"I don't think the blog was stupid at all. I told you, I think it was a brilliant way to deal with a painful situation."

"Thanks. I appreciate that. But yeah. The house is going." Grace stood.

"Are you considering staying in Wyndham Beach?"

"I honestly don't know. I don't think I'd mind it, though. There's something so peaceful and easy about being there. Life is slower than it is in the city. Of course, then I run the risk of being the unemployed, thirty-two-year-old woman living with her mother."

"You could get a job," Natalie suggested.

"I'm still thinking about what I want to do. But right now I'm going to head out. Thanks for hanging out with me last night and for letting me stay."

"You're always welcome here. Anytime." Natalie walked her sister to the front door, where Grace had left her overnight bag. "Next time you need to teach me how to make a killer omelet like the one you made this morning."

"Aw, you make me almost sorry for all those times when I was so mean to you when we were kids." Grace picked up her bag, then turned to hug her sister. "Almost."

Natalie laughed. "Stay well, you. Drive safely."

She stood in the doorway and watched Grace drive away. When the car disappeared around the corner, Natalie closed the door and went into the kitchen to clean up from breakfast. Then she carried in her laptop and set it on the table. She checked email—so few since school ended for the semester. One student who wanted to argue his grade, another who thanked her for helping him improve his listening and reading skills. One from Glenn Patton, asking if she'd like to go with him to the Mann Center on Sunday afternoon for a concert. And one from Joe Miller, her would-be half brother. She clicked on his email and began to read.

> Natalie,
>
> Well, I haven't heard back from you, so I'm assuming you have decided not to be in contact with me. I understand, and it's okay. I do have something exciting to share with you, though, before I disappear from your life (unless you change your mind someday). I have been in contact with my birth father. I spoke with him over the weekend. We will be getting together sometime soon, and I am beyond happy. Nervous, but happy. I hope you're happy for me. He told me I have not one, not two, but three younger sisters! Mind blown!
>
> I'm still hopeful that one day things might work out that I could meet you, too. A guy can't have too many sisters.

"Wait, what?"

Confused, Natalie read the email again. "That's impossible. Dad's been gone for two years."

And then she noticed the PS several lines below Joe's name.

> By the way, the genealogical site has identified several second and third cousins. Do you know a Polly Wakefield Drummond? Or a Claire Lloyd Anderson?

Natalie slumped back against the pillows.

"Holy shit."

Chapter Fifteen

MAGGIE

"I think I want to move some of the iris over by the garage," Maggie told Liddy. "I think the purple flowers against the weathered gray wood will be stunning."

"Okay. Let me get a shovel." Liddy sat on the bottom step of the deck, looking over the array of garden tools Maggie had laid upon the grass.

"We'll use the new spade. It's the one with the blue handle." Maggie pointed to the tool, and Liddy held it up. "Yes, that one."

Liddy handed over the spade and Maggie proceeded to dig up the clumps that had sat neglected under the shade of a forsythia that had been permitted to grow wild and unchecked. Earlier that morning, she'd pruned the shrubs to a more manageable size and shape, and it was then she'd discovered the iris.

"These must have been my mom's," Maggie said as she dug. "She used to have a patch of them. She loved iris. And I see they've done their thing and multiplied. There must be fifty or sixty plants out here."

"Well, since it appears the previous owners didn't do much gardening, they probably were your mother's. I know iris can hang on for a long time even under poor conditions. But they'll be happier over there in the sun."

"I'll have to divide these clumps before I can replant them." Maggie wiped the sweat from her forehead with her forearm.

"Want me to dig a bed next to the garage so all you have to do is drop in the tubers?"

"That would be great, Lid, but you don't have to. You can sit and watch." Maggie knew there was no way in hell Liddy would sit in the shade and watch Maggie work.

"What, and miss an opportunity to tell everyone how you worked me like a dog? Ha. Not a chance." Liddy picked up a shovel. "I think the iris should go right here." She pointed to a short stretch of ground along the side of the garage.

"Perfect." Maggie began to divide the clumps.

"Where's Grace this afternoon?" Liddy dug in and turned over a shovelful of dirt.

"She went into town to pick up some things from the general store and the wine shop. Natalie and Daisy will be here tomorrow afternoon, so we're planning a reunion dinner." Maggie smiled at the thought of seeing her daughter and her granddaughter again.

"How long are they staying?" Liddy bent down and shook dirt from a clump of grass, then resumed digging.

"Natalie wasn't sure. I told her I'd love to have them, but if she wanted to leave and then come back, she was welcome to do so. Whatever fits her schedule."

Liddy knelt to remove some weeds, and Maggie stood watching her.

"What?" Liddy asked without turning around.

"What *what*?"

"What is it you're not saying?" Liddy stood and leaned on the shovel. "I can feel your eyes on my back, and it's spooky. Out with it."

Maggie sighed. "It could just be me. But I got this strange feeling from Nat last night on the phone. Like there was something she wasn't saying."

"Maybe she has a new boyfriend," Liddy suggested. "Maybe she's running off with Chris and wants you to know before the tabloids get their hands on the story."

Maggie laughed. "That's not likely to happen. Not that I'd mind." She knelt and began to pull apart the iris tubers. "It's probably nothing. I know she's been busy with the end of classes."

"It's a busy time of the year." Liddy resumed digging. "Did you hear old Mr. Lattimore is retiring?"

"Fred Lattimore, who owns the bookstore?"

"Yep. Word is his son wants him to sell it."

Maggie paused her work. "I hope that's just a rumor without substance. We'd have no bookstore in town. Unless someone buys it." She considered the loss to the community. Grace stopped in at least twice a week for a new book or magazine, and Maggie often accompanied her. "What are the chances someone will buy it?"

"Pretty damned good."

"What have you heard?" Maggie stretched. She hadn't realized how out of shape she was. Time to get back to yoga. And maybe running, as she'd talked about doing. She should call Dee Olson, get some tips on training. *Run a marathon* was still on the list.

"I heard a certain woman with whom you are quite friendly—one might even say a BFF—is looking into the possibility," Liddy said, her tone a tease.

"What? When would Emma have time to . . . ?" Maggie stopped and stared at Liddy's back.

"Turn around."

When she did, Liddy was grinning.

"Liddy? You're thinking about buying the bookstore?"

"Fred's son and I had a long chat yesterday afternoon. You know Fred is in his eighties, and he's showing signs of Alzheimer's. Carl—that's Fred's son, I don't know if you ever met him, but he runs the hardware store—he said Fred's becoming increasingly forgetful. Some days he forgets to open the store, so whoever is working that morning has to call Carl to come and unlock it. Other days, he forgets to lock up when he leaves. Or he forgets to leave. Carl said he's had to run down there some nights at ten or eleven o'clock to pick him up. And a couple of nights, Brett has found him wandering around town late. He's brought him to Carl's several times."

"That makes me so sad. I remember Mr. Lattimore always being in the store in the summers when Mom and I would take the girls for story hour. What a shame." She brushed the dirt from off the back of her shorts and motioned for Liddy to follow her to the deck. "Hold that thought. I'm going to run in and get some drinks. Stay right there."

She dashed into the kitchen, grabbed two glasses and a pitcher of ice tea, and took it all outside. Liddy held the door for her, and they sat at the round black iron glass-topped table Maggie had brought with her from her Bryn Mawr house.

"Talk," Maggie said as she poured tea. "Tell me what you're thinking."

"I'm thinking I should be doing something with my life besides feeling sorry for myself. I've always loved that store. I used to take Jessie there every week to pick out a book. I spend so much time in that place I might as well buy it." With a forefinger, Liddy traced the condensed drips of water that ran down the side of the glass. "I want to do something useful. And I don't want Wyndham Beach to be without a bookstore. It's too important for the town."

"Can't argue with that. You'd be a great bookseller. You know books, that's for sure. Yes, I could see you owning that store, Lids."

"Thanks. I told Carl to call me after he decides how much they want for it. They own the building, but he's not sure he wants to sell it. Maybe just rent the space. He's going to talk to their lawyer and get back to me."

"Well, if it wasn't so hot, I'd suggest we toast this bit of news with wine, but I know I'd fall flat on my face after just one glass." She raised her ice tea and tilted it in Liddy's direction. "So let's drink to this new venture."

"Possible venture."

"This new possible venture, and we'll cross our fingers and hope for the best."

"And now, I suggest we get those iris in the ground," Liddy said after she drained her glass. "Otherwise, when I tell the story about how I had to redo your garden for you, I might have to admit to being complicit in killing off your mother's iris."

~

Maggie spent the evening preparing for Natalie and Daisy's arrival the next day. The guest room across the hall from Maggie's was fluffed, with a vase of fresh daisies set upon the dresser. Thinking ahead to visits from her granddaughter, Maggie had ordered a double bed for Natalie with a trundle bed that pulled out from underneath so Daisy would have her own special place to sleep. When she got older, Daisy could have her own bedroom. The list Maggie had given Grace to take to the general store included some of Natalie's and Daisy's favorite foods, and several bottles of wine the three adults could enjoy. She was so excited when the car pulled into the driveway a little after four, she raced outside and flung open the rear passenger door to greet Daisy in her car seat.

"Sweet pea! I've missed you!" She swooped in and kissed the little girl's face. "Hi, Nat! I'm so glad you're here!"

"I missed you, Nana." Daisy struggled to release her seat belt.

"Hold up, baby. Let me get that." Maggie tried but once again was foiled by the intricacies of the car seat.

"I'll do it, Mom." Natalie got out of the car and walked around.

"It's different from the one she had before," Maggie noted.

"Yeah, well, she's growing." Natalie proceeded to help Daisy out of her seat with ease.

The first clue Maggie picked up was the cool tone of Natalie's voice. The second was the realization that her daughter hadn't greeted her with a hug. The third? A refusal to meet Maggie's eyes.

"Nat? What's wrong?" Maggie took a step back.

"We can talk about it later." Natalie went around to the back of her car to retrieve their bags.

"Here, let me help you." Maggie reached to help but Natalie stepped aside.

"I've got them, Mom."

"Mommy, where's the beach?" Daisy stood in the driveway, looking around. "You said there was a beach at Nana's new house."

"We'll go see it as soon as we get our things inside." Natalie started up the walk to the front porch. "Come on, Daisy."

Daisy reached her hand to Maggie, who gave it a little squeeze. Whatever had gotten under Natalie's skin apparently hadn't been shared with her daughter.

Daisy chatted away, accompanying Maggie into the kitchen for a snack. Seated on a booster seat at the island, Daisy drank a glass of milk and ate a freshly baked oatmeal cookie while she told Maggie all about the ride and how she kept asking when they'd be here and how far was the beach and was Nana going to get a dog or maybe a cat now that she lived here and could she see the backyard and was there a swing set . . .

"Daisy, you're making my head spin." Maggie laughed. "Let's do one question at a time."

But before Daisy could resume, Natalie came into the kitchen.

"What are you eating?" She peered into her daughter's hand. "You know you're not supposed to snack before dinner."

Before Natalie could take the cookie, Daisy shoved the remains into her mouth. Her "Nana gave it to me" was barely discernable.

"Mom, we don't snack between meals. You know that." Natalie was clearly annoyed, but she did not look her mother in the eye. "Finish your milk, Daisy. We're going for a walk."

Natalie stood next to Daisy's chair and watched her daughter empty the glass. "Good. Let's go." She helped Daisy out of the seat and stood her on the floor. Without looking at Maggie, she asked, "Where's Grace?"

"She ran into town to pick up some things for dinner," Maggie said softly. "Natalie, what is your problem?"

"Later." Natalie dismissed her mother and started toward the front door. "When she gets back, tell her we went to the beach."

"Natalie, you're being very rude." Maggie could barely keep the hurt from her voice.

"Sorry," Natalie said, still on her way to the door.

"You're not acting very sorry." Maggie followed them to the foyer, her arms crossed over her chest. "And it's not like you to be secretive."

Natalie turned, her eyes blazing with anger. "Then that would make two of us."

"What?"

A confused Maggie watched Natalie and Daisy walk toward the beach.

She went out onto the porch and relived every conversation she and Natalie had had over the past few weeks, but there'd been nothing—*nothing*—she could point to. There'd been no arguments, no cross words. On the contrary, they were both looking forward to this visit and the opportunity to spend some fun time together.

Baffled, Maggie was still standing on the steps, staring in the direction of the beach, when Grace pulled into the driveway and parked behind Natalie's car. She opened the rear passenger door and took out a shopping bag and hurried toward the house.

"Yay! Nat and Daisy are here! Are they inside?"

Maggie gestured. "Your sister took Daisy to the beach."

"I'll run down and join them as soon as I get this stuff into the house." Grace hoisted the bag onto her hip and went inside. When she came back out, she said, "I couldn't get the wine you wanted, but I did find a really nice . . ." She fell silent, apparently noticing her mother's demeanor.

"Mom, are you all right?"

"I was until your sister got here." Maggie turned to Grace. "I don't know what I did to make her angry. I've never seen her like this."

"What are you talking about?"

"I'm talking about Natalie. She's being . . . obnoxious. Rude." She made no effort to disguise the hurt.

"That's so not like her. No hint why?"

Maggie shook her head. "I asked her, and she just said 'later.' Which I guess means after Daisy goes to sleep. She didn't mention anything to you?"

"No. The last time I talked to her, she was excited about coming and spending some time with us. What the hell could have happened between then and now?"

"I have no idea."

"Look, I'll get the rest of the stuff out of the car, then I'll walk down to the beach and see if I can figure out what's going on." Grace gave her mother a hug. "She's probably in a snit over something that has nothing to do with you, Mom. Not that she should take it out on you, but we'll get to the bottom of it and help her get through it, and all will be well."

"I hope you're right."

Maggie helped Grace bring the groceries into the house, then unloaded the bags while Grace went to join Natalie and Daisy on the beach. She began to organize dinner—steaks to go on the grill, a big salad, oven-roasted potato wedges, and fresh green beans. She'd finished the salad, cut the potatoes and tossed them in olive oil and herbs, and trimmed the green beans, and her daughters still hadn't returned. *Well, maybe Natalie needed to unload to her sister,* she thought as she opened a box of crackers and arranged them on a platter. *I guess that's what sisters are for.*

Suddenly feeling very sorry for herself that she and Sarah never had those moments to share as adults, she poured a glass of wine and let the melancholy roll through her before tossing it off and reminding herself she had nothing to feel sad about. Her daughters were both here with her—Natalie's snit aside—and her one and only grandchild was here, and they were all healthy and reasonably happy.

That had been her last thought before Natalie, Grace, and Daisy came in through the front door and one of them went dashing up the stairs to the second floor.

"Was that Grace I saw running upstairs?" Maggie asked when Natalie followed Daisy into the kitchen.

"Well, there are only two of us, and I'm here, so good guess." Natalie walked past her mother and went straight to the island, where Maggie had set out the wine goblets. Pouring herself a glass of merlot, she took a long sip.

"Excuse me?" Maggie set her glass on the counter. "Are you speaking to me in that tone?"

Natalie made a pretense of looking around the room as if searching for someone else. "Do you see anyone else?"

"What in the name of God is going on with you?"

"I don't feel like talking about it right now." Natalie helped Daisy onto one of the island's barstools.

"And I don't feel like being the target of your rudeness. Whatever it is that's gotten under your skin, we can talk it over, Nat."

"Maybe we should have had that talk long ago, Mom." Natalie opened the refrigerator, took out a block of cheese, and began to thinly slice it. She added the cheese, piece by piece, onto the platter where Maggie had placed the crackers.

"If you're going to keep poking at me, you might as well just come out and say whatever is on your mind."

Natalie raised an eyebrow but didn't comment.

"Natalie, I have no idea what this is about."

"Oh, really? You can't think of one thing . . ." She bit her lip and went silent.

"Nana, can I put the grapes on the plate with the cheese?" Daisy knelt on the seat and, leaning on the island, reached for the bowl of fruit, her little hands hovering over the cluster of green grapes.

"Of course, sweetie. Thank you for being such a good helper girl."

Oblivious to the drama around her, Daisy beamed and nodded. "I am a good helper. I help Miss Julie at school every day."

Maggie leaned next to Daisy and ran a hand over the girl's head. "I'm sure you do."

To Natalie, she said, "No, I cannot think of one thing that would excuse your behavior. Now go upstairs and get your sister, and let's get dinner on the table. See if we can get through a meal without you biting my head off."

Natalie put her glass down with more force than necessary, left the room, and stomped up the steps to the second floor.

Maggie took a deep breath and turned her attention to her granddaughter. "Are you hungry, Daisy?"

"I am very hungry, Nana." Daisy picked the grapes off their stems one by one and put them onto the cheese plate, chatting away about the beach and the birds they saw and the shells she found.

All the while, Maggie fought off the feeling of dread that something terrible was about to happen, but she was at a loss to understand what, or why.

Grace and Natalie came downstairs looking very much like conspirators, Natalie's jaw set and Grace's eyes rimmed in red. Maggie decided to let it ride for the time being. Her daughters took their glasses and a bottle of wine and the cheese platter out to the deck, leaving Maggie to prepare dinner on her own, which she normally wouldn't have minded. But she had the sense their turning their backs on her was a joint protest, and she was already weary of trying to figure out what was at the bottom of it. She slipped a CD into the player on the counter and filled the room with music, dancing with Daisy between putting the potatoes in the oven and getting the steaks ready to grill. For a few moments, she forgot about Natalie and whatever it was that had her in such a mood.

When dinner was ready, Maggie sent Daisy out to the deck to bring the others to the table. A minute later, Daisy came back inside and announced her mommy and Aunt Gracie wanted to eat on the deck.

"Well, then, go tell your mommy and your aunt Grace they can set the table out there."

Maggie got out the plates, salad bowls, flatware, and napkins and placed them on the counter. She arranged the potatoes and steaks on serving platters and slid the green beans into a bowl. When Natalie, Grace, and Daisy came in, she merely pointed to the items that had to be carried outside. They each grabbed what they could, and moments later they were seated at the round table. Maggie's hopes for a fun, carefree, lively dinner together disappeared the second she realized not only was Natalie avoiding addressing or even looking at her, but Grace had adopted her sister's attitude. Only Daisy's constant chatter kept the meal from being more like a wake than a family dinner.

"Daisy, I think it's time to start getting you ready for bed," Natalie announced as soon as she'd finished eating.

"I didn't have ice cream. Nana said I could have ice cream if I ate my beans." Daisy pointed to the empty spot on her plate, where several green beans had been lined up earlier.

"Well, Nana doesn't get to decide," Natalie said sharply. "Mom, I'd appreciate it if you left it to me to decide what she can eat and when."

Too angry and hurt to speak, Maggie nodded without looking at her daughter and bit back her words. She and Natalie were going to have this out tonight, but not in front of Daisy.

Natalie helped a pouting Daisy from her chair.

"But Nana said—"

"Nana isn't Mommy," Natalie snapped.

"Mommy, you talked mean to me and to Nana. You should say you're sorry." Daisy's bottom lip quivered.

"I'm sorry. Now let's go upstairs and get your bath." Natalie took Daisy's hand and led her through the back door to the kitchen.

Maggie turned to say something to Grace, but Grace was following Natalie into the house.

"Shame on me for having raised such brats," Maggie grumbled. "And shame on me for not realizing it until now."

Maggie cleared the table, stacked the dishwasher, washed the pots and pans, and cleaned off the grill. She tried to get her emotions under control, but the anger inside her burned like hot coals, and the hurt had pierced her heart. She'd devoted so much of her life to raising her daughters, and now they'd both seemingly turned against her without explanation.

Well, she mused as she polished off the last bit of wine in the bottle, *for better or for worse, that's probably going to change within the hour.*

She took her wine outside onto the deck, where she watched the sun drop into the harbor, determined not to give in to the feeling of dread that had engulfed her. She'd just closed her eyes and tried to think soothing thoughts when Natalie opened the door and said briskly, "Mom, would you come in here, please?"

As if facing her executioner, Maggie rose and went into the kitchen.

"Sword or ax?" She glanced from one daughter to the other.

"Funny, Mom." Natalie gestured to the barstools.

"Mom, won't you join us?" Maggie quipped sarcastically in her most saccharine voice. "Why, of course. I always enjoy spending time with my loving daughters."

Natalie sighed heavily. "You're not funny, and you're not making this easier. Mom, do you know someone named Polly Wakefield?"

"Sure. She's my mom's aunt," Maggie said.

"How 'bout Claire Lloyd?" Natalie tossed out the name.

"She's my mom's cousin. My second cousin, I guess." Maggie grew more confused by the second. "But what do either of them have to do with anything?"

Natalie went to her bag and pulled out several sheets of paper. "These are emails I received over the past few months. I think you should read them."

Mystified, Maggie grabbed her glasses from the counter, where she'd left them, and slid them on as she took a seat. Natalie handed her the papers, and Maggie began to read.

Time stood still as she attempted to understand what she was reading. She read the first printed page with her mouth open, one hand on her heart as if trying to keep it from leaving her chest.

> My name is Joe Miller and I think I'm your half brother. Actually, according to the DNA results, I'm pretty positive I am.

"Oh. Oh . . . oh . . . ," Maggie whispered, too stunned to speak beyond that one simple word.

Tears fell from her eyes, rolling down her face in a steady stream to leave their mark on the pristine sheets of paper, a mixture of pain and joy at odds within her.

Caught completely off guard, she was oblivious to the presence of her daughters and the fact that their discovery of her deepest secret had driven a wedge between them. For a moment, knowing her son—her son!—was reaching out was more than she could process.

"Joe. His name is Joe," she whispered.

Maggie'd never given him a name. In her heart, he'd always simply been *my baby boy*. She'd believed naming him would be the prerogative of someone else, but seeing his name in print, saying it aloud . . . somehow it sounded right to her. *Joe. Joseph.*

"Mom? Oh my God, Mom. I'm sorry. I'm sorry." Apparently realizing the anguish her actions had caused, Natalie reached for the emails to take them back. "I didn't think. I didn't know. I didn't . . ."

Maggie held the pages she'd read in one shaking hand, out of Natalie's reach. Then, sobbing, she read through to the last page.

"Mom, please . . . I'm so sorry." Natalie began to cry. Grace observed both her mother and her sister as if watching a play.

> I have been in contact with my father. I spoke with him over the weekend. We will be getting together sometime soon, and I am beyond happy.

Maggie felt she'd been struck by lightning.

"What?" she yelled, the tears forgotten. "He . . . what? He *knows*? Son of a bitch."

Natalie and Grace both jumped, obviously jarred by their mother's curse.

"Who knows what?" Natalie dabbed at her face with a tissue.

Maggie slammed the handful of paper onto the counter and hopped off the stool. "When I get my hands on him . . ."

She grabbed a handful of tissues and paused to wipe off her face before tossing them into the trash, then headed out the front door, her bag over her shoulder, cursing under her breath every step of the way.

"Wait, Mom!" Natalie raced to catch up.

"Not now, Natalie." Maggie was already out the door and halfway to the sidewalk and showed no sign of slowing down, muttering all the way down Cottage Street. "Brett Crawford, you have a lot to answer for . . ."

~

Maggie stormed into the municipal building as if she were being chased by a demon, which in a sense she was. She forced some semblance of control as she rounded the hall toward police headquarters and took a deep breath as she opened the glass door and approached the receptionist.

"Hey, Maggie. What's up?" Coraline Webster asked as she hung up from a call.

"I'd like to see Br . . . the chief. Is he still here?"

"I think he's still here. Let me check." Coraline hit a button on her phone and, seconds later, said, "Chief, Maggie Flynn is here to see you. Sure." She hung up and glanced at Maggie, clearly curious. "He said go on back." Turning to point to the left, she added, "The chief's office is—"

"I'll find it." Maggie headed toward Brett's office, her anger boiling over. When she saw Brett standing in his office doorway, leaning against the jamb as if he hadn't a care in the world, as if this were a social visit he'd been expecting, she almost blew.

"Inside and close the damned door," she growled as she drew near him.

He took a step backward, his eyes widening, a look of confusion on his face. He stepped aside for her to enter, then did as she'd demanded. He closed the door softly.

He opened his mouth to speak, but she cut him off.

"Joseph Miller." She threw the name at him in a fast volley.

Brett stared at her, his face blank.

Maggie moved closer and repeated the name, more slowly this time. "Joseph. Miller."

Brett continued to stare, obviously caught off guard.

"Do I have to say it again?"

"Ahhh . . . ," he finally said after clearing his throat.

"How long have you known?"

"Known what? That I had a son?" He sat on the edge of his desk, his expression no longer confused, his eyes no longer defensive. It appeared

Brett had gone on the offensive. "That's something you've never let me forget."

"How long have you known?" She ignored his attempt to put her on the ropes. This was her showdown.

He walked around the desk and sat on the worn brown leather seat. "He contacted me about a month ago. He's been looking for—"

"A month ago?" She leaned on the back of the guest chair, too amped up to sit. "When were you going to tell me?"

"I've been trying to let you know he's been looking for us for months, but every damned time I tried to talk to you, you blew me off."

"How did he know . . . how did he find you?" She was embarrassed she couldn't get her thoughts out in a coherent fashion, but she was angry and confused.

"He'd done that DNA testing thing on one of those genealogical sites, and they showed a match to my sister, Jayne, who'd joined the same site. He contacted her at the end of last summer, since she was identified as an aunt. Jayne and I are the only children in our family, so it wasn't hard for her to figure out whose son he was. I tried to tell you at the reunion he was making inquiries, but you kept walking away from me. I wanted to give you a heads-up, but I couldn't make you listen."

"You could have called me."

"If you wouldn't listen to me when I was standing right in front of you, why would I think you'd have picked up my call?"

He paused, no doubt collecting his thoughts, but she wouldn't have it. She gestured with her hand for him to continue. "Keep going. The rest of it."

"So Jayne asked me how she should respond, and I told her the truth." Another pause, this one longer, but Maggie's emotions were too jumbled for her to press him. He sighed deeply. "She asked me if she could tell him who his father was, and I said yes. Long story short, we met for coffee one morning about a week ago."

"You met him? You actually *met* him?"

Brett nodded.

"And . . ." Maggie gestured for him to continue, but it was obvious his emotions were getting the best of him. Tears were in the corners of his eyes, welling up like bubbles, but they didn't fall.

"And there was no doubt he was who he said he was." Brett wiped the tears away with the back of his hand. "He's built like me. He looks like me. But he has your eyes." Brett closed his hand around a coffee mug that had been sitting on the desktop and held on to it as if it were his lifeline.

"Did he ask about me?" she whispered.

Brett nodded. "Yes, of course he asked about you. He wanted to know all about you. Who you were, what you were like. What you looked like."

"What did you tell him?" She couldn't hold back the tears.

"I told him you were the most beautiful girl in the world and that all my life I'd loved you with my whole heart and soul. That you were the smartest woman I'd ever met, and the kindest."

She rolled her eyes. As if she wanted Brett's flattery at that moment. "I mean what did you tell him about why . . ." She couldn't say the words: *Why I gave him away. Why I walked out of the hospital, leaving him behind. Why I wasn't brave enough . . .*

"I told him the truth. That things were different forty years ago, that there was a stigma then that doesn't seem to exist today. I told him your parents forced you to give him up and I . . ." Brett swallowed hard. "I didn't stand up for you, or for him. That I talked you into it, mostly because I wanted to go to Ohio State and play football and go to the pros. I told him if it had been up to you, you would have brought him home with you. You would have found a way to raise him with or without me. But I talked you out of it." He was openly crying, something Maggie hadn't known he was capable of.

"Stop." Her voice caught.

But he went on. "I convinced you it would be better for him to grow up in a stable home with two adult parents. I made you believe there would be other babies for us. I told him the truth. I told him I was a selfish, self-centered bastard who only thought about myself and the future I wanted."

"In the end, it was my decision. I was the one who walked away." She was whispering, the truth so hard to speak aloud.

"The day you were leaving the hospital . . . remember?"

"Please don't . . ." Her arms wrapped around her middle like a shield against his words.

Ignoring her protest, he continued. "You asked me, *begged* me, to walk down the hall with you and look at him. 'Just look at him. He's so tiny and so beautiful. If you see him' . . ." His voice broke, and he made no attempt to hide his tears or the wave of regret that washed over him.

"Please stop." Maggie covered her face.

He closed his eyes, his face a mask of anguish. "But I really didn't want to because I was afraid you were right. If I saw him, would I be able to leave him there? Was I too much of a coward to look at my own son? But then I—"

Coraline's voice came through the intercom. "Chief, there's a guy on the phone who—"

"Take a message, please. And hold my calls." He hit the button to turn off her voice. He cleared his voice as if to compose himself and, to Maggie, said, "When he contacted me, of course I wanted to meet him."

"What's he like?"

"He's . . . he's pretty terrific, Maggie. He's more forgiving than I ever would have expected him to be."

"The people who raised him . . ."

"His parents, Maggie. Those were his parents, not us," he said. "They were great people. Gave him everything we would have wanted him to have. Love. Stability. A happy home, a great education. He said he'd always known he was adopted but never felt he was less than their son."

"Bless them for . . ." Maggie began to sob, and Brett started to get up to comfort her, but she shook her head no.

Brett backed away and waited until the worst had passed. When her sobs subsided, he said, "He wants very much to meet you."

"I'm afraid," she whispered. She hadn't wanted to appear weak in front of him, but there was no point in pretense. "I'm so afraid of what he'll think of me, leaving him like that. I never tried to find him. I just let him go."

"Maggie, he knows everything. And he understands. If he's holding a deep-seated grudge against us, he's hiding it well. In all our conversations, there have been no recriminations, no accusations on his part. He just wanted to know who we were." He paused before correcting himself. "Who we are."

"Did he tell you he found Natalie the same way he found Jayne?"

"He did. He said he'd contacted Natalie, but her response was he must be mistaken."

"What did you tell him? About meeting me?"

"I said it wasn't my call. I didn't know if you'd told your husband, your kids. He said Natalie hadn't been receptive, so he decided not to pursue it with her. He didn't want to rock the boat as far as your family is concerned."

Maggie opened her bag and rummaged through its contents, searching for tissues. She wiped her face and blew her nose. "I don't know what to do."

"I'm afraid I can't offer you any help there."

"I wasn't asking you to."

"Fair enough."

They stared at each other across the flat surface of his desk. The room was so quiet she could hear the round schoolhouse-style clock ticking off the seconds on the wall behind her.

Maggie turned toward the door. She needed space. "Thanks for your time."

"If you decide you want to get in touch with him, I can . . ." He started to walk around the side of the desk, but she backed away before he could reach her.

"I'll let you know." She opened the door before he could open it for her and left the office, her nerves a jumble, feeling his eyes on her back the entire way down the hall.

She wondered how she could get past Coraline without the woman noticing her swollen eyes and red nose, but Coraline was on the phone, her back to the hall as Maggie hurried past.

Once outside, Maggie took several long, deep breaths, trying to even out her emotions so she could think. When she realized deep breathing wasn't helping, she walked to the corner and started up Cottage.

But when she approached her house and saw her daughters' cars in the driveway, she knew she wasn't ready to continue that conversation just yet. Not sure when she might be, she headed for the beach. She kicked off her shoes and walked on the pebbly sand to the lifeguard stand. She climbed up and sat at the top, her legs drawn up to her chest, and watched the calm water of the bay ebb and flow as night began to fall, and she tried to rationally think through everything that had happened. On the one hand, she was relieved to finally know what had put the bee in Natalie's bonnet, but at the same time, she herself was annoyed. Did her daughters really think they had a right to know everything about her past? What was it about discovering the truth that had made them both so indignant?

Then there was Brett. She'd tried to ignore the nagging little voice that had warned her moving back to Wyndham Beach might not be such a good idea. She hadn't been back for long, but already she'd run into him once in the general store, and another time in the post office. Both times he'd tried to speak with her, but she still wasn't ready to hear a declaration of love when he'd never really acknowledged the reason they'd broken up so many years ago. Somewhere in her heart she'd felt there might be too much history between them for the future to hold anything that mattered, but seeing him break down had broken something inside of her, and the rancor she'd kept inside for forty years had begun to crack. She'd had no idea how much he'd suffered—he had so many regrets. Now she understood why Brett had been so persistent in his efforts to speak with her privately, away from prying eyes and ears.

And now there was Joe. Her son, no longer nameless, wanted to meet her. The reunion she hadn't believed would ever happen was suddenly the one thing she wanted most—and all she had to do was say yes. Was she strong enough to face the child she'd abandoned so long ago? How would she know what to say? Could she tell him she'd wept every year on his birthday because she'd never stopped trying to picture him as he grew? That she'd prayed every night his mother and father loved him and had given him a happy life? That she'd never gotten over the pain of losing him?

She sat on the stand until the stars blinked their way into the evening sky, and slowly, one by one, all the pieces of her life began to fall into place. It would take strength and honesty. It would mean facing the truth unflinchingly. But if she was very lucky, in the end, the payoff would be healing and understanding, and maybe even love. It was all within reach, if she could only step up and accept the challenge, knowing her life would never be the same.

She'd begin where she needed to. She climbed down and headed for home, and the conversation she never thought she'd have.

Chapter Sixteen

GRACE

"I don't believe she walked out on us like that." Grace had been loaded for bear, and the fact that her mother had left the house before she'd had a chance to say one word had infuriated her.

"God, I can't believe I did that to her." Natalie covered her face with her hands.

"What could she possibly have to do that would be more important than explaining to us how she'd had this son she never bothered to tell us about? And seriously, Nat? You're feeling sorry for her?"

Before Natalie could reply, Daisy stumbled into the room, half-asleep and rubbing her eyes. "Mommy, I can't sleep. I'm lost," she said, her voice small and frightened, and Grace couldn't blame her sister for picking up the child and taking her back upstairs. She'd thought Natalie would come right back, but Grace was still sitting alone in the kitchen when she heard the front door open and close quietly.

Grace fixed her mother with her most lethal stare, and she was annoyed even more that Maggie ignored it.

"Where's Natalie?" Maggie asked.

"Upstairs with Daisy." Grace got up and opened a new bottle of wine. If she didn't do something to relax, she was going to blow, and right then the only sure thing in sight was the bottle of pinot grigio sitting on the counter. She took a glass from the cupboard, poured, and drank.

"I'll have one of those." Maggie poured a glass for herself, then sat at the island, toying with the fruit in the bowl, rearranging the oranges, apples, and bananas. Finally, she said, "If you have something to say, go ahead, Gracie. Get it off your chest so we can get past this."

"You think we can just have a nice chat and then we'll be *past* this? How do we get past the fact you had a child you never told us about? That I have a brother I never met?" Grace knew her face was headed to ugly town, but right at that moment, she didn't care. "Did Dad know? Did he know his perfect wife had this deep secret?"

"Whoa, Grace." Natalie came into the room in a rush. "That's none of our business. Whatever was between Mom and Dad was just that. Between them." She touched her mother on the shoulder, and when Maggie turned, Natalie drew her in. "Mama, I'm so sorry. I didn't think about how this would hurt you. I acted like the worst kind of brat, and I'm so embarrassed I could die."

"Oh, honey." Maggie hugged her, and Grace could tell both her sister and her mother were close to tears once again.

"Oh, please. Natalie, you have nothing to apologize for. But Mom, you have some explaining to do."

"Grace. For God's sake . . ." Natalie turned on her.

"Nat, I'm not talking to you. I'm talking to Mom. She owes us an explanation." Grace was aware she sounded like a shrew, but she couldn't stop herself. Her whole life she'd believed her parents had had this fairy-tale marriage, this once-in-a-lifetime love. She'd always wanted to be just like her mother—her hero!—but never felt she measured up. She'd believed her mother was pretty damned near perfect. Apparently, her perceived perfection had been a figment of Grace's imagination. Watching her mother fall off her pedestal was more than disappointing. It was excruciatingly painful.

"Thank you." Maggie held Natalie's hands, then said, "Pour yourself some wine and join us. Grace is apparently determined to re-create the Inquisition, so you might as well fortify yourself."

"Mom, you don't owe us an explanation." Natalie reached across the island for the wine.

"Grace obviously believes I do." Maggie directed her gaze to her elder daughter. "Let me preface this by saying I don't believe I owe you anything. My life is my own, just as your life is yours. And if I recall correctly, recently you needed a hefty dose of understanding after your life imploded. I was more than happy to be there for you, Gracie. Apparently, it's too much to ask I be given the same respect and understanding I so willingly gave you."

"Mom, it's not the same. It's—" Grace began, but her mother cut her off.

"It's my turn, Grace. You want to know how come I never told you I'd had a child before I met your father? You want to know about the baby I wasn't permitted to keep?" Maggie was speaking softly, so softly Grace had to lean in her direction in order to hear her. "I was eighteen, my senior year, when I got pregnant in the spring. The old cliché of prom night . . . well, it doesn't matter. My boyfriend and I had been together for three years. We planned to get married after college. There was never a doubt in my mind that would happen. I loved him more than I can say. Even now, forty years later, I know I loved him with my whole heart and soul. And he loved me." Maggie took a sip of wine, then took another before proceeding.

"When I found out I was pregnant, I wanted nothing more than to keep my child. But my parents were adamant I give the baby up for adoption. My boyfriend agreed—I'm not letting him off the hook. The three of them were relentless. My parents didn't want to have to deal with the embarrassment. My boyfriend didn't want his football career to suffer. He had plans to play professionally, which he did."

"Your high school boyfriend played professional football?" For some reason, this sounded incredible to Grace. "Seriously? Who'd he play for?"

"What does it matter? Geez, Grace." Natalie shot her a dirty look. "Go on, Mom."

"So the end of August came around and my friends all took off for college. I pretended I was going, too, but I was really going to spend the next few months living in a cabin in Maine my mother's brother owned. He only used it in the summer, so he let us move in until after the baby was born." Maggie paused. "I don't think my mom told him why she wanted to stay there. We stayed in Maine until the baby was born, and a few weeks after, because I was such a wreck. My mom stayed with me, but once I went into labor, my dad flew up to be with us. And the day after I gave birth, my boyfriend came to the hospital." She smiled sadly. "It wasn't exactly a happy reunion."

"Mom, I can't even imagine what you felt, having to leave your child behind. That must have been horrible for you." Natalie had tears in her eyes.

Maggie nodded. "There are no words to express how painful." She glanced across the table at Grace. "You want to know why I didn't tell you? Why I didn't tell your father? It wasn't because I thought he'd be angry or because I was afraid he'd stop loving me. Your father was one of the kindest people I've ever known, and he loved me unconditionally. I didn't tell him because it hurt too much for me to talk about it, to say the words out loud. I wanted to tell him, believe me. I thought about it a thousand times, rehearsed over and over what I'd say. But every time I tried, I couldn't get the words out. Because it hurt too much that I'd given my baby away."

"And I made you say it. I threw it in your face and made you say it. I don't know how you could ever forgive me for putting you through this, Mom." Natalie's face was white with anguish.

"It's all right, Nat. It's out in the open now. And if we look on the bright side, we could say you brought me the answer to a prayer I've held inside for forty years. It means everything to me to know my son is alive, that he sounds happy. He says he's had a good life. What more could I ask for, under the circumstances?"

"I still think you should disown me." Natalie sniffed.

"Oh, sweetie. That would never happen." Maggie hugged her.

Grace glared from the opposite side of the island.

"So who's the father?" Grace asked.

"Mom, you don't have to answer," Natalie hastened to say.

"I'm not sure that is your business. In any event, it's not something I feel like discussing right now." Maggie crossed her arms over her chest. "When—if—I decide to share that with you, I'll let you know."

Their mother may have been forgiving of Natalie—Natalie, who'd started this whole mess!—but she wasn't sending Grace the love. Not that Grace expected or wanted her to. She couldn't understand how Natalie could cave in and forgive Maggie just like that. Natalie, who'd been so angry and indignant when she'd first told Grace about their mother's secret love child, had backed down the minute Maggie had turned on the tears.

"So what are you going to do now?" Grace asked. "About him."

"I need some time to think about it. I've been told he wants to meet me, and I'd like to meet him, but I need to think it through." Maggie rolled an orange on the island top, back and forth between her hands.

"I'd like to meet him," Natalie spoke up. "He sounds really nice. Maybe you could invite him here, and we could all meet him."

"And do what, Nat? Hold hands and sing 'We Are Family'?" Grace shook her head. "No thank you." She glanced at her mother. "And if you invite him here, to this house, I won't be here."

"As you wish, Gracie." Maggie tossed the orange into the bowl. "This is my house. You are my daughter, and you are welcome here. He is my son, and he is welcome as well."

"Count me out." Grace got up and walked out of the room and straight out the front door.

~

Grace walked toward the center of town, her mind replaying the facts over and over. Her mother had gotten pregnant by her high school boyfriend on prom night, had the baby, and gave it away. If Grace had been asked to guess the most unlikely scenario—her mother having landed a spacecraft on the moon or having a secret baby—she'd have been hard pressed to choose between the two.

Her anger kept her company while she walked. When she arrived at the corner of Front and Cottage, she turned left and walked two blocks before taking a right onto Jasper Street. She was just starting to calm down when she heard someone calling her.

"Gracie, is that you?"

She turned in the direction of the voice and realized she was passing Liddy's house.

"Hey, Liddy," she called but kept her stride. The last thing she wanted to do was talk to her mother's best friend.

"Come on up here on the porch and have a margarita with us. Liddy makes the best margarita on the entire Massachusetts coast."

When Grace looked closer, she could see Emma standing on the front porch with Liddy.

"Oh, thanks, but I just had some wine, and I don't think . . . ," Grace declined, but the ladies were adamant.

"Well, in that case, just have some of this delicious guacamole. We're doing Cinco de Mayo, Wyndham Beach style." Liddy came down the front steps, margarita glass in hand.

Crap. Seeing no gracious way out, Grace joined Liddy on the walk, then followed her up the stairs to the porch.

"May fifth was a month ago," Grace said. "You know that, right?"

"So we're a little late." Emma tilted her glass in Grace's direction as a sort of toast.

"Right," a slightly tipsy Liddy said. "It's Cinco de Mayo somewhere."

"Actually, it's Cinco de Junio, but whatever," Grace said.

"So what are you doing out walking in the dark?" Liddy sat and pointed to a chair for Grace to sit in.

"It seemed like a nice night, so I thought I'd get a little air." Grace sat and crossed her legs.

"Have some guacamole." Emma passed her the bowl and a plate of chips.

"Oh, no thank you. My stomach's a little unsettled." Grace was already regretting having stopped. She should have simply waved a greeting, then continued on her way. Walking had helped dispel the anger and the hurt, but she was still on edge and uncomfortable, and she'd be foolish to think neither Liddy nor Emma would notice.

"What's going on, Gracie?" Emma leaned over and patted Grace's knee. "You don't look like yourself."

"Why, you've been crying," Liddy announced. "Oh, sweetie, I hope you're not still pining for that ex-husband of yours. Exes are always best left in the past, where they belong."

Grace felt the tears well in her eyes. She shook her head, not trusting her voice.

"It's the job thing, right? You're upset about leaving your dad's law firm. You'll find another job with another firm, honey. I know it won't be the same, but Art would totally understand. He loved you and was so proud of you," Emma said softly.

"No. It's not that. I'm okay about Zach, and I'm almost okay about Flynn Law. It's Mom." Grace began to cry and babble at the same time. "Natalie got an email from Joe and she showed it to Mom and now Mom wants to meet him, and I'm upset because we didn't know about him. She never even told Dad about the baby."

Liddy and Emma exchanged a long, confused look, then both turned to Grace.

"What baby?" they asked.

Chapter Seventeen

NATALIE

"Mom, where do you suppose Grace went?"

"She's probably walking it off. My guess is one loop around town should be enough for her to calm down."

"Who'd have thought she'd react this way?" Natalie paused. "I mean, I did at first. I was pissed off, too, but once I saw how devastated you were, I couldn't be mad at anyone except myself for not talking to you privately. I made it about myself when it had nothing to do with me."

"In a sense, it does have something to do with you. He—Joe—is your brother."

"I always wanted a big brother when I was growing up." Natalie was trying to sound upbeat. "Well, better late than never."

"You want to meet him?"

"I do. He sounds so kind and understanding. Wanting to meet me but not wanting to push. Telling me he was okay if I didn't want to meet him, that he respected whatever I wanted to do." She reached for a banana from the bowl and peeled it. "He said he discovered he has three other half sisters."

"I believe that's true."

"Do you know anything about them?"

"Not really. I think one might be around your age—not certain about that, though—one might be in her teens. One might be young, like maybe six or eight? I'm not sure."

"But you know this because you know their father?"

"Right."

"I'm not going to ask you who he is," Natalie assured her.

"Thank you."

"Even though it's killing me," she whispered, and Maggie laughed.

"When the time comes, when I can put it all together, you'll know," Maggie assured her. "Until then, that door is closed."

"Got it." Natalie had peeled the entire banana but had yet to take a bite. She broke off a piece and offered it to her mother.

"Thanks." Maggie reached for the pile of emails she'd left on the island and began to read through them while she ate the fruit.

"When do you think you're going to meet him?" Natalie couldn't help it. She wanted to meet Joe in the worst way but thought Maggie should be allowed to meet him first.

"Soon, I think. Now that it's out there and we all know about it, I don't see any reason to wait too long to contact him." Maggie grabbed a napkin and wiped her hands. "It may take me a day or so to get my head in the right place. This"—she pointed to the emails—"has come as such a shock. I never expected to know what happened to him. I never thought he'd look for me or his father." She smiled. "Who could have known forty years ago that someday you'd be able to send your spit away and that act would lead you to lost relatives?"

"When I signed up, all I wanted was to find some of Dad's relatives he'd lost track of. It never occurred to me someone might be looking for me." She amended that to, "Or for someone with my DNA."

"Well, then, I guess it was meant to be." Maggie got off her stool and went to the sink to rinse her glass. "I'm exhausted from all this." She waved her hands around the island. "I think I'm going to turn in. Maybe read for a little while. Will you remind Grace to lock the front door when she gets back? Sometimes she forgets." She kissed the top of Natalie's head. "Good night, sweetie. And don't lose any sleep over the emails. I think it was probably the right time for it all to come together."

Maggie left the kitchen, the emails in her hand.

Natalie straightened the kitchen and turned off the overhead lights before going into the family room. She searched for something to watch on the TV, but nothing appealed to her. She scanned the bookshelves and tried to get into three different novels, but she couldn't concentrate. She kept thinking about the dilemma her mother had faced, and about the brother she'd yet to meet.

The right time for it all to come together. Maggie's words played over and over in Natalie's head. Somehow it seemed to imply something more than just Joe Miller.

Just Joe Miller, Natalie mused as she flipped through a magazine without really seeing the articles. *Just my long-lost brother.*

She heard the front door open and close, and got up to peek around the corner. "Grace, did you lock the door?"

Grace paused halfway across the foyer. "You sound just like Mom. Did she tell you to wait up to see if I could remember to lock up on my own?" Grace went back to the door, locked it, and said, "Locked."

Natalie could have pointed out that apparently someone did need to remind Grace about the lock but decided she was better off not commenting. Judging by the look on her sister's face, teasing would not be appreciated.

"Where'd you go?" Natalie plunked down on the sofa next to the magazine she'd been paging through.

"I went for a walk." Grace turned on the TV and, after jumping from channel to channel, settled on the opposite end of the sofa.

"I hope you cooled off a bit. Honestly, Grace, I don't understand why you're taking this thing with Mom personally. I mean, I did at first, but it really has nothing to do with—"

"Do you know she didn't even tell Liddy or Emma? Her best friends? She never said a word to either of them about that baby." Grace looked pissed off all over again.

Natalie shrugged. "So? She wasn't obligated to tell either . . . wait, how do you know she didn't tell them?"

"Because they told me."

"What, they just came out of the blue and said, 'By the way, your mom never told us she had a baby after graduation.'" A feeling of dread welled up inside Natalie's chest. "Grace. You didn't."

Grace turned her face to the TV.

"Grace. Tell me you didn't tell Liddy and Emma." When Grace didn't respond, Natalie threw her magazine at her sister. "You told them. How dare you! That wasn't your story to tell."

"I didn't know they didn't know. I assumed they did."

"So, what, you walked out of here and went over to Liddy's or Emma's—"

"Liddy's. And I didn't leave here to go there. I was walking and I went past Liddy's house and she and Emma were on the porch. They talked me into going up and sitting with them, and it just all sort of came out."

"You always did have the biggest damned mouth. You couldn't wait to blab Mom's secret, could you? You were angry at her, and you couldn't wait to let everyone else know how pissed off you were."

"I didn't know, Nat! I swear. The three of them have been so close for so long it never occurred to me she hadn't confided in them. They could tell something was bothering me, so when they asked, I said we'd just found out about Mom's baby and I was upset about it." Grace looked sorry for the first and only time that night. "And then they both said, 'What baby?'"

"Grace, this is really bad. Mom's going to kill you when she finds out, and I won't blame her one bit. You shouldn't have told them."

Too late, Natalie saw Maggie in the doorway.

"She shouldn't have told who *what*?"

Chapter Eighteen

MAGGIE

Maggie drifted into wakefulness the same way she'd drifted to sleep, minute by minute, the scent of salt air surrounding her. She glanced at the clock—only five thirty. A quick storm had rolled through at some point. The wet spray blowing in through the window had awakened her, and she'd gotten up to close the window, then fallen back into bed. Turning over, hoping for at least another hour of sleep, the drama of the previous evening replayed in her head, and she knew there'd be no more rest for her that morning.

She expected to have a rocky night, but she'd gotten herself ready for bed, climbed in, and pulled up the covers, her mind bouncing from one scene to another. Natalie's revelation. Grace's unexpected and unreasonable reaction. Natalie's reversal from anger to kind understanding and apology. Grace spilling the beans to Liddy and Emma—and God only knew what the two of them were thinking. But the hardest punch to her gut had been Brett confessing his true feelings after all these years. She'd never suspected he'd suffered as she had.

The discovery that her son was reaching out.

My son is reaching out.

Of course she would meet him. Nothing could keep her from that longed-for reunion, regardless of how nervous she might feel, how afraid she might be of how he might judge her. What did he look like? Brett had said he looked like him, but what did that mean beyond he had blond hair and he was tall? Lots of tall men were blond.

"He has your eyes," Brett had said.

She tossed the covers aside, stood, and stretched, then went into the bathroom, where she turned on the light and stared into the mirror.

Were his eyes the same shade of green, the same shape? Were his lashes long and thick like hers? Did they darken when he was angry, as hers did? Did the corners crinkle when he laughed?

Would she see anything else of her in his face or his mannerisms, the way she could see herself in Natalie and in Grace? Or would his gestures favor his adoptive parents, the people who raised and loved him? She thought about them, wondered who they were. She'd been given the option to meet them in the hospital, but she'd declined. Her eighteen-year-old self thought of them as the people who were taking her baby from her. Now, with so much time between the girl she'd been and the woman she'd become, she could honor them for who they were. They were the ones who tended to his scraped knees and kissed him good night, sat at his bedside when he was sick, read to him, and put up with his teenage antics. They gave him a life and made him the man who could reach out to a half sister he'd never met and wish her a beautiful, happy life, even if she chose not to be a part of his.

They'd given him their name when she could not give him hers.

"Thank you," she whispered. "Whoever you are, thank you."

~

Twenty minutes later, Maggie sat at the kitchen table, her laptop in front of her, trying to compose an email to Joe Miller. She'd started it a dozen times but couldn't find the words to make it sound exactly the way she wanted. This would be his first impression of her, and she couldn't seem to strike the right balance between stiff and formal, and between familiar and chatty. It was so much harder than she thought it would be. There was no point in pretending she didn't want to meet him, so she might as well set the ball in motion. Why waste more time?

Should she take Brett up on his offer to call Joe and set it up? Was that the coward's way out? Did that make her seem weak, too tentative?

An email from her to him was definitely the way to go. She couldn't hide behind Brett. If only she could say what she wanted and have it come out right.

She was still sitting there, staring at the blank screen, when she heard a knock at the front door. She glanced at the clock—7:25. Who knocked on your door at that hour of the morning?

Maggie peered through the glass panel in the door, sighed, and opened it. She should have known.

"Neither of us could sleep," Liddy announced as she stepped inside.

"I called her at six thirty and told her we needed to address this head-on." Emma followed Liddy.

"Come on in, then." Maggie gestured in the direction of the kitchen.

"I don't smell coffee." Liddy sniffed the air. "Why don't I smell coffee?"

"I didn't get to it yet," Maggie explained.

"Looks like you had time to start working on something." Liddy pointed to the open laptop as she went right past Maggie and began filling the coffee maker.

Maggie slid Joe's emails to Natalie under the laptop and closed it. She eyed both friends. "Go on. Spit it out. Say what you have to say."

"Okay. You twisted my arm. I'll go first. I—we—are hurt and offended you didn't trust us enough to tell us what you were going through." Emma needn't have told Maggie she was hurt. Her eyes said it all.

"It wasn't that I didn't trust you . . ."

"Oh, I call bull." Liddy opened the refrigerator and took out the half-and-half. "If you'd trusted us, you'd have shared this with us. It had to have been terrible, but did you take us into your confidence so we could offer you moral support? No. You kept it to yourself. You deceived us and lied to us all summer long." Liddy slammed the carton of creamer on the island top. "'Maggie, want to come to the beach with us?' 'Oh, no, thanks. I have to help my dad in his office.'"

"I couldn't go to the beach. I couldn't put on a bathing suit. I was okay in street clothes—by the time I started to really show, you'd already left for college."

"You could have told us the truth instead of lying all summer long. Friends don't lock out friends when something bad happens. It's thick and thin, not thick and thick." Liddy's eyes reflected her anger. "I'm really pissed off, Maggie."

"I can tell, and I'm sorry. I don't know what else to say." Maggie took the mug of coffee Liddy offered her and set it on the counter. "I understand why you're angry. I wish I could have told you back then what I was going through. It was a very painful and confusing time."

"Did you think we'd judge you? Start rumors? Tell the whole town?" Liddy hadn't lost her edge.

"No, of course not. You'd never have done that to me."

"Then why? Even after all this time, you never told us. We had to find out by accident from Grace. After all the things we've gone through together, all the times when we had to be there for each other. When Harry flipped out at Emma for siding with Chris because he didn't want to follow in Harry's footsteps . . . the death of our parents . . . when my daughter took her life . . . the three of us were solid. We held each other up. Why didn't you let us do that for you?"

"I think what Liddy is saying is that when you're very close to someone, and they're going through something very difficult, you want to share their burden because you love them," Emma said softly. "We love you, Maggie. We would have been there for you. We are hurt because you wouldn't let us share in what must have been the worst thing that ever happened to you."

"I didn't think of it that way. I was constantly badgered by my parents, who were insisting I give the baby up and go on with my life as if nothing had happened. Brett sided with them, and I couldn't make him or them believe I could keep the baby and still have a life. I could still go to college. He could still go to college." Maggie's sigh was deep and came from her heart. "I was very confused and very scared."

"We could have shared that with you." Emma reached out her hand, and Maggie squeezed it. "We would have taken your side."

"I know you would have. But there was so much drama. I just wanted the talking to stop—the arguing and the cajoling and all the talk about facing reality and stop being selfish and think of the baby and what's best for it. Him," she corrected. "That whole summer was a blur. I was embarrassed and scared and my parents were on me about disgracing them, and Brett's father went on these rants about how I was ruining Brett's life and how if he had to worry about me and a baby he wouldn't be able to focus on football and he'd never make the pros."

"Brett's father was an asshole." Liddy sat next to Maggie. "Everyone in town knows that."

"I'm surprised Brett didn't stand up for you." Emma sat across from the others.

"He'll never admit having let his father bully him, but I think that may have influenced his wanting me to give the baby up." Maggie rubbed her head. As always in times of stress, her head began to pound.

"So what did you do?" Emma asked.

Maggie explained how she and her mother had gone to Maine and stayed there until the baby was born.

"It hurts me to know you went through this. And while I respect your reasons for keeping it to yourself, I wish I could have been there for you." Sweet, softhearted Emma was crying.

"Me too." Liddy got up and went into the adjacent family room.

"Bring the box, Lids," Maggie called to her.

"What box?"

"The box of tissues I know you're looking for. It's on the mantel," Maggie told her.

"So what are you going to do now?" Liddy returned with the box in her hand. She took a tissue and passed the box around.

"You mean about Joe?" Maggie explained: "His name is Joe. Did Grace tell you? Brett met him and said he's wonderful. Which, of course, he would be, just meeting for the first time."

"Well, yeah, he'd be on his best behavior." Liddy nodded. "He wouldn't want to come off like an ax murderer when he meets his birth father for the first time."

Maggie laughed. "I have the emails he sent Natalie. He sounds so nice."

"Can we see?" Liddy asked.

"Liddy, those are personal," Emma admonished her.

"Oh, like we have secrets now?" Maggie lifted the laptop and slid out the emails she'd stashed away. She handed them over to Liddy. "Pass them on to Emma when you're done."

"Well, if you're going to have one secret, might as well make it a good one." Liddy began to read, passing the sheets of paper to Emma as she finished each one. "Oh my God, he does sound like such a nice kid."

"He's not a kid," Maggie reminded her. "He's forty."

"Yes, but he's your kid." Emma smiled as she read. "Aw, he was so nice to Natalie." When she finished reading the last email, she wiped away a tear and asked, "So when do you think you'll meet him?"

"As soon as we can arrange a mutually agreeable time and place." Maggie arranged the emails in a neat stack. Maggie looked from Liddy to Emma. "You didn't tell Grace that Brett was the father."

"No. We didn't tell her anything. We just let her talk."

"If she'd known, she would have mentioned it. When she didn't, I figured she didn't know," Liddy added.

"Thank you. One less explanation to make. Guys, I have to admit, I'm scared to death. Curious and excited, but mostly I'm scared."

"He's going to love you. I know it." Emma patted her heart.

"I'd be happy if he just liked me." Maggie's shoulders were hunched. "So. That's where we are."

"So that's why you and Brett broke up. It all makes sense now," Liddy said. "We could never figure out why. After you moved to Seattle to be with him, we kept waiting for the call telling us you'd set the date for your wedding. But then you called and said you were moving to Philadelphia and you'd decided marrying him wasn't what you wanted after all. We figured maybe he'd cheated on you." Liddy glanced across the table at Emma, who nodded.

"Brett wanted to get married right away after we graduated from college. Like, as soon as I got to Seattle. But I just couldn't decide what to do. That first year out there, he was so busy trying to make the team. Over the summer I'd obtained my teaching credentials so I could teach, so that kept me occupied. Then when the season ended, he wanted to plan a wedding for the spring." Maggie shook her head slowly. "But I was so broken up about that baby, and he seemed to have put it behind him, and I couldn't understand how he could do that. The more it haunted me the less it seemed to bother him. After a while, I felt I couldn't love him the way I had, so I started looking for places to move to. I found a job in a private school outside of Philly that seemed to suit me, so I took it. Then I had to tell Brett, and that wasn't a fun conversation. But in the end I felt it was the right thing to do. So I went my way, and he went his."

"I don't know what to say, except that's one of the saddest stories I ever heard." Liddy put an arm around Maggie and gave her a hug, then smacked her lightly. "That's for not letting us be there for you."

"Give her a pop for me, too," Emma said.

"Not necessary. I get the point, and I apologize. But now you have the whole story." Maggie sighed. "Could we talk about something else now? There's nothing more any of us can say on the subject."

"Except where you all go from here." Liddy sipped her coffee. "Especially you and Brett."

"Don't go there, please." Maggie turned to Emma. "Talk about something else. Anything else."

"Okay. Well, Liddy has news." Emma looked pointedly across the table and said, "Liddy, tell Maggie your news."

"What news?"

Liddy brought the coffeepot over and topped off everyone's mugs. "So I told you about Fred Lattimore thinking about selling the bookstore."

Maggie nodded. "Right."

"Well, he did." Liddy's grin lit the room. "He sold it to me."

"Liddy, that's wonderful!" Maggie got up and gave her friend a hug. "Congratulations."

Still grinning, Liddy said, "The sale won't be final for about six weeks, but I'm taking over as of Saturday. I'm so excited I can hardly stand it. I've always loved that little building. Did you know the lot goes back almost to the harbor? I'm thinking I could do something out there. Not sure what. Looks like there could have been a patio. Anyway, Carl's going to show me how to do the books—no pun—and how to take inventory and invoice vendors and all the bookkeeping stuff. Payables. Receivables. I have an accountant, but Carl said I need to understand the business before I hand everything off to someone else." Liddy rolled her eyes. "He suggested I set up a website and start offering internet sales—about which I know nothing. Do some sort of internet promotions. Ditto, I know nothing. Carl said he tried to get his father to get online, but he wasn't interested, and Carl didn't have the time to do it for him. So I'm going to have to find someone who knows how to design a website."

Grace came into the kitchen dressed in sleep shorts and an old tee. She glared at her mother before acknowledging their company. "I thought you two were never going to speak to my mom again. I thought the plan was to do away with her in a very painful way and toss her remains off the side of a boat in Buzzards Bay. Feed her to the fishes. That was the plan, wasn't it?"

"That was last night's plan. This morning, your mother explained everything." Emma added a little more sugar to her coffee. "We love her, and we've forgiven her. I suggest you give serious thought to doing the same."

"Maybe," Grace grumbled. "You guys drank all the coffee."

"Yes, and I had to make it myself because your mother was otherwise occupied. I'm pretty sure you can handle making the second round." Liddy pointed toward the coffee maker.

"So who needs a website?" Grace began to make another pot of coffee.

"I do." The grin returned to Liddy's face. "You are looking at the new owner of the Wyndham Beach Bookstore."

"Get out." Grace turned, wide eyed. "You bought the bookstore? Seriously?"

"Actually, I'm in the process of buying it, but I'm going to be running it as of Saturday." Liddy explained the current owner's situation.

"That's so exciting. The bookstore is my favorite place in Wyndham Beach. I'm sorry to hear about Mr. Lattimore, though," Grace said. "He's such a sweet man. But now that you mention it, he was acting a little strange the last time I was there."

"Strange in what way?" Maggie asked.

"He kept calling me Ellen, like he thought I was Gramma. And he told me that once upon a time, he'd 'courted' my sister." Grace made a face.

"My aunt Helena was my mom's sister," Maggie told her. "She ran off with a woman who taught poetry at Yale. It was a huge scandal, back in the day."

"Wow, I'll bet." Grace filled the coffee maker and turned it on. "Are they still alive?"

"The last I heard they were living in an old villa in France and making goat cheese, but that was years ago."

Natalie and Daisy ambled into the room. Like her sister, Natalie wore shorts and a tee she'd slept in. Daisy wore a rainbow-striped bathing suit with a glittery unicorn on the front and pink cowgirl boots and carried a fairy wand.

"If I'd known we had company, I'd have gotten dressed." Natalie paused. "Nah, probably not. You show up before nine a.m., you take what you get."

Natalie hugged Liddy and Emma. "Daisy, can you say good morning to Miss Liddy and Miss Emma?"

"Good morning." Daisy waved.

Emma patted her lap. "Come sit with me for a minute, sugar. I haven't seen you since you were a baby. And I love your boots."

"I'm not a baby now." Daisy readily climbed into Emma's lap, then held up both legs to show off her boots.

"Liddy is buying the bookstore," Grace told Natalie. "How cool is that?"

"Really? That's wonderful." Natalie opened first one cupboard, then the next. "Mom, where's the cereal?"

"Two doors over."

"Got it. Yay, Daisy's favorite O's." Natalie found a bowl and poured in the cereal, then placed it in front of her daughter. "So are you going to have story hours for the kiddos? And maybe a book club for the big kiddos? Is there a café there? I haven't been there in years, but I seem to remember some cozy chairs."

"I'd love to do all that in time, but it's going to take me a while to learn how to do all the things there. If I think too much about it, I get queasy," Liddy admitted. "But we are quickly moving into summer, and I guess at the very least we should be thinking of story hours for the kids."

"What do you mean 'we'?" Emma teased. "We are not buying the store. You are."

"All for one, one for all?" Liddy said hopefully.

"Of course, we'll all help where we can," Maggie assured her.

"I can do your website," Grace offered.

"And I can help set up a story hour. I'd be taking Daisy anyway if you had one. Then when I go back home, it will be up and running." Natalie smiled. "I'd love to do that. I can sit in one of those chairs . . ."

"If you're thinking of those big soft chairs Fred had near the back window, they'll be the first thing I toss. They're old and smell musty. Sort of like Fred, now that I think about it. And no, there's no café there, but maybe there could be. Come in sometime next week and take a look, all of you, and we'll see what we can do with the place."

"There's that 'we' again," Emma pointed out.

"Oh, I have a couple of wingback chairs in the attic," Maggie said. "I brought them with me from Bryn Mawr, but I have no place for them. You can have them for the shop."

"Thank you. I'm not too proud to beg these days. Now, we all know none of you would pass up an opportunity to put in your two cents. This time I'm asking you to. Take a tour of the place next week, and let me know what you think about the possibilities. I have some ideas, but I'd love to have yours." Liddy got up and went to the sink, rinsed her mug, and set it on the counter. "I have to get back home. I need to talk to the bank and call my insurance agent and my accountant and my lawyer."

"And I need to get to the art center." Emma, too, rose, and eased Daisy onto the floor. "Natalie, you should sign up Daisy for the children's classes. We'll be starting in another two weeks."

"If we're still here, I'll definitely do that," Natalie assured her.

Maggie walked her friends to the front door to see them off. They'd arrived together in Emma's car, but Liddy chose to walk. *She wants to go past the bookstore,* Maggie thought. *It's too early for it to be open, but she just wants to see it and know it will soon be hers.*

She closed the door behind her and went back into the kitchen, where Grace and Natalie were discussing their plans for the day.

"I think I'm going to play with a potential website for Liddy's bookstore," Grace was saying. "It might take a while to get the look right, but I can at least set up the platform."

"I didn't know you knew how to do that," Natalie said.

"Oh, sure. I took a class in college, and at the firm we had a really good IT guy. He showed me how to do all sorts of different things." Grace rolled her eyes. "And we all know what I did with that information."

"Ah, yes. My sister the blog star."

"I can almost laugh at that now. Almost," Grace said.

"Whatever happened to your blog anyway?" Natalie asked.

"The FBI took it as evidence against Amber."

"Do you miss it?"

Grace shrugged. "Sometimes I wonder how some of the women are doing, but all in all, not so much. I don't really need it anymore."

Maggie listened to the exchange as she cleared away the abandoned coffee mugs. *Good for you, Grace.*

"Mom. I owe you an apology." Grace touched Maggie's arm. "I am very, very sorry. The only thing I can say in my own defense—not that there is a defense for the way I spoke to you last night—is just that I was so shocked. I'm still sort of in shock, actually, and to be honest, I still don't know how I feel. I'm still trying to work my way through the fact you didn't tell us until you had to. I mean, if Joe hadn't contacted Natalie, would you have ever told us?"

Maggie answered as best as she could. "I don't know."

"Well, regardless of how I feel, I shouldn't have said the things I said."

"Yes, you said things I wish you hadn't. I'm not going to say I wasn't hurt. I was. But at the same time, I do understand you'd been totally blindsided. I get it."

"I acted like a total brat. Especially after you were so kind and good and nonjudgmental when I screwed up so badly you had to sell Daddy's law firm."

"Don't carry that guilt for too long, Gracie. I may have sold it eventually, who knows? Your situation merely served as a catalyst to get me off my duff so I could move forward with my life. I doubt I would have taken even one step forward if I'd stayed in Bryn Mawr, in that house."

"I think you would have found a way. You're resourceful and smart, Mom."

"I don't know. I was in such a rut. The house had too many memories. I think over time I'd probably have adopted about twenty cats and had my groceries delivered so I never had to go out again." Maggie watched Daisy dig into her dry cereal. "Don't you want milk or maybe some strawberries with your cereal?"

"I like it like this." Daisy grabbed a handful of cereal from the bowl and ate it one piece at a time.

"Okay." Maggie ran her fingers through Daisy's long blonde hair and smiled. Having her only grandchild with her made her happy. It reminded her that regardless of what had happened in her past, she'd made the right decision to marry Art. It was through him she'd had these two girls—trying and contrary, even occasionally bratty. But she loved them with her whole heart. And through Natalie—thank God Nat was braver than her mother had been and had kept her child!—Maggie had this wonder of a girl to love and watch grow. This was her reward for having survived her life's storms.

And now life held one more plum: her son was being returned to her. The reunion could very well be painful, but she felt certain it would be worth it.

Bring it on.

~

Maggie struggled with the email to Joe all day and well into the night. She wrote and rewrote, deleted, and started over more times than she could count. After another sleepless night, she forced herself to sit at her laptop and write what was in her mind and her heart.

> Joe:
>
> I'm sure by now you know I am the woman who gave birth to you and terminated my rights to you in favor of your adoptive parents. I never knew their names or where they lived. The only thing I knew about them was that the adoption agency thought they were the best people to raise you and that they wanted you very much. I'm sure you have questions after all these years, and I'd be happy to meet with you.

She struck that last part.

> . . . and I'd very much like to meet with you whenever you like.

She paused and considered replacing that with "as soon as possible" but didn't want to put pressure on him.

Thank you for reaching out to Natalie, and to your father . . .

She added "birth" before "father."

. . . and eventually to me. All my contact information follows—please feel free to contact me when you feel the time is right.

She debated on how to sign off and eventually decided.

Looking forward to hearing from you.

Maggie Lloyd Flynn

She hit "Send" before she lost her nerve. *And now to wait.*
She didn't have to wait long.
She'd taken Daisy into the backyard and let her pick a bouquet of flowers for the kitchen. Of course, Daisy needed to know the names of every flower and tree, and by the time they'd made the rounds of the entire property, almost an hour had passed since she'd sent her email. When they returned to the kitchen, she saw the voice mail light on her phone blinking.
She'd expected an email reply and so wasn't prepared for the strong male voice that greeted her.
"Hi. Oh, I don't know what to call you. Is Maggie all right? This is Joe. Joe Miller. Okay, you probably figured that out. I was so happy to get your email. I was hoping you'd want to meet me as much as I want to meet you. Maybe not as much, but at least you're willing to see me. I can be in Massachusetts any day that's convenient for you. I have a project in Boston I check in on every other week, and I can drive out there where you are or meet you anyplace you want. Just let me know

where and when. I was really happy to hear from you. Okay, I already said that once, but I am. I hope to hear from you soon."

Maggie played the recorded message over and over several times, listening to the cadence of his voice. She detected a definite New England accent, not Boston, but more northern, like maybe Maine. She wondered what kind of project he had in the city. What did he do for a living? Had Brett told her? Her mind was buzzing to the extent she could barely think beyond the reality she was going to meet her son. She didn't trust herself not to sound weepy or overly excited on the phone, so instead of returning the call, she sent a text, which she rewrote four times. She finally decided on, Thanks for getting back to me so quickly! Does Thursday of this coming week work for you? Maybe we could meet halfway for lunch? What works best with your schedule?

Less than ten minutes later, he replied, Thursday is good. There's a place in Brockton called Eleanor's. It's easy to find, right on the main road going into town. If that is convenient for you, we could meet there at noon. Your call. (Did you know the first department store Santa was in Brockton?)

Maggie sent a text confirming, then after he confirmed back, she sat at the kitchen window and stared out it for a long time. Finally she got up, pocketed her phone, then set out through the front door.

"You look like a woman on a mission." Natalie sat in one of the rocking chairs, watching Daisy play with a train set she'd brought with her and set up on the porch. "Where are you off to, Mom?"

"I'm just going to walk up to the beach for a few minutes."

"Want some company, or . . . no, you don't look as if you do," Natalie observed.

"I think I'd rather fly solo, but thanks. I don't expect to be long."

"We'll be here."

The walk to the beach was a short one. Maggie took off her shoes and made her way through driftwood and tangled loops of seaweed that had washed ashore in the recent storm. She climbed the rocks but didn't go all the way to the end of the jetty. She sat facing the harbor and the bay, with its islands beyond. She was happy and scared and wondering if somehow she might regret her upcoming meeting with Joe Miller. What would they talk about? They didn't know each other and very well may not have a thing in common.

She tried to think of topics that might be nonthreatening. His job would be a good place to start. What kind of projects did he work on? Where did he go to school? What did he major in? He hadn't mentioned a wife, but he could be married. If he was married, did he have children?

If he had children, she had grandchildren she'd never met. She covered her face with her hands. It was almost too much to grasp. After all this time, it was almost too much, too soon.

The sound of shells crunching beneath footsteps drew her attention. She looked back toward the road, and her heart caught in her chest.

"Hey," Brett called to her across the beach. He was in uniform, except for the Red Sox cap, which she was pretty sure wasn't department issued.

"That's a good way to ruin those policeman shoes you're wearing," she called back, her heart beginning to thump. *Keep it casual.* "The sand's pretty wet out here."

Could she do casual where Brett was concerned? Now, when the son they'd made together was coming into their lives?

"I'll dry them off and knock the sand out later." He drew closer, and with his aviator glasses covering his eyes, he looked more like the boy she used to know than he had the last time she'd seen him. Of course, that time he'd been sitting behind his desk in the police department. This time he was more in his element. He'd always loved the beach and the water. "Natalie told me I'd find you here. I hope you don't mind me stopping by. I won't stay long if it bothers you."

"It's okay." She sighed, then said something she hadn't realized she'd needed to say. "I'm sorry, Brett."

"You're sorry? For what?" He scoffed. "You have nothing to be sorry about."

"I flew into your office like a harpy. You'd been trying to tell me about Joe, and I kept blowing you off. I should have listened."

"The important thing is now you know. But as soon as Jayne told me he'd contacted her, I should have tried harder to get in touch with you. You shouldn't have had to find out the way you did." He lowered himself to sit on a rock near her.

"Still, I said some things that . . . well, I'm sorry."

"I'm sorry, too. For everything. I know I can't go back and change things, but I've been needing to apologize to you for years."

"Brett, now's not the time to—"

"There's never been a time. So will you please listen, let me get this all off my chest? This isn't what I came here to do—but things being the way they are right now, I don't know if I'll ever have this chance again." Without waiting for her to reply, he said, "I'm sorry I didn't pay more attention when you tried to tell me how much you hurt inside. It hurt me, too, but I wanted to be strong for you. So I tried to pretend it was all going to be okay. That we'd have other children and we'd go on to have a happy life together. I wanted that to be true. But it seemed no matter how hard I tried, you just got more and more sad as time went on. After a while, it was like there was you before the baby, and you after the baby. And being the jerk that I am, I tried to love the one and ignore the other. I want you to know how sorry I am for not trying harder to understand what you were going through. I'm sorry for not letting you know how much I was hurting, too."

She sat still as a stone, listening to words she'd waited forty years to hear. When he stopped, she tried to process everything he'd said before nodding. "I get it. I do. Maybe you couldn't deal with the fact I couldn't get over it, couldn't leave it in the past. I can understand that. What I can't understand, what's bothered me all these years, is that you wouldn't see him. You wouldn't look at him." She fought a wave of tears. "He was so tiny and so beautiful, and you wouldn't even walk down the hall to look at him."

"But I did," he said, his voice so low it was almost a whisper.

"What? When?"

"I went to the nursery the day you were leaving the hospital. I didn't plan on it, but when I got off the elevator, the nursery was right there. I went up to the window, and I saw the little bed they had him in. I saw the name—Lloyd—on a white card trimmed in blue, and I remember thinking it should have said Crawford, because he was mine. The nurse was wrapping him up in a blanket, and she held him up. 'Yours?' she asked. I started to say yes, but then I noticed a couple standing close to the glass. Before I could answer, they both said, 'Yes.' They were so excited they were beaming." Brett's voice cracked. "It was the only time I let myself wonder if we were doing the right thing."

"Why didn't you tell me?"

"What difference would it have made? We were going to walk out of the hospital and leave him behind, and that's what we did."

"All this time, a part of me has hated you because I thought you were ignoring the fact he was born."

"How the hell could I have ignored he was born? He was mine as much as he was yours." He took off his ball cap and ran a restless hand through his hair, his cowlick sticking up stubbornly before disappearing again under the cap. "He was ours, and we were giving him away. I hadn't wanted to see him because I knew some other guy was going to walk out of there with my son. Only then it would be *his* son. I thought if I didn't see him it wouldn't have been as hard to leave him. But that day, I knew it was my only chance, probably forever. So I stopped at the nursery window. I watched the nurse wrap him in that blanket, and I knew they were getting him ready to go home. But not with us."

"All this time, I thought you didn't care."

"Of course I cared. How could I have not cared?"

"I wish you'd have communicated that a little better."

"Maggie, for a long time, neither of us could talk about it. Then when we did, all you did was cry. I knew giving him away had broken your heart, and I knew it was my fault. I talked you into doing something you didn't want to do." He looked at her across the space separating them. "And I couldn't undo it. I could never make it up to you. When you left me in Seattle, I knew it was what I deserved. I hadn't fought for you when you needed me to, and I can never make that right."

"It wasn't just you. My parents . . . your father . . ."

"It shouldn't have mattered. I should have stood up to them. Should have backed you. I never would have lost you if I'd been less of a coward and more of the man you needed me to be. After you left me, I didn't run after you and beg you to come back, because I knew I didn't deserve you."

"Oh, Brett."

"When I didn't hear from you, I figured you just wanted to put it all behind you. And I thought I should give you that much. But something inside me never stopped hoping you'd come back. When I heard you'd gotten married, I thought, *Okay, she's found someone else to love. She's moved on. I should, too.*" He tried to smile. "Took me a little longer, and I have to say, I wasn't as good as you were about getting it right."

She raised her eyebrows, as if questioning him. Before she could respond, his phone rang. He took it from his belt, where it sat next to his holstered service pistol.

"Crawford . . . what? Where? Okay, secure the scene and get the witnesses' info. I'll be there in five minutes."

He turned to Maggie. "Hit-and-run over on Pratt Street. I need to go. But there's something else I need to tell you. About me being married three times. Something else I deeply regret." His expression was sober. "I married three very good women whose only failing was that they loved me. And I hurt them because I couldn't love them the way they deserved to be loved." He paused, took a deep breath. "Because the problem was, I wanted them to be you, and none of them were. It wasn't their fault. It was unfair and stupid of me to have married a woman while wanting her to be someone else. They deserved to be loved for themselves, and I couldn't do it, and I realize what an asshole I was. The truth is I never really loved anyone but you. I'm pretty sure I never will."

She wanted to cover her ears, but she couldn't move. His words hung between them for what seemed like a lifetime. Then Brett stood and stepped down from the rock he'd been sitting on. "So that's the story. Start to finish. We have a son together, and he wants to know us. He seems almost too good to be true. You'll understand once you've met him. I'm glad he's reached out to us. I'm glad you're back. Where any of this will lead is anyone's guess. But I'm keeping my options open." He started to walk away, zigzagging slightly to avoid the wettest part of the sand.

"Do you love your children?" Maggie called after him.

He stopped and turned. "Of course I love them. What kind of question is that?"

"You said you regretted having been married three times. Three marriages. One child from each wife, you said at the reunion."

"So?"

"So if you hadn't married each of those women, you wouldn't have those children. If you changed the past, those kids you love wouldn't exist."

Brett stared at her for a long time. "Huh."

His phone rang again, and he answered as he walked away, leaving Maggie with way too much to think about. Today, for the first time, he'd told her exactly how he'd felt forty years ago, and the confession had left her speechless. Forty years too late, she might have said, but then, as she'd pointed out, changing the past meant changing everything, and that she would not do.

She walked back to the house, thinking maybe she, too, should keep her options open.

~

On Thursday morning, Maggie stepped into the cavernous closet the prior owners had built. Even with every piece of clothing she owned housed there, she'd barely filled the space. She stared at her skirts on their hangers, her shirts, her jackets, blouses, and tops, trying to decide what to wear. Something plain but not dowdy. Casual but not too. The weather was projected into the low eighties, so something light. She decided on a navy pencil skirt and a white button-down long-sleeve shirt. She'd roll the sleeves up to her elbows and wear a necklace of glass beads Natalie had picked up for her on a trip to Italy. Nothing fussy, nothing she had to think about once she put it on. She wanted her focus to be on Joe, not herself.

The drive took over an hour, but it was an easy one. She kept to local roads as much as she could, avoiding the busy highway. She needed a slow-and-easy ride to calm her nerves. What if he didn't like her? What if he decided this meeting was a mistake and at the last minute decided not to come?

She turned into the restaurant's parking lot at 11:55 and parked in the first space she saw. Pulling down the visor, she checked her appearance in the mirror. No lipstick on her teeth. No mascara flaked on her cheeks. She fluffed her hair just a bit, took a deep breath, and got out of the car, the strap of her bag slung over her shoulder, her sunglasses covering her eyes. There were several others about to enter the restaurant when she arrived at the door, a party of five or six, and one young man who stood outside. They made eye contact briefly, and he smiled. She smiled back, a force of habit, and then he opened the door for her. Thanking him with another smile, she stepped inside, and he followed. She was taking off her sunglasses when she realized he was behind her. She turned and took a good look at him.

"Hello, Maggie." She'd dismissed him immediately because at first glance he hadn't looked old enough to be her forty-year-old son.

"How did you know it was me?" she asked.

He held out a hand to her, and she took it, barely noticing he hadn't answered her question.

"I'm so glad you're here." To the hostess, he said, "Reservation for Miller."

"I have two for noon." The pretty hostess smiled at him. "Would you prefer the dining room or the patio?"

Joe turned to Maggie, who peered past him. The patio tables were almost empty, promising some privacy.

"The patio looks lovely," she said.

The hostess led them to a table shaded by a fully leafed-out maple tree. Joe held Maggie's chair for her, then sat across from her at the small table.

"Your server will be with you in a moment," the hostess said as she handed them their menus.

"Thank you for coming," Joe said. "I was afraid you'd change your mind and decide not to come."

"After forty years?" She smiled. "Nothing could have kept me away."

He's almost too beautiful, she thought after he'd taken off his dark glasses and hung them from the open neck of his shirt. He was wearing the male equivalent of her outfit: navy Dockers and a white button-down shirt with the sleeves rolled to the elbows. She could indeed see her eyes in his, just as Brett had said. And she could see Brett in him as well, in the dimple on the left side of his cheek, the shape of his face. She couldn't help but smile.

"What?" Joe asked.

"You have a cowlick in the same place as Brett."

"That was the first thing I noticed when I met him, and believe me, I didn't thank him for it. I've wrestled with that thing all my life. I never could tame it." He self-consciously tried to force it down, but it didn't stay, and when it popped back up, they both laughed. "Well, at least I know I came by it honestly."

The waitress came by for their drink orders and to explain the specials. They ordered ice teas, a burger for Joe, and a strawberry salad for Maggie, who had little appetite and who'd barely looked at the menu. She was mesmerized by the fact of where she was and who she was with. The miracle was not lost on her.

"Tell me about yourself," she said. "I know you have a lot of questions, and I'll answer what I can, but could we first learn a little about each other before we talk about the past?"

"Sure. What do you want to know?"

Everything.

The waitress returned with their drinks, and Maggie waited until she left before responding, "Where you grew up. Went to school. What you studied. What you do for a living. Are you married? Do you have children?" Maggie was suddenly overwhelmed by everything she didn't know about this man, this newly found son. She sipped her tea to keep from asking more. There was so much to learn about him, about his life, but she had to slow down, take small bites instead of big gulps, lest he feel he was being interrogated.

"I grew up in a small town in Maine. Cape Elizabeth, near Portland. Less than ten thousand people. My dad ran the local medical center. He'd gone through med school on an ROTC scholarship, so he owed the army a few years. But once his debt was paid, he went back to his hometown, opened a clinic, and met my mom there. She was an RN. So was my wife." The index finger of his right hand began to tap slowly on the tabletop, measured beats against the white cloth. "We lost my parents and my wife during last year's pandemic."

Joe's eyes misted, and he cleared his throat.

"Oh, Joe, I'm so sorry. I am so very sorry." Maggie reached across the table to take his hand.

He nodded, an almost imperceptible acknowledgment of her condolence, before continuing. "Thank God, my kids and I survived. I have a son—Jamey, he's twelve—and a daughter, Louisa, seven. We call her Lulu."

Jamey and Lulu . . .

He cleared his throat again. "Anyway. I grew up there, great town. Good schools. Went to Bowdoin, then U. Maine for grad school, studied engineering."

"You didn't want to be a doctor, like your father?"

"I liked to build things. Engineering seemed a better fit. My parents didn't care. They just wanted me to find something that I liked doing."

"That was good of them," she said, thinking of parents she'd known who'd pushed their children to be what they wanted them to be, or tried. Chris Dean came immediately to mind.

"They were wonderful people, Maggie. Very fair, always, about everything. Try everything, but you get to decide what you like and what you don't. I was their only child, and they gave me a great life." His voice carried the weight of his emotions, his love for the parents who raised him, and his sadness at having lost them. "That's what I told Brett, and what I want you to understand, too. My wanting to connect with you and with Brett is not a reflection on them. I couldn't have had better parents. I'm not looking to replace them." He paused and took a few seconds to compose himself, his emotions so close to the surface. "I just want you to understand that. I loved my parents. I still do. Always will."

"Of course you do—and you will. You should. I understand completely. I don't have words to tell you how grateful I am to them."

"I was afraid you'd think I was searching for you because I was hoping to find something better because they weren't good parents."

"I never thought that for a minute, Joe."

The waitress delivered their meals, apologized for the delay, then topped off their ice teas. "Anything else I can get you?" she asked, and they both declined.

They made small talk while they ate, but when they finished, Joe took his phone from his pocket and scrolled across the screen, a smile on his face. "You asked how I knew you were you." He passed the phone to her.

The face of a little girl with curly blonde hair and huge eyes—blue like Brett's, not green like hers—filled the screen. "Lulu looks like you."

"Oh, look at her." Maggie zoomed in on the picture. "Actually, she looks so much like my daughter Grace at that age. She's thirty-two now and dark haired, but she was blonde when she was a child."

"So you have two daughters? Natalie and Grace?"

Maggie nodded as she returned the phone to Joe. He scrolled some more, then held the phone out to her again. "My son, Jamey. He definitely resembles his mother."

The boy had sandy blond hair and dark eyes. He stood in front of a lacrosse net, a stick in his hand, a broad grin on his face.

"He's very handsome, Joe." Maggie gave him back his phone.

Joe nodded. "Yeah. He's a good kid. Smart and kind and good natured. Heck of an athlete, too." He smiled. "Brett picked that up right away by the way he's standing. He'd scored three goals in that game. His best day ever."

"He looks very proud of himself." She picked at a lone strawberry she'd left on her plate, trying to decide how to ask her next question.

"And you look like you have something to say. Go on. You can ask me anything," Joe assured her.

"I was just wondering why now. Why you waited all these years to look for us." As soon as the words left her mouth, Maggie knew the answer. He'd lost everyone—his parents and his wife. He was looking for a connection to someone beyond himself and his children.

"Like I said, I'm an only child. I always knew I'd been adopted—my parents never hid that from me. But once they were gone, and Josie, my wife, was gone, I felt the kids and I were adrift. My son, my daughter—they had no cousins, no aunts or uncles. No one they could look to for . . ." He held his hands palms up in front of him while he searched for the words he needed.

"People who maybe looked a little like them? People with whom they shared a common background?" she offered.

"All of that. It took me months to get up the nerve to have my DNA tested at that genealogy site. When the results came back, I hit pay dirt. I found you both."

Joe grinned, and in his smile she saw Brett. For a moment, it dazzled her.

"Beginner's luck," he said. "You know how it went from there. Brett's sister, Jayne, popped right up. I contacted her because I wasn't sure how she fit into the story, since she was identified as an aunt. She got back to me pretty quickly. She said she knew who I was looking for, and if it was okay with me, she would have him contact me. And he did." Joe was still smiling. "Then Natalie popped up as a sister, and I almost couldn't believe it. The thought I had a sister . . . I can't explain what that meant to me." Joe paused. "Do you have any siblings?"

"I had a sister. Sarah." Maggie explained the circumstances of Sarah's death.

"My son has extreme sensitivity to insect stings, but I don't know how serious he takes it. I should make sure he always has his EpiPen with him. His sensitivity doesn't seem as serious as your sister's, but still . . ."

"Safe, not sorry," Maggie said.

"Yeah."

"So now you know you have sisters. And I know I have a grandson and another granddaughter. How amazing."

"I hope you want to meet them someday."

"You're kidding, right?" Maggie laughed. "Natalie has Daisy—she's three. Grace is divorced and has no children. Do I want to meet your kids? Oh yeah."

"I'll need to explain to them who you are, who Brett is. He's said he'd like to meet them, too." He finished the tea in his glass and shook his head to decline a refill when the waitress appeared at the table with a full pitcher. "I want to know more about you."

Maggie told him about growing up in Wyndham Beach, how she'd gone through school there.

"So you and Brett went to school together," he deduced.

"Yes. We started dating when we were fifteen. Right after he and his family moved to Wyndham Beach." She hesitated, not sure how many blanks she wanted to fill in right then.

"I'm not going to ask you anything personal," he assured her. "You're afraid I'm going to ask you things you might not be ready to talk about right now. I won't."

"I appreciate that. There will be a time for those questions." Maggie talked about her time at the University of Pittsburgh, how she'd gotten a degree in early childhood education, then moved to Seattle after graduation. She could tell Joe had questions, like why after she'd moved to the opposite side of the country she and Brett hadn't married, but he didn't ask. "Then I moved to Philadelphia. Taught kindergarten. Met my late husband. Got married. Had two kids. Raised them. My husband passed away two years ago."

"I'm sorry, Maggie."

"Yeah. Me too. Art was a great guy. A good husband and a wonderful father."

"And then I took a DNA test, and here we are."

"And here we are," she repeated, and reached for his hand.

"Do you think we could meet up again?"

"Of course. I didn't consider this a one and done. This has been one of the best days of my life, Joe. Thank you from the bottom of my heart for meeting me. For not resenting me or hating me. Or thinking I didn't want you, I didn't love you." Without warning, tears flooded her eyes and rolled down her cheeks. *Damn.* She'd promised herself she would not cry.

"Please." Joe moved to the seat between them. "I don't feel any such thing. I've wondered about you for most of my life, but never with resentment or judgment. I've wondered what brought you to that place where you made that decision, but that's something you may someday want to talk about. Or not. Either way, it's all right. I am grateful to you for giving me life, and I'm grateful to you for giving me a chance to know you."

He put his arm around her shoulder, and his comfort felt like the most natural thing in the world. "So you think about what you want to come next and let me know."

"You mean, think about if I want you to be part of my life?" She thought about what that might mean not only to her, but to her daughters. "Yes. I do. Of course I do. I believe Brett does as well."

"We've already talked about him meeting my kids, and me meeting his daughters. You've met them?"

"No, I never have."

"Really?"

Maggie nodded. "We haven't been particularly close over the years."

"I'm sorry. The way he talks about you, I thought . . . well, no matter."

"It's complicated."

Joe walked Maggie to her car, and they hugged.

"You have my number," Joe reminded her. "Please call me. Anytime. I want this to be a beginning."

"So do I."

He opened her car door, and she slid behind the wheel and turned on the ignition.

"You'll hear from me," she promised. She backed out of the parking space and drove toward the exit. When she checked the rearview mirror, he was still standing where she'd left him, watching her drive away.

Chapter Nineteen

GRACE

"Good morning." Grace pushed open the bookshop's front door.

"Hey, early bird." Liddy stood behind the front counter, going through some papers.

"I thought I'd stop by before customers started coming in so I could get a few pictures for the website." Grace swung the camera case from her shoulder and placed it on the floor. She looked around the shop and noted, "The lighting could be better."

"Feel free to wander around. Take whatever shots you want. I'm leaving the whole internet thing in your hands."

Grace scanned the front part of the store. The morning sun high-lighted the faint haze on the large front window, probably the result of not having been properly cleaned in a while. Judging by the dirty floor, Grace suspected Fred hadn't been big on housekeeping. She walked through the shelves of books, and it occurred to her that the store lacked display areas, making it hard for customers to find the books they wanted. The shelves went almost to the ceiling, too high for most people to reach while at the same time cutting off much of the natural light from the windows, and didn't seem to follow any particular order. Funny, but she hadn't realized how haphazard the arrangement was when she was browsing the shelves. She paused throughout the store to take photos, none of which inspired her when she reviewed them.

"Get any good shots?" Liddy asked when Grace returned to the front of the store.

"Not a one."

Liddy took off her glasses and set them on the counter next to her little handheld calculator. "Why not? I thought that's what you came to do."

"There just aren't any."

Liddy stared at her. "What's that supposed to mean?"

"Here. See for yourself." Grace showed her the pictures she'd taken. Liddy watched silently as the images scrolled past. "See anything you think might attract customers?"

"Humph."

"The place lacks ambience. It's dark and uninviting. We love this place, but it's pretty dingy. And it's in need of a really good cleaning." Grace looked down at the carpet that was bunched between her feet. "And frankly, this rug's gotta go before someone trips and breaks a bone or two. I'm surprised no one's fallen over it."

"Well, I know one person who has."

"Who? Did they sue Fred?" Grace asked.

"Me, and no, I did not."

"That's not the only problem with this place, Liddy."

"Do tell, since you seem to be on a roll."

Grace took a deep breath. "The bookcases are too high. They're one of the reasons it's so dark in here. And they're not well organized."

"Excuse me, but we're not the public library."

"You'd never know it by the way the store is set up."

"And you have how many years of experience in retail?" Liddy's ire had been fully stoked.

"None, but it doesn't take a marketing expert to know the space isn't utilized well," Grace countered. "Look, it's like being married to someone for a long time and not noticing they're going gray or gaining weight until someone else points it out to you. You get used to things looking a certain way, and it's okay. Until it isn't."

"All right then. How would you rearrange things?" Liddy challenged.

"I'd take up the carpet. I bet there's a wood floor under there, but it might need to be refinished."

Liddy came out from behind the counter, glaring, her hands on her hips. Before she could speak, Grace continued her critique as she walked through the store.

"I'd turn the bookcases around so they're facing the front of the store. Adult fiction in the very front—bestsellers on a table there in the center—children's books all the way in the back." Grace knew she was dumping a lot on Liddy, but she was on a roll. "These chairs are perfectly awful. Take Mom up on her offer to give you those chairs she isn't using. You could have story hour here. Maybe get a small rug you can unroll just for story time. You know, like a magic carpet?"

Liddy acknowledged the suggestion with a sort of grunt Grace took to be agreement, though her hands were still riding on her hips.

"And over here . . ." Grace pointed to the wall of shelves on the left side of the shop. "The space is not utilized well. If you moved those bookcases over there"—she pointed toward the opposite wall—"you could have a little coffee bar. Nothing fancy, but just a place where your customers can pick up a little something while they look over their selections or chat with friends." She gestured for Liddy to follow her to the back window. "You have a beautiful view out there. If that wild hedge was trimmed, you'd be able to see the harbor. I bet if you put in a patio, nothing expensive, you could have book club meetings out there in nice weather."

"Huh." Liddy tried to open the back door, but it was stuck. "Probably hasn't been opened in years," she grumbled.

"Let me help." Grace put her shoulder into it, but it still wouldn't budge.

"Do you need a hand there?" a male voice called from the front of the store.

Grace turned around in time to see a tall dark-haired man around her age make his way around one of the ill-placed shelves. He had a three-day scruff of beard and wore a blue T-shirt and cargo pants. The first word that popped into her mind when she looked at him was *pirate*.

"Damn door's stuck." Liddy stepped aside while the man wrestled with the door for several seconds before it opened with a groan.

Dried leaves and the ancient corpses of dead bugs danced in through the doorway on a light breeze.

"And now there's a damned mess," Liddy complained.

"You did want it open, right?" The man appeared to be fighting a grin. He winked at Grace. "I can close it back up again if . . ."

"Stop it." Liddy gave his arm a light smack. "You always were a smart aleck."

"I think you need a little WD-40 on those hinges, and it should be okay." He knelt to get a closer look. "I might have some in my truck."

He rose and started toward the front of the store.

"Got a broom in there, too?" Liddy asked.

"You're on your own there, Ms. Lydia." He kept walking and left the store.

Grace went out through the still-open door and walked around the grounds behind the bookstore. Judging by the overgrown hedge, the area hadn't been maintained any more recently than the interior of the shop. But like the shop itself, it had possibilities. A few flower beds, a patio large enough for maybe ten or twelve chairs, and it would be perfect. Grace walked toward the door, then noticed the man had returned and was working on the hinges. She stood outside, watching him administer the oil.

"So how's that cranky old grandfather of yours?" Liddy asked him.

"Old and cranky," he replied. "That's never going to change."

"How's his health?"

"He's hanging in there." He stood up and noticed Grace standing outside.

"Linc, you ever meet Grace Flynn? She and her sister used to spend summers at her grandmother's house over on Cottage."

"Our paths may have crossed when we were kids." He turned to Grace, and the only thought in her head was that his eyes were the color of chocolate. Deep and rich and delicious. "Nice to meet you, Grace Flynn."

"Same," she managed to say.

He wiped his hands on a red bandanna he'd pulled from his back pocket, then held the door for Liddy. "You want to try it out?"

Liddy gestured for Grace to step inside—"Just in case he's not as good as he thinks he is"—and closed the door. It reopened with ease. "Thank you, Linc. Put it on my tab. Now that you're here, I want you to scrap the plans for the carriage house we talked about, and take a look around this place for me. My decorator here"—she nodded in Grace's direction—"thinks we need a little work done."

He glanced around the shop. "You really needed to call in a decorator to tell you that?"

Liddy rolled her eyes. "Grace, why don't you tell him what you told me? Maybe he'll have some ideas about moving stuff around." Liddy walked toward the front of the store.

"Don't you want to . . . ," Grace began when she realized Liddy had removed herself from the conversation.

"No, I do not. You two decide what needs to be done and let me know." Liddy continued on to the front counter.

"Oh. Well." Grace felt slightly flustered. She'd offered her thoughts about the shop to Liddy because Liddy had asked. She hadn't expected her observations to be taken as anything more than suggestions. "I mentioned that I thought the bookshelves should be repositioned—see how they block the light? Makes the place look dark and"—she lowered her voice—"uninviting. A little creepy, frankly."

"Like you wouldn't want to be locked in here alone after dark," Linc said, and she laughed.

"Exactly like that." She walked through the comments she'd made earlier to Liddy, Linc occasionally nodding but not saying much beyond a few *yeah*s and *okay*s. When they got to the wall where she'd suggested Liddy consider a coffee bar, he pulled a retractable tape measure from his back pocket and began to measure out the space.

"You're thinking maybe a counter here and a place behind it for one person—no matter what we do, you'll never have room for more than one person there—a sink, a coffee maker, supplies, a couple of shelves. Anything else?" he looked up and asked after he'd walked the space, measuring here and there.

"You'll have to ask Liddy. It's her shop."

"She seemed to be handing the renovation off to you." He grinned, and the pirate image flashed back into Grace's head. "Which is probably the best thing she could do. I've done some remodeling for Mrs. Bryant before, and left to her own devices, she'll change her mind sixty times. She's had me working on plans for that old carriage house of hers for the past four months. We're on our third set of blueprints."

"And now we're putting that project on hold," Liddy called. "Just about everything I have went into buying this place, so the carriage house will have to wait. But I like the idea of income property, so I will ask you to take a look upstairs and see what we could do to make apartments on the second and third floors. Got time to take a look?"

"I don't right now, but I can stop back later in the week."

"Just let me know when." Liddy leaned on the counter. "Think you can come up with some plans for this place?" She waved her hand around the shop.

"It won't take much. Your decorator here has some good ideas. Easy to implement, not much in materials. You're going to end up paying mostly for my time and some paint," he told her as he walked to the front of the shop.

"And whatever you'll need to make the coffee bar," Grace reminded him as she followed along.

He rubbed his chin. "I think I might have something back home we can use for that. I'll work up a plan and drop it off."

"Don't take too long," Liddy told him. "I want to get this place done by July Fourth."

Linc shook his head. "Not gonna happen. I'm booked solid for the next month. If you need it done sooner, you need to call in someone else."

Liddy looked annoyed but shook her head. "I'll wait."

"It's up to you," he said.

"Shelby and Son's been doing for me for most of my life. I said I'd wait."

"Just want to make sure you understand you have options." He took a step toward the door.

"So you're a contractor, then." He had an easy way about him that Grace was drawn to. He was also easy on the eyes. Very easy, pirate or no.

"Most of the time."

She had to ask, "What do you do the rest of the time?"

"Fish." He smiled again. "Sometimes I sell to a couple of the restaurants in town. Depends on what's running and whether or not they're biting."

The front door opened, and a woman in her midforties entered. Grace recognized her as one of the shop's sales staff, Evelyn Marshall.

"Morning, Liddy. Carl told me to expect you to be here. He told me about your arrangement. I'm thrilled. This place desperately needs new blood." The woman smiled at Grace to acknowledge her, then said to Linc, "We had some of that cod you dropped off the other day. It was delicious. Thank you. My husband really enjoyed it."

"Good. Tell him I'll be going out again sometime next week, and I'll stop by to see how he's doing."

"Fishing was always Matt's thing. Since his accident, he hasn't been able to take the boat out." The sadness reached Evelyn's eyes. "Damned drunk driver."

"You tell him I'll be happy to take him out with me as soon as he's up to it." Linc patted her on the arm. To Liddy, he said, "I'll get back to you soon."

"Thanks, Linc. And thanks for getting that back door open."

"Sure." He smiled at Grace. "See you, Grace."

The three women watched him leave, then Liddy sighed. "If only I were twenty years younger."

"Twenty?" Grace smirked.

"Okay, twenty-five to thirty." Liddy nodded.

"Linc got that back door open?" Evelyn asked. "That thing's been stuck for as long as I've been working here. I'm going to take a look."

"Help yourself." Liddy moved the stack of papers she'd been working on earlier. "Now that Evelyn's here, I think I'll take these back into the office. Gracie, want to join me?"

"Thanks, but I need to get over to the general store. I told Mom I'd pick up a few things for her."

"How's that going? With your mother."

Grace shrugged. "It's okay, I guess. I love my mom, but honestly, this thing with Joe. She told you she met him for lunch last week, right?"

"Right."

"Well, she's talked to him on the phone several times since then." Grace paused and looked out the window. "Did she tell you she wants to invite him and his kids for the Fourth of July? For the parade and the picnic and everything else?"

"She mentioned it. I take it you're not happy about including him?"

"I hate that I'm always the family bitch. Natalie's thrilled. Even Daisy is excited to meet cousins, though she has no idea what that means. Honestly, I don't know if I can handle it." She picked up a book that was left on the counter and leafed through it absently.

"What is it exactly that you can't handle, Grace?"

"The whole thing. I hate we never knew about him until now. That she kept this deep dark secret all these years. And I hate that Dad never knew."

"Grace, I love you, sweetie, but that's between your father and your mother to work out in the next life. It has nothing to do with you." Grace opened her mouth to protest, but Liddy cut her off. "And if I may say, it's really none of your business. But everyone who's met Joe says he's a really great guy."

"Who's everyone?"

"Your mom. Brett." Liddy came around from behind the counter.

"Brett? You mean the police chief?" Grace frowned. "Why would he . . ." It was as if lightning had struck her brain. Her jaw visibly dropped.

"Oh my God. The cop? Seriously? My mom and *the cop* . . . ?"

Liddy squeezed her eyes shut. "Whoops."

Chapter Twenty

Natalie

Daisy burst through the back door, her hands filled with shells. Natalie followed, towels hanging off her shoulder.

"We were waiting," Daisy announced to Grace, who was loading the morning's breakfast dishes into the dishwasher.

"Waiting for what, pumpkin?" Grace asked.

"She means wading," Natalie explained as she hung the damp towels over the back of a chair.

"That's what I said." Daisy held up one bare foot. "A shell scratched my toe, and I bleeded. And we had sand on our feet, so we couldn't put our shoes on."

Grace leaned over as far as she could to inspect the cut. "Yes, I see. Need a Band-Aid?"

Daisy nodded. "One with Olaf."

"I don't know if Nana has any Olaf Band-Aids. You might have to settle for a plain one." Natalie went into the powder room and came back empty handed. "I thought Mom might have left a box in there, but I didn't see one. We'll have to ask her when she comes in."

"Comes in from where?" Grace asked.

"She's out front talking to someone in a police car. When I first saw it parked out there, I got scared that something happened while I was gone. But she's just talking."

"Police car?" Grace went to the front window and peered out. "Yup, it's him, all right."

"Him who? Who's him?" Natalie laughed from the doorway. "Who are you talking about?"

"Chief Crawford. Brett Crawford." She lowered her voice to a whisper. "It's *him*."

"Grace, you're not making any sense." Natalie went back into the kitchen and lifted Daisy onto a stool at the island. "Let me look at that little cut again. Oh, it looks fine, Daisy. It's already closed itself up."

"I can't believe she's out there talking to him *so publicly*." Grace was scowling as she came through the doorway.

"So? What's the problem?"

"The problem is that Brett Crawford, the police chief—you know who he is, right?"

"Sure. Daisy and I ran into him in the coffee shop yesterday. So what?"

"He's Joe's father, Nat," Grace whispered.

Natalie wasn't sure she'd heard correctly. "Say again?"

Grace spoke slowly and deliberately, pronouncing every word distinctly. "Brett Crawford is Joe Miller's father."

"And you know this how?" Natalie got a juice box from the fridge for Daisy and the pitcher of ice tea for herself.

"Liddy. She slipped yesterday."

"Really? Huh." Natalie thought for a moment, then grinned. "Well, he is sort of hunky. I'll bet he was really hot when they were in high school. Yeah, I could totally see Mom with him."

"Is that all you can say? He's a middle-aged hunk?"

"I didn't say middle-aged. But yeah, he's very good looking." Natalie poured herself a glass of ice tea and offered some to Grace, who declined. "I wonder if Mom kept her high school yearbooks."

"Really, Nat? You want to see if there are pictures of them together?"

"Why not? I bet they were really cute. I've seen pictures of Mom from back then, and she was a knockout. And now that I think about it, I could totally see him being an athlete. He's still a big guy, shoulders still broad. And yeah, he still looks really good. So what's your problem?"

"Doesn't it bother you he was so awful to her about . . . you know." Grace glanced at Daisy, who was paying attention. "About Joe? And then she sells our house in Bryn Mawr and moves here knowing he's here?"

"Hey, neither of us knows how things went down between them back then. And the house was hers to sell or to keep. And furthermore . . ." Natalie had started to return the pitcher to the refrigerator when Maggie walked in, and she fell silent.

"Wow, it's really heating up out there. I guess it's really summer," Maggie said.

"I need a Band-Aid, Nana," Daisy told her. "An Olaf one." She held up her foot for Maggie to inspect her cut.

"Nat, don't put away the tea." Maggie turned her full attention to Daisy. "I'm afraid I do not have any Olaf Band-Aids. But we can walk into town and see if the drugstore has any. Would you like to do that?"

Daisy nodded. "I would."

"You drink your juice, and I'll have a glass of ice tea, and then we can go." Maggie reached for the glass Natalie had filled for her. "Thank you, Nat."

"So Mom." Natalie grinned. "You and Chief Crawford, huh?"

"Oh, we were just talking." Maggie waved her off. "Oh, wait. You mean . . ."

Natalie nodded. "Grace spilled the beans."

"And who spilled to Grace?" Maggie asked. "Wait, let me see if I can figure this out." Maggie did her best Church Lady imitation. "Hmm. Who could it be? Could it be . . . Liddy?"

"She thought I knew, Mom," Grace said in Liddy's defense.

"And now you do." Maggie sipped her tea. "Is there something you wanted to say about that?"

"Nope." Grace pretended to zip her mouth closed.

"Natalie?" Maggie turned to her.

"Just that I could totally see you together, and he's still a hunk. Oh, and you could have just told us."

"Yes, because telling you the rest of it went over so well." Maggie shook her head. "Anything else you want to know?"

"Yes. Did you move back here to be with him?" Grace asked.

"No. Did I know he lived here? Sure, I did. Did I plan on seeing him? Only when it couldn't be avoided."

"You could have avoided seeing him just now," Grace pointed out.

"When I moved here, things were different than they are now," Maggie told her.

"Because of Joe."

"Of course because of Joe, Gracie. He's my son. And yes, he's Brett's son. And I can't wait till you meet him. I promise you'll like him. He's your brother."

"Half brother," Grace reminded her.

"I'd like to think this is a family where there are no 'halves,'" Maggie said softly.

"So we just accept this guy and welcome him with open arms just because—"

"Yes," Maggie interrupted. "Just because."

"I don't know if I can do that. I'm not going to pretend I can if I don't know."

"Fair enough. Wait until you meet him," Maggie said. "Please. Just reserve judgment until then."

"He's dying to meet you, Grace," Natalie piped up. "He's so impressed that you're a lawyer. He said his son wants to be a lawyer. He's twelve and he—"

"Hold on. You've met him, too?" Grace asked.

"No, but I can't wait to. We've spoken on the phone a few times. He's smart and he's funny and he sounds like just the guy you'd want to have as a big brother." Natalie draped an arm over her sister's shoulder. "Please keep an open mind until we all get together on the Fourth of July."

Grace turned to her mother. "By all, does that include Chief Crawford, too?"

"You can call him Brett, and yes, that includes him," Maggie said.

"Seriously? Will we set up a firepit in the backyard and roast marshmallows and tell ghost stories around the fire?"

"Hmm. Actually, that's not a bad idea." Maggie pretended to think it over. "Thanks for suggesting it, Grace."

Natalie's phone pinged to alert her to an incoming message. Grinning, she grabbed it from the counter, swiped the screen, then laughed.

Grace slanted her a look, then turned back to Maggie. "Come on, Mom. This is all moving a little too fast for me."

"I'm sorry you feel that way, sweetheart. But it's been a long time coming for me. Forty years, to be exact. Try to keep an open mind and an open heart. For my sake."

Natalie typed something into her phone, smiling broadly.

Grace nodded slowly. "Okay, I'll try. I promise. If that's what you want."

"It's what I need," Maggie told her.

Another ping. Another burst of laughter.

"Natalie, what is so freaking funny?" Grace glared.

"FaceTiming." Natalie held up her phone to show Grace the image.

"What am I looking at?" Grace leaned close, her eyes narrowed. "What—who is that?"

"It's Mr. Potato Head," Natalie whispered, pointing to Daisy, who was drawing a picture with an orange crayon.

"Mr. Potato Head?" Maggie grabbed the phone and stared.

Natalie nodded and held a finger in front of her lips.

"Are we supposed to guess who's wearing it?" Grace whispered.

"Hold up." Natalie giggled. "Daisy, someone wants to talk to you."

Seconds later, a male voice came through the phone. "Is Daisy there? Miss Daisy Doodle Dandy?"

Daisy all but flew to the phone, jumping from her stool to her mother's.

"I'm Daisy Flynn, not . . . who you said." Daisy looked into the phone.

"Do you know who I am?" the man in the Mr. Potato Head suit asked.

"Uh-huh." Daisy nodded. "You're Chris."

"No." The man in the suit tried unsuccessfully to hide his laughter. "I'm Mr. Potato Head."

Daisy pointed a finger at the screen. "No. You are Chris."

The man removed the head portion of the costume.

"See." Daisy looked up at her mother. "It's Chris."

Natalie suppressed a grin as her mother and sister both gaped.

"I guess I can't fool you, Daisy," he said. "I guess next time I'll have to come up with a better costume if I want to trick you."

Daisy nodded enthusiastically. "Next time be . . . a dragon."

"A scary dragon?" he asked.

"Uh-huh. But no fire," Daisy told him.

"Chris Dean in a Mr. Potato Head costume?" Grace shook her head. "Why?"

"Hi, Gracie!" Chris waved. "Hi, Mrs. Flynn."

"Chris." Maggie waved.

"Hi, Chris." Grace turned to Maggie and said under her voice, "What is happening?"

Maggie shrugged. "No clue."

Daisy, having lost interest, went back to drawing.

Natalie retreated to the back door and continued her conversation while still listening to her mother and sister. She wasn't sure who was more amusing, Chris or Maggie and Grace.

"Daisy, how do you know Chris?" Natalie heard Grace ask.

"From when he was at our house. He's Mommy's friend. He brought me a book." Daisy was focused on her drawing. "About a frog girl."

Natalie whispered into the phone, "My sister is interrogating my daughter."

Chris laughed. "Can you get close enough for me to hear?"

"I'll try. Hold on . . ."

"When was that?" Grace asked.

"Can you hear?" Natalie whispered, and an amused Chris replied, "Yeah. Tell Grace I said she has a future with the CIA."

"That time." Any time in the past was *that time* to Daisy. "The first one."

"The first one?" Grace was wide eyed. "How many times were there?"

"Nat," Chris said, "you better go bail out the kid before your sister brings out the water board."

"Talk to you later." Natalie turned off her phone.

"Sometimes"—Daisy continued to draw—"he comes to have dinner with Mommy and me."

Natalie placed the phone on the island and casually picked up her glass and took a sip. "That's a beautiful pumpkin, sweetie." She pointed to Daisy's artwork.

"It's not a pumpkin." Daisy looked up at her. "It's Nana's car."

Maggie leaned close. "Why, so it is. I always wanted an orange car." She tapped Natalie on the shoulder. "Is there something you want to tell us? About you and Chris?"

"Is there something you want to tell us, about you and Chief Crawford?" Natalie smirked.

"Don't change the subject," Grace said. "Mom and the chief are old news—sorry, Mom—but since when has Chris been visiting you? And does he stay over?"

"My, aren't we nosy?" Natalie finished her tea and rinsed out the glass.

"Natalie. Fess up," Grace whispered. "Are you and Chris . . . ?"

"We're friends. We've always been friends. You know that."

"Well, I consider him a friend of mine, too, but he doesn't visit me." Grace turned to Maggie. "Mom, make her talk."

"I'm sure if Natalie had something she wanted to share with us, she'd do it. Wouldn't you, Nat?" Maggie said pointedly.

"You two are a riot." Natalie laughed. "There's not a lot to tell. Chris was on his way to New York about a month ago, and his plane landed in Philly for some reason. So he called and asked if we could have dinner. I was just getting ready to put Daisy to bed, but I told him he was welcome to come over if he felt like driving." She shrugged. "He rented a car and drove to my place. I ordered takeout to be delivered, and we had dinner, and then he drove back to the airport and caught his plane."

"His plane?" Grace raised her eyebrows.

"Yeah. He has a little jet. Why?"

"Did it occur to you maybe he had the plane stop in Philly on purpose?"

"I did wonder about that," Natalie confessed.

"I think it was intentional," Grace said.

"It's not important." Natalie lifted Daisy from her seat. "Come on, Daisy. Let's find your sneakers. I'll walk into town with you and Nana to look for special Band-Aids."

"And I'm going to work on Liddy's website before this day gets any weirder. You should have taken a screenshot of him in that costume. Any one of those gossipy entertainment rags or TV shows would have paid you handsomely." Grace paused to plant a kiss on Daisy's head as she left the room.

There were no Olaf Band-Aids to be found at the general store or the pharmacy, but a stop at the ice-cream shop served just as well to heal Daisy's toe. After they returned to the house, Maggie headed out back to do some weeding in her garden. Daisy wanted to help, so the two of them went outside. Natalie grabbed a book from the stack she'd brought with her from home and went out to the front porch. She pulled one of the rocking chairs closer to the porch rail, sat, and rested her legs on the railing. Fifteen minutes later, she realized she was still staring at the first page.

She'd known Maggie would ask her about her relationship with Chris on that walk into town, so she'd prepared herself, but when her mother asked, "So how long have you been seeing Chris, and does Emma know?" Natalie forgot her rehearsed lines.

"We've been in touch since Grace and I went to his concert," she'd responded honestly. "And no, Emma doesn't know."

"Is there a reason neither of you mentioned it to your mother?"

"Yes. So you wouldn't be asking the questions you're asking now. So you wouldn't think we had some great romance going on. We don't. We're just friends."

"How often has this 'friend' found his way to Philly on his private jet?"

"Several times."

"Well, let's see. Several is more than a couple, which would be two. So somewhere between three and whatever?"

"Yeah. Three and whatever." Natalie laughed. "Four. He's stopped in four times."

"Four times in the past month?"

Natalie nodded.

"And . . . ?" Maggie gestured for her to continue.

"And . . . he calls. We FaceTime. We text." Natalie could have added, *At least once a day, every day.* But best to play it down. "No big deal."

"Okay. No big deal." Maggie had turned her attention to Daisy, who'd stopped walking and was about to pick one of the neighbor's prized peonies. "Those are not ours, Daisy. You can help me pick our own flowers when we get back to the house."

And that had been the extent of the conversation about her relationship with Chris. It was more complex, more nuanced than she'd let on, but she was conflicted about her own feelings. She knew he cared about her—he'd said as much—but she also knew he'd been seeing some high-profile women. She'd have died before she'd admit it, but she'd become addicted to those gossipy TV shows. She'd yet to pass by any supermarket magazine that had Chris's face on the cover without picking one up. Last week she'd actually found herself hiding in the paper goods aisle hunched over a tabloid story about how he'd rescued an ex-girlfriend from suicide after he'd dumped her via text—a story he'd sworn was absolute rubbish when she'd chided him about it.

"Seriously, Nat? You know me better than that. Dumping someone by text? And, by the way, she dated my manager, not me. I've never been alone with her, I've never sent her a text of any kind, and if she'd tried to commit suicide, this is the first I've heard about it."

"Why would they make up a story like that?"

"To sell magazines, why do you think?" He'd shrugged. "They make up crazy crap all the time so people will pick up the magazine and talk about it. Crap sells."

Their relationship was hard to define. Yes, they were friends. The things that had drawn them to each other years ago still attracted. They both laughed at the same things. They liked the same books and movies and disliked the same television shows. They both loved *Game of*

Thrones and had seen every episode more than once, and had read each of the books. Classic rock? Yup. Butter pecan ice cream and taco salad? Yes indeed. Environmental awareness? Absolutely. *Mad Men? The Office? Seinfeld?* Bring on the reruns. They saw eye to eye on almost every political issue. They never ran out of things to talk about.

One thing they didn't agree on was where their relationship was headed. Natalie was struggling to keep things in the friend zone. Chris wanted to move it toward something else. He'd made certain she understood that, by his words and by the way he kissed her. He never left her house without kissing her goodbye and making sure she understood he was game for more, but not unless and until she was.

Then there was his reputation of being a player. As much as Natalie cared about him—wanted to test those waters with him—she had yet to determine how much of his rep was hype and how much had roots in fact. If their relationship became romantic and didn't work out—*And why would it,* she asked herself over and over, *because he can have his pick of anyone*—how awkward would that be? How could they maintain a friendship after a bungled romance? He was so affectionate with Daisy, and Natalie loved watching them interact, but how would her daughter feel if Chris disappeared from their lives? If things ended really badly, how might that affect their mothers, who were such close friends? Maybe best to avoid future regret, as they said in those late-night commercials, and forgo the love story.

But there was that little voice inside her that teased with thoughts of how it could be if it *didn't* end badly. What if they really did fall in love? What if they could live happily ever after?

What if she could tell Chris he was right, the reward would be worth the risk?

"Would you ever move back to Wyndham Beach?" he'd asked her as he was leaving after his last visit.

"I don't know. Would you?"

"I would if you would," he'd told her. She'd searched his face for a sign he was teasing, but she'd found none.

"I don't see you doing that," she'd said.

"Not right now. Maybe not for a while," he'd admitted, "but someday."

"Maybe someday."

"Someday for sure," he'd said right before he'd kissed her goodbye. "You and me, Nat. Someday . . ."

Chapter Twenty-One

MAGGIE

Letting go of the anger Maggie'd held on to for so many years felt like dropping a hundred-pound weight she'd been carrying on her back. Relieved of the burden that had caused her nothing but sorrow, she was free to open her heart completely not only to Joe, but to Brett. It had shocked her to learn he'd suffered, too, and while she wished with all her heart he'd opened up to her sooner, she had no regrets in the way her life had turned out. She'd always believed things turned out the way they were meant to.

On the Monday after her lunch with Brett, Maggie walked into town and stopped at Ground Me for coffee and doughnuts, then made her way across the street to the police station.

"Hey, Maggie. Nice to see you again." From her post, Coraline checked out the carrier holding two cups of coffee and the bag with Ground Me on the front. "And so soon."

"Good morning. Is Chief Crawford in?" Maggie ignored Coraline's scrutiny.

"He's in his office. I'll let him know you're here." Coraline buzzed him, relayed the message, then hung up. She pointed toward the hall. "You know the way."

"I do. Thanks."

Maggie tapped on Brett's open door with the back of the hand holding the bag.

"Hey, Maggie. This is a surprise." He stood and walked around the desk. "Is that coffee . . . ?"

"Yes, and a doughnut. Glazed. You used to like those, so I thought . . ." She handed him the bag.

"If I didn't know better, I'd think this was a peace offering." He moved a stack of files from one of the visitors' chairs and gestured for her to sit.

"I needed an excuse to come and see you." She sat and took the top off her coffee to have something to do with her hands.

"You never need an excuse, but I'm glad you're here." He opened the bag and smiled. "No one in town does a better glazed doughnut than the guy they have working in the back at Ground Me."

"I met Joe. We had lunch on Thursday," she said.

He raised an eyebrow. "How'd it go?"

"Great. He's . . . well, you met him. I don't need to tell you what he's like." She sipped her coffee.

"I'm so happy it went well for you, and that you saw what I saw in him." For a moment, his hand holding the doughnut paused in midair. "Meeting him made me wonder what if . . ."

"No." She waved a hand at him. "We're not going there. Not today, not ever. He is who he is because of the people who raised him, and we're going to accept that and not speculate or talk about anything different, hear me?"

Brett nodded. "I hear you, and you're right. We should focus on who he is, not . . . well, not anything else."

"I really like him. I can't wait to see him again."

"I feel the same way." Apparently sensing it might be time to change the subject, Brett said, "So Liddy's buying the bookstore from Fred. It's about time. Poor Carl really had his hands full, trying to run the hardware store and keep track of his father at the same time."

They talked for a few more minutes, but then Brett got a call, reminding them both he had a job to do. Maggie left after he picked up the phone, and waved goodbye from the doorway.

On Wednesday, she brought coffee to the office again, and on Friday, she picked up lunch for them to share at his desk. Maggie was beginning to look forward to spending a half hour or so with Brett every few days, and it appeared he did as well. They were more relaxed and friendly with each other than she ever expected they could be, and she enjoyed his company. More than ever, she knew she'd done the right thing in moving back to Wyndham Beach. It had been an emotional decision, the first step in shrugging off the mantle of sorrow she'd worn for much of her life, beginning with the death of her sister, continuing with the loss of her baby, her parents' divorce, the continued grief for her son, the eventual breakup with Brett, and the death of her mother, and ending with Art's passing. So many times during his illness, Art had urged her to seek happiness after he passed, to not spend the rest of her life in mourning. At the time, she hadn't believed her future held much joy, but there'd been more laughter than tears as that heavy mantle began to slip from her shoulders. She'd made her peace with Art when she'd sold their home and made the decision to move on with her life. Now, with every day that passed, life seemed brighter, the future more hopeful, than she'd ever imagined possible. She was beginning to believe something wonderful was waiting for her, if she'd only reach for it. If she only believed.

~

On Saturday morning, Maggie walked up Cottage Street following her run. Sweat ran down her face, and she swore even her eyelashes were sweating. She was wiping her face with the bottom of her T-shirt when she heard a car pull up next to her.

It would be him, she inwardly groaned after she glanced over her shoulder and saw the blue-and-white police car stopped at the curb.

"This is a new look for you," Brett said as he got out from behind the wheel.

"Nice of you to notice." She pulled her shirt back down and tried to pull up her ponytail.

"Hard not to. I haven't seen you sweat like that since you were on the track team back in high school."

"I'll have you know I'm in training for a marathon," she told him.

"Do tell." Looking faintly amused, he leaned back against the passenger-side panel.

"It's been on my bucket list. And after talking to Dee Olson at the reunion luncheon, I was inspired. Do you know she runs marathons?"

"I do. She runs the Boston Marathon every year. She's quite the accomplished runner."

"Well, she told me she'd help me get started if I was serious about it. I thought I'd run a few miles every day before I called her. You know, build up to it." She rested her hands on her hips. "It would be really embarrassing to go out with her and pass out after the first quarter mile."

"Yeah, I can see where that'd be a problem." He rubbed his chin to hide a grin.

"So have you talked to Joe this week?" she asked.

"Yeah, this morning. That's what I wanted to talk to you about." He took off his sunglasses, their eyes locked, and inside her head she heard that old familiar buzz. "We were thinking about dinner tomorrow night. You, me, Joe." He studied her face for a long moment before putting his glasses back on. "What do you think? You ready for that?"

"I . . . yes. Yes. I'd love that," she heard herself say, pushing away all thoughts of it being too soon or feeling too much like a family dinner.

"I thought maybe Crossen's, out on the Cape."

"I haven't been, but I heard it's really good. Sure."

307

"So I can tell him you're in?"

"I'm in. Yes. Definitely in."

"Great." Brett nodded and pushed away from the side of the car. "So how 'bout I pick you up around six?"

"Oh. Sure. Good." Maggie nodded. "Yes."

"I'll see you then." He walked around the front of the car to the driver's side and opened the door. He stood for a moment, and Maggie had the feeling he wanted to say something more, but all he said was, "Bye."

She raised one hand in a sort of half wave, then when the car pulled away from the curb, she resumed walking toward her house, already second-guessing her decision. Would it feel strange, the three of them together? Lunch with Joe had been fine, and Brett's dinner with him apparently had gone well. And her visits the past week and a half with Brett had gone really well. But was it too soon to have the three of them together?

Would it feel strained to Joe? To her? One minute she thought it was a great idea, the next, the worst ever.

Her biggest fear? That it would feel too much like what might have been.

~

The drive to the Cape wasn't as awkward as it could have been. Brett may have sensed her unease, or maybe he felt a lick of anxiety himself. He kept the conversation light, ignoring the elephant in the room, for which Maggie was grateful. She didn't want to talk about how she felt, and she didn't want to know his feelings about what they were about to do. Instead, he entertained her with stories about dumb criminals and dogs, like the guy who burglarized a house, was attacked and chased by the homeowner's dog, then called the police to report the dog bite. Or the guy who kidnapped a pricey best-in-show-winning pug and left a ransom note written on the back of an envelope that had his full name and address on the front. By the time they reached their destination, laughter had helped Maggie relax enough that she could shake off her worries.

Joe had waited inside at a table overlooking the water, with a spectacular view of the sunset over the dunes. He'd risen when Maggie and Brett approached the table, offering Maggie a hug and extending both hands to shake Brett's. After making their drink selections—beer for Brett and Joe, wine for Maggie—the conversation easily drifted from one topic to another.

"Jamey had a swim meet this afternoon," Joe told them after Maggie asked what his kids were doing for the summer. "He said he wanted a job to start saving for law school, but I reminded him there was time for that and he should concentrate on being a twelve-year-old."

"Right. Don't want him growing up too fast, or to push him into something he doesn't want to do," Brett commented.

"You played football from the time you were what, seven?" Joe asked, and Brett nodded. "Did you ever feel pushed?"

Brett hesitated. "Maybe a little. My dad played when he was in high school and was good enough to get a scholarship for college, but he wrecked his knee his freshman year, so there went the scholarship, and there went college. So he had really high expectations of me."

"Which you fulfilled in spades," Maggie reminded him. "And I don't remember you wanting to do anything else. You loved playing."

"You're right." Brett turned to her. "I did. I don't regret a minute of it up until the time I got hurt. There was nothing else I wanted to do."

"How did you feel about that? About not being able to play anymore?" Joe asked, something Maggie herself had wanted to ask. She'd been there through his entire journey, except for the end.

"It sucked." Brett shrugged. "And I can't say I handled it very well. But in time I came to accept the fact my playing days had come to an end."

The rest of the evening passed smoothly, with Joe discussing his work as an engineer and the part he played in the design and construction of several major industrial projects in New England, and Maggie talking about her daughters and their lives. He was particularly interested in meeting Natalie, he said, since they'd corresponded.

"She's dying to meet you," Maggie told him. "Grace, on the other hand, is having a bit of a problem with this. She wishes . . ." Maggie swallowed hard. This was no time for anything short of total honesty. "She feels I wasn't honest with her father—which, admittedly, I was not."

"I understand," Joe said. "I hope she comes around."

"So do I," Maggie said. "Which reminds me. I'm having a cookout for the Fourth of July, which is a big deal in Wyndham Beach. Parade, followed by games for the kids at the town park. This year there'll be carousel rides as well, and we top off the day with fireworks."

"Which are always spectacular," Brett told him.

"So I was wondering if you would like to come and bring Jamey and Lulu, and spend the day with us." She turned to Brett. "You're invited, too, of course. I meant to ask you earlier."

"I'll be working most of the day," Brett told her, "so I won't be free until after the fireworks."

"You have to eat sometime. Come over when you're done."

"It's a date," Brett told her.

She felt a little flush rise up her neck to her cheeks. Had she intended the invitation to feel like a date? Up until that moment, she hadn't thought it through.

"It sounds like a great day. I'd love to come, and I think the kids will, too. Thank you for including us." Joe paused. "But are you sure you want to open that can of worms after, well, after keeping me a secret for forty years? Are you sure you want to go public in front of the entire town now?"

Maggie nodded slowly. "I'm not ashamed or embarrassed about you. You are my son." She felt the tears welling in the corners of her eyes. "I waited a very long time to be able to say that out loud. At this stage of my life, I'm not afraid of what people will think or what they'll say."

Joe reached for her hand. "Thank you."

"I'm with Maggie," Brett said. "Besides, anyone looking at you would know whose son you are. No point in denying paternity."

"Well, yeah, the resemblance is tough to ignore." Joe pointed to his hair. "The cowlick would give it away if nothing else."

After coffee and dessert, they walked out to the marina behind the restaurant, making small talk while they watched a few boats being moored, taking their time, trying to delay saying goodbye.

Finally, Brett glanced at his watch. "I need to call it a night. I have an early meeting in the morning."

"Well, I'll see you both soon. Fourth of July. It's a definite yes." Joe embraced Maggie and placed a kiss on her cheek, and the warmth filled her with hope for the future.

"It went well, don't you think?" she asked Brett on the way home. "I was afraid it would feel awkward."

"It felt . . . normal. Like three people who like each other getting together for dinner. It just felt normal."

She sighed and rested against the headrest. Maybe not parents out for dinner with their adult son, but yeah, like three people who like each other getting together for dinner. Exactly like that. It had felt normal, and normal was more than she could have asked for.

"I really do appreciate the invitation for the Fourth," Brett said. "Are you sure you want to include me? I mean, what will your daughters think?"

"Grace could be horrified. Natalie will think it's about time."

Brett laughed. "And what do you think?"

"I think maybe it's about time, too." Maggie paused before asking, "You?"

"Past time." He reached across the console for her hand. "Think there's any chance we might ever . . ."

"Don't push your luck," she said good-naturedly. "Let's just see how it goes."

"It's your call," he told her. "I'm just grateful you didn't say no."

She held his hand for a few minutes, then dislodged her fingers and reached for the radio "On" button.

"Do you mind?" she asked.

"Not at all. There's a seventies station and an eighties station. Which would you prefer?"

She thought about it. "Surprise me."

He hit a button, and music surrounded them.

Ambrosia. "Biggest Part of Me."

Maggie groaned, and Brett laughed.

"I could pull over to the side of the road, and we could dance," Brett said, a twinkle in his eye.

Maggie laughed in spite of herself. One thing she'd always loved about Brett was his sense of humor. Good to know that hadn't changed.

~

Maggie walked around the Tudor-style bookstore's spacious backyard, taking note of existing plantings and where sun and shadow fell.

"I think we could move some of my iris back here once you get that boxwood hedge trimmed. It's really out of control. It forms a nice barrier between the alleyway on the left and the parking lot for the ice-cream shop on the right, so I wouldn't take it out unless you wanted to install fencing. Which is an expense you probably don't need right now."

"No, I don't need to add anything else. If I could afford it, I'd hire a landscaper to do the hedge, maybe trim back that crab apple tree, plant some flowers, put in a patio, but none of that can happen for a while. Buying the store pretty much cleaned me out," Liddy admitted. "I had to put the renovations to the carriage house on hold until I get caught up."

"Why'd Carl decide to sell the building along with the store? I thought he only wanted to sell the business?"

"I don't know. I guess holding on to it, collecting rent, sounded like a good idea for a while. But when we sat down to negotiate, I think he figured he might as well unload the whole thing, and I'm glad he did. I love this building, and once it's fixed up, it's going to be great. Fred lost a lot of business to online retailers and the bigger chains because the place was so shabby, no one other than locals bothered to come in. To tell you the truth, even I hadn't realized what a mess this place was, because I was here so often."

Maggie nodded. "The familiar often goes unnoticed. After a while, we don't see the flaws."

"Exactly. And as far as his stock was concerned—let's face it, Fred's orders weren't always up to date. Sometimes bestsellers were a month or more late, and his displays were haphazard. And he never advertised. With just a little effort, he could have pulled in more customers from the academy and visiting parents. The school has a lot of big weekends he could have capitalized on, but judging from his sales history, he never took advantage of the influx of out-of-towners."

"Good point. I hadn't thought of that. The school brings a lot of people into town, so maybe you should plan events around their schedule. The sailing school in the summer could bring in more sales, too."

"That's what I'm hoping. Then there's the space on the second and third floors. I think I could get zoning approval for apartments."

"Did you ever see yourself as a shop owner slash bookseller slash landlady?" Maggie teased. She knelt to push aside dead leaves from what might have been a flower bed, but nothing of interest grew under the debris.

"No. But this town needs a bookstore, and I needed something positive to do with my life. The more I thought about it, the more it seemed right, so I figured, why not? It's a nice reminder all life's surprises aren't necessarily bad ones."

"You're preaching to the choir there." Maggie smiled, recalling the surprise that had popped into her life recently. Definitely not a bad thing. "I'll work out back here for you, see if I can make it look a little nicer. Not as good as a professional landscaper, but I can improve what's here."

"That would be great, Mags, thank you. I won't turn down help. You have such a great eye, I'm sure it will look fabulous when you're finished. But are you sure you want to spend your time working here when you could be with your girls?"

Maggie held up her tattooed left wrist. "Waves of the same sea, girlfriend."

"Ah, there is that." Liddy started to hug Maggie just as Maggie's pocket buzzed.

Maggie took her phone from her pocket. "That's my reminder I need to get going."

"Appointment?"

"Sort of." Maggie smiled. "I'm meeting Brett for coffee at Ground Me."

"Going public, are you? You know it'll be all over town before noon." Liddy lowered her voice to a stage whisper and mimicked a gossip. "You'll never believe who I saw having coffee together this morning. Our chief of police and that nice widow, Maggie Flynn. You remember Maggie Lloyd, Ellen's daughter? She grew up here, moved to Philadelphia, and married some hotshot lawyer. He died and she moved back, bought the Wakefield house. Didn't she and the chief used to have a thing . . . or am I thinking of someone else?"

Maggie laughed. "Well, people might as well get used to seeing us together."

"You and Brett are . . . what are you doing, anyway?"

"We've been talking a lot lately. And there's been a lot to talk about, what with me living here and Joe finding us. It's like the past smacked us both in the face, and we're trying to deal with that. We both know we want a relationship with Joe, so it's only natural we have some sort of relationship with each other. We'll see how it goes."

"You're not thinking about . . ."

"Right now, I'm trying not to think. I just want to take things day by day. I never dreamed our lives would play out this way. Now we share a son and a couple of grandchildren. We both want to know them and want them to be part of our lives. As for Brett—I'm leaving my options open."

"Wow. Just . . . wow."

"Like I said, day by day. I don't feel any need to look beyond right now. Oh, except I invited Joe and his kids for Fourth of July. We'll do the parade, then go back to the house for a cookout, fireworks at the park later."

"Don't forget the carousel. Emma said Owen Harrison promised he'd be back in time to have it set up in the park for the kids. I'm not sure how she managed to talk him into it."

"Ha. It must have been Emma's charm."

"Are you sure you're ready to have everyone together so soon?"

"The sooner the better. I figure it's like ripping off a Band-Aid. One swipe and it's done."

"Grace and Nat are okay with it?"

"They're both on board, and so far no one's voiced any objections, so I'm taking that as a good sign. Even Grace is trying. I think she'll be fine once she meets Joe." She hoped Grace would be fine. Her daughter had promised to keep an open mind. "You'll come over after the parade, right?"

"Wild horses couldn't keep me away. What can I bring?"

Maggie's phone rang, and she answered it. "Yes, I'm on my way. Five minutes. Order a coffee for me, a . . ." She laughed. "Right. Thanks for remembering. See you soon."

Liddy raised an eyebrow. "Tell me he remembers how you take your coffee."

"He does."

"That's amazing. After all these years . . ."

"Nah. It's only since Sunday night. We had dinner with Joe." Ignoring Liddy's dropped jaw, Maggie grabbed her bag from the grass. "Gotta go. Talk to you later." She stepped inside the shop. "Oh, and since you asked, bring potato salad. No one makes better."

"I was thinking more along the lines of margaritas." Liddy was right behind her. "Chips and salsa. But wait. You had dinner with Joe and Brett and you didn't tell me?"

"I just did."

~

True to his word, Brett had her coffee, along with a cherry cheese danish, waiting for her when she entered the shop.

"So what have you been up to since Sunday night?" he asked after she'd taken a few sips of coffee and a bite of her danish.

"Just trying to get things organized for the Fourth. I found horseshoes up on the garage loft, so I thought maybe we could play games if things seemed awkward. You know, get everyone up, break the ice if we needed to." She hesitated before asking, "Are you going to have any of your kids this summer? Would you want me to include them?"

"Jenna lives with Kayla, and they go to Kay's mother's on Martha's Vineyard every year for the entire summer." Brett rested a forearm on the table. "My oldest, Chloe, will be with Beth, her mother—my first wife—and her stepfather in Austin. Alexis, my fourteen-year-old, wants to come for the summer, though, and Holly, her mother—"

"Wife number two," Maggie interjected. Holly, the California surfer girl who was quite a bit younger than Brett. She wasn't about to admit it, but Maggie had googled all three of his wives.

"Right. Alexis always spends most of the summer here. She's intrigued by the idea of a secret older brother. She wouldn't miss this get-together for the world."

"You told her about the Fourth of July at my house?"

Brett nodded. "We spoke last night, and she asked me what she could do here this summer, and that's the first thing that came out of my mouth. Party at Maggie's."

"Did she ask who I am?"

"I told her you're Joe's mother. She's processing all that. Alexis is really smart. She'll figure it all out. I still need to come up with something for her to do while I'm working, though. There's the beach. Emma said there will be classes at the art center, but that's only for a few hours on Tuesday and Thursday. I can't leave her alone in the house all day."

"Think she'll miss the California life?"

"Doubtful. She has very little interest in board surfing or windsurfing. She's more of a bookworm. She likes biking and likes to go on hikes, but water sports, not so much."

"Maybe Alexis could babysit for Daisy while Natalie's still here. She wanted to get involved with the renovation of the bookstore, since Grace and I are pitching in."

"I'll ask her. She'll be here next week."

"Great. Liddy's planning on some nice changes. She'll have a grand reopening once all the work's completed."

"Does she need anyone to paint? I'm hell with a paintbrush."

Maggie laughed. "Yes, I seem to recall the hellish job you did on that first place we had in Seattle. We could have been evicted if the landlord had seen the mess you made before we got it all cleaned up."

"I made a mess of a lot of things back then. I know I can never say I'm sorry often enough to make up for any of it. Hindsight's a bitch, isn't it?"

"You've apologized, Brett." She was aware the older woman at the next table was listening and watching from the corner of her eye.

"I was an asshole back then." He lowered his voice. "I don't know how you could have loved me, but you did. I screwed up your life, and I screwed up my own at the same time."

"Listen, there's something I need to say to you. I didn't intend to do this today, and certainly not here. But there are things you need to know, and I guess . . . well, I guess now is as good a time as any." Maggie took a deep breath and whispered. "I've had a lot of time to think about things. A lot of time to look back and try to remember how things really were. Brett, I could have stood up to you. I could have defied my parents. I could have—I *should* have stood up for myself, and for our baby. But I didn't. I let everyone else make that decision, because it was easier for me. And I made you the villain, and I've played the victim ever since. I made you pay for the fact I didn't have the courage I should have had." Maggie swallowed hard. "So this apology is on me. I shouldn't have put all the blame on you."

He started to speak, but she shook her head. "Ultimately, the choice had been mine." Another hard swallow. "And yes, hindsight is a bitch. We can't change what happened back then. But we can appreciate where we are now. Joe said he had a great life. He's happy and successful, and he's appreciative of the gift we gave his parents. Yes, at a cost to us, but still, things have worked out. I married a man who loved me. My girls are the light of my life. You have kids you love. Joe is back in our lives. I believe with all my heart that things happen the way they're meant to." She held his hand, tugged it a little closer, and leaned in. "We can't go back, Brett, but we don't have to be defined by things that happened thirty or forty years ago."

"Then why can't we start over? Like start at the same place we started the first time around. I ask you out on a real date. You say yes."

"Do you remember our first date?"

Brett groaned. "I was hoping you'd forgotten. That party at Moose Jorgensen's. His parents were away for the weekend, his brother was home from college, and he brought a keg. The whole football team was there. I was the new guy, and all the other guys were drinking. Everyone got drunk and sloppy and sick. Okay, I didn't get sick, but I'm pretty sure I wasn't at my best." He shook his head at the memory. "I could have kicked myself. Here I'd been in Wyndham Beach for two whole weeks and I'd snagged a date with the most beautiful girl in the entire school, and I got drunk. I'd been so nervous all day, thinking about you, I couldn't eat. I drank one beer because besides wanting to fit in, I thought it would help me calm down, and when it didn't, I drank the second. I'd never gotten drunk on two beers before or since. I was sure you'd never speak to me again."

"Aw, I was already a little bit in love with you, but your drunken solo rendition of 'You Make Me Feel Like Dancing,' followed by 'Hotel California'—well, you had me from the opening line."

"What an idiot I was back then." He rested his elbow on the table and his chin in the palm of his hand, and looked into her eyes, his fingers still laced with hers. "Even with that memory so fresh in your mind, would you like to go to dinner with me tonight?"

"I'd love to."

"Wow. If I'd known it was going to be that easy, I'd have asked you out long ago."

"Timing is everything." She disengaged his fingers from hers. "And speaking of time—tonight?"

"How about seven? There's a new place in Acushnet I hear is really special."

"Sounds perfect." She picked up her bag and stood. "See you then."

~

"Ooh, fancy mama." Natalie whistled when Maggie came into the kitchen. Daisy was still eating, and Grace was still at the bookstore plotting the renovation with Liddy. "You look like a woman who has a hot date."

"I do." Maggie turned slowly. "What do you think? Too much? Too . . . anything?"

Natalie looked her over from the top of her head to her shoes. The dress was one Maggie'd bought on sale before she'd left Pennsylvania. Sleeveless, deep red chiffon with a print in subtle shades of gold, it had a low ruffled neckline and tiny fabric-covered buttons down the front. It was light and summery, and the skirt fell just above her knees and had a flirty touch of swing, just enough to give it a little motion. With it she wore round gold earrings set with large citrines in the centers, gold bangles on her left arm, and a large ring of hammered gold on the middle finger of her right hand. She wore strappy gold-leather sandals and had a camel-colored cashmere wrap over her arm.

"Too perfect. You're gorgeous. Brett will fall in love with you all over again." Natalie paused. "Assuming, of course, Brett is your date."

Maggie nodded. "Does it bother you I'm going out with him?"

"Why would it bother me? Because of Dad? Or because of Joe?" Natalie shook her head. "Don't answer, because it doesn't matter either way. You deserve to have a good time and be happy. For as long as I can remember, you always made everything about Dad and Grace and me and Daisy. Now it's your turn. And if you don't mind me saying so, I think it's romantic that you and Brett are going on a date." She paused thoughtfully. "Unless of course it doesn't work out again. Then maybe not so much."

Maggie gave her hair one last look, moving a strand here and a strand there. "You know I loved your father, don't you?"

"Of course I do. You two were great together." Natalie grabbed a paper towel to sop up the milk Daisy'd spilled on the table. "But I think you loved Brett, too."

"I did." Maggie took a deep breath. "Maybe I still do."

"No time like the present to find out. Mom, life's too short."

"Oh, this from my daughter who has yet to turn thirty?"

"I'm closing in on that big three-oh. Nine more weeks and I'll be over the hill."

"Here's a secret, sweetie. Every time you've made it up the hill, the hill moves. Thirty this year doesn't seem so bad. So you start thinking the hill is really forty. Until you hit forty. And suddenly the hill is—"

"Fifty. Yeah, I get it." Natalie tilted her head in the direction of the front of the house. "I think I heard a car."

Maggie looked out the window, but it was Grace, not Brett, who pulled into the driveway. Moments later, she came in through the back door, a fat folder under her arm, and took one look at her mother. "Where's the party?"

"Mom has a date for dinner. With Brett," Natalie spoke up before Maggie had a chance to open her mouth. "I think it's pretty cool. And doesn't she look fab?"

"She does. I mean, Mom, you do. Look fab, that is." Grace set her folder on the counter.

"That's all you're going to say?" Maggie watched her daughter's face for a sign of disapproval but didn't find one.

Grace shrugged. "Inevitable."

"How'd your meeting with the Meehans go?" Natalie asked.

"They loved my ideas, and they're totally on board. Hired me on the spot." Grace turned to her mother. "Have you met the Meehans? They own Ground Me and a couple of other shops in town. Dress Me Up. Dazzle Me. You get the *Me* connection, right? Anyway, they were talking to Liddy, and she was telling them how I was working on a website for the bookshop, and they mentioned they were looking for someone to do something for them. They called. I looked up what they already had. Lackluster, to say the least. They own all the shops on the Stroll, so in addition to working up something for each of the shops, I mentioned they might want to merchandise the Stroll separately. You know, in addition to the individual shops, and link everything together. I drew up some samples and met with them for a 'brief' meeting this afternoon. Lasted three and a half hours, but I left with a contract and a check in my hand."

"Fabulous! Congratulations!" Maggie gave her a hug, and Natalie followed suit.

"Yeah, it's pretty cool. I'm thinking I might want to do more of this. It's fun and creative." Grace looked very pleased with herself. "I never realized I was so creative. If I get enough clients, maybe I'll forgo the law and just do fun stuff."

"I'd hang on to the law degree," Maggie said. "You worked hard for it."

"You have a point." Grace turned to Natalie. "What did you have for dinner, and are there any leftovers?"

"Daisy and I had takeout eggplant stacks from Jim's and potato wedges. I just put it all away. And there's salad on the top shelf of the fridge."

"Great. Thanks." Grace stood in front of the open refrigerator door while she decided what to take out first.

"Oh. Knock on the front door. I'll get it." Natalie flew out of the room.

"You do look fabulous, Mom. I hope you have a good time." Grace put the container of eggplant on the counter and opened the cupboard for a plate.

"Thank you, Grace." There was more Maggie would have said— such as, *Why the sudden change of heart?*—but the voices from the front hall drew closer. She turned as Natalie came into the kitchen with Brett close behind. He held a huge bouquet of summer flowers.

"Oh my." She gasped and held out her arms. "Come to Mama." She held the flowers to her chest. "All my summer favorites. They're gorgeous, Brett. Thank you so much."

"You're welcome." He looked mildly uncomfortable, with both her daughters standing there watching and her granddaughter staring at him. He said hello to Grace and hi to Daisy, who continued to stare.

"Mom, let me take those flowers and put them in water for you." Natalie reached out, and Maggie handed them over.

"Thanks, sweetie. We'll see you all later." Maggie grabbed her clutch bag off the table in the foyer on their way out.

Brett stopped at the passenger door and opened it. Maggie got in and began to fasten her seat belt. Before he closed the door, he looked down at her. "You look beautiful. You were beautiful when you were younger, but now you're spectacular."

Her stunned "Thank you" was lost in the sound of the door slamming.

Brett walked around the front of the car and slid in behind the wheel. He started the car and pulled into the driveway to turn around.

"What?" he asked. "You look like you have something to say."

"You caught me off guard." She tilted her head in his direction.

"Why, 'cause I said how beautiful you are?" Brett shrugged. "You are. You take my breath away. You always did." He drove toward the center of town as if he'd stated an accepted fact that was not noteworthy. "And I do find you even more beautiful and more sexy than you were when you were fifteen or nineteen or twenty-four." He smiled. "I can't remember you being uncomfortable at a compliment."

"I'm not uncomfortable. I'm just . . . surprised, that's all."

"Why? Didn't you look in the mirror at some point tonight? Check to make sure your hair wasn't sticking up in the air or that you had both earrings in? Nothing green hiding between your front teeth?"

Maggie laughed self-consciously. "Yes, I looked in the mirror, but I didn't see . . ."

"Didn't see what?" he asked softly.

"Didn't see what you think you see."

"Maybe you can call and get an appointment with Dr. Almquist. Get your eyes checked. You are beautiful. Maybe you just need to be reminded a little more frequently." When she didn't respond, he said, "Hey, what is it?"

She turned her head to the window and looked out to avoid his gaze. "I'm almost sixty. If I didn't color my hair, there'd be lots of gray on this head. My boobs are starting to move south, and I have cellulite on my thighs. I don't feel sexy."

"What's cellulite actually look like, anyway?" he asked. "I've heard the term, and I know it's something women seem to worry about, but I don't know what it looks like."

"Think of an orange peel. All those little tiny puckers." Maggie was sorry she'd brought it up. "If you saw my thighs, you wouldn't have to ask."

"Oranges are my favorite fruit. And for the record, I would love to see your thighs again. As I recall, you had the best legs in the entire state of Massachusetts."

She rolled her eyes.

Brett laughed. "Come on, Mags. For one thing, you're not 'almost sixty'—you're fifty-eight and will be for another few months. But even so, what's the big deal? It's a number. You look at least ten years younger. Fifteen years younger when you smile." He checked the rearview mirror, then pulled to the side of the road and stopped the car. "I don't care if you're gray under all that blonde. I don't even care if you're blonde. We all have moving parts that are starting to slide just a bit. No big deal. And I repeat: you always had great legs, and you're still beautiful. And still very, very sexy. So what are you worried about?"

It took her a moment to pull her thoughts together. "I guess . . . it's just the last time we were together, I was younger . . ."

"So was I, Maggie. We've both aged."

"I don't think of you that way."

"Then you should understand when I say I don't think about you that way, either. You'll always be my prom queen, Mags. No matter how old you are, how gray your hair is, or how far your boobs slip."

Finally, she laughed.

"You'll always be the love of my life, whether you ever love me again or not." He'd lost the tease in his voice, and he lifted her hand to his lips and kissed the palm.

She tried to ignore the sudden racing of her heart. "What woman could resist a man who says things like that?"

"I'm hoping you can't when I make my big move." He put the car in drive and eased back onto the highway. "That won't be for a while, though, in case you're wondering."

"Oh? Why is that?" She felt lighter, as the fear she hadn't known she harbored—fear of being compared to her younger self—began to float away in the wake of his reassurance.

"It's not complicated. You need to learn to trust me, and I need to know if you could love me again." He put his turn signal on and waited for traffic to pass before pulling into the parking lot. "I wanted to get all that out of the way so we can just enjoy each other's company and not worry so much about what comes next. We're headed in the right direction, Mags. Let's take our time getting there, just let it unfold as it's meant to."

How he'd been able to intuitively tap into her insecurities was a mystery. In the past, Brett had rarely inquired about her feelings—other than how she felt about him—and almost never acknowledged his own. This older version was more sensitive than his younger self, more self-aware in the best sense. This new one had been totally unexpected, and she liked it.

"So. We're here. Pretty setting, isn't it? Great view of the bay." He'd parked at the far end of the lot near a narrow stretch of beach. The day had been mild, the wind light enough to move the sailboats lazily across the water.

"Very."

He reached over and tucked a stray curl behind her ear. "So we're good?"

Maggie nodded. "We're good."

~

The restaurant was beautiful, the service attentive, and the food proved to be out of this world.

"Why did you decide to become a police officer?" Maggie asked over their shared dessert, an enormous slice of chocolate cake that the waitress served with two forks. "I don't remember you ever expressing an interest in law enforcement."

"I'd never given it a thought. I guess in my testosterone-saturated mind, I thought I'd play football until I was ninety or so, and then I'd just die. I never had a backup plan, never thought I'd need one." His shoulders slumped just a little. "Until of course I did. Then all of a sudden, I was out of a job. I had no idea what to do with myself. I was in California, living alone in a cottage on the beach. As soon as I got traded, Beth left me and took Chloe with her." He paused to take a drink from the beer he'd ordered with his scallops. "I met some guys who hung around the beach, taught me how to surf. That's when I met Holly."

"Love at first sight?"

"No. Holly was beautiful and young, and I felt old and broken. My ego was shattered, and she built it back up." He paused, as if debating what to say next. "Okay, here's the thing. I wasn't kidding when I said I'd never loved anyone but you. When you left, I felt if you didn't love me—after all we'd been through—that must mean I wasn't worthy of being loved. So when someone said they loved me, I figured, there—see, someone does love me. I can't be that bad if this nice woman loves me. And that's how I ended up married three times."

He said it lightly, but Maggie could see the toll it took for him to make that admission.

"I'm so sorry, Brett. I know it sounds trite to say it wasn't you, it was me, but that's how it was. I couldn't stay with you when I was having problems living with myself."

"And if I hadn't been so much of a jerk, so focused on myself, I would have understood that. So maybe we should accept the fact we both made mistakes."

Maggie nodded thoughtfully.

"Okay. So. Why I'm a cop. There was a guy who was in the California Highway Patrol who used to windsurf at Holly's place. He was into the whole law enforcement thing, serving the public good and all that. The more I got to know him, the more we talked, the more I realized nothing I ever did in my whole life was as important as what he did every day. Then Holly and I broke up, and I didn't know what to do with myself. Then I found out my dad was dying, and I came home, figuring I'd just stay till the end." He picked up the spoon next to his plate and tapped it softly on the tablecloth. "Do you remember Chief Hawthorne?"

"Sure. He was the chief of police when we were growing up."

"He was a good friend of my dad's, and he visited every week until my dad passed away. He told me they had a vacancy on the force, hadn't been able to fill it. Suggested that I apply to the police academy. I think it had been in the back of my mind for some time, so when he brought it up, I thought it was a sign. And that's how I ended up where I am. Patrol officer. Detective. Then chief when the old chief retired." There was a touch of pride in his voice that made her smile.

"And you like it." It wasn't a question.

"I love it. I loved playing football, but don't think it's sour grapes when I say I love being a small-town cop. Something inside me settled the day a badge was pinned on my chest."

She'd seen him in town, talking to the older residents who needed reassurance in their safety as well as the young kids who were inching their way toward trouble. It was such a natural fit for him, and it was obvious he took great pleasure in serving his community.

"I'm glad you found something that makes you happy. The town is lucky to have you."

"And what about you? What makes you happy?"

"My family, of course. Other than that . . ." She shrugged. "I guess I'm still figuring that out."

"You were a teacher, right?"

"I was. And I suppose I could become certified in Massachusetts and teach, or substitute if I couldn't find something full time. But right now, I don't feel pressured to make any decisions about my future. I want to enjoy the summer with my kids and my granddaughter. Grandchildren," she corrected herself. "And I want to help Liddy get her bookstore spruced up. I'm lucky Art left me well off. He had a lot of life insurance, and . . . oh, I sold his law firm."

She shared the story of Grace's cheating husband that led her to start *TheLast2No* and to Grace's eventual outing as the spurned wife who took to the internet and invited other women similarly situated to join her and bash their unfaithful husbands.

"That was actually a pretty damned clever thing for her to do. Innovative. It's a shame she had to abandon it," Brett said. "I can see where it could be helpful to have a judgment-free place to express your anger. It would sure go a long way to cutting down the number of domestic calls we get if people felt they had a safe place to vent."

"That's pretty much what Natalie said. Unfortunately, few in Philadelphia saw it that way. Grace was ridiculed and practically run out of the city."

"And that's why you decided to sell the law firm and move back to Wyndham Beach?"

"One of the reasons," she conceded.

"Going to tell me what the others were?"

She smiled at him over the rim of her wineglass. "Not tonight."

Chapter Twenty-Two

By the June solstice, summer was already well established in Wyndham Beach. Maggie spent two weeks busily preparing for the party on the Fourth. She took stock of the patio furniture and found seating was sorely lacking. She drove to the hardware store, because she'd seen their ad for outside chairs in the local paper.

White-haired Carl Lattimore was behind the counter chatting with a customer when Maggie walked in. He turned his attention to her when he was free.

"Hi. Can I help you find something?" he asked her.

"I saw your ad for the folding chairs, and I wanted to see what you have in stock," she told him.

"Right over here's what we have left." He pointed to a wall display. "If there's something in particular you're looking for, I can maybe special order it. Can't guarantee the sale price, though, but I can see what I can do."

"I like these turquoise ones. Do you have maybe half a dozen of these?" She was drawn to the color, which looked tropical to Maggie. With maybe some coral table accents, the backyard could look almost tropical on the Fourth. Not exactly red, white, and blue, but she liked the idea.

"I don't think so, but I can check. I know I have more of the navy, though, Miss . . ."

"It's Maggie. Maggie Flynn."

"Oh. I heard about you," he said.

Uh-oh. "You did?" She hated to ask but felt obligated to.

"Sure. You're Liddy's friend. She told me you were helping her out at the bookshop. Going to fix up the backyard for her, right?" Before she could respond, he went on. "I know it's in a sorry state, but between running this place, and my wife being sick, and my dad's health, well, you know how it goes."

"I do totally understand. I had to let some things go when my husband was ill." *Like myself.* "So no apologies necessary. I'm happy to be able to help Liddy any way I can. We've been friends forever."

"Yeah, I heard you were from here. Ellen Lloyd's girl, right? I knew Ellen for years. Lovely woman."

"She was. Thank you."

"And you bought Ellen's place, I heard. Must be nice to be back in your family home. Grew up in that house, did you?"

"I did. And so did my mother. And it's wonderful to be back."

"We're glad to have you, Maggie. Now let me see if I can locate some chairs for you . . ."

Carl disappeared through a doorway.

Maggie wandered through the store while she waited for Carl. She turned a corner and bumped into a woman she recognized but couldn't remember her name.

"Maggie?" The woman slipped off her sunglasses. She must have realized Maggie was drawing a blank, because she introduced herself. "I'm Marian Coster. Emma's assistant at the art center."

"Nice to meet you." Emma had mentioned she had a part-time assistant. Maggie shook the woman's hand.

"I saw you at the opening of Jessie Bryant's show. I've been working with Emma since she opened the center, but I'm taking the next few weeks off. My daughter just took over the florist shop on Locust Lane—Jack Schuster retired, you know—and she's in over her head, so I told her I'd give her a hand. Emma's very understanding, and she offered to let me come back part-time again if I want. After we get things straightened out at the shop."

"Well, I wish your daughter all the success. The town definitely needs a florist. I'll stop over one day."

"We'll be having a grand opening right before the Fourth. Please come. Joanna—my daughter—is hoping to have some centerpieces ready for the holiday."

"I'll definitely be there."

"Oh, there you are, Maggie." Carl appeared around the corner. "Be with you in a minute, Marian."

"No rush. I'll just wander a bit." Marian turned to Maggie. "I'll make sure you know when the shop opens."

"I'm looking forward to it." Maggie smiled, then looked over the chairs Carl carried.

"No more of the turquoise. I can order those, but they won't be here for four weeks, I'm afraid. I have lots of the navy, though. And the red's been popular this year as well."

Maggie looked over the available color selections and went with the red, which had that sort of faded Nantucket vibe she liked, so in her mind, the color scheme was once again red, white, and blue. Carl offered to have one of his guys deliver the chairs, and she readily agreed.

Before she left, she found a badminton set and a firepit, and asked Carl to have those delivered as well, along with some tiki torches and two big red-and-white-striped planters she could fill with flowers for the front porch. At checkout, she noticed a bin of blue-and-white-striped crepe paper streamers, so she bought some of those to wrap around the front porch railings.

Next year—window boxes. Mr. and Mrs. Gribbin would have been proud.

~

The Fourth of July promised to be a hot one, and humidity was rising along with the heat. Not the best weather for all-day outside activities, but you took what you got in July. With luck, the wind would shift and blow ashore from the harbor, and by afternoon, the air would be bearable if not pleasant. Maggie woke early and dressed in holiday-appropriate garb of a white denim skirt, a navy-and-white-striped T-shirt, and red sandals. She'd always loved the Fourth of July celebrations in Wyndham Beach for their winning combination of patriotism and the showing off of local pride.

But this year was unlike any other holiday. Today all the threads of her life were coming together, and she prayed the eventual result would be seamless and beautiful. She planned an early but simple breakfast for her immediate crew—fruit and scrambled eggs—and put on a pot of coffee. The preparations made, she stepped out to the patio, a mug of coffee in hand, and eased herself into a comfy chair while she waited for her daughters to join her. She sat back and closed her eyes and took a deep breath of air heavy with salt from the harbor and floral from her garden, an odd but surprisingly pleasant combination.

She was tempted to pinch herself, so unlikely would a day like today have been even one year ago. Today everyone who meant the most to her would be under her roof. She still wasn't certain what the outcome would be, but she knew the time had come. Hopefully everyone would find a way to get along.

Last week, she and Brett had met Joe and his two children for dinner. Lulu had enchanted them both. She was a fairy child, a garden sprite with almost ethereal beauty with a shy smile. Jamey had been tougher, but Brett had won him over with tales of his football days as well as his years on the police force. That Brett had played multiple sports just like Joe and Jamey had won him big points. Maggie, not so much, but she was okay with that. After all, it had been their first meeting, and Joe had assured her in time Jamey would be eating out of her hand. She hoped he was right.

Alexis, Brett's fourteen-year-old California-raised daughter, had arrived the previous week. Maggie'd met up with them when she'd taken Daisy to the ice-cream shop in town, and Alexis had taken to Daisy immediately and had offered to babysit anytime.

Grace questioned the wisdom of tossing everyone together all at once, but Maggie had stood firm in her belief it was best to simply dive in. Would time make the journey easier to take? Maggie doubted it. The situation was what it was, and it wasn't going to change. Why put it off and miss out on whatever time they all might have together? Maggie knew all too well tomorrow wasn't promised to anyone.

Natalie hadn't waited to take that dive—earlier in the week she'd met Joe for dinner and had come home singing his praises. She couldn't wait to report to Grace how wonderful he was, that he was exactly the way she'd pictured him, that they'd had a great time.

"I felt like I'd known him my whole life," Natalie'd said. "He's the brother I always wanted. You're going to love him, Gracie. I promise."

Maggie mentally marked an imaginary scoreboard: one down, one to go.

The back door opened, and Grace wandered out, coffee mug in hand, followed by Natalie and an even-chattier-than-usual Daisy, who couldn't wait for all their guests and the parade and rides on the carousel. She wasn't really sure what a carousel was, but she was excited about it all the same because the grown-ups seemed to be. After a quick breakfast, there was a sort of dead silence while they all watched the clock, waiting for their guests to arrive.

"Did you have enough breakfast?" Maggie asked. "I can go in and . . ."

"We did," Grace told her. "Thanks for leaving everything pretty much prepped."

"Nana, Mommy said today I get to ride a carousel with big horses that go up and down." She climbed into Maggie's lap. "Do the horses bite? What color are they? Do they have horns like unicorns?"

"Yes, you will get to ride the carousel, but no, the horses don't bite. We'll have to wait and see what colors they are, and I don't think there are any unicorns on Mr. Harrison's carousel. I rode that carousel when I was a little girl, and so did your mommy and Aunt Grace when they were little."

The sound of a car door slamming got everyone's attention.

"That must be Joe." Maggie lifted Daisy from her lap, stood, smoothed her skirt, and hurried into the house.

She went straight to the front door, then out onto the front porch. Joe approached on the sidewalk, his hand holding an uncertain Lulu, Jamey following behind with obvious reluctance. Maggie stood at the top of the steps to welcome them.

"I'm so glad you're here. And you're right on time." She smiled and held out her hands to Joe. He kissed her on the cheek, and she noticed Jamey turn his head. "Come on in and we'll get ready for the parade. We should leave in a few minutes."

The threesome followed her inside, where they met Grace, Natalie, and Daisy.

"Hey, Natalie. Good to see you again," Joe said. "And this must be Grace. I've heard so much about you. I'm so happy to finally meet you."

Natalie offered a hug, and Grace a brief handshake.

Joe turned to his children. "Jamey, Lulu, meet your aunt Natalie and your aunt Grace."

Lulu smiled shyly and offered a tiny wave. Jamey glared and half waved in their general direction.

Oh boy. It was clear both children felt unsure and awkward, not totally understanding their place with these three women who were new to them, a normal reaction. But Maggie had high hopes the activities of the day would go a long way toward helping them relax and enjoy themselves. The butterflies in the pit of her stomach may not have been convinced, but she covered her doubts so well no one would have suspected there had been a moment or two when she wondered if perhaps Grace had been right. Perhaps it was too soon. Maybe they should have taken more time to get to know each other. Was she trying too hard to make up for lost time?

Well, she thought, *it's a little late to examine my motives or question my wisdom.*

"Guys, it's going to be hot as blazes later, so you're going to want to bring water to the parade. I do have a cooler we can take for water bottles, but I think starting out, we should each take a bottle." She held a cool bottle out to Lulu, who whispered, "Thank you." Jamey shook his head to decline, but Daisy walked over and took the bottle from Maggie's hands.

"Mama says we have to drink lots of water when it's hot," Daisy told Jamey matter-of-factly, all but forcing the bottle into his hands. After he took it silently, she reminded him, "Now you say thank you."

Being schooled by a three-year-old apparently stung. Jamey's mumbled "thank you" was the first words he'd spoken since he'd arrived.

Maggie zipped up the cooler, and Joe stepped in to take it.

"I'll carry that. Anything else you need?" Joe asked.

"No. I think we're good." Maggie pointed to the front door. "Lead the way."

As if trying to escape, Grace was first out the door, but Joe, with his long legs, easily caught up to her on the porch.

"So Grace, Nat tells me you collect first editions. So do I. Is there any particular genre or time period you favor?" Joe asked.

"Oh." Grace sounded as if she'd been taken off guard. "Well, I love the old detective mysteries. Mickey Spillane. Raymond Chandler. Dashiell Hammett."

"Hey, me too! My autographed copy of *The Maltese Falcon* is my most prized possession."

"I'm so jealous! I have a first edition, but mine is not signed."

"Did you know Spillane wrote comic books before he wrote novels?"

"No!" Grace smacked him softly on the arm.

Joe nodded. "Superman. Batman . . ."

"My dad collected those from the nineteen fifties."

"So did mine . . ."

Listening to the exchange, Maggie sighed with relief. It appeared Grace had forgotten her preconceived dismissal of Joe, and all it had taken was the discovery of a shared love.

"And we're two for two," Maggie muttered as she locked the front door.

Behind her, Natalie laughed. "Relax, Mom. It's going to be a great day. Fourth of July in Wyndham Beach, and we're all together. What could be better?"

They fell in step with the slow-moving group headed for the center of town.

Grace led the way, walking with Joe on one side and Daisy skipping along on the other. Jamey and Lulu followed close behind their father, not speaking, both looking slightly lost and clearly feeling out of place. Maggie hoped that would change by the end of the day.

Liddy and Emma stood at the curb in front of the bookstore. By the time Maggie caught up with her group, the introductions had already been made. Two blocks away, the parade was beginning to take form, the long line of participants snaking out from the town's largest parking lot. Brett's police cruiser was at the front, followed by the Mid-Coast Regional High School Marching Band and a caravan of convertibles carrying the mayor and other municipal leaders.

When the lead car approached the bookstore, it stopped, and Alexis jumped out.

"Alexis!" Daisy jumped up and down with joy to see her new friend. Alexis ran to the side of the street and picked up the three-year-old, apparently as happy to see Daisy as Daisy was to see her.

Maggie gave Brett a thumbs-up before he drove away, leading the parade around the corner toward Prescott Street and the route that would wind the parade all through Wyndham Beach.

"Where's Chris this weekend?" Liddy asked Emma.

"He's doing some holiday charity concert out on the West Coast." Emma's exasperation was evident. "I just wish one time he'd say no to one of those big gigs that always seems to fall on a holiday weekend. Just once I'd like him to be home. Just. Once."

"Don't hold your breath, Em. What does Wyndham Beach have that can compete with the life that boy is living? He's an international celebrity, and you need to remember that and what it means to be one of the most eligible bachelors in the world," Liddy told her.

Maggie watched Natalie's face as she listened to the exchange.

Oh, sweetie, we all love Chris, we really do. But please, don't . . . In that moment, Maggie feared for her daughter's heart even more than she had when Jonathan had walked out on her.

Almost defiantly, Natalie turned on her phone and started to record the parade as it passed by.

"Saving Daisy's first Wyndham Beach glorious Fourth?" Maggie asked.

"No. It's to send to Chris so he can see what he's missing," Natalie said.

"Oh."

"He asked me to, Mom." There was a touch of challenge in Natalie's voice, as if she expected Maggie to question Chris's interest in his hometown parade. "He really hasn't forgotten where he came from."

"I wouldn't expect him to, sweetie. I'm sure he'll get a kick out of watching it."

Natalie resumed her video as the marchers filed by, and Maggie wondered just how interested Chris would be in seeing the local DAR float and the float honoring the one-hundredth anniversary of the founding of the Wyndham Beach Historical Society, or the floats for the local cultural alliance, followed by a flatbed truck carrying several of the teachers from the art center, displaying representative samples of their work. A contingent from the local Vietnam Vets marched by, and there were the usual fire trucks with volunteer firefighters riding on the backs, tossing candy to the children along the route. The widely acknowledged highlight of the parade was the Alden Academy Faculty Marching Kazoo Band, composed of teachers and administrators of the local prep school. There were seemingly miles of kids on bikes decorated in red, white, and blue crepe paper streamers. The junior high marching band, playing an off-key version of "The Stars and Stripes Forever," brought up the rear, followed by one lone police vehicle, lights flashing, no siren, to officially mark the end of the parade.

"Remember when we used to ride our bikes in the parade?" Liddy came up behind Maggie and put an arm around her shoulder. "We'd wrap them in miles of crepe paper, and if it rained, we'd be covered in dye."

"And the dye would get on our clothes, and our mothers would be all over us for it," Emma said. When neither Liddy nor Maggie commented, Emma frowned. "No? Just mine?"

"I'm afraid so." Liddy patted her on the back.

"So what's next on the agenda, Mom?" Grace asked.

"Footraces in the park." Maggie gestured toward the sidewalk on the opposite side of the street. "Just follow the crowd."

The crowd spilled into the street and undulated like a fat snake as it headed for Harrison Park, where the festivities would continue. The park was on the grounds of the old Harrison mansion. Built in the late eighteen hundreds, it was unlike anything the residents had ever seen, in parts Gothic, Victorian, Tudor, and Georgian in architecture, depending on the side of the house viewed. Other than the staff in residence—on call when someone was there, otherwise acting as security and maintenance—no one in recent memory had been inside, though it had been the object of speculation for years.

Jasper Harrison had set aside five acres of his vast holdings to be used as a park for the residents of the town, with money from the estate earmarked to maintain and add to it as the town council requested. There was a set limit to what they could spend, but it had been more than adequate. Over the years, they'd added an elaborate wooden play structure for children, a ball field, and a gazebo, which had been intended to be used for summer concerts, but which served only as a backdrop for wedding and prom pictures. No one remembered a concert ever having been held there.

Every year on the Fourth of July, the park overflowed with locals and their visiting friends and relatives. The American flag was raised as the crowd pledged their allegiance. Then the high school band played "The Star-Spangled Banner," which everyone was expected to sing. The president of the local Boys & Girls Club then announced the order in which the footraces would be held, from the youngest to the oldest, and pointed out the area where the runners were to gather. The script hadn't changed since Maggie was a girl.

Jamey declined to participate, despite his father's reminder he was one of the fastest kids in his grade, but Lulu ran with her age group, easily outdistancing the next closest runner. She proudly returned to the group, holding up the blue ribbon and small trophy to her father and her brother, who'd been mostly silent since his arrival. Alexis, who had possibly the longest legs Maggie had ever seen on a young girl, like Lulu, outran everyone else in her field.

"Dad!" she'd cried when she spotted Brett on the sidelines. "Check it out!"

Maggie watched Brett hug his daughter and admire her small trophy engraved with the date. He put an arm around her and crossed the field to join Maggie and the others.

"Some runners in this family," he grinned as he high-fived Lulu, and she beamed under his praise.

Maggie noticed Jamey kick the ground with the toe of his sneaker, a frown on his face. He was clearly distancing himself, and she wished she knew how to pull him in, but she'd only had daughters, who'd always been pretty vocal in how they felt. She didn't know Jamey at all and wondered if he'd ever permit her to. She watched Joe's face as he leaned over and spoke to his son. He gave the boy's shoulder a squeeze before turning his face back to the crowd as the last race lined up.

After the field activities, they walked farther into the park to witness the unveiling of the carousel. Maggie remembered it well, her memories of having ridden on the hand-painted mounts throughout her childhood and her teen years still vivid.

"Hey, remember when . . ." Brett slipped up behind her and whispered.

"I was just thinking about that." She smiled at the memory. Once they'd ridden side by side. Every time the ride's circular motion had hid them from view, he'd leaned over and kissed her. "We were sixteen."

"Maybe we can hitch a ride on one of those ponies later," he said, his eyebrows wiggling up and down suggestively.

"The ride will be back in its barn by the time you're off duty tonight, Chief. But I cherish the memory."

"Maybe we can catch a few moments alone." His eyes met hers, and she detected a touch of veiled amusement.

"Doubtful. I suspect we'll still have a full house by then."

"Looks like things are going pretty well." He tilted his head in the direction of Joe, Grace, and Natalie, who were engaged in conversation.

"Better than I'd hoped. It seems Joe and Grace share a love of detective novels' first editions. There just might be a bit of sibling rivalry brewing, though. They apparently covet the same authors. He has a signed first edition of *The Maltese Falcon* she'd kill for. She has a copy of Mickey Spillane's *I, the Jury* I suspect he may be willing to trade for his firstborn."

"It's a good start."

"It is. Alexis has been great entertaining Daisy and Lulu. The only one I'm concerned about is Jamey. He's not given an inch since he got here. Doesn't want to talk to anyone, didn't want to run in the race, doesn't show any interest in anything or anyone."

Brett watched the boy from a distance. His body language reinforced Maggie's assessment. "Everyone and everything is new. He doesn't know how he's supposed to feel about all these people who are supposed to be related to him and who seem to assume he's going to like them. He'll be all right once he figures out his place."

"I hope so. He hasn't said a word to me all day." Maggie fell into an old habit of biting the cuticle of her left thumb. Brett pulled her hand away from her mouth.

"Stop that. You're not fifteen," he teased. "Don't be upset. It's going to work out. I promise. Trust me. Jamey just needs time."

"How can you be so sure?"

"I was a twelve-year-old boy myself once." He gave her hand one last squeeze. "I need to make my rounds here. Lots of people to see and greet. I'll see you after the fireworks."

Maggie watched him walk away, watched as people stopped him for a handshake or a pat on the back. It was obvious he was well liked and respected in Wyndham Beach, and she felt no small amount of pride in him. He was still that same sweet boy she'd met in homeroom sophomore year. Despite the years and the unexpected turns his life had taken, he was still the Brett she'd known and fallen in love with back then. She had a feeling history might repeat itself.

Sometimes life did move in circles.

Maggie noticed Emma talking to the tall man with the receding hairline and wire-rimmed glasses she recognized from the art center. Owen Harrison had promised to deliver the carousel and had. Someone walked past and handed her a brochure with a picture of the carousel on the front, and Maggie skimmed the text describing the history of the Wyndham Beach amusement. Purchased and brought to Wyndham

Beach by Jasper Harrison II in 1905, the horses had been hand carved by one of the two greatest artists of the carousel world, Marcus Illions.

"There are two other Illions carousels I know are still in operation," Owen was telling Emma when Maggie approached them. "One's here in Massachusetts, in Springfield, and another in the Columbus Zoo in Ohio. Not sure if others survived."

"The workmanship is just glorious." Emma moved closer to the ride.

"Oh, yes. Illions was known for the flamboyance of his creations. He was truly an artist."

Owen took Emma's elbow and walked along with her. For as long as Maggie could recall, Emma had shown no real interest in any man who'd shown an interest in her, and there'd been more than a few since Harry's death. Yet here was Emma being guided along, apparently deeply fascinated with carousel horses. Will wonders never cease?

She thought the shake of her head was unnoticeable. Liddy apparently noticed.

"Yeah, how 'bout that?" Liddy gestured in Emma's direction. "That man hasn't taken his eyes off her since we walked over."

"Nice. She's been alone for a long time, and between you and me, Harry wasn't the greatest husband."

Liddy nodded in agreement. "There were rumors about him and Darlene Fitch, who worked at the bank . . . I don't believe Emma ever heard them, but still. And the way he treated Chris—no wonder the kid was always sneaking off to the garage to play his guitar."

"I'd say it worked out pretty well for Chris, though," Maggie pointed out.

"Emma misses him. She's alone too much. It would be nice for her to have a distraction," Liddy said. "Even if it's only now and then. I heard he"—she nodded toward Owen—"has a town house in London and a place on Florida's Jupiter Island. Someone in that family invested all that shipping and lumber money really well."

An announcement came over the PA system that the first ride of the season was about to begin, so the children who were interested needed to line up at the place designated by a huge flock of balloons tied to a stake in the ground. One by one, the children stepped up to the platform and selected their rides. Maggie took her phone from her pocket and snapped pictures of the elegantly draped horses. Natalie stood in line with Daisy, who danced excitedly.

"I want the black horse, Mommy." Daisy pointed.

Emma turned at the sound of Daisy's voice. She said something to Owen, who nodded.

"Daisy, would you like to ride that black horse?" Emma held her hand out.

"Yes! Yes, please!"

"Come along and we'll ride the carousel together." Emma helped Daisy onto the platform, then lifted her onto the horse. Daisy's beaming face said more than words could have.

"Nat, take a picture to send to Chris," Maggie urged.

"Already did." Natalie held up her phone. "He's going to love seeing his mom having a good time."

The carousel filled, the music began, and Owen started the ride. Slowly the carousel turned, the horses on the posts bobbing up and down as the music played. Maggie opened the brochure and read a few lines.

"The horses that move up and down are called jumpers," she told Natalie. "Daisy's horse is a prancer, the front legs in the air and the back legs on the ground."

Daisy's ride came to an end, and she ran excitedly to her mother to relate the wonderfulness of her experience on the black horse as the next round of riders chose their horses and the music began to play again.

Liddy stepped away to greet a tall dark-haired man accompanied by three children. She ruffled the hair of the oldest child, a boy of about eight, then knelt to speak to the two girls, twins of maybe five or six.

Maggie noticed Grace watching, her attention not on the children but on the man. The expression on Grace's face was unreadable, though Maggie thought she detected a hint of disappointment.

"Who is that with Liddy?" Maggie asked Emma, who'd followed Natalie.

"Oh, that's Linc Shelby. Remember Emmett Shelby, three classes ahead of us? Linc's his son. Listen, Maggie, would it be all right if Owen joined us at your house for the cookout?" Emma asked quietly.

"Of course. I'm sure everyone will love to talk to him about his amazing carousel." Smiling, Maggie leaned closer to Emma. "So. Owen."

"Stop." Emma laughed self-consciously, her cheeks pink. "He lives all over the place, travels all over the world. I was surprised he actually came this weekend. If it weren't for my nagging reminders, I doubt he'd even have remembered. Though he does seem interested in the carousel now that he's here."

"I think he's interested in more than the carousel."

"One could hope."

"Two could hope. I'm pulling for you," Maggie said. "He seems like a very nice man."

"He is. And he's interesting, and he . . ." Emma laughed. "Never mind. Whatever I say, you're going to pick up and run with it."

"Damn right."

"He's just here for the weekend, and then he's off to someplace I never even heard of." Emma paused. "Just like my son. Here today, gone today."

It was on the tip of Maggie's tongue to ask if Chris had said anything to Emma about Natalie, and it took all her willpower not to. She hadn't been blind to the number of pictures Natalie had taken and how many times she appeared to be texting. She suspected all the texts and the photos were being sent to Chris, who might be onstage performing to a gigantic crowd even as Natalie was trying to get his attention.

She'd previously thought Chris and Natalie would be good together, but she wasn't so sure once the reality of who he was when he wasn't in Wyndham Beach became clear. The last thing she wanted was for Nat to be involved with someone who would leave her like Jonathan had. Like Zach had left Grace.

Too heavy to think about when the entire day lay before her.

After Lulu and Alexis each had their turn on the carousel, Maggie herded the group together and they headed back to Cottage Street. Emma would join them later with Owen, and Liddy would be over after she ran home for her contributions to the feast.

And it really did turn out to be a feast. Joe worked the grill, so the hot dogs, hamburgers, and barbecued chicken Maggie'd prepared the night before were expertly tended to. There were folding tables to be set up in the backyard after being wiped down to remove any spiders and cobwebs, the new chairs to be set up, and dishes of cold food to be carried out and placed on a long table that served as a buffet. There were a cooler filled with soft drinks and bottled water and a tub of beer on ice. Grace assisted Joe on the grill, and from what Maggie overheard they were engaged in a lively discussion about rap and whether or not it constituted poetry.

Alexis wanted to teach Lulu and Daisy to play hopscotch—after having politely asked Maggie if it would be okay if she chalked up the front sidewalk—but Natalie was nowhere to be seen.

"Gracie, where's your sister?" Maggie asked.

"She's inside watching TV," Grace told her.

"Watching TV?" Maggie frowned. While they had guests? On the Fourth of July?

"Yeah, DEAN is playing in that big concert, and it's being televised."

Of course it would be. Maggie started toward the house.

"I love DEAN," Alexis said. "They're my favorite band."

Maggie paused halfway across the patio. "You know Emma is Chris Dean's mother, don't you?"

"She is not." Alexis stared at her and repeated, "She's not."

"She most certainly is." Maggie pointed to Daisy. "Tell her, Daisy."

As she was about to go inside, Maggie realized Jamey was missing as well. Maybe he was watching the concert with Natalie.

But when Maggie walked into the family room, she found only Natalie.

"Mom, watch this. I sent Chris videos of the parade." She backed up the image on the screen until she arrived at the place where Chris and his bandmates could be seen mounting the stage.

"Are you recording this?" Maggie asked.

"Of course. Here, watch. Watch his face." Natalie giggled.

Chris was at the microphone, singing for several minutes. Then his hand went to his pants pocket, and he pulled out his phone. He kept singing but turned his head and laughed before sticking the phone back into his pocket.

"I sent him the kazoo band. He loved it."

"Obviously."

"No, he did. He texted me when he got off the stage."

The image on the screen continued to run, and Maggie stood in the doorway, watching as Natalie sat without moving when Chris began to sing a slow song, something about shooting stars that appeared to have an effect on her daughter.

Oh dear. Maggie inwardly sighed. *This might not end well.*

"Nat, we might have to have a talk later about Chris and you."

"Don't go there, Mom. We're good. So please don't ask me to put a label on our relationship. I don't want to call it anything. Just leave it be."

"All right." Maggie still perceived danger ahead but let it go for now. "Have you seen Jamey?"

"Not since he asked me where the beach was, but that was a while ago." Natalie's attention was still on the screen.

"If anyone asks, I went to find him."

Maggie could tell Natalie had barely heard her even as she opened and closed the front door.

Chris was a good kid. God, she sounded like Emma. A good guy. He'd never intentionally hurt Natalie. He wouldn't take advantage of her or their friendship.

Then again, he was a guy. A guy with an international reputation and about a million young women willing to throw themselves at his feet. She wondered what the chances were Chris was as infatuated with Natalie as she appeared to be with him.

Maggie walked to the end of the street and removed her sandals before stepping onto the beach. She scanned the rocks, then saw him atop the lifeguard stand. She walked across the sand and took a deep breath before she began to climb. He might not want company, but he was going to have it.

"Jamey." She stood on the top rung of the ladder and motioned for him to scoot over to make a place for her to sit. "We missed you."

"Why?"

"Because I—"

"Don't say because you're my grandma. You're not." He stared straight ahead, not blinking.

"Well, in one sense, you're right. But in another . . ."

"You're not my dad's mother."

"I didn't raise him, that's true. But I did give birth to him."

"And you gave him away because you didn't want him. You abandoned him, and my grandparents had to find him and bring him home because you didn't want him. You didn't love him then, so why are you wanting to hang around with him now?"

"Well, that's a very deep question, Jamey. I can see you've been thinking about this, and you deserve an honest answer. So I will tell you the absolute truth."

"Right."

"You asked a question. I want to answer. You want to hear it or not?"

After a long moment, he nodded, but he still hadn't looked at her.

"I did not abandon your father." She paused. "You're old enough to understand what adoption means, right?"

"Yeah. It's when you don't want your kid, so you give it away."

"Jamey, I was very young when he was born, and I knew I could not take care of him. I wanted to, but I knew I could not. My parents were not accepting of the situation I was in. Your grandparents wanted him desperately. They were very special people, and I knew they would give him a wonderful home and the happy life he deserved. Things I couldn't give him when I'd just turned eighteen."

"You were eighteen?" He frowned.

"Yes. Not much older than you. You think you'd be ready to raise a baby in six more years?"

"That's not the point."

"Then tell me what is."

"You didn't love him. They were the ones who loved him."

"I always loved him, even when I didn't know him." She touched his arm.

"That doesn't even make sense." He pulled away. "My gram was the best." He began to cry, and Maggie understood this was not about her.

"I know she was," she said softly. "Your father told me all about her. How wonderful she was. That she was kind and good hearted and how much she loved you and your sister."

"I loved her and my grandpa. Why did they have to be taken away?"

She put a hand on his back, and this time he made no move to pull away.

"I wish I had an answer for that. There are so many times in your life when you will wonder why this or why that, questions you may never find the answer to." She felt like crying along with him. "Jamey, Brett and I don't want to take the place of your grandparents. We never

349

could, and we would never try to. I know how much you loved them and how much you hurt. We are honored they chose to raise our . . ." She had to say it. He had to know how she felt. "That they chose to raise our son. We just want to have a place of our own in your life and in your sister's life. We don't want you to ever forget your grandparents. They loved you. But we want to love you, too. We both hope in time you might grow to like us. But whatever happens, I promise you, I will never try to take your grandmother's place. Do you understand what I'm saying?"

He wiped his face on his bare arm, his nod barely perceptible. They sat in silence and watched the sandpipers run along the waterline and two gulls argue over something one of them had plucked from the sand.

"I'm never going to call you Grandma."

"I'm never going to ask you to. You can call me whatever you want."

"Can't I just call you Maggie?"

"Of course."

"Are you and Brett married?"

The question caught her off guard. This kid had a lot on his mind.

"No. We thought we would be, long ago, but it didn't work out that way. I married someone else—Natalie and Grace's father—and Brett married someone else, too. Alexis's mother." *Among others, but no need to get into that now.* "My husband died a few years ago, and Brett is divorced."

"So you could be married, if you wanted to be."

She glanced in his direction. She'd raised two kids. She knew sly when she saw it.

"I think it's time to get back to the house." She patted him on the knee. "Your dad is grilling burgers. Are you hungry?"

He nodded. "Yeah."

They climbed down from the stand and walked back to the house.

"What's everyone been doing?" he asked.

"Making food. Your sister and Daisy are playing hopscotch with Alexis. And Natalie is watching the concert on TV."

"Oh, yeah. I heard about that. I wanted to see it. Guess I missed it."

"Talk to Nat. She recorded it. I'm sure she'll play it for you later."

"Why'd she record it? She's like, old, right?"

Maggie suppressed a grin. Natalie—her baby—old? "You know who DEAN is?"

"Sure. Everyone knows DEAN."

"Well, did you know Chris Dean is from Wyndham Beach? My friend Emma is his mother. He and Natalie have been friends since they were kids. They're like this." She crossed her fingers and held them up.

Jamey stopped dead in his tracks. Maggie smiled and continued up the steps and into the house.

Dinner had been loud in a good way, loud in a way Maggie was not accustomed to. Male voices predominated, even though there were only three guys in the group. Owen had arrived with Emma and had taken his turn at the grill while telling the story of how his great-great-grandfather, Jasper Harrison, had brought the carousel to Wyndham Beach for his terminally ill daughter. He'd wanted to do something that would make her happy every day of what was to be a short life, so he'd had the carousel built, and when she died at the age of thirteen, he shared it with the other children in town to keep her memory alive.

"I never heard that story before," Liddy remarked. "Huh. That's very cool."

After everyone finished eating and all hands volunteered in the cleanup, they walked as a group back to the park for the fireworks. They carried blankets on which they sat clustered together, watching the lights in the sky, oohing and aahing at every display, laughing and covering their ears at the loudest booms.

The show ended, and they gathered their things and walked back to Cottage Street, still in a group, still clustered together.

Like a family, Maggie thought as she trailed behind, watching their interactions, listening to their teasing and their laughter. She saw Joe look around, then look behind until he saw her. Then he dropped back and fell in step with her.

"This was the best, Maggie. I don't know how to thank you . . ." He draped an arm over her shoulders.

"Please." She shook her head. "I want to thank you for . . ." Her words caught in her throat. "You've no idea what you've given me. I will never forget this day."

"This is just the beginning, Maggie. We're not going away. We're here as long as you want us."

"Of course I want you. You and Jamey and Lulu. Always." She started to tear up. "So you and Grace seemed to hit it off."

"I can't believe I have a sister who collects the same books I do. And I'm sure you're thrilled she's staying in Wyndham Beach for a while and starting up her web company."

Maggie was just about to ask *She is?* when a car parked in front of her house. Brett got out and stopped on the sidewalk when he saw them.

"Hey," he called to them. "Enjoy the fireworks?"

"Never saw better," Joe said.

"Come inside and grab something to eat." Maggie took Brett's arm, happy to walk between him and their son. *Miracle.* She heard the word as clearly as if it had been spoken but had no idea where it had come from. *Great-Aunt Ida, maybe,* she mused.

"What's the joke?" Brett asked as the threesome climbed the steps.

"Just thinking about my great-aunt Ida," she told him.

"Who was she?" Joe asked.

"A story for another day." They went inside, Joe heading straight for the backyard, where everyone was waiting for Emma to serve her trifle.

In the kitchen, Maggie fixed Brett a plate of cold chicken and the rest of the potato salad.

"I'm sorry there's not much else left," she said. "This group was like a bunch of locusts. And there weren't that many people here."

"This is perfect. Thank you." He ate a few bites. "So how was it, having everyone together? Any fights? Bloodshed?"

She shook her head. "As it turns out, we have a very well-mannered family." She realized what she'd said, then tried to amend it. "You know what I mean. Group."

"I liked *family* better. It is our family. Like the saying goes: yours, mine, and ours."

"Jamey had a few rough moments." She told him how the boy had disappeared and how she'd found him on the lifeguard stand. "He was afraid we were going to try to take the place of his grandparents. He was very close to them."

"What did you tell him?" A few more bites and he'd finished his late dinner. He took the plate to the sink and rinsed it, then set it on the counter.

"I told him we would never do that. That we want our own place in his life."

Brett reached for her and pulled her into his arms. "I do want a place in his life, and in Lulu's." He nuzzled the side of her neck. "And in yours, Maggie. I want to be a part of your life again."

"You always have been," she assured him. "Always will be."

He kissed her, a long, deep kiss, the kind of kiss they used to share in the back seat of his car, and she smiled.

"What?" he asked. "Is there something funny about kissing me?"

"No one kisses like you, Brett. You'd think I'd have forgotten, after all these years, but I haven't." She leaned back and grinned. "For a minute there, I felt like we were back in that old Jeep you used to have."

"I'll get an old Jeep if it would make you happy. Who says you can't relive your youth?" He'd started to kiss her again when the back door opened.

"Oh God. Stop. Get a room." Grace started to laugh, then hastened to say, "No. No room. Forget I said that."

Maggie laughed, especially when she realized Brett looked mildly embarrassed.

"Come on out and get dessert," Grace told them as she went back outside. "Emma's made the most amazing trifle. White chocolate, dark chocolate, and pureed raspberries. To. Die. For."

"How could anyone resist?" Brett took Maggie's hand, and they followed Grace as far as the back door, where he paused, looking out at the gathering.

"Did you ever dream a day like this would come?" Brett asked her.

Maggie shook her head. "I prayed I'd meet Joe someday, but I never dared pray you and I would find each other again. And this? No. Never. It's beyond a dream."

He stood behind her and wrapped his arms around her. "This is nice. It feels almost like we're a normal couple."

"Are you implying there's something abnormal about us?" she teased.

"I just meant it doesn't feel like we've been apart for forty years."

"It's more like thirty-six."

"Still, that's a long time. Lot of water went over that dam in thirty-six years. I'm still trying to wrap my head around the fact we're here, we're together again, and Joe's with us. We have grandkids together." He shook his head. "How did this happen?"

"Just lucky, I guess. Blessed." She rested against him, and they swayed together slightly. "Back then, when we were young, this is exactly where I thought we'd be at this stage of our lives. Celebrating a big holiday in Wyndham Beach with our family and our friends."

"It's different from the way we thought it would be, but it can still be good, right?" There was just a tinge of worry in his voice.

"It can be very good." She leaned into him. "It will be very good."

"I like the sound of that." He kissed her on the cheek and reached for the door handle.

"You go on out," she told him. "I'm going to put coffee on. I'll be out in a minute."

She watched him cross the patio and join the others, who were toasting marshmallows.

She caught Liddy's eye and held up her left arm to show off her tattoo.

Liddy grinned and returned the gesture.

Friendship is complicated, Maggie thought. *Families are complicated. Love is complicated.*

But still and always, waves of the same sea.

ACKNOWLEDGMENTS

Huge thanks to my readers, who have stuck with me from my early contemporary romance days through my suspense days to my current works of women's fiction. Thanks to my Facebook family and friends—you've been so much fun and so helpful in so many ways. When I was searching for just the right tattoo for Maggie, Liddy, and Emma in this book, you rallied and offered some fabulous suggestions. Special thanks to Paul Bellefeuille, who gave me the idea for the tattoo my characters get on their trip to Charlotte—I never would have thought of it myself, but it's perfect and, by the way, looks great on you! I want to give a shout-out to Betsy Meehan-Bittner and her daughter, Kate, who helped me out when I had questions about tattoos in general.

To the editors I've had over the years who have taught me so much, especially Lauren McKenna—much love and many thanks. And to the Montlake editors who worked with me on this book—Maria Gomez and Holly Ingraham—so many thanks to you both for putting so much time and thought into my story and my characters. The copyeditor (James!) and the proofreader (Jill!) cleaned up my errors, helped tighten up my story, and pointed out all those little inconsistencies that drive readers insane. Many thanks to you both. Thanks to Lauren Grange, production manager, for keeping it all on track.

My family is my best reason for doing, well, everything—my husband Bill, who is facing down a dragon with resolve and determination and his characteristic good humor; our daughters, Kathryn and Rebecca; their husbands, Mike and David, respectively; and the five incredible, amazing, adorable little people they've brought into this world.

(Update: Make that *six* incredible, amazing, adorable little people to include the latest: Gethin Peter William Jones!)

ABOUT THE AUTHOR

Photo © 2016 Nicole Leigh

Mariah Stewart is the *New York Times*, *Publishers Weekly*, and *USA Today* bestselling author of several series, including The Chesapeake Diaries and The Hudson Sisters, as well as stand-alone novels, novellas, and short stories. A native of Hightstown, New Jersey, she lives with her husband and two rambunctious rescue dogs amid the rolling hills of Chester County, Pennsylvania, where she savors country life, tends her gardens, and works on her next novel. She's the proud mama of two fabulous daughters who—along with her equally fabulous sons-in-law—have gifted her with six adorable (and yes, fabulous) granddarlings. For more information visit www.mariahstewart.com.